As a child, Nyrielle Tam dreamed of being a soldier.

We can't release Harryn Stormblade from his bondage, Steel said, *but Queen Sheshka can. And as one of the most powerful warlords in Droaam, she'll undoubtedly be in attendance at this diplomatic gathering, as will you.*

"So," Thorn said, "I just need to find a statue, kidnap the queen of the medusas, force her to reverse a curse, and smuggle a legendary warrior out of Droaam, all without causing an international incident."

Instead, she became a spy, a saboteur, and when necessary, an assassin.

Sheshka's death is an acceptable loss, provided Breland can't be blamed for it.

Thorn's mind raced as she considered the variables. This was what she'd been trained for, and after months of rehabilitation at the Citadel, it was good to have a challenge.

**She became
Thorn, Dark Lantern of Breland.**

THORN OF BRELAND

By Keith Baker

The Queen of Stone

Son of Khyber
Coming Fall 2009

EBERRON

Merry Christmas Jacob!

THE QUEEN OF STONE

THORN OF BRELAND

Enjoy! Stephen

KEITH BAKER

Wizards
OF THE COAST®

2018

Thorn of Breland
The Queen of Stone

©2008 Wizards of the Coast, Inc.

Cover art by Wayne Reynolds
Map by Rob Lazzaretti
First Printing: November 2008

9 8 7 6 5 4 3 2 1

ISBN: 978-0-7869-5009-6
620-21823740-001-EN

U.S., CANADA,   EUROPEAN HEADQUARTERS
ASIA, PACIFIC, & LATIN AMERICA   Hasbro UK Ltd
Wizards of the Coast, Inc.   Caswell Way
P.O. Box 707   Newport, Gwent NP9 0YH
Renton, WA 98057-0707   GREAT BRITAIN
+1-800-324-6496   Save this address for your records.

Visit our web site at www.wizards.com

Last Chants

Forgotten Choir

Crimson Wind

Byeshk Mountains

Wind Howlers

Cazhaak Draal

*Sheshka, the
Queen of Stone*

Brass Talons

Drul Kantar
Thrakelorn

*The
Daughters' Domain*

Blackwater
Lake

The
Watching
Wood

The Great
Crag

Xor'chylic

Graywall

*The Dark
Pack*

Scar River

The Gnoll Clans

Graywall Mountains

Tzaryan Keep

Tzaryan Rrac

Gorodan Ashlord

*Kethelrax the
Cunning*

N
W E
S

0   *miles*   250

To everyone who's joined me in exploring Eberron over these last few years, who has helped to make this dream a reality - and to Malcolm, whose courage and integrity has always been a source of inspiration.

CHAPTER ONE

✷ ✷ ✷

The City of Graywall
Droaam

Eyre 11, 998 YK

The scents of sweat and blood filled the common room of the Bloody Tooth. A minotaur covered in matted black fur bellowed in triumph as he shook blood from his horns. Across the room, a tattooed ogre fell back against the rough stone wall of the tavern, baring three-inch fangs as she clutched her gory shoulder. As the horned beast moved forward to seal his victory, the ogre suddenly rose to her full nine-foot height. A swift snap of her hand sent her blood flying into the eyes of the minotaur. The crowd roared its approval as the two giants grappled again. The shrill voices of goblins mingled with the deeper cries of brutish bugbears and the chortling laughter of hyenalike gnolls. Gargoyles hissed and scratched the floor with stony talons, and the only two dwarves in the bar set aside their bone dice to concentrate on the match. As the brawlers clashed, onlookers spread slivers of precious metal and the teeth of fierce beasts on the tables and floor, tokens of value in a nation yet to mint a coin.

None of the patrons noticed the woman in black as she moved along a wall, just another shadow in the faint and flickering light. Thorn wasn't the only woman of the Five Nations in the Bloody Tooth, but anyone with human blood in this place was likely a cutthroat, bandit, or worse. Thorn had no friends in that tavern—not even the man she had agreed to meet.

Thorn slid a short dagger from its sheath, keeping the dark blade hidden behind her forearm. In this room, bare steel would be seen as a challenge, and the last thing she needed was a fight with a drunken bugbear.

"Where's your gold?" she murmured quietly into the stale air. "Scars or horns?"

You're looking for a goblin. The voice was a cool whisper, as clear as if the speaker were breathing into her ear, but Thorn knew no one else could hear it. *I'm searching for the amulet now.*

"The ogre's a safe bet," Thorn said as another cheer rose from the crowd. "You're just afraid to take a chance."

I have nothing to wager. Steel's voice was detached and indifferent. *And I question your judgment. The ogre has already been injured twice. Her opponent possesses superior natural weaponry. I expect the contest to end soon.*

"I'm sure it will," Thorn said. "Look at the scars. She's seen worse than this. He hasn't."

As if in answer, a roar rose up from the center of the room. As the minotaur charged, the ogre caught his horns in her calloused hands. Grunting from the exertion, she slammed the black-furred beast face-first into the stone floor. The minotaur spat blood and broken teeth, struggled to pull free as the ogre raised him up for another blow.

Thorn smiled. "Where's the mark?"

The aura is strong, but it's out of sight. The crevasse in the left corner. He's about seven feet down the passage. The southern wall of the Bloody Tooth was a sheer rock face, marred by a number of crevasses and small tunnels. *Gnoll tunnels,* Steel explained. *This place must have been a lair. The young seek spaces too small for their parents to interfere with them.*

"A game?" Thorn said, dodging around a chanting

gargoyle as she moved toward the tunnel mouth. Behind her, the crowd cried out again as the ogre smashed her enemy into the floor.

If you call murder a game. They're quite competitive.

"Lovely." Thorn paused at the edge of the passage. A goblin—or young gnoll— might have no difficulty fighting in the tunnel, but it would be a tight fit for her. "Is he alone?"

I can sense only magical emanations. There's one additional aura. I believe it's some type of container, but it's difficult to read. It's an excellent abjuration effect—it can't have been made by his own kind.

"So you don't know what's inside."

No. But I can tell you it's more than it appears. I doubt there's a sorcerer in this city who would notice even that.

"Fine. Let's go." She slipped the dagger into its sheath and stepped out of the tavern and into the dark passage. As Thorn squeezed through a tight corner, her vision shifted into a different spectrum, each stone highlighted in sharp black and white. Thorn slid a finger along her enchanted ring that provided this gift. As useful as it was in her line of work, Thorn was still uncomfortable with darkvision. She'd received the ring only two months ago, just before the mission at Far Passage.

The crevasse came to an abrupt end. A goblin sat on the floor, a rough burlap bag at his side. He wore the gray rags of a laborer, and his skin was covered with dirt and sores. Looking up at Thorn, he plucked a withered tick from one leg and swallowed it.

Thorn saw no sign of weapons or wands, and at this range she could strike before he could complete the workings of a spell. But the Silent Knives of Darguun were trained to kill with their bare hands, and Thorn knew better than to underestimate the little man. She dropped into a crouch and held out her hands, palms up. "Silence is sharp as a blade," she said.

"Yes," said the goblin, his voice low. "Thorn of Breland, is it?"

Thorn gave a slight nod. "Kalakhesh of Darguun?"

"Yes," the goblin said, speaking slowly and deliberately. "Many tales I've heard of you, lady. Much for one so young, though perhaps it is the long-eared blood in your veins that keeps your skin so smooth. I felt sorrow when I learned of the death of Magister ir'Torath of Arcanix . . . all his research lost in that remarkable fire that consumed both house and bone."

"It's always a tragedy when knowledge is destroyed." Thorn said. "I remember hearing about the Arcanix blaze in Sharn, when I was serving with the Royal Guard." She smiled, but behind the mask she was surprised. Not even the Royal Eyes of Aundair knew she'd killed the old wizard, yet it was clear that the goblin knew the truth.

"Oh, so you were not involved?" Kalakhesh smiled. "Pardons—we know so little of your nations. And the damage at Far Passage, you were surely not part of this. We know your Citadel was the moving hand, but it is said all those involved were killed. And here you stand."

Thorn stiffened, hating herself for reacting, knowing that the goblin had seen it. She could still hear Dellan's screams. And she still carried the crystal shards of the explosion in her flesh, embedded in her neck and spine. The stone at the base of her skull pulsed, the pain as sharp as a dagger pressed against her neck.

"We have business in the here and now," she said, ignoring the pain. "I suggest we tend to it."

"Yes," the goblin said. "We do have that." He slid a hand into the worn sack on the floor, producing a large book bound in black leather and gilded with strips of gold. The image of a sword gleamed on the spine, inlaid with bright silver. A figure in relief rose up from the cover—the full-sized image of a man's face. Strong features, jaw set, a slight cleft to his chin . . . familiar, but too faint to recognize.

"I'll need to verify it," Thorn said.

"Do as you must. My hand does not leave until I am paid, and it would be unwise to try to remove it any other way."

Thorn nodded. The goblin hid his feelings well, but she could see the tension in his stance, preparation for battle or betrayal. But she intended neither. She drew her dagger and passed it slowly over the heavy book. The furrow of crimson steel running down the center of the blade burned with a faint light. Thorn said nothing, waiting for the whisper in her mind.

Tell him to open it, Steel said.

Thorn relayed the request, and Kalakhesh turned to a random page. Light filled the room, vellum glowing with a pale white radiance. The image of a knight in silver armor facing a dragon with blood-red scales and flames dripping from its vast maw caught Thorn's eye. The artistry was astonishing, both the sharpness of the lines and the brilliance of the color. Thorn half expected the flames to burn through the page, or to see the image take life as the warrior leaped to dodge the snapping jaws. With a conscious effort, she pulled her eyes away from the picture and glanced at the facing page.

The sheet was covered in words written in gleaming golden ink. In her peripheral vision, she'd seen a spidery, alien alphabet. Yet as she looked at the text, it flowed before her eyes, resolving into new shapes and intelligible words. It was an account of the action seen in the picture—the legendary knight Harryn Stormblade's encounter with Sarmondelaryx, the Bane of Thrane.

Fascinating. It was the first time Thorn had heard any hint of surprise in Steel's voice. *I can't imagine how this was made. This is what we are looking for, Lantern Thorn. Pay him and return to safer ground.*

And then I want some answers, Thorn thought. She couldn't voice her questions around the goblin, so she sheathed the dagger and nodded to Kalakhesh.

"Satisfied?" The goblin closed the book and the light faded.

"Yes." Holding out her hand, Thorn stared at her palm, tracing an arcane pattern with her thoughts. With her mind, she reached into her glove, into the small pocket of space mystically bound to the leather. She pulled, and a leather pouch appeared in her palm. Tugging at the cords, she held the bag open so Kalakhesh could see the glittering red stones within. "Twenty thousand galifars in Narathun rubies. Do you want to inspect them?"

"Unlike you, I have confidence in my allies," Kalakhesh smiled, his eyes cold. "I doubt your Citadel would risk the wrath of the Silent Knives for such a small sum." He slid the book toward Thorn, reaching out for the treasure bag. He released the book as his fingers tightened on the pouch, and he rose to his feet.

Thorn ran the fingers of her left hand across the cover of the book. Even through her gloves, the leather felt warm and soft, all too close to human flesh. She pressed her palm against the book and concentrated; the tome vanished, drawn into the space vacated by the pouch of gems. "How did you get it?"

She didn't expect a response, but the goblin surprised her. "Luck, more than anything," he said. "And not a risk I'd take again, knowing what I would gain. I'd hoped to find a treasure for my people, not a curiosity for yours that would drive me from this country. I am glad to be done with it, and it is well enough that I am done with this place and still alive." Kalakhesh put the gems in his sack and threw the larger bag over his shoulder. "Give me a few steps before you follow."

Thorn nodded and moved out of his way. "Good fortune on your return."

"And you. Stay to the shadows. This is a bad place for my kind, and far worse for yours."

Kalakhesh disappeared around the bend in the tunnel.

The sounds of the brawl had ended, and Thorn wondered if the ogre had won her bout. If so, she'd probably be fighting again by the time Thorn emerged. They didn't call it The Bloody Tooth for nothing. Thorn resolved to give him the count of two hundred before she followed.

Five.

Ten.

PAIN!

Every nerve in Thorn's body burned in agony. She fought against the pain, refusing to pass out. She clung to it, analyzed it, anything to distract her from the torment. And then it was over, leaving her shaken but still standing.

Kalakhesh. The alien voice hissed in Thorn's mind. It sent a shiver of fear through her, like a nightmare she had thought she'd forced from her memory. *You have taken something from the Daughters of Sora Kell, silent singer. I will have the book, and your secrets with it.*

"Lovely," Thorn whispered.

CHAPTER TWO

✳ ✳ ✳

The City of Graywall
Droaam

Eyre 11, 998 YK

The pain fades soon, little thief. The thought rose in her mind, carrying an awful sense of violation and shame, horribly different from her psychic rapport with Steel. *The pain fades soon, and I will feast on your knowledge. All that I wish, you will tell me. All that remains, I will devour.*

Whatever was out there, it wanted the stolen book. She had to escape before Kalakhesh revealed the book's new owner, and there was only one way out of the Bloody Tooth. But Thorn had no intention of charging blindly into the unknown. She whispered a phrase she'd learned at the Citadel, letting her fingers dance along with the syllables, and as she spoke she could feel the power building within her. A tingling sensation swept over her skin as the last syllable left her lips, but there was no time to evaluate the results of her spell.

As soon as she'd made the final gesture, she began again, working her way through another incantation. This one was more difficult, and she could feel the energy fighting her; just speaking the words of the spell was a challenge, each syllable forced through her lips. This was a ritual of invisibility, and as she finished she saw her hands fade before her. A wondrous gift for a spy, but with limitations. The veil lasted for only a few minutes, and it required a balance of intention—the magic hid her from enemies, but if she harmed another, the spell would shatter and she would be revealed.

Thorn mouthed a silent, instinctive prayer to Olladra as she crept along the fissure, and thought of her father. He had raised her in the faith of the Sovereign Host, before the gods abandoned him to die in the Last War. She quietly drew her sharpest dagger—even if Olladra was listening, trust in her blades was more reliable than trust in any miracle.

There was no time to discuss the situation with Steel, and she trusted that he'd keep silent; she couldn't afford distractions. It took only a moment to reach the mouth of the tunnel, and trusting her invisibility, Thorn stepped into the open room.

Kalakhesh stood before her. His muscles were rigid, veins standing out like thick twine, and his bag lay on the floor beside him. The patrons of the Bloody Tooth watched from the shadows—goblin, gnoll, and gargoyle alike shocked into silence by the presence of the creature walking slowly toward Kalakhesh. The stranger wore a robe of black and red silk, with a high collar rising around his head. He was as gaunt as an old man, skin stretched tight across his bones. But this was no man. His oily flesh was the pale green of a dying toad. Four tentacles emerged from his chin, writhing and clutching at the air. His eyes were pale, bloated orbs with no trace of iris or pupil. His appearance was horrifying, but worse, as he drew closer, Thorn could feel the creature's thoughts wash over her . . . a ripple of malevolence, an echo of every humiliation she'd tried to forget.

Mind flayer, Steel whispered.

Despite the growing influence of the Daughters of Sora Kell, the land of Droaam was a realm ruled by fear. Ogres and harpies easily terrified humans, but it took something truly horrifying to frighten *them*. Mind flayers could read thoughts and crush the willpower of any being, and they fed on the brains of the living. This tentacled monster wasn't lying. He would enslave Kalakhesh, and when the goblin had revealed everything, the flayer would consume what was left of his mind.

Xorchylic, Steel said. *The lord of Graywall. Any flayer would be dangerous, but you cannot fight this one. We must leave. NOW!*

Thorn knew he was right, and yet she hesitated. The mind flayer moved slowly, basking in the terror of the audience. Paralyzed by psychic pain, Kalakhesh could only watch his death approaching. An awful way for anyone to die, but worse still for a spy. Knowing that he would be forced to betray his country, that every secret would be stripped from him . . .

What are you waiting for? Steel hissed. *Go!*

Thorn sidled up to Kalakhesh, carefully studying his neck. A revolting shiver of joy swept over her, the triumph of the flayer as it reached out for its prey. As Steel shouted in her thoughts, Thorn seized the goblin's head with one hand and struck with the other. Kalakhesh jerked as the enchanted blade severed his spine and drove into his brain, but it was pure reflex; it was a perfect killing blow, and Thorn knew he was dead on his feet.

She slammed the heel of her hand against the goblin's head, forcing her blade free of its grisly sheath and driving the corpse forward. Blood and brain matter burst from the wound, spattering her right hand. But that was the least of her concerns. As Kalakhesh's corpse fell to its knees in front of the mind flayer, a tingling sizzled across Thorn's skin as her bloody blade appeared before her. Thorn had sought to spare the goblin from a horrible death, but for all that it was merciful, it was an act of aggression. Thorn had shattered her invisibility, and as the first drop of his blood struck the granite floor, she flickered into view.

She knew she couldn't fight Xorchylic. He was too strong, one of the chosen lieutenants of the Daughters of Sora Kell. The master of Graywall would shatter her will and consume her mind, and no one would drive a dagger through her brain. There was only one thing she could do. As she shimmered into view, she stared directly into the mind flayer's eyes.

For an instant she saw her image reflected in the pale white orbs, saw the snakes coiling around her head and the scales covering her skin. Then Xorchylic jerked away, raising his hands to shield his eyes, a satisfying pulse of pure terror radiating from his mind.

It took something terrifying indeed to frighten a mind flayer.

Thorn snatched Kalakhesh's bag off the floor and leaped forward, racing toward the arch leading to the street. The creatures in her way cried out in shock and fear, turning away and covering their faces. As she ran, Thorn thrust her hand inside the sack. Dropping her weapon into the space within, she formed an image of the bag of rubies in her mind, and as she'd hoped, she felt the contents shift and the purse rise into her grasp.

STOP!!! The thought was carried on a wave of agony. All around Thorn, creatures twitched and screamed. A goblin collapsed, and a gargoyle dug furrows in its stony skin with its claws. But the pain flowed around her. She could feel the flayer's fury, though it was a distant echo; something pushed it away from her mind. Thorn didn't waste time questioning her good fortune. In his anger, the mind flayer had inadvertently stunned anyone who might have tried to block Thorn's path, including his own minions. Three ogres and a troll wearing the armor of the Flayer Guards spanned the archway, but all were moaning and clawing at their skulls.

She slipped between the wart-covered legs of the troll, pulled the gem pouch from the sack and scattered the contents behind her, littering the floor with rubies. The stones would make for treacherous footing, and she could already hear the yelps of gamblers as greed warred with fear. Trusting that the chaos would buy her a few moments, Thorn leaped through the open arch and into the night that lay beyond.

CHAPTER THREE

✗ ✗ ✗

The City of Graywall
Droaam

Eyre 11, 998 YK

Three full moons hung in the sky over Bone Lane. Graywall was a nocturnal city, and those creatures that shunned the sun came out to barter and fight under the light of the moons. Bursting out of the Bloody Tooth, Thorn ran headlong into the milling throng of monsters. She pressed into the crowd, darting between the legs of giants and leaping over goblins, weaving her way through the maze of flesh and fur. An orc stepped into her path, a squat warrior with steel-tipped tusks and an ugly cleaver. As soon as he caught her eye, the orc gave a strangled cry, dropping his blade and hurling himself out of her way.

A narrow alley lay to her right, and Thorn ducked into the opening. She'd done some scouting before her meeting—a little labyrinth of narrow passages hid that way, too small for any ogre or troll to follow. She took a moment to rest and to remember the path to return to the palace.

A puddle of water lay ahead of her, and Thorn studied her reflection. Her skin was covered with coppery scales, her teeth sharp needles, and her hair was a mane of living serpents, coiled as if ready to strike. The face of a medusa. It was the first spell she'd cast in the Bloody

Tooth—an illusion to cloak her appearance, disguising herself as this monster. The people of Droaam dealt with medusas, and they knew the deadly consequences of meeting a medusa's gaze. Though Thorn's eyes lacked that mystical power, the fear was sufficient to shake even Xorchylic. The disguise wouldn't hold up under long examination, but it had served its purpose. Her reflection blurred as the mystical energies faded, and Thorn could see her own true face. She reached into Kalakhesh's sack and retrieved her dagger.

"We're safe," she whispered.

I doubt it, Steel said. *Disguised or not, you revealed yourself to Xorchylic. He'll be able to track your thoughts.*

"Please," Thorn said. "I know we haven't worked together before, but I *am* a Dark Lantern. I learned counter-divination my first year."

And Xorchylic is a mind flayer, one of great power. Your technique is impressive, but we can only guess at his mental abilities.

"You didn't see his eyes," Thorn said. "Whatever powers he might have, he was too surprised to get a lock on me."

Then he will find another way. The trackers of the Znir Pact can follow a trail better than any hound, and your scent is all over that tavern.

"I have a plan," Thorn said. "And I don't need to explain every detail to my dagger." She returned the dagger to its sheath before Steel could respond.

Thorn had learned only a handful of spells . . . brief invisibility, disguise, the power to leap a great distance or cling to a sheer surface for a few moments. Her greatest trick was a ritual that concealed her scent and hid all traces of her passage. Thorn had planned to use it to cover her escape, but her ability to draw on magical energy was limited—and she hadn't expected to cast so many spells in the Bloody Tooth. She reached out with her thoughts, flexing her fingers and whispering the first syllable of the spell, but it was no use. Without the power, the words had no effect, and she couldn't draw from the source of the magic. But there were other ways to block pursuit.

Thorn moved deeper into the maze of alleys. The three moons above spread light and shadow across her path. Rhaan's pale blue radiance blended with the reddish light of Aryth to cast a purple hue across the city. Faint Sypheros was shadowy even when it was full. The orange moon, Olarune, wouldn't be truly full for at least a few days, but this was the month of Eyre, and her moon was especially bright. Once it was high in the sky, Thorn imagined the night would be nearly as bright as full day.

She emerged in a small courtyard, a convergence for alleys leading to the major streets. The air was filled with a foul stench, hot blood and bitter chemicals, and even though she'd been prepared for it, Thorn had to pause to hold back the bile in her throat. The pavement was dark, crusted stone, and Thorn realized she was walking across dried blood.

A high, sharp scream rang out to her left, only to be cut off by the sound of steel on stone and a bugbear's laughter. Thorn didn't reach for her blades. There was no danger here. The sounds and the blood both came from a slaughterhouse, where the bugbear butchers were preparing meat for a city of monsters. The tannery next door processed the hides produced by its neighbor, and together the industries produced the vile odor that permeated the courtyard. The smell was enough to turn Thorn's stomach, and it would be a thousand times worse for any creature with a sensitive nose. All she had to do was mask her scent, rubbing some of the offal from the killing floor across her clothing. Even if they used trackers, the stink would cover her true scent, making her indistinguishable from any other slaughterhouse worker. She had only one problem: the beast sitting in front of the slaughterhouse gate, calmly devouring a pair of equine legs.

Her first impression was of his face. He looks like King Boranel, she thought, knowing that was madness. The strong brow, prominent nose, wide cheekbones, even the thin mustache and goatee . . . all strikingly reminiscent of Breland's king. Of course, the creature's head was twice the size of Boranel's, and his bloodstained mouth was lined with a double row of vicious teeth. Red, leathery wings spread out as the creature met her gaze, revealing the tawny flanks of a lion. A manticore.

Thorn had seen manticores before. During a mission in the Mror Holds, she was set upon by a gang of dwarf separatists mounted on manticores. This beast was larger than she remembered, his features less bestial than his Mror cousins. And where the eastern manticores had clusters of quills along their tails, this beast had a scorpion's barb. Wings and stinger . . . part wyvern, she thought idly. And part king. I wonder what Steel will make of this.

"Are you hungry, little one?" the manticore rumbled. Blood dripped onto the stones as he spoke. "You're welcome to a leg. I assume you don't want an arm."

He leaned down and Thorn heard the crack of snapping bone. When he rose again, a human arm dangled from his jaws. Then Thorn saw the bare and bloody torso, the stump of the neck—the corpse of a centaur. The manticore raised his head and wolfed down the arm, keeping one eye fixed on Thorn as he swallowed.

Though Thorn's first instinct was to flee, she held her ground. Compared to the mind flayer, this creature was almost mundane. And the manticore seemed more curious than aggressive; it was testing her.

It was an opportunity.

"I've had all the horse I can stomach for one evening. How's your appetite for flesh?"

"My hunger is all-consuming," the manticore replied. "But you have chosen your shape well. I have no taste for elf, and I see the taint of the old ones in your features." He sank his teeth into the centaur's chest, tearing out the heart and swallowing it. "What brings you to this place?"

"I wanted to take in the air." Thorn took a deep breath and managed not to choke. "I've heard so much about the night breezes of Droaam."

The manticore laughed, thunder echoing off the walls of the square. "I see there is strength within you, despite that fragile frame. But it's not safe to be walking the back paths at night, not with Olarune on the rise."

"That's what I've heard," Thorn said. "But I've never been one to take advice from strangers."

"And are we strangers?" The beast looked at her, a smile on his bloody lips.

Thorn was puzzled by the manticore's increasingly jovial demeanor, but it served her purposes. "Stranger than most."

"Yes," he said, "We are at that."

"Of course, the best place to take in the air is in the air," Thorn said. "Could you help me with that?" Masking her scent was a good plan, but flying out of the square would be even better.

The manticore considered this as he chewed on the centaur's other arm. "You would sit on my back? Hold fast to my mane?"

"That's what I had in mind."

"And you have no fear of my venom?" The stinger twitched, a drop of poison glistening on its tip. "My spite has laid dragons low."

"Give me your word that you'll give me safe passage and I'll trust you."

"And why would you say such a thing, little elfblood?"

"You have an honest face." The truth was harder to explain. She just *believed* it. She felt as if she'd seen this beast in a dream, that this had all happened before.

The manticore licked a paw and dabbed at his chin. "And the reward? What do you offer for the might of my wings?"

"What do you want?" Thorn knew this was coming, but she didn't know what to expect. The creature had no hands. Did he have any use for gems or gold?

"A story."

"Well, I'm no Phiarlan sage-singer, but—"

The beast laughed again, the rumble echoing around her. "No," he said. "It is *your* story that I wish to hear. A tale of my choosing, a truth from your past."

Thorn's doubt was echoed by the shard of crystal embedded in her neck. As her eyes narrowed, the stone grew warm and shivers of pain flowed along her spine. Did the beast know her true profession? Did it want some secret of the Lanterns?

"Very well," she said at last. "But it must be my story, and mine alone. I will not reveal any secrets that could harm my friends."

"Acceptable," the manticore said. He had cleaned the blood from his fur and face. He rose and stretched his front legs. His movements revealed powerful muscles—a sinuous grace in his leonine limbs, a touch of draconic majesty in his outstretched wings. He knelt before her. "Mount, lady. I will not harm you on this journey."

"And when we reach our destination?"

"You will not feel my sting under the light of these moons, little one," he replied. "You are safe until I have my story, and there will be another time for that."

Hardly a reassuring answer. But the image of Xorchylic still lingered in her mind, and the memory of the pale white eyes of the flayer drove Thorn onto the creature's back.

The manticore rose to his feet, and Thorn sank her fingers into his fur. She was already beginning to regret the decision. The Mror riders had saddles and stirrups.

"Before I take to the air, I should know where you wish to land."

"The Calabas," she said. "Someplace quiet. I don't want to cause a disturbance, especially at this hour."

"Of course." Thorn could feel the manticore's rumbling laughter shaking his sides. Then the beast leaped forward and rose sharply into the air, and suddenly laughter was the least of her worries.

Thorn didn't speak as they flew over the streets of Graywall. The wind drowned out all other sound. Thorn twisted on the creature's back, shifting her balance to keep from falling. Was this all a cruel game? The manticore promised that he wouldn't harm her, but that left Thorn free to kill herself.

Balancing on the creature's back took most of her concentration, but Thorn was able to take in the view of Graywall stretched below her.

Humans typically built cities on flat land, clearing obstacles from their way. Graywall was built in a mountain pass, a valley choked with tors and chunks of stone, but the city absorbed and assimilated them. Buildings merged into the edges of cliffs. Stonework was bound to hills that had served as lairs for gnolls and gargoyles long before the architects came. Beyond this blend of raw stone and artifice, the city had the same bizarre traits she'd noticed on the ground.

At a glance, the buildings seemed rough, functional, almost perfectly uniform. The roofs were an odd design—wide slabs of stone interlaced like a deck of cards, presumably supported by plaster or pillars below. The stone had the same subtle patterning she'd seen on the alley walls, and the faint shadows seemed to ripple in the moonlight, like the surface of a quiet pool. It was bright enough to discern each building under the light of the three moons, but the appearance would be quite different on a dark or cloudy night, when the moons hid their faces from the world.

The Calabas was something else entirely. It might

have been plucked from another land and dropped into Graywall as punishment. This was the foreign quarter, home to merchants, explorers, exiles, and others who dared deal with the savage creatures of the west. Built by the architects of the dragonmarked House Tharashk, it was designed for the comfort of humans and their kin. Coldfire lanterns spread light across the streets. Ogres or trolls would have to crouch to fit through the doorways of most buildings, and many of the hostels and taverns had painted walls and windows of glass—sharp contrast to the stark stone of the city proper.

True to his word, the manticore descended in a quiet spot behind a Tharashk warehouse. Most of the inhabitants of the Calabas kept the hours of their homelands, and compared to the bustle outside the Bloody Tooth, the streets of the quarter were peaceful.

"What story do you want to hear?" Thorn asked, once she'd stumbled to the ground. Her legs were weak and the world was spinning around her, but she kept her mind fixed on one simple thought: don't vomit on the manticore.

"No. Now is not the time," the manticore said, looking down at her. "You have forgotten the story I wish to hear. We will meet again, under different moons."

"What do you—"

He was gone before she'd finished the sentence, leaping over her and rising into the sky. He circled above her, and for a moment his shadow passed across the orange face of Olarune. Then he was lost amid the darkness and the stars.

The manticore's words followed her as Thorn made her way to the plaza known as the Roar. Even as her balance returned and her stomach settled, the memories of the conversation haunted her. *Are we strangers?* What did he mean by that? What tale from her past could interest a creature from this savage land? Could he have fought in the war? In the final years of the war, House Tharashk had brokered the services of monstrous mercenaries . . . could this manticore have served under a Brelish banner?

She wondered if he knew her father.

No, she thought. More likely he was toying with her, taking pleasure in sowing doubt and confusion. Whatever the truth of it, he had served his purpose; Thorn had reached the Roar.

The plaza was lined with taverns, shops, and hostels, all built to cater to travelers and expatriates who longed for a last hint of home in this strange city. It took its name from the bronze statue at the center of the plaza—a mighty dragonne, with the body of a lion and the wings and scales of a dragon. It stood on its hind legs, wings outstretched, roaring at the sky. This was the sigil of the dragonmarked House Tharashk, the House of Finding, and the Tharashk fortress was the most imposing building on the square.

The Tharashk keep was one of the most important outposts of the house beyond its homeland in the Shadow Marches, serving as a central point for prospecting operations along the Graywall Mountains and a recruiting center for the mercenaries the house brought out of Droaam. As governor of Graywall, the mind flayer Xorchylic had granted Tharashk the power to administer justice in the Calabas, and since Thorn had arrived within its bounds, she felt safe from pursuit.

Thorn studied the dragonne. After watching the manticore tear out a centaur's heart, it was hard to be impressed by this chunk of lifeless metal.

Quiet as the plaza was, there were still signs of life in the early hours of the morning. A handful of orcs and half-orcs dressed in Tharashk livery wrestled and laughed. Two dwarves sang a Mror chant outside Dorn's Flagon, a tavern known more for the size of its tankards than the quality of the ale.

The black garb Thorn had worn for the meeting with Kalakhesh would have drawn bemused glances from the

Tharashk laborers, so she'd changed on her way to the Roar. Shiftweave allowed Thorn to transform her clothing with a simple thought. Her options were limited to only a few different styles, but the ability to switch garments was invaluable in her line of work.

She changed her outfit to the dress of a courtier traveling on diplomatic business, the bear of Breland embroidered on her breast. A few jewels glittered on her traveling gown—not so many as to invite thieves, but enough to suggest her importance. Her dagger hung from her belt—in Droaam, only a fool would be completely unarmed.

The Tharashk keep was a true fortress, built to withstand riots. By contrast, the building that lay directly across the plaza could have served as a summer palace in the golden age of Galifar; it was built for beauty, not war. Whorled marble pillars supported a sloping roof. A hound carved from basalt stood just beyond the gates, frozen in mid leap. The head and forequarters of the dog were bronzed, sharply visible in the coldfire and the light of the moons. The hindquarters were glass and shadow, as if the dog were appearing from the darkness. Beyond the hound, the five heads of a golden hydra adorned the arch, staring down at approaching travelers. But the walls of the building truly caught the eye: polished black marble that glittered with points of light. Even in brightest daylight, this was a glorious citadel of shadows—a Twilight Palace. The staff were recruited exclusively from the Five Nations and trained to provide comfort to those wealthy travelers who wished to forget they were in Droaam.

The proprietors of the Twilight Palace also went out of their way to erase the scars of the Last War. The décor drew from Galifar at its height. Tall tapestries depicted heroes of the unified kingdom, carefully chosen from each of the Five Nations of Galifar. It was a symbolic effort; more than a picture of Bright Kethan would be needed to bring a Karrn and a Thrane together at one table. But Thorn was always fascinated to see the world of her great-grandfather, a world in which the people of the Five Nations stood as one.

A steward caught her eye with a questioning glance. Thorn wanted a drink. She wanted dreamlily . . . anything that would make the pain of the burning stones go away. But as she raised her hand, she saw the tapestry that hung behind the steward, the image of the knight with the flashing sword and the fierce red dragon. Harryn Stormblade.

She had no time to waste. Thorn pulled a bottle of dark liquid off the tray of a passing steward, silencing his complaints with two gold coins. She made her way to her room and slid the cover off the coldfire lantern. Passing her hand over the bed, she called the book forth from the space within her glove. She drew the dagger with the crimson furrow, staring at the red circle on the black pommel.

"Steel," she said. "We need to talk."

CHAPTER FOUR

✠ ✠ ✠

The City of Graywall
Droaam

Eyre 11, 998 YK

When she was a girl, Nyrielle Tam wanted to be a soldier, to fight for Breland like her father. She'd been raised on tales of Brelish bravery and the noble values of her homeland and her king. Other nations were full of villains and madmen. The Thranes were blinded by zealotry. The Cyrans were arrogant cowards, and they would surrender the kingdom to elves and goblins. The Karrns desecrated the bodies of the dead to create zombie armies, and who could say what horrors would fill the world under a Karrnathi king. And the people of Aundair relied on dark magic to slaughter their enemies. By the time Nyrielle was a teenager, though, Aundair and Breland were allies, and people didn't tell those stories as often.

In childhood stories, Breland was a land of opportunity, a place where even the nobles respected the common man, where the lords were truly servants of the people. It was a land of industry and progress, the greatest hope for the future.

As she grew older, Nyrielle learned to recognize propaganda. She could even imagine what the children of Thrane or Karrnath might have been told about Breland. Its people placed gold above honor. Its industrial might spawned corruption and crime. The nobles had no control over their subjects, and the people had largely abandoned their faith in the gods. Slander and lies, but all with the same hint of truth as those childhood tales of other lands.

The people of Breland were more pragmatic than their cousins in other lands, less devoted to Sovereigns and Flame. And there were those who said that the noble families—even the great King Boranel, a hero who'd fought in the vanguard of many a battle—were no longer necessary. It was the royal succession to the throne of Galifar that had brought about a century of war; many believed that the proper response was to abandon the institution of the monarchy and start anew.

For all that, Nyrielle believed in Breland. Her homeland wasn't the paradise of her childhood. But she believed that the king was a good man, that he believed in justice and the rights of his people, and that when the war was over he would tend to the wounds of the nation.

Whenever her father returned home, those wonderful weeks or months before the battles began anew, she forced him to teach her the ways of sword and shield. When her father was away, Nyrielle would wrestle and race with her brother Nandon and the other Khoravar children, building her strength and speed and waiting for the day that she could serve alongside her father on the field of battle.

That day never came. On the 12th of Barrakas, 992 YK, a courier arrived. Her father was dead, killed in a skirmish with Cyran troops. She barely remembered her mother Jaelari, who had left when Nyrielle was just a child. Her father told her that Jaelari had returned to Aerenal, the distant land of the elves, but that she had left a great treasure behind—four beautiful emeralds in the green eyes of her twin children. But those emeralds wouldn't pay her father's debts. Their home was sold and the children put to the streets.

Nyrielle and Nandon were luckier than most orphans of the war. The Khoravar—those who carried the blood of human and elf—of Wroat looked after their own. Nyrielle's father had no relatives in the neighborhood, so others took turns providing shelter for the teenagers. But it was hard for Nyrielle to be grateful.

After the death of his father, Nandon turned against Breland, spitting on the war and all Five Nations. For Nyrielle, the dream of serving Breland was all she had left. Her father had died in the war, but he'd believed it a cause worth dying for. She devoted every moment to her dream, drilling with sticks, chasing rats to build her speed, and waiting for the day she would follow in the footsteps of her father.

She enlisted three years later, and in the training camp she met Zane. At the time, he appeared to be a handsome lieutenant; she learned that it was only one of his many faces. He was impressed by her talents and her lineage; he'd known her father. Zane said that if she truly wished to serve Breland, he knew better ways to do it—battlefields more dangerous than the Crying Fields or the Thrane front. Zane gave her an introduction to the King's Citadel, the hidden hand of the Brelish crown.

The Citadel had many branches. The King's Shields were charged to protect members of the royal family. The King's Wands were the magical experts of Breland, and they provided mystical tools and training to the other branches. The King's Swords were the fist of Breland, deadly soldiers called in when force was the only answer. Nyrielle had first hoped to be a Sword, but her greatest strength wasn't her skill with weaponry. That honor went to her cunning and her speed, her ability to observe and adapt. And so she was inducted into the King's Dark Lanterns.

As a child, Nyrielle Tam had dreamed of being a soldier. Instead, she became a spy, a saboteur, and when necessary, an assassin. She became Thorn, Dark Lantern of Breland.

✳ ✳ ✳ ✳ ✳

Open the book to the final page, Steel said.

"Why?"

Are you questioning your orders, Lantern Thorn? Steel's voice was a chilly whisper in her mind.

"I don't take orders from a piece of metal," Thorn snapped. "And I don't like being kept in the dark about the nature of a mission. What aren't you telling me? Why is Zane keeping secrets?"

I have been part of the Dark Lanterns for one hundred and twelve years, Steel said. *I remember when the Lanterns served the King of Galifar, not simply Breland. I have aided true heroes, and if you think shepherding a wounded agent is some sort of honor, you—*

Thorn dropped the dagger and the voice ceased abruptly. She ran her fingers over the shard embedded at the base of her skull, feeling the pressure of crystal on bone and the fire in her nerves. Thorn hated herself for giving in to the pain. She took a deep swig from the open bottle and almost choked. It was iced tal, and if that wasn't bad enough, it was sweetened with honey. *I didn't think they served children here,* she thought bitterly.

The red circle on the dagger glowed with a faint light, but Thorn ignored it. She picked up the sack she'd taken from Kalakhesh and studied its contents. A small loop of leather cord, just large enough to fit around a finger. A much longer coil of lightweight silk rope. A few sets of rags, the clothes of a goblin servant; a clink of glass against glass revealed vials of dark liquid wrapped up in the filthy clothes. She found a raven's quill and a few folded pieces of parchment covered with writing in the goblin alphabet.

Thorn examined each item, opening a vial to sniff the potion within, considering the cipher used on the parchment notes, testing the quill on the blanket—as she expected, it was enchanted to write on any surface.

Finally, she opened the leather-bound book, turning to the last page.

Light suffused the vellum. Golden ink flowed like quicksilver, settling into words. Half the page was taken up by a picture. It showed a statue of a handsome knight, his hands at his sides, his sword absent. A woman leaned close to him, a woman with golden skin and a mane of snakes for hair. Stone monsters flanked the knight and the medusa; a mighty griffin reared up behind the warrior, a fierce hydra stood across from him. Thorn looked at the words below the image.

Without his sword, the Knight of Storms was a man divided, bereft of his past and his glory. In this state he faced the Queen of Stone and met her pitiless gaze. Now, he who had been the most loyal servant of the King was made subject to the Queen of Stone and left among the ghosts of the Crag. Three keys are needed to free him from his eternal slumber— his sword, his past, and the forgiving kiss of the Queen of Stone.

Thorn picked up the dagger. "I'm listening."

Harryn Stormblade is alive. Steel's voice was cold, but he said nothing about her earlier outburst.

Every child heard the stories. The Knight of Storms, the child of Thronehold, one of the greatest champions of unified Galifar. "He disappeared over two hundred years ago," Thorn said.

In Droaam. And now he's been found.

"In a picture book?" Thorn shook her head. "I'm impressed with the glowing pages and the magic ink, but what makes you think this is anything but a goblin scam to lighten the Brelish treasury by a few thousand galifars?"

Because we've found the statue. It's in the Great Crag. Kalakhesh confirmed it when he contacted us.

"Well, if Kalakhesh said it, it must be true." The crystal in her neck reacted to her frustration, and the pain increased with her anger. She struggled to calm her thoughts and quiet the stone.

The Silent Knives have nothing to gain from it, and you know that. Kalakhesh said that we wouldn't betray Darguun for such a sum—the same holds true for his masters. We have independent confirmation of the existence of this statue—a sketch made by one of our envoys, when the Daughters sought to be recognized at Thronehold. At the time, we assumed it was no more than a monument, a mockery of a fallen hero. Now we know it is the hero himself, most likely given to the Daughters as tribute. Your mission is to recover Harryn from the Great Crag.

Harryn Stormblade. It was easy to see why the Citadel wanted to recover the knight. Few people in Thorn's line of work believed that the current peace would hold, and the support of a true hero of legend would be a powerful tool for any leader who sought to claim the throne of Galifar. "And what of my original assignment?"

That is equally important. You must find a way to accomplish both goals.

"Lovely." But Thorn smiled as she considered the challenge, and the pain began to fade. "So what am I supposed to do? Steal the statue and bring it back to Breland? I don't think it's going to fit in my glove."

If that were the goal, I wouldn't have even mentioned the mission. You won't be stealing a statue. You'll free the man.

Thorn looked at the dagger. "That sounds more promising. How do we do that?"

'The kiss of the Queen of Stone.' Spells can reverse petrification, but they're useless in this case. Sheshka, the so-called Queen of Stone, is no ordinary medusa. We've recovered a few of her victims in the past, and we've never been able to restore them. But 'the medusa's kiss' is a ritual the creatures themselves use to negate the effects of their deadly gaze. There is great power in that book—magic of transformation and divination. I believe that what it says is the truth. We can't

release Harryn Stormblade from his bondage, but Queen Sheshka can. And as one of the most powerful warlords in Droaam, she'll undoubtedly be in attendance at this diplomatic gathering, as will you.

"So I don't need to steal a statue," Thorn said. "I just need to find a statue, kidnap the queen of the medusas, force her to reverse a curse, and smuggle a legendary warrior out of Droaam, all without causing an international incident."

Yes. Sheshka's death is an acceptable loss, provided Breland can't be blamed for it.

"Oh, that was the only thing I was worried about." Thorn's mind raced as she considered the variables. This was what she'd been trained for, and after months of rehabilitation at the Citadel, it was good to have a challenge. "I don't suppose you've got some sort of trick hidden in your pommel for protecting me from a medusa's gaze?"

You'll be protected.

"Is there a 'how' somewhere in this conversation?"

No. We both have our orders, Lantern Thorn. I am to give you the information you need, when I decide you are ready to receive it.

The angry spark was burning in the shards again. "And why is that? Why do I suddenly have a metal nursemaid?"

There were some at the Citadel who were concerned about you returning to the field so soon after the incident at Far Passage. Master Zane hoped that this book would be a false lead, and that you would not have to undertake this mission. However, even with your injuries, he believes you are best suited to the task.

"So you're keeping secrets from me for my own good."

You're angry, the cold voice whispered. *Is that normal for you?*

Thorn cursed under her breath, but she knew the dagger was right. The memories of Far Passage, the pain of the stones . . . they were playing games with her emotions. This wasn't who she was. She closed her eyes and took a deep breath. She thought of her father, of the smile on his face when he saw her after a long absence. She thought of the mission and the challenges she had to overcome. The pain receded, and she was herself again.

"Reconnaissance is first priority," she said. "I'll need the information if I'm going to manage the rescue . . . and I think we'll have to leave quickly once it's done."

I concur.

"Is there anything else I need to know tonight?"

There is nothing more that I may say.

Thorn narrowed her eyes. "That's not quite an answer, is it?"

Steel said nothing.

"That's fine. I need the sleep. I think tomorrow will be an interesting day."

Thorn closed the shutter on the lantern, and the room fell into darkness. Through the blinds of the windows, the moonlight cast purple shadows across the floor.

CHAPTER FIVE

✠ ✠ ✠

The City of Graywall
Droaam

Eyre 12, 998 YK

The laughter of ghosts woke Thorn from her sleep and she sat up. As her thoughts cleared, she realized that the laughter wasn't a remnant of her nightmare . . . it was a sound outside her window.

Gnolls. Lots of gnolls. Thorn reached for her shiftweave and gauntlets.

"Delegates of foreign lands!" The voice was curt and rough, loud enough to echo across the plaza. "Present yourselves! We leave with the setting moon!"

Thorn relaxed. The manticore hadn't betrayed her, and the Pact hadn't tracked her to the Calabas. This was simply business; this was why she was in Droaam.

For a thousand years, the land to the west of Breland had been a savage frontier. Trolls lurked in mountain passes while harpies and wyverns circled the peaks. Many bold warriors traveled west to slay horrors in the name of Galifar; few returned. But over the centuries, these monsters posed little threat to the lands beyond the Graywall Mountains. The creatures weren't organized. Warlords laid claim to land and then fought the other monsters to hold it. Now and again, a flight of harpies or pack of worgs would venture east to prey on human settlers, but for the most part the monsters had more interest in battling their own kind. Then came the Daughters of Sora Kell.

Thirteen years ago, the hags appeared in the west accompanied by an army of ogres, trolls, and other fearsome creatures. Through sheer force and fear they bent the warlords to their will, but they wanted more than power—they wanted a kingdom. The Daughters declared the land west of the mountains to be the sovereign territory of Droaam. Soldiers scoffed at the idea that the beasts of the west could create any sort of nation; surely it would collapse within a decade, and the name of Droaam would be forgotten.

Cyre fell before Droaam. While the Mourning destroyed the heart of Galifar, Droaam built cities and roads, expanding the city of Graywall and the capital, the Great Crag. The hags asked for a voice at the Treaty of Thronehold, but the lords of the eastern nations scoffed at the idea. It was bad enough that Darguun and Valenar were sitting at the table, but those nations had armies and had fought in the Last War. Droaam was a joke, and surely it would be gone in a year. Perhaps, with the war over, Breland would take the time to cleanse the area once and for all.

If it was a joke, no one was laughing any longer. Three years had passed since the Treaty of Thronehold, and Droaam was stronger than ever. Through House Tharashk, the monsters of Droaam found employment as mercenaries and laborers, and the people of the Five Nations saw for themselves the power these creatures possessed. The leaders of the Thronehold nations began to wonder what forces the Daughters of Sora Kell had at their disposal . . . and then the invitations arrived. The hags had asked the leaders of the twelve nations recognized under the Treaty of Thronehold to send representatives to the Great Crag, to reconsider counting Droaam among their number.

It was hard to imagine King Boranel accepting a hag or a mind flayer as a fellow monarch. But it was an excellent chance to get a spy into the heart of Droaam. Thorn's original mission had been a simple one: Observe. Gather information. Find out as much as possible about Droaam's capabilities and intentions. Watch the delegates of the other nations. Breland wouldn't be the only nation with eyes—or knives—at the assemblage.

Thorn had wanted to bathe, but she had no time with the convoy to the Great Crag already gathering. She pulled on her courtier's dress. Dark brown with russet trim and the bear of Breland on the breast, it complemented her auburn hair and dark green eyes. Next came the traveling cloak, and finally her gloves.

Like the rest of her wardrobe, her gloves were made from shiftweave, and she adjusted them to match her outfit; leather gauntlets transformed to long silk gloves. Their appearance meant little to Thorn—what mattered was the pocket of space mystically bound to each glove. One held her rapier; in a fight, she preferred something with more length than a dagger. The other held the book— the chronicle of Harryn Stormblade.

Thorn mentally checked the placement of the dozen professional tools hidden on her person and hid Kalakhesh's sack inside her traveling bag. Shouldering the bag, she made her way into the hall. A polished marble orb was set on a pedestal at the top of the landing. Thorn placed her palm on the orb and felt a slight breeze blow across her skin. The cleansing stone was an Aundairian innovation. As its energy passed over her, it drove dirt and oil from skin, clothes, and hair. In addition, it dispersed the lingering odor of the slaughterhouse, replacing it with a hint of fresh rain. Thorn didn't think any of the creatures outside would be looking for her, but it never hurt to be careful. She took a loaf of brown bread from a silver platter in the atrium and walked onto the Roar.

Seven long wagons were spread across the plaza, their interiors hidden beneath canopies of painted cloth. Dozens of gnoll warriors moved around the convoy, and a knot of gargoyles circled in the sky above the square. Thorn examined the closest soldier—seven to eight feet in height with spotted reddish fur, blunt snout, gleaming green eyes, and strength to rival bugbears. His limbs were long and lanky, and his legs were jointed like those of a dog. Despite the awkward appearance, none of them had any trouble standing or walking upright. The nearest gnoll wore a jerkin of black leather set with iron rivets, and he held a bow taller than Thorn. He glanced at her and grinned. It was difficult to tell if it was meant to be friendly or aggressive.

"People of foreign lands!" The gnoll who had called them out to the Roar shouted. "I will tell you what carriage to ride in. I will hear no argument, and my soldiers will prevent any battles between you. Leave your struggles in this place. I care nothing for your nations, for crimes done to you or your brood. My task is to bring you safely to the Three, and if you must be chained for your safety it will be done."

Thorn glanced around the plaza at the other delegates. The dwarves from the Mror Holds, with jewels and finery fit to rival the King of Breland. The Aundairians—but which was the wizard, and which the spy? Everyone had fallen silent, waiting for the gnoll to speak.

"Aundair! Brown coach!"

Thorn watched the delegates as they moved. Both the servants had hidden pouches and pockets woven into the lining of their cloaks. One would be carrying the many tools of arcane magic—pinches of sulfur, cat whiskers wrapped in paper, little balls of guano from which to conjure fire. The other would have poisons, weapons, lock picks, and tools . . . the same things Thorn had hidden on her person.

Unless, of course, they were both sorcerers *and* spies.

"Breland! Blue coach!"

Gray was about as close to blue as anything on the

plaza, so Thorn made her way toward the gray wagon. She spotted two soldiers in the red and gold uniform cloaks of the Brelish Royal Guard, escorting a familiar figure.

"Nyrielle! There you are!" Lord Beren ir'Wynarn beamed as he caught sight of her, and his escorts turned to face her. "Gentlemen, Nyrielle is here as my aide. Nyri, meet Toli and Grenn, the worst layabouts my cousin could find. I'd say the bear was trying to kill me, but I think you and I could take on these brutes ourselves, eh?"

Thorn laughed, but it was Nyrielle who answered. "Normally, I could fight an even dozen, my lord, but I slept poorly last night. You'd be unwise to rely on me today."

"Then I suppose it falls to me," Beren grumbled, grinning behind his beard. "Good thing I'm up to the challenge. Did I ever tell you about my victory over the champion of Kalnor Pass?"

"I've had the honor of hearing the tale, Lord Beren, but I've always heard it said that your royal cousin King Boranel fought that battle."

Beren waved this aside. "Oh, I let it be spread about that way, yes. Good for morale. But you ask Boranel where the brute's axe is . . . and then come to my manor and see what hangs above the hearth."

Thorn liked Beren, though she doubted that she'd ever be invited to his mansion. A senator and cousin of the king, he'd spent his younger years in battle. Age was beginning to take its toll; streaks of gray snaked through his golden hair, and there were new lines in his face. But he retained strength and pride. He might not be able to fight a dozen gnolls, but he was likely a match for either of his bodyguards.

Thorn guessed that this was how he'd drawn the assignment. The Crag Summit might be an excellent opportunity for espionage, but the diplomatic goals were equally important. Breland needed someone brave enough to sit across the table from a medusa, and someone smart enough to match wits with Sora Katra herself. Beren might not be a hero of legend, but of all the senators she'd met, he was the best.

Thorn doubted Beren knew everything about her mission—especially this business with the Stormblade statue—but Zane had told her that Beren would give her a free hand. She might be attached to the delegation as his aide, but Lord ir'Wynarn was a capable man. She suspected that he wouldn't call on her too often over the course of the summit.

She considered the guardsmen as they climbed the ladder into the coach. Despite Beren's jibes, she knew Boranel wouldn't leave his cousin in the hands of fools. Grenn was a dwarf, and his ease with his armor and the notches on the hilt of his sword spoke of long service. He smiled at Thorn, but if there was any interest in his gaze, it was simple lechery. This man was a soldier, chosen for strength and courage. Thorn was certain he'd lay down his life for his charge without a second thought—provided he saw the enemy coming.

Toli was cut from different cloth. He was taller than Beren, and his dark skin hinted at Seren Islander blood. Thorn could tell that the guard's breastplate was uncomfortable for him; she hated inflexible armor herself. The true tell was his eyes. It was subtle; he was a professional. But Thorn could see him studying her, searching for concealed weapons or other threats, just as she'd done with the Aundairians. King's Shield, she thought. One of the elite bodyguards of the realm, trained to protect the king himself. Good thing, she mused. With a rescue and a kidnapping to plan, I won't have much time to keep him safe.

Toli knew his work. He stopped Beren from climbing into the wagon, carefully testing each rung himself. He disappeared into the wagon for a moment, then appeared at the door of the carriage and offered his hand to Beren. "Please enter, my lord."

The interior of the wagon confirmed Thorn's suspicions. *Troop transport.* The weapon racks were empty, as were the hard wooden benches. But the odor remained, and it didn't take the nose of a gnoll tracker to recognize the scents of oiled steel, sweat, and damp bugbear fur. Bugbears and gnolls were taller than humans, and the benches were too high and wide for comfort.

As they tried to settle themselves, a gnoll climbed up into the wagon. Unlike his cousins, his fur was black, with a crest of red-orange running from his forehead to the base of his spine. Like most gnolls, he had spotted fur; gray patches mottled the coarse blackness. All together, it gave the impression of a line of flame along his back, with flecks of ash blowing across his body.

Thorn could see Toli tensing, his hand slipping to the hilt of his sword. The gnoll wore a small, wedge-shaped shield on one arm. The lower end tapered to a narrow point, sharpened on either side, and Thorn could imagine it being used to disembowel a foe at close range. His other hand held a long axe with steel at both ends. One head was a heavy crescent blade. The other was a spearhead, sharpened along the edges. The ugly weapon showed as much wear as Grenn's sword; Thorn was certain this beast knew the business of war.

"Ghyrryn." The gnoll pounded his chest with the blunt edge of his shield. He spoke slowly, straining to form words in the common tongue around his snout full of sharp teeth. Nonetheless, his voice was clear and deep. "You are in my charge. Breland, this side." He gestured to his right.

"Lord Beren will sit where he chooses," Toli snapped, moving between the nobleman and the gnoll.

"We'd be happy to have Lord Beren ir'Wynarn on our side of the wagon," came a voice from the back of the carriage. The speaker had climbed up moments ago, and Thorn hadn't seen him behind the gnoll.

Toli looked as surprised as Thorn, and that made her feel a little better. It was the bodyguard's job to notice such things, after all. She took measure of the newcomer, and liked what she saw. Human, male, late twenties—the picture of a young courtier. His short brown hair was perfectly groomed. His white silk shirt was spotless and bright. Black breeches. Tall boots of oiled leather. A fine black doublet with glittering silver embroidery along the collar and cuffs, woven into patterns of silver flame. His amulet caught her eye: a small silver arrowhead with the image of a flame engraved on the surface.

"Breland, on the right," the gnoll growled. "Thrane, left."

Toli frowned. Twelve nations, seven wagons. Some of the delegates would be sharing coaches. "Lord Beren. Please sit here, between Grenn and myself."

"Oh, I'd planned to speak with Nyri during our trip," Beren said cheerfully. "I hate to leave a lady without a suitable companion, and Olladra knows the two of you are terribly dull."

"I'm certain your aide can take care of herself," Toli said, with a meaningful glance at Thorn.

"So Lord Beren *won't* sit where he chooses?" Thorn asked innocently. She saw the corner of the Thrane's mouth twitch slightly.

Toli wasn't amused. "Lady Tam, I hope that you understand the dangers we face in this place. We will do our best to defend you, but our first priority is to protect Lord Beren. Please let us do that."

Beren raised a hand. "Look here, boy—"

"He's right, Lord Beren." Thorn nodded to Toli. "I'm sorry for being rude. But you must listen to your guards."

The gnoll was tired of the discussion. "Sit now," he growled. "Others wait outside. Caravans leave before sun rises."

The Brelish took their seats on the hard bench. The

Thrane diplomat sat across from Thorn, flashing a brilliant smile at her. The gnoll moved deeper into the wagon, making room for the remaining members of the Thrane delegation. First came a soldier dressed in a lightweight shirt of polished chain mail. Her sword was drawn, and the engraved blade gleamed in the fading moonlight. Thorn guessed that the steel was mixed with silver. The Thrane warrior studied Beren and his guards with obvious distaste, but sheathed her weapon and took a seat alongside her countryman.

A second soldier helped an elderly elf woman up the ladder into the wagon. The elf wore the habit of a priestess of the Silver Flame, and judging from the pale parchment of her skin and her sunken eyes, she had to be at least four hundred years old—almost as old as the church itself. Apparently, the Thranes weren't concerned about having a delegate who could defend herself if a brawl broke out—or they trusted that the Silver Flame would protect her. For a moment the priestess met Thorn's gaze, and looking into the pale eyes of the elf made Thorn think of her mother. Where was she now? What had led her to Khorvaire thirty years ago, and why had she been so quick to leave?

This was no time to ponder the past. A few more gnolls climbed into the wagon, and they spoke in their own tongue—a strange mix of hoots, whines, and fluting sounds that she never would have expected from creatures with such canine appearance. At long last the black gnoll that had called himself Ghyrryn closed the back flaps of the wagon and sat down next to Thorn. He gave a long cry, and a moment later, the wagon lurched forward. The journey to the Great Crag had begun.

CHAPTER SIX

✠ ✠ ✠

The Korlaak Pass
Droaam

Eyre 12, 998 YK

The benches were uncomfortable, and the wagon bumpy and unsteady on the rough road. The passengers had to clutch the edges of their seats to keep from sliding or falling. Toli and Grenn had passed the first hour of the trip glaring at their Thrane counterparts. For their part, the Thranes sought to project cool disinterest, but the tension was there.

Toward the end of the war, Thrane had been one of Breland's greatest rivals. Beset on all sides and hamstrung by the betrayal of its mercenary forces, Cyre had been pushed into a desperate position, struggling to defend its remaining territory against the constant pressure of Breland, Karrnath, and Darguun. Breland had formed alliances with Aundair and Zilargo, and Karrnath was too far away to pose a true threat. Which left Thrane as the most significant danger to Brelish security.

Early in the war, the people of Thrane had turned away from the rule of royalty and fully embraced the Church of the Silver Flame, and the faith served them well in the struggle. When the conflict began, the standing army of Thrane was far smaller than that of Breland or Karrnath, and it lacked foundries to produce the weapons of war.

But whereas its army was small, its civilian militias were vast. The followers of the Silver Flame were charged to fight against darkness, and villagers trained with spear and bow. Two centuries earlier, they had exterminated the werewolves and shapechangers of the western woods; that same zeal gave them the courage to defend their nation against human foes.

Beyond the courage of the commoner, the priests of Thrane were true miracle workers. The people of Breland were pragmatists by nature, never fond of things they couldn't measure or prove. The work of a wizard was based on formulas and arcane science, and the Brelish could grasp it. But the magic of a cleric was a thing of pure, trusting faith, and when it came to faith, few people could match the Thranes.

"How did you come to be in civil service, Lady . . . Tam, was it?" They were the first words the envoy had spoken since the trip began. "I thought I knew the sixty families of Sharn as well as the royal lines of Galifar, but I don't recall ever hearing the name Tam."

Thorn studied the man sitting across from her. Perfect skin, not a hair out of place, fine clothes—unusual for a nation driven by such an ascetic faith. The priestess had an aura of serenity, and her habit was far simpler than her comrade's garb, with his glittering embroidered flames. No sign of a weapon, no wand that she could see . . . was he truly just a diplomat?

"My father was a soldier," Thorn said. "In Breland, you don't need gold or noble blood to serve the nation. And what of your lineage? I'd hate to sully your ears with my common speech."

The man laughed. "No fear of that. I am Drego Sarhain, milady. And surely, I am as common as they come."

Thorn glanced at his gleaming cuffs. "Rather fine work for a common man."

He waved his hand dismissively. "Your father was a

soldier; my mother, a seamstress. We each have our heir-looms." He gestured at the dagger Thorn wore on her belt. "Your father's blade?"

Perfect!

"Yes, it's been in my family for generations." She drew the blade from its sheath. The eyes of the gnolls and the Thrane soldiers locked on her, but she simply laid the dagger across her legs. "I've always wondered what stories it could tell, if only it could talk."

Very funny, Steel whispered in her mind. *Give me a few moments and I'll see what I can find.*

"An interesting design," Drego said, studying the dagger from across the wagon. "Balanced for throwing, yes? May I take a closer look?" He extended his hand.

"I'm afraid not," Thorn replied. "My father was a very superstitious man, and he left strict instructions concerning treatment of the blade. I'm sure your mother wouldn't want to see me wearing your clothes, would she?"

"Probably not," the Thrane said with a smile. "But I wouldn't mind."

Thorn raised an eyebrow, glancing slightly toward the priestess. "Why, Lord Sarhain, should you be saying such things in the presence of Minister Luala—a holy woman?"

"You labor under a common misconception, Lady Tam. We have our political differences, but my faith is based on defending the innocent from *supernatural* threats. So unless you're some sort of disguised demon temptress, I need not shield myself from your presence. And if you must be formal, it's Flamebearer Sarhain. But if we're going to spend the next few days sharing a wagon, I'd prefer Drego."

"Then it's only fair for you to call me Nyrielle," she replied. "So . . . tell me all about Drego Sarhain."

The diplomat launched into his story—born to parents of low status, studying the courtly ways of his mother's customers, reading romance stories in addition to the holy texts of the church, becoming an apprentice to a minstrel until his magical talents were discovered, and, much to his surprise, drawn into government service. It was a good story; some of it might have even been true. But Thorn hadn't been listening to Drego.

Be careful, Steel said. *The priestess is wearing protective charms. She's safe from poisons, and her thoughts are protected from all divinations. Standard diplomatic warding—Lord Beren has much the same. Our guard Toli has a few tricks hidden away. And the two Thrane soldiers have spells strengthening their armor and potions of healing in those belt pouches. But your friend Drego—nothing at all.*

". . . so I was asked to perform for Cardinal Krozen himself," Sarhain was saying.

"Really? How is that possible?" Thorn tapped Steel as she spoke, continuing to feign interest in Drego's story.

Either he has the same sort of training you do—in which case he's very good—or he's using some sort of tool to protect himself from my examination. Either way, it means that he has something worth hiding. He's not just a simple envoy. The question is whether he's an envoy at all.

"That's fascinating," Thorn said to both Steel and Sarhain, and the Thrane beamed at her. Whatever he was hiding, he certainly had an enchanting smile. She examined him more closely. No gloves. No cloak. Not even a backpack or a satchel. Only the silver amulet around his neck and an unmarked copper band around one finger. What secrets was he protecting?

"And what of you?" he asked her, having reached the end of his long tale. "What does Nyrielle Tam have to say for herself?"

"Nothing so interesting," she replied with a shy smile. "I thought I'd follow my father to war, but you know how it is. I'm just not cut out for bloody work."

Oh, you're a lamb, Steel said.

"Honestly, I'm not even sure why I carry this," she said to Sarhain, returning the dagger to its sheath. "I'll probably end up hurting myself." She looked down the bench. "Lord Beren! I'm sure Flamebearer Sarhain would love to hear about your deeds at Kalnor Pass."

"Ah!" Beren cried, leaning out to look past his guards. "A man after my own heart, always keen to hear a tale of blood and battle. Now tell me, lad, have *you* ever faced an ogre in battle?"

Thorn continued to deflect further inquiries from Drego Sarhain, turning the conversation toward his companions or the difficulties of the journey. This was complicated by the fact that the Thrane priestess—Minister Luala—had taken a vow of silence, saving her words and her wits for the business at Flamekeep. Surprisingly, the gnolls proved to be more loquacious than the Thranes. Thorn noticed that each of them wore cords around their necks or wrists, with bits of metal, hair, or cloth, bound by leather. Their leader, Ghyrryn, explained that gnolls of the Znir Pact retained souvenirs to remember each kill.

"The Keeper takes us all," he told Thorn. "When you come to the final lands, the prey of past hunts will be waiting. Honor them in life and they will honor you in death. Let them be forgotten, and they will be hungry and filled with rage."

Ghyrryn showed her each of his totems—links of chain mail, knots of hair, claws, fangs. Jharl, the archer sitting across from her, was a tracker; he carried strips of cloth and leather taken from his victims' clothes or skin. He seemed especially intrigued by Thorn's scent, sniffing her hand and hair a few times. Thorn also noticed that he paid a great deal of attention to Drego Sarhain. The interest was subtle, but when the Thrane envoy looked away, the gnoll would breathe deeply, tasting the air around him.

Hours passed, and the well of conversation ran dry. Thorn was considering lying down on the floor to try to get some sleep when the gnolls rose to their feet. Ghyrryn hooted and whined.

"What is it?" she said to Ghyrryn. Around her, the soldiers of the Five Nations had hands on their weapons, ready to defend their charges.

"You are not concerned," he told her.

"Humor me."

"Korlaak Pass. Long crossing. The Pact will pass first and last, secure the bridge. You have no fear."

Thorn could hear gnolls moving around the wagon, forming into squads. Around her, the human bodyguards drew their weapons. Toli was clearly suspicious and prepared for gnoll treachery. Outside, squad leaders barked commands and Thorn heard the troops moving forward. A few moments later, the wagon began rolling again. The bumpy road beneath the wheels shifted to smooth stone. Lifting the back flap of the wagon, Thorn could see a massive span stretching across a deep gorge—an impressive piece of architecture that seemed beyond the skills of the architects of Graywall. Three more wagons rolled across the bridge behind her, surrounded by gnoll soldiers. A trio of gargoyles circled in the sky above.

The wagons continued to move forward, and Thorn let the flap close. They rolled another fifty paces, then a shriek of alarm pierced the skies—the cry of a gargoyle scout, quickly picked up by another. Toli clenched his fist and a shield appeared—an oval formed from dark energy—and he moved his arm to protect Beren. Thorn watched Drego Sarhain, but the Thrane took no action; was he oblivious, or did he have such great confidence in the Thrane guards that he had no fear? She drew Steel, keeping the blade hidden against her inner arm.

Then the song began . . . and moments later, the screaming.

CHAPTER SEVEN

✠ ✠ ✠

The Korlaak Pass
Droaam

Eyre 12, 998 YK

The song was the most beautiful sound Thorn had ever heard, but it was too far away for her to make out the words. She needed to move closer, to find a place where she could hear the lovely song. Then a second voice chimed in, and a third, a chorus coming from all around her.

The first scream came within moments, and it didn't come from a human throat. It was a wailing howl, a gnoll's cry of terror, and it faded too quickly for comfort. The scream snapped Thorn free from her reverie and into chaos.

With each passing moment, a new scream rose outside the wagon, but Thorn was more concerned with the situation within. The dwarf Grenn had drawn his sword and began cutting a hole in the canvas covering the wagon. A dreamy, distant look filled his eyes, and Thorn remembered the urge to follow the exquisite music, to reach its source. The effect had completely taken hold of Grenn. And he wasn't alone. One of the gnolls had leaped out the back of the wagon. Drego Sarhain was holding onto the old priestess while the two Thrane soldiers were cutting their own holes in the canvas. Toli wrestled with Lord Beren, struggling to keep the diplomat inside.

Harpies, Steel whispered, confirming Thorn's thoughts. She could imagine the scene outside the wagons. Harpies beyond the bridge, calling out in their beautiful voices . . . and gnolls and guards leaping to their deaths in a doomed quest to reach the miraculous sound.

What can I do?

Someone else had an answer. Ghyrryn dropped his axe and drew an object out of a pouch on his belt—a round stone about the size of a human eyeball. He threw it to the floor and a thunderous explosion shook the wagon. There was no flame—just an immense boom that replaced both song and screams with a dull ringing.

Thorn shook her head, catching her bearings. Grenn was missing, but the deafening blast had shattered the harpy's seductive power, and the others were clutching their heads and gathering their wits. Three gnolls were still in the wagon—Ghyrryn, the archer Jharl, and a halberdier who hadn't spoken during the journey.

Ghyrryn snatched up his axe and struck the flat against the canopy to attract attention. Once all eyes were upon him, he made a sweeping gesture encompassing the passengers, then pointed at the floor. The meaning was plain enough—*stay here!* He turned and jumped off the wagon, accompanied by the archer. The halberdier moved into the center of the coach, lowering his weapon to block the passage.

Toli pushed Beren back onto the bench. The lord's hand was on the hilt of his sword, and his lips were drawn back in a scowl. Toli was right—as a diplomat, Beren needed to stay out of danger. But the soldier in him surely wanted to take the fight to the enemy. Thorn knew the feeling intimately.

The canvas of the coach offered no sanctuary. Deafened as she was, Thorn didn't hear the arrows tearing through the cloth, or the cries as they bored into flesh. Toli staggered under the impact of an ash shaft that drove through his breastplate and into his shoulder. Bad as it was, he was still alive; one of the Thranes wasn't so lucky. Younger than Thorn, she wouldn't see another season; an arrow passed fully through her throat, and two more lodged in her chest. She collapsed against the edge of the wagon, leaving a trail of blood as she slid down. The old priestess pushed Drego aside and bent over the young woman, and silver fire blazed around her wizened hands. But whatever sacred powers she possessed, it was too late for the Thrane; the flames sealed the flesh, but she could not catch her spirit.

Toli was still standing. His magical shield had doubled in size and was almost the height of a man. He'd forced Beren behind it, leaving himself exposed. A spreading bloodstain darkened the fabric of his cloak, and his gritted teeth and the shaft of the arrow were mute testimonies to his devotion to his homeland.

The gnoll soldier still guarded the back of the wagon, but Thorn had no intention of sitting and waiting for the next volley of arrows. Grenn had left a wide hole in the canopy next to her. Given the horrors surrounding them, it was reasonable for the courtier to faint—and an unfortunate coincidence that she slipped into the gap in the cloth and fell through it. Thorn saw Drego Sarhain turning toward her, reaching for her, but he wasn't fast enough to catch her.

It was a short fall, but Thorn was able to twist in the air and get her feet under her. As she landed, she took stock of the world around her.

It was worse than she'd imagined. A trio of harpy archers swept overhead, raining arrows on the blue wagon. She saw the corpses of at least half a dozen gnolls, though she took some comfort from the broken body of a harpy smashed against the bridge.

The worst part was the chaos. The gnolls that had managed to deafen themselves could resist the harpies' song, but they couldn't coordinate their actions. As she took in the situation, Thorn could see that the passengers weren't the only ones threatened by the magical compulsion; the beasts of burden were equally vulnerable, and some were trying to respond to the song Thorn could no longer hear. Beyond the blue wagon, a pair of gnolls was helping a group of gnomes and halflings out of an orange-brown coach, practically throwing the small folk to the ground. Ahead of them, two more gnolls were struggling with the creatures pulling the wagon—massive horses with scaly skin and sharp teeth—while a third gnoll fought to cut the tethers binding the beasts to the vehicle. It was no use. The bizarre horses knocked the handlers aside and charged toward the edge of the bridge. A low lip was all that separated the edge of the stone span from the chasm below, and the horses leaped over the edge, the wooden front wheels shattering as the carriage was pulled after them.

This is an unwise course of action, Steel told her. Though Thorn's ears were still ringing from the thunderstone, the voice of the dagger was perfectly clear. *If you reveal your talents in front of the other delegates—or worse, the gnolls—you'll place the entire mission at risk. Let the soldiers and the bodyguards handle this. You are a political aide, not a warrior of legend.*

"Just tell me how many harpies we're dealing with," Thorn said, hoping Steel could hear her. She couldn't even make out the sound of her own voice.

A gargoyle was sprawled on the ground near the blue wagon, riddled with arrows—no small feat, given the toughness of the creature's stony hide. Thorn seized hold of a leg and dragged the corpse beneath the carriage; she expected it to be a chore, but the body was surprisingly light, as if stuffed with straw.

There are fourteen harpies in the air, Steel told her. *However, in planning such an ambush, I would have placed the singers beneath the bridge, where they could be shielded from attack.*

Weaving a spell proved to be a challenge. Thorn couldn't

hear her own voice, and her chosen incantation always required a little improvisation. She was afraid she might miss a syllable, dispersing the mystical energy.

Focus, she told herself. Stone and strength. Horn and wing. With her gestures and whispered words in the Draconic tongue, she painted a picture of the gargoyle, and she felt the familiar tingle as the illusion took shape around her. The wings were the weakest element. She couldn't stretch the disguise very far beyond her own body, so her illusory wings were folded against her sides. Like her medusa guise at the Bloody Tooth, it wouldn't hold up under close inspection, but it would serve her purpose.

"I hate this part," Thorn muttered, still unable to hear her own words. The next incantation was shorter and simpler, but the spell required a certain talisman to trigger its effect. As she completed the final gesture, Thorn felt the mystical potential building around her. She pulled a box from a hidden pocket, a tiny container too small for even a ring. Flipping it open, she inhaled quickly, drawing a little spider into her mouth. She swallowed before it could start to crawl. Damned spiders.

With a thought, she drew her rapier out of the magical pocket in her right palm and let it fall to the ground. She'd need Steel for the work that lay ahead, and until then she'd need both hands. Each glove could hold only one object, and she wasn't about to leave the magical book on the ground.

What are you— Steel's words were cut off as Thorn drew him into her glove. With all her preparations in place, she leaped out from beneath the wagon.

The battle on the bridge raged around her. Gnoll archers had killed a few harpies and injured a handful, but another wagon was teetering on the edge of the bridge. The remaining harpies targeted the gnolls who were working to control the coaches, and it was a deadly game. The gnolls fought viciously, and a few of the foreign soldiers and even delegates were scattered among them. One of the gnomes Thorn had seen earlier was pointing a wand of pale wood at the sky, unleashing bright bursts of mystical energy that chased his harpy foe no matter how she ducked or swooped. Another gnome lay stretched out in a pool of blood.

Thorn darted along the span and then over the edge of the bridge. To anyone watching, the sight was ordinary— a gargoyle joining the fight, leaping off the bridge to take to the air. But Thorn didn't jump from the bridge—she slipped over the stone lip and set her hands against the sheer surface of the outside wall. Using the energy of her second spell, she crawled down the bridge like a spider.

Though her clothing was hidden by the illusion, Thorn could feel it moving against her skin, the cloak falling over her shoulders as she descended head-first down the wall. Deafened as she was, her world was reduced to sight, smell, and touch. An unconscious glance down into the gorge revealed the corpses scattered along the riverbed far below. It was a discomforting sight, but Thorn was a gifted climber even without the aid of magic. She shook off her concerns and proceeded carefully.

It took only moments for Thorn to reach the lower edge of the bridge, and she peered under the stonework. Steel's theory was accurate. Three harpies were perched on the struts below the bridge—the closest less than twenty feet from Thorn. A handful of gargoyles was clustered around the creatures, and for a moment Thorn was mystified. Then she realized that the harpies were still singing, even though she couldn't hear them. The gargoyles had been drawn to the object of their fascination, and they listened to the song, blissfully unaware of anything around them. The harpies ignored the gargoyles, and that would make her job all the easier. She would appear to be just one more victim, slowly making her way toward certain death.

As Thorn reached the nearest strut, another of the huge

horses tumbled off the side of the bridge, plummeting hundreds of feet. It had been cut free from its harness, but the loss of any of the beasts was surely a problem for the caravan. She needed to act quickly, but without alerting her prey.

For the moment, her slow pace gave her time to consider her target. The harpy had the torso of a human woman, her skin weathered and deeply tanned, her hair wild and windblown. Dark leathery wings sprouted from her shoulders, and as she sat in repose, these were folded against her back. Her legs were those of a bird of prey, with long talons clutching the stone. A host of possibilities ran through Thorn's mind, but she most wanted a swift kill.

As Thorn had hoped, the harpy didn't even glance up as she pushed her way through the gargoyles. The creature's eyes were half-closed, as if lost in the beauty of her own song. Thorn wondered if the harpy considered it an art as well as a weapon. The haunting melody seeped into her thoughts, and a part of her wanted to pause, to listen to the music.

A thought brought Steel into her hand, and Thorn could hear the dagger's protests. Grabbing hold of her victim's hair, Thorn drew the blade to the side, slashing through flesh. Steel had a supernatural edge; he couldn't cut though iron or stone, but he tore through the harpy's neck like soft cheese. Warm blood spattered across Thorn's arms, and the bird woman fell from the bridge, plummeting toward the bodies of those drawn to their deaths.

You might have— Steel didn't get to complete the sentence. As soon as she'd completed the stroke, the dagger was back in her glove. Thorn was just another gargoyle among the others, and she had just enough time to cast a quick spell. She could see the dawning confusion on the faces of the creatures around her, and looking toward the southern end of the bridge, she could see a distant harpy staring at her fallen sister, face frozen in shock. In a moment, the foul creature would gather her wits and begin her song anew—if Thorn gave her the chance. Trying not to think about the broken bodies that lay below her, Thorn leaped out into the space between the struts.

Thorn couldn't fly, but anyone watching might have guessed that the gargoyle could. Her recent spell enhanced her momentum when she jumped, allowing her to cover great distances. Even so, a standing jump to a narrow beam was a terrible risk.

She'd hoped for a safe landing on the strut, for the chance to fight the harpy on her own terms. Instead, Thorn slammed into the creature itself, sending them both tumbling off the beam. The harpy was at home in the air, but Thorn had the advantage of surprise. Before her enemy could shake her free, Thorn wrapped her legs around the harpy's waist and dug fingers into the tough flesh of the creature's throat. The harpy's wings beat against the air as it struggled to push her away; fortunately, the claws on its fingers weren't as long or as sharp as the talons on its feet.

Above them, Thorn saw gargoyles swarming over the third harpy under the bridge. If it had managed to continue its song, it hadn't captured the minds of the gargoyles in time. Thorn had achieved her goal—the only question was whether she'd survive.

The two spun through the air, the harpy beating her wings wildly to counter for the unbalanced weight of her enemy. Her chest heaved from the exertion, and her fingernails dug furrows in Thorn's stomach. But Thorn kept her hands locked around the creature's throat, denying her air.

The creature was desperate, weaving erratically through the sky. Thorn squeezed harder and felt the harpy's throat collapsing under the pressure. Then an unexpected impact forced the air from her lungs. The harpy had smashed into the wall of the gorge, ramming Thorn into the rough stone.

Sharp rocks tore at her flesh, and her right leg slipped from the harpy's waist. She just needed a second to catch her breath, to regain her grip . . .

She didn't have time. The harpy was mad with pain and only wanted to take its foe with it into the darkness. Thorn saw a rocky outcropping rushing toward her, and then the world went white. When her vision cleared, she caught a glimpse of the harpy crumpled against the ledge above her, blood smeared around her crushed skull. Thorn's head throbbed, and her left arm was in agony. Was it broken? Dislocated? Distracted by the pain, it took her an instant to realize the greater concern.

She was falling. And the bottom of the gorge was only seconds away.

CHAPTER EIGHT

✗ ✗ ✗

The Korlaak Pass
Droaam

Eyre 12, 998 YK

For a mad moment Thorn tried to spread her wings, to reach out and catch the howling wind. The delusion passed quickly. Her cloak was flapping around her, and jagged rock lay directly below. She had only moments before impact . . . plenty of time for a woman trained in the City of Towers. The spires of Sharn stretched thousands of feet into the sky, and she'd learned to leap between the bridges, descending a dozen levels in a single jump. But even the best bridge runner missed a step, and sometimes you needed to reach the ground as quickly as possible. And that's why you carried a feather token.

The wind tore at Thorn's cloak, pulling the clasp against her throat. She couldn't move her left arm. She still had strength in her right hand, enough to reach down and touch the buckle of her belt. The air grew thick around her, and Thorn's stomach heaved in protest at the sudden change of velocity. She drifted gently, cushioned by the wind. She had just enough time to shift position, landing on her hand and knees as she struck the rocky floor of the gorge. She grimaced in pain, but it was the pain of falling against cobblestones, not the deadly plummet it could have been.

Thorn rolled onto her back and stared at the bridge and the sky above. She could see figures whirling about, but she couldn't tell if they were gargoyles or harpies. Her heart pounded, and the pain she felt as she gasped for breath suggested a shattered rib. Gritting her teeth, she slapped her hand against her right thigh.

Nothing happened. Thorn didn't have the energy to curse. She had a tattoo on her leg, a mark that had been applied when she was assigned to the mission. Power was stored in the symbol, but it wasn't a form of magic she was used to; it was imported from the distant land of Riedra. "It channels the powers of the mind," the provender had said as he applied it to her skin. "It's not like drinking a potion. You have to want it to happen."

Thorn placed her hand over the symbol, and this time she silenced her thoughts, pushing the pain away and focusing only on the tattoo. "Heal me."

She felt the lines of the symbol itch as power spread through her body. Agony was swept away by soothing warmth as the energy healed flesh and bone. The healing took only seconds, and Thorn raised her left arm, carefully flexing her fingers, then rose to her feet. Cuts, bruises, even the broken rib had been restored. "I might just move to Riedra," Thorn murmured.

Corpses were scattered all around her, broken remnants of human and gnoll. The scent of blood filled the air, and the vermin were already gathering, flies and pale brood-worms burrowing into the bodies.

Thorn had seen worse sights during the war, but the carnage still gave her pause. As her gargoyle disguise faded away, she called Steel out of her glove.

I see you're still alive, he said.

"And you may have noticed that the rain of gnolls has stopped."

What resources did you consume in all this chaos?

"A feather token, a healing tattoo . . . a spider."

That's half your reserves. I hope you don't plan on falling again soon.

Thorn tossed the dagger in the air, then caught it. "This was never part of the plan. I don't recall a briefing that covered the delegates being killed before they reached the Crag. If I'm supposed to be Beren's aide, we need Beren."

The guards—

"Weren't having much success, from what I could see. And I like to keep my options open. Someday, the Citadel just might need a warrior of legend."

Fine. Thorn felt a faint shiver in her mind . . . a psychic sigh, perhaps?

"As much as I enjoy these little chats, I was wondering if you had any insight into the attack. Did the Daughters do this?"

A moment of silence lingered before Steel responded. *The Daughters of Sora Kell are unpredictable. They might do such a thing without telling our gnoll companions. But it seems unlikely. The Daughters put considerable effort into arranging this summit, and the deaths of diplomats would anger the leaders of the other nations. Unless they're trying to start a war, I see no gain.*

"Which means someone else is playing."

Indeed, Steel said. *And if you want to stay part of it, you'd best find a way to return to the caravan.*

"You think so?" Thorn smiled as she returned the dagger to its sheath and shifted her clothing to her envoy's gown. This outfit was still fresh from the coach, so Thorn smeared a little blood and dirt onto the fabric. Then she pried a dented shield from the broken arm of a dead gnoll. A few gargoyles were still circling around the bridge, and Thorn used the shield to catch the light of the sun. After a few tries, she drew the attention of the scouts.

Lured off the edge by the harpy's song, fortunate to have that souvenir from Sharn . . . Thorn composed the story in her mind as the gargoyles came to her rescue.

✕ ✕ ✕ ✕ ✕

"A souvenir from Sharn?" Drego Sarhain laughed. "That's the most ridiculous thing I've ever heard."

Beren ir'Wynarn shook his head. "Have you been to the City of Towers, Flamebearer Sarhain? When you're walking the edge of Skyway, staring at the hard stone a mile below, you might find that peace of mind is worth a few galifars. And I'd say it was gold well spent."

"I suppose so," Drego said. "I apologize, Lady Tam. Blessings to the Flame for sparing us all."

Thorn's daring attack had given the defenders the opportunity they needed to rally and destroy the remaining harpies. But three of the wagons were broken timber on the floor of the gorge. When the gargoyle carried Thorn up to the bridge, she discovered chaos. Diplomats demanded explanations from guards who couldn't hear them, and gnolls struggled to get everyone moving away from the bridge. They called a halt to regroup as soon as they were a safe distance from the span, and the deafening effects of the thunderstones finally faded.

After some animated discussion, growling, and whining, the gnolls drew the entire group off the main road and into a forest, setting up camp beneath the gnarled trees. With the camp settled, the surviving gnolls drew together and appeared to be evaluating the damage and determining how to proceed. Movement in the sky caused a stir among the travelers, but it proved to be the gargoyles bringing salvaged supplies from the shattered wagons.

Night was falling, and the light from the full moons fell through the trees. The passengers of the blue wagon sat around a crackling fire, watching one another uneasily. Jharl, the gnoll tracker who had ridden in their wagon, studied the sky silently, outside the circle, an arrow held to his bowstring. The buzz of flies filled the air, and Thorn fought to push the image of writhing broodworms out of her mind.

The old elf approached Toli. The bodyguard had bandaged his own wound, but he winced whenever he shifted his weight. The priestess reached out her hand, but Toli pulled away, glaring at her.

"Minister Luala only wishes to tend your wounds," Drego said. "She's a gifted healer. Unless you enjoy pain?"

"I'll take the pain over the touch of a Thrane," Toli said, glaring across the bonfire.

"In this, she acts not as an emissary of Thrane, but as a servant of the Silver Flame," Drego said, and the old woman nodded gravely. "We both lost comrades in this attack, and you fought to defend us all. The light of the Flame touches any brave heart, regardless of your nation or your faith. Let us ease your pain."

The minister reached out again, and this time Toli pushed her hand aside. "I saw the light of your Flame at Vathirond, Thrane. I wasn't defending you, and I don't want your help."

Thorn said nothing, watching as the silent priestess returned to the other side of the fire. She understood his anger. The city of Vathirond lay on the border with Thrane and what had once been Cyre. Few Brelish towns had suffered as much during the war, and it took more than a few years of peace to ease the tensions of a century of war.

Soon a gnoll hunter arrived, carrying a brace of large rabbits. Jharl prepared them over the flame, quartering them with his knife and passing chunks out to the travelers. With no spices and only water to wash it down, it wasn't a meal worthy of the Twilight Palace, but it was better than nothing. Beren and Drego took turns asking for explanations of the attack, but all Jharl would say was, "Wait."

At last, the black-furred gnoll emerged from the deepening shadows around their camp. Jharl rose and bowed his head to Ghyrryn, and the larger gnoll addressed the travelers.

"No delegate is dead," he said. There was no hint of apology in his stance or his voice. "You travel in the morning."

Beren was on his feet. "I'll need a better explanation than that, lad. Who did this? How do we know you weren't involved?"

"You are alive," the gnoll growled.

He's got a point, Thorn thought. Despite her earlier doubts, if the gnolls had turned on the travelers on the bridge, it would have been a bloodbath.

"Then who was responsible? Will they come after us again?"

"We will know by morning. Before we travel." Everything Ghyrryn said was a statement. If he had any doubts, he didn't show them. "A messenger is sent ahead. Troops from the Crag will secure the way."

"And they couldn't have done that sooner?" The silver embroidery on Drego's doublet glittered in the firelight.

"No need was seen. No delegate is dead."

The bear was the symbol of Breland, and in his anger, Beren had the menace of an angry bear. Although he was a diplomat, he spoke with the authority of a man who believed he served the most powerful nation in Khorvaire. "One of my men is dead," he growled. "A man I chose myself. You tell me why he died."

"You knew the danger of this land, or you would not have guards," Ghyrryn said, speaking more clearly than usual. "We promised your protection. We do not protect the others."

Both Drego and Beren began to protest, but the gnoll snarled and straightened his back, towering over the humans. His eyes gleamed in the firelight. He didn't raise his weapon—he didn't need to. This was no guardsman to be ordered about by angry aristocrats. He was a creature of the wild, a predator, and when he showed his teeth, the humans fell silent. Toli rose to his feet, sword in hand,

and Thorn moved closer to Beren. But silence was all the gnoll wanted.

"Your enemy will suffer when found. Know this and be satisfied. It is the only answer you will have from me. Now sleep. We will protect you in the night." He took a step backward, his eyes locked on Toli, then turned and stalked into the woods.

✠ ✠ ✠ ✠ ✠

Perhaps it amused the Daughters of Sora Kell to put Thrane and Breland in the same wagon, but even the hags didn't force them to share a tent. Jharl and the gnolls set up pavilions made from stitched hides. Each was built to shelter four persons, and as Thorn entered the tent for her group, the extra space was a painful reminder of Grenn's death.

Beren fell asleep as soon as he bedded down, but to Thorn's dismay, Toli remained awake, glaring at the Thrane tent. Thorn wondered what horrors the man had seen at Vathirond, and when he quietly rose from his bedroll, she feared that he might seek vengeance. Moving quickly, she bunched her blanket around her traveling bag. It wouldn't fool anyone under close inspection, but at a distance in the moonlight, it would serve.

Toli was careful and quiet, but he was a bodyguard by trade. A Dark Lantern lived and died by the art of stealth. The light of the moons was almost a match for the sun, and the trees broke the light into deep shadows. Thorn clung to this darkness. Her nightclothes were another version of her shiftweave wardrobe—though her blacks were a better choice for such work, she wanted to play the part of the innocent aide if she were discovered creeping about the camp.

She needn't have worried. Murder wasn't what the bodyguard had in mind—he sought only a secluded place to empty his bladder. A few moments later, he returned to the pavilion.

Thorn had other plans. She shifted to her dark outfit. An enchantment woven into the black cloth drew the shadows around her, helping her blend into the gloom. She raised her hood and drew her mask up over her face; even if she ran afoul of a gnoll guard, it was unlikely that he'd recognize the Brelish lady. The bracelets she wore on her wrists were multiple overlapping sections, and she drew them back to cover her forearms, activating the defensive magic bound within. She drew Steel, turning the blade against her wrist and keeping him close to her body as she slipped into the woods.

Is there a reason for this late night stroll?

Thorn spoke in a low whisper. "I want to learn about the attack. The gnoll said he'd know by morning. That means they're doing something now—and I want to eavesdrop."

A valid concern.

"I'm glad I have your approval," Thorn said. "Given the size of gnoll ears, I don't think I should be whispering to my dagger while I'm trying to avoid them. If you notice anything interesting, let me know. Otherwise, let the Lantern do her work, yes?"

Understood.

Thorn made her way through the woods, staying just beyond the light of the campfires. The halflings of the Talenta Plains had brought their own sentry—a large lizard that stood on two legs and glared into the woods, sniffing the air and flashing inch-long teeth. If the beast detected Thorn, it made no move.

Although the gnolls were spread out among the various campsites, the creatures also had a camp of their own. As she made her way toward it, she paused to avoid a pair of gnolls . . . and became aware of a problem. In the absence of any humans, the two were speaking in their own tongue. It was difficult for her to recognize that the hooting and whining was actually communication; it sounded like the noise of wild beasts.

Steel was able to identify a few key words. The gnolls were waiting for someone to arrive. Thorn decided to wait and learn the identity of the newcomer. But if it was another gnoll, she might not be able to understand much.

As she moved closer to the gnoll camp, she heard a sound in the woods behind her. It was no rabbit; it was the crack of a foot snapping a fallen twig. Thorn slid around the trunk of a gnarled oak, taking cover while searching for the source of the sound.

I sense no magical emanations, Steel said. *Most likely another sentry.*

Thorn wasn't so sure. The gnolls were larger and heavier than humans; the snap had sounded like the work of a smaller creature. Reluctantly, she abandoned her position, moving deeper into the shadows of the forest. A moment later, she heard the rustle of an arm brushing against bark. She glanced toward it . . . and saw nothing. The magic of her ring let her see clearly in the gloom, but she saw only empty air.

And yet . . . she knew something was there. She'd always had sharp eyes and keen ears, and now she *felt* a presence in the woods—more by instinct than anything else. Though her eyes denied it, she *knew* someone had slipped around the tree ahead of her.

Thorn couldn't ask Steel's opinion without warning her prey. But she wasn't about to let this stranger escape. She had come to find out about the attack—and some invisible creature was skulking around the perimeter. She carefully closed the distance to her target.

Focusing her thoughts, Thorn spun around the tree. She saw nothing, but she *knew* where her target was, and she rammed her forearm into the place where a man's throat might be. Her bracer struck a soft target, what felt like flesh. She raised Steel, ready to drive the blade into her hidden foe.

Finding the invisible man was challenge enough.

Predicting his movement was something else entirely. His kick caught her off guard and knocked her backward, just enough to put her out of reach. His invisibility had the same limit as her own magic; his hostile action shattered the enchantment. The air rippled as Drego Sarhain appeared before her, his hands wreathed in silver fire.

"Well, Lady Tam," he said quietly. "It seems we have something in common."

CHAPTER NINE

✻ ✻ ✻

The Duurwood Camp
Droaam

Eyre 12, 998 YK

Adrenaline surged through Thorn's veins, and the crystal shrapnel burned along her spine. Her first instinct was to charge, to rush in and slash her enemy's throat before he could begin an incantation. She'd fought wizards and sorcerers before, and she'd found that steel, applied directly to the flesh, was the most effective counterspell. Still, Drego had landed a solid kick; he knew his way around a brawl. She couldn't afford a long, loud fight . . . but, odds were, neither could he.

"Flamebearer Sarhain," she murmured. "This is a surprise. Unless you're trying to attract the attention of every gnoll in the woods, I suggest you douse your pretty hands."

Drego flexed his fingers, and Thorn tightened her grip on her dagger, ready to leap at the first sign of a mystical gesture. He lowered his hands, and the flames flickered and died.

"Wisdom *and* beauty," he said with a smile. He'd seen through her disguise in an instant, but he hadn't bothered with one; he still wore his embroidered doublet. Of course, an invisible man had little need to conceal his identity. "Does Lord Beren know what an exceptional assistant he has?"

"I'm just as surprised to see your talents at work," Thorn said, tapping the hilt of her dagger on the word *surprised*. "Given that your minister isn't speaking, I doubt she authorized this walk in the woods."

No explanation, Steel whispered in response. *I'm still not sensing any magical auras. Whatever he can do, whatever he's carrying—I can't help you.*

Drego bowed his head to acknowledge the point. "I don't like to burden the minister with such trivial things. Between prayer and preparation for the task ahead, she has much on her mind."

"You're taking quite a risk, wandering the woods like this. If something were to happen to you, who would speak for your minister? Could she even ask for breakfast?" As Thorn spoke, she slid one foot forward. If it came to combat, she needed to end it with a single stroke, before they could draw the attention of the gnolls. Throwing her blade was too risky. She needed to be quick and close.

Thorn wasn't the only one prepared for battle. Drego had lowered his hands, but his fingers were still spread wide, ready to weave a spell. The danger of magic was that it was unpredictable. Thorn had no idea what powers Drego could unleash. Though he wore no armor and carried no sword, he had the confident presence of a predator. If Thorn had struck to kill on her first attack, he'd be dead now . . . but he showed no hint of fear. A moment passed as they stared at each other, poised on the edge of violence.

A burst of laughter broke the silence. No, not laughter—the hooting voice of a gnoll, coming from the main campsite.

Thorn kept her eyes on Drego. He surprised her. He slowly raised his hands and brought them together, interlacing his fingers into a tight double fist. It was a terrible position for anyone who relied on magic. To cast a spell, he'd have to pull his hands apart, and in the heat of battle, every second mattered.

"This is foolish," he said. "We should be allies." Since she'd met him, he'd always had a condescending air, as if he knew a joke no one else could see. Now he was calm and serious, placing himself at her mercy. Was this the true Drego Sarhain, or just another mask?

"Why is that?" she said, still ready to strike. "I haven't seen the Korranberg Chronicle recently. Has the Keeper of the Flame recognized King Boranel's right to the throne and made reparations for the war?"

He didn't rise to the jibe. "You're not in Breland, Nyrielle." She'd given him permission to use her name when they were leaving Graywall, but after the mocking "Lady Tam," it was strange to hear it. "And I'm not in Thrane. You and I—we both know that the war isn't over. But I don't believe Galifar will ever be reborn. All I want now is to protect my people from harm."

Thorn had been trained to read people. Either Drego was serious, or a remarkably skilled liar. Since he was a spy, it was an even bet. She said nothing.

The gnoll calls rose again, and Drego tipped his head toward the sound. "Another place, another time, we might be enemies," he said quietly. "Your king, my queen, my Keeper; they might never be friends, and the best we can hope for is that this stalemate will last through our lifetime. But you were on that bridge. This is no place for humans. We are the outsiders here, and if we don't stand together, we may all find ourselves falling." The hint of a smile returned. "Without any souvenirs from Sharn."

Thorn rubbed a thumb along the pommel of her dagger. "Quite a speech. But why should I trust you?"

"I can give you three reasons," he said. "Were you actually sent here to kill a Thrane spy? My task is to gather information about what is going on in the heart of Droaam. I see no reason why Breland shouldn't have this information—if there is danger here, it threatens us all."

"That's one."

He gestured with his thumbs, pointing toward his chest. "I know you like my doublet. If we both survive this, I'm sure my mother would weave you a gown."

Despite her best efforts, Thorn found herself smiling. "And the third?"

"Clearly, you don't speak the language of the gnolls, or you'd know that last call was gathering the squad leaders. If you don't get moving, you'll miss the introductions . . . and unless I'm with you, you're not going to understand them."

"I see why your minister doesn't feel the need to speak," Thorn said. "You have a way with words. But I don't know about working with a Thrane . . . let me consider it."

She wanted a chance to hear from Steel, and he seized the opportunity.

I think you should let him live for now, he whispered in her mind. *He's attracted to you, and we can use that. Let him believe you are only here to gather intelligence. If he learns about Stormblade, he'll have to die.*

"Yes. I believe you're right." Thorn inclined her head toward Drego. "Shall we see what our gnolls have planned?"

Though Drego was a spy, he proved the adage that magic was no substitute for skill. He conjured new invisibility, and although it probably served him well on the city streets, he had little experience in the wild. He scraped against trees and shrubs, trampled dry leaves, and left countless traces of his passage. Though she couldn't see him, Thorn was aware of his location almost constantly.

Fortunately, the gnolls made plenty of noise of their own. Most of the healthy soldiers guarded the delegates. The gnoll camp was filled with those injured during the attack, and they whined and growled as the healer moved among them. The old gnoll was dressed in dark brown robes, and his fur was patchy and gray. Lacking the magical powers of the minister of the Silver Flame, he relied on mundane methods to do his work—bandages, powders of questionable potency, foul-looking salves and tinctures. Thorn winced as she saw him setting broodworms against a particularly ugly wound. She'd heard that such creatures devoured infected tissue. As a child, though, she'd lost a dog when broodworms had entered a cut and ultimately burrowed into its brain. The memory still haunted her.

Beyond the tending of the wounded, considerable activity was underway. Two young gnolls sorted through the goods salvaged from the broken wagons. A soldier sharpened blades with a whetstone, while another carved new arrows. Amidst all this commotion, not even the patrolling sentry noticed Drego's clumsy footsteps.

Thorn had seen similar activity a hundred times during the war. Aside from the fur and sharp teeth, it could have been any camp on the Cyran front in the days before the Mourning. She detected no explanation for the attack, no sign of betrayal; if anything, the wounds of the soldiers proved that they'd put themselves in harm's way to protect the foreigners.

But one thing was missing. She didn't see Ghyrryn, or the gnoll with the horned helmet. These were the common troops . . . where were the officers?

Thorn began to circle the edge of the camp, moving cautiously along the tree line. The sound of Drego's footsteps followed her closely. Thorn silently cursed the noisy Thrane; if he drew the attention of a sentry, *she* was the one the gnoll would see. But despite their large ears, the gnolls seemed to lack the keen senses of other beasts.

A hand closed on her shoulder. Her immediate instinct was to lash out, thrusting Steel beneath her arm and burying her blade in her enemy's chest. But she knew it was Drego, and she checked her aggressive impulses. His fingers traced a slow path down her arm, finally tugging at her hand. If he doesn't have a good reason for this, I'm going to take one of his fingers as a keepsake, she thought. But she let him lift her hand. A finger tapped her glove. He pointed.

Four gnolls were gathered a few hundred feet from their camp. They were spread across a moonlit grove, weapons drawn but not ready. Thorn saw a familiar silhouette among them, and a smile spread across her face.

She reached out and placed her hand against the chest of the invisible man, gently pushing him away. She raised a single finger to her lips, then pointed at the ground, hoping he'd get the message. *You're too noisy. Stay here*.

No such luck. As Thorn crept closer to the four officers, she heard him moving behind her. She stopped, looking over her shoulder to glare at him.

"You need me." The whisper was quieter than his footsteps, which was worth something. "You can't understand them."

In such a situation, Thorn always sought to avoid all unnecessary sound and motion. She didn't shrug, didn't sigh in resignation, didn't nod her head. But all of those thoughts passed through her mind as she started forward again. It's just four gnolls, she told herself. Probably the most skilled soldiers in the camp, but just four gnolls. Surely, if it comes to a fight, the two of us can handle four gnolls.

The officers muttered to one another, and none of them seemed to hear Drego as he and Thorn drew closer. A thicket of ghoulbriar grew on the edge of the grove, and Thorn dropped to one knee behind it. The brambles weren't too dense and allowed a good view of the gnolls. If they were discovered, Thorn hoped any pursuers would charge into the briar without recognizing their danger.

A minute later, the others arrived.

A dark shape emerged on the far side of the grove, a shadow the size of a pony with eyes that glowed in the moonlight. It was a wolf, the largest Thorn had ever seen.

Its fur was dark as Khyber, and its teeth gleamed. For a moment Thorn thought the gnolls would fight the beast, but they fell silent and turned to face it. The gnoll leader, the armored officer who'd addressed them on the Roar, raised his weapon to salute the beast. Thorn could feel a faint breeze against her skin, and she gave thanks that she was downwind from this creature.

Other newcomers followed the massive wolf. A young and handsome elf with silver hair and pale skin. A large man whose muscles and gray skin spoke of orcish heritage, with a heavy bundle thrown over a shoulder. Both wore loose clothing dappled in patterns of black and gray, along with harnesses bearing a wide assortment of weapons and tools.

Something wasn't quite right. When Thorn first laid eyes upon them, a chill passed through the crystal shard at the base of her spine, and that faint sensation lingered as the strangers approached the gnolls.

Two more wolves arrived. While fierce in demeanor, these were the sort Thorn was accustomed to—strong and better fed than those she'd seen in the King's Forest, but no match for the beast that led this pack into the grove. Despite their mundane appearance, Thorn felt the chill again as one of the wolves passed her hiding place.

"My mother sends her greetings, brother Gharn." The elf spoke. His voice was soft and clear, and Thorn heard a hint of menace in his tone. It was clear that he held himself above the gnolls.

The armored gnoll inclined his head. "The children of Zaeurl are welcome in this place. Reveal our enemy." Like Ghyrryn, Gharn spoke in statements, never asking a question. He was almost three feet taller than the elf. Yet instead of barking out orders as he had on the plaza in Graywall, he was almost polite.

The half-orc threw his burden to the ground, and the wrappings fell away. It was a harpy—or the remains of one. Her wings were fractured in multiple places, her feathers were soaked with blood, and Thorn could see pale bone protruding from flesh. Her broken wings were wrapped around her body like a cloak and bound with heavy rope. Her face was bruised, her chin stained crimson, and Thorn thought she was dead. Then her eyes opened. The harpy stared right at Thorn. Yet even if the harpy had seen Thorn, her eyes were empty. She was broken, little better than dead.

"Wind Howlers," the elf said, placing his heel on one of the broken wings and grinding his foot against it. "As expected. Callain couldn't resist such choice prey, not with the storm approaching."

"Callain lives." Again, a statement, not a question.

"Such were my orders." The elf prodded the harpy again, but received no reaction. "The old bird's working with one of the others—the Ashlord, Tzaryan Rrac, Sheshka—and our ladies wish to draw out the game. You're to take this one with you to the Crag for questioning." He reached into a pouch, producing a piece of glistening pink flesh. "I made sure to find one that knew how to write."

He tossed the tongue to Gharn, who closed his fist around it. "Go, then. Guard our path on the journey ahead."

Perhaps Gharn had grown too bold, too dismissive. The half-orc scowled, his hand falling to the haft of a hatchet. The massive wolf drew its lips back from vicious teeth . . . and spoke.

"Mind your tongue, two-legs," it snarled, its voice deep and rough. "Or we may take yours next. Watch how you speak to the blessed."

The gnolls raised their weapons and shields, and Ghyrryn barked out a phrase in their strange tongue. Wolf and gnoll faced each other, teeth bared.

And then Thorn's knee slipped against the soft ground and damp grass. Perhaps she'd leaned too far forward, trying to see the wounded harpy. Maybe it was a cruel trick of a malevolent god. She caught herself with her left hand and saved herself from tumbling into the ghoulbriar. But it was too late. When she looked up, all eyes had turned toward her.

CHAPTER TEN

✳ ✳ ✳

The Duurwood Camp
Droaam

Eyre 12, 998 YK

Fight, or flee? Make a run for it, trusting the poisoned barbs of the ghoulbriar to slow pursuit? Stand tough and take down as many monsters as possible? Shift to nightclothes and play dumb? Had it only been Ghyrryn or even Gharn, the last option might work. But the image of the harpy's broken wings and empty eyes chilled her, and she didn't want to fall into the hands of this wolf pack. They might not hit the briar, and she couldn't outrun a wolf. She'd fight.

She reached her conclusion in less than a second, and her enemies hadn't moved. On the heels of their argument, both sides were cautious, waiting for the other to act. The tension broke when the elf moved forward, drawing a curved sword with one hand as he gestured to his wolves with the other. Thorn prepared for the attack.

A burst of sound and motion shook the briars and branches to her left. All heads turned, including Thorn's. A bird of prey—a hawk with dark feathers and a wide wingspan—broke through the canopy and rose into the moonlit sky. In a second, it was gone.

Thorn froze, holding her breath. Unless the breeze changed, she was still downwind from the wolves. As long as they blamed the disturbance on the bird . . .

"Go," said Gharn. He turned back to the hunters.
Behind him, Ghyrryn and the other gnolls were ready for
battle. "You have your task. Leave us to ours."

The elf stared at the horned gnoll, then glanced over
his shoulder, following the path of the bird. "Very well,
brother," he said, a razor edge to his soft words. "Have no
fear. We'll be watching your path all the way to the Great
Crag." His eyes drifted to Ghyrryn. "And beyond."

Ghyrryn gave a low, trilling whine, staring at the elf.
The large wolf growled again, but this time the elf turned
his back on the gnolls. "Come," he said, beckoning to his
wolves. "We have other matters to attend to."

The gnolls remained until the hunters and their beasts
were out of sight. Then they huddled together, hooting
and growling. Thorn couldn't understand their words—
but she could see that Gharn was angry and taking it out
on Ghyrryn. Finally, one of the other gnolls picked up the
wounded harpy and the quartet turned back to their camp.

✠   ✠   ✠   ✠   ✠

"All I'm saying is that *I* wasn't the one who almost got
us both killed."

"Which is a miracle, with all the noise you were making.
I've seen drunken tribex quieter than you. Perhaps it was
my fear that they'd hear *you* that caused me to slip."

"And yet—"

"Fine." Thorn said. "I acknowledge your skill, mighty
Drego. Your gifts, and your gifts alone, prevented that
battle, saved our lives, and avoided an international incident
that would have sent the world spiraling into war."

"There's no need to exaggerate," Drego said
reproachfully.

"Once I start, it's hard to stop."

Drego and Thorn sat in the woods on the edge of the
Brelish-Thrane campsite. Jharl had spotted them as they

returned to camp, but Thorn had already changed her clothes to her traveling gown. As she explained to the gnoll, the two were just enjoying the night and debating the issues that lay between their two nations.

"Impressive work, though," Thorn said. "You summoned the hawk, and the casting didn't break your invisibility. But why didn't I hear the words of the spell? Summoning can be noisy magic."

"Not for me," Drego said. He waved a finger in the air, and a spark of silver light flickered on the tip.

Duly noted, Thorn thought. She knew it was possible to cast spells without speaking—certainly a useful talent for a spy. But it took vastly more energy to cast a silent spell, and it was a difficult skill to learn; Thorn had tried with no success. It occurred to her that the Thrane minister Luala had remained silent while performing her healing magic earlier . . . apparently, the Thranes had a gift for it. Still, it was unwise of him to flaunt it. Now she knew that if she ever needed to subdue Drego, she'd need more than a gag.

Drego stared into the tiny flame. Thorn reached out and ran her fingers gently across his other hand. "So what happens now?" she said.

Her touch broke his concentration and the spark of light vanished. He turned to meet her gaze. His eyes were gray, but the light of the moons turned them silver. "What do you mean?"

"I'm not proposing marriage, and if I see you in Breland I'll probably cut your throat. But as long as it's us versus them . . . I think we can work together."

"I'm glad to hear it." He smiled, lifting her hand and touching his lips to her gloved fingers. "And the marriage will have to wait until you convert, anyhow. I have my faith to consider."

"We have other things to discuss. What did you make of that meeting?"

Drego released her hand, a pained expression on his face. "Very well, my lady, very well. To the matter at hand."

"Droaam is a young nation. The Daughters of Sora Kell arrived less than twenty years ago. Before that . . ."

"Chaos," Drego said. "My people know more of it than most. Crusaders of the faith would often venture into the savage lands of the west, dedicating their lives to destroying all the evil that they could until they themselves fell in battle. Few returned, but some journals have been recovered."

"And what qualifies as 'evil' in this tale?"

"Any monster that would threaten the settlers to the east . . . people of Breland, I'd like to point out. So my ancestors gave their lives to protect yours. If not for my great-great-grandfather, you might never have been born."

Thorn refrained from pointing out that her mother wasn't even from Khorvaire. "So we're practically brother and sister."

Drego placed his hand over hers, and his smile wasn't exactly fraternal. "I wouldn't go that far. But in those days, there was no semblance of a nation. Ogres, trolls, giants—the stronger creatures enslaved the weak. When Galifar collapsed into war, the beasts of Droaam became more aggressive, but their attacks were still random, uncoordinated."

"And then the Daughters of Sora Kell arrived."

"Yes. Force is the only language these warlords understand, and thirteen years ago, the hags appeared with an army of trolls and other creatures. I don't know about you, but we've never been able to determine how they gathered such a powerful force in secret. Within a year, their opponents were either dead or sworn vassals. And here we are today."

"Sworn vassals are only as good as the oaths binding them," Thorn said. "From what I've heard, some in this land are glad to serve the Daughters. The gnolls are supposed to be a loyal bunch. But fear is the mortar that holds Droaam together, and if you're a tyrannical giant, it may hurt to bend your knee to some tiny crone."

"Which brings us to tonight's encounter. Did you recognize the name Callain?"

It meant nothing to Thorn, but Steel whispered in her ear, and she repeated the words aloud. "Callain of the Final Word. Leader of a flight of harpies accused of multiple counts of banditry."

"The Wind Howlers."

"Yes," Thorn said. "I believe so."

"So it seems that we're bait," Drego said. "The Daughters invite delegates to the Great Crag, ostensibly to negotiate full recognition as a sovereign nation. Death of a delegate at the hands of monsters would be an embarrassment at best—at worst, a cause for war. If any of these warlords wants to challenge the Daughters, all they need to do is kill the delegates. Small wonder your gnoll friend isn't promising to keep the rest of us alive. I imagine they'll have their paws full as it is."

"There's more to it," Thorn said. "That elf . . . he said that Callain couldn't resist the opportunity because of the 'approaching storm.' What did he mean? And what did Ghyrryn say that made those hunters so angry?"

"That was odd," Drego said. "The worg warned the gnoll leader about speaking to 'the blessed.' Then our friend said . . . what's the best way to put this?" He closed his eyes for a moment, running his fingers along the back of Thorn's hands as he considered it. "Less blessed by the day. Less? Or . . . a blessing more common? It's not an easy translation."

Thorn mulled things over. "So the Daughters don't trust their vassals, and they're probably using us to draw out traitors. All this against the backdrop of a coming storm and a fading blessing." Her eyes widened. "Could they be talking about House Tharashk?"

Drego frowned. "What do you mean?"

"Think about it. Those people in black were trackers. One was a half-orc. We know House Tharashk has dealings with Droaam, and the half-orcs of House Tharashk carry the Dragonmark of Finding—the perfect tool for a bounty hunter, and the pillar of their house. What if that 'blessing'—their dragonmark—is fading away?"

"That seems far-fetched. One of the hunters was an elf, but that doesn't mean Aerenal is involved."

"You're right." Thorn sighed. "And I've never heard of Tharashk having a great love of wolves. Blessings and wolves . . . no clever ideas?"

"I'm afraid not," Drego replied. But Thorn saw a flicker in his eyes—a moment of doubt.

"What?"

"It's nothing," he said.

"Don't hold back on me now," she said. "There's still time for me to return that wedding dress."

"No," he said. "Really, it's nothing. I don't know what this is about. But it sounds like something may be afoot in the Crag that concerns both our nations after all. I suggest we get some rest. Perhaps the sun will shed new light on this."

"You're wise beyond your years," Thorn said. "Until the morning, then." She began to stand, then paused. Drego was still holding her hand.

"I said that *we* should get some rest," he said, a slight smile on his lips.

"I see," Thorn said. "And would you like to come to my pavilion? I'm sure my friend Toli would be happy to see you."

"With you at my side, I would need no tent but the sky, no blanket but the grass," he said. She looked down at him. He was a handsome man, with cheekbones a kalashtar would envy, and piercing eyes. Even after their adventure in the woods, his skin was flawless, his hair perfect. She considered Steel's words . . . *he's attracted to you, and we can use that.*

"Not tonight, Flamebearer Sarhain," she said, pulling her hand free. She smiled at him. "You'll have to convert me first."

He slid down to the ground, placing his hand over his heart and giving a heavy sigh. Thorn turned her back on him and walked toward the Brelish pavilion.

CHAPTER ELEVEN

✗ ✗ ✗

The Duurwood Camp
Droaam

Eyre 13, 998 YK

The brilliant light of the moons made it difficult to
sleep. Thorn remembered seeing four full moons in
the sky when she was a child, marveling at the multihued
light they cast across the land. The moons waxed and
waned at different rates, and now Dravago and Nymm
were growing wider and brighter. Within a few nights, six
of the twelve moons would be full.

While Thorn had little interest in history and the aca-
demic significance of such events, the topic had come up
on the long wagon ride. Drego explained that over two
centuries had passed since the last such spectacle. It was
a natural wonder, but for Thorn it was simply annoying.
She was a restless sleeper at the best of times, and the shimmering light was too much. She pulled her blanket up over
her head. It was scratchy and hot, but anything was better
than the glare.

The darkness was a blessing, but Thorn's thoughts were
troubled. The campfire spat and crackled, and the sounds
mingled with images of the battle with the harpies—the
crushed corpses at the bottom of the gorge and the smell
of blood. Thorn tried to push the thoughts away, but the
charnel stench grew stronger with each moment. She heard

moans, sobs, and distant cries of pain. She was certain it was all in her imagination; it was too distant, too faint, and she'd heard no sounds of battle.

Then she heard the sound of a steel blade shifting in a mailed fist, the rasping noise of armor plates brushing against one another. A soldier in full plate mail, and only a few steps away from her. Thorn threw aside the blanket and rose to her feet, reaching for Steel.

But Steel wasn't at her side. And she wasn't in the camp anymore. Wagons, tents, even the others who had been sleeping around her—were nowhere to be seen. She couldn't even say if it was still night, because the sky was filled with thick clouds of smoke, reflecting the light from fires burning across the land before her.

She saw that she was dressed in a gown of red and black glamerweave, better suited to the ballroom than the battlefield. Illusions had been woven into the cloth, giving the red pigments the liquid intensity of fresh blood. Red leather covered her arms and legs: thigh-high boots stretched up beneath her skirts, and gloves rose past her elbows. The fingertips of the gloves were open, revealing long, curved nails painted with black enamel. The only familiar aspect of the scene was the pain at the base of her skull; the upper gem was throbbing against her flesh.

Everything was different, yet somehow it was familiar. Had she been here before?

She'd been right about the sound. The man was wearing full armor, and he clutched a longsword in his outstretched right hand. But he was sprawled on the ground, his beautiful armor covered with mud and ash. The sound of the sword was the man's effort to maintain his grip on the hilt, not a preparation for attack. He coughed, and Thorn could smell the blood in his mouth. He was broken inside, and he wouldn't last much longer. "Why?" he croaked.

Thorn wanted to help him, to ask him what had happened . . . but she couldn't move. Her body betrayed her, acting with a mind of its own. Instead of assisting the injured man, she found herself laughing at him, her lips twisted in a cruel smirk.

"Because it amuses me." Thorn could feel her mouth shaping the words, but she didn't stop them; she was an observer in her own body—if this *was* her body. She walked toward the fallen soldier, and Thorn could see details beneath the mud and grime. The seal of old Galifar was engraved on the soldier's breastplate, along with the rising sun emblem of the goddess Dol Arrah. It was a princely suit of armor, the raiment of a general or lord.

As she drew closer, the man forced himself up on one elbow—an impressive feat, given his injuries and the weight of his armor. He swung his blade in a low arc, putting all his remaining strength into the blow. Thorn's instinct was to leap back, but her body had other ideas. A surge of energy flowed through her and she dropped down and caught the blade with her hand. Despite the force of the blow and the razor edge of the sword, there was no pain and no blood. Thorn felt the steel against her skin, but the stroke didn't even cut the fine leather of her glove. She felt as if her muscles were on fire, burning with a power she could scarcely contain, and her hand closed around the blade and tore it from the grip of the weakened soldier.

"This isn't about you, little prince." She placed the heel of her boot against the knight's chest and pushed him down to the ground. "I don't care about you or your kingdom."

"Fiend . . . " the knight struggled, but he'd spent all his strength on that last blow. He couldn't even raise an arm.

"You know so little of the world," Thorn found herself saying. "I'm no fiend. My kind bound the demons at the dawn of time. I am more than any pathetic devil, and greater than any of your gods." She tossed the longsword into the air, catching the hilt in her hand and placing the point of the blade against the soldier's chest.

Leaning into her work, she slowly gouged a slash across

the symbol of Dol Arrah. "Look at your people, so devout, so confident that their goddess will come to their defense in their hour of need. Yet here we are. I have burned your hall and your holdings. I have devoured those you love and savored the taste of their blood.

"Your Dol Arrah is the Sovereign of the Sun, but my fires have sent the sun into hiding. Now we will see what path your people will take when this pillar is broken. Shall they cling to their faith even when the Sovereigns leave them to die? Might they embrace a new mystery, or take up the banner of those death-worshippers to the east? Or will they worship me, raising altars to the Angel of Flame?" She laughed again, and Thorn could feel the cruel joy within her. She'd caused the deaths of thousands, tens of thousands. Thorn couldn't quite grasp the memories, but she *knew* it was the truth. And she felt no remorse. It was just a game, played with human lives.

"The Sovereigns . . . " The man was speaking again, struggling to form words. "With us. They know . . . will punish . . . "

Thorn shoved her boot against the man's chest, cutting off breath and speech. "If any god was going to punish me, it would have happened long ago. You are alone in this world, prince. And you will go alone into your death. No realm of glory awaits you—just the slow dissolution of your memories, of everything you are. You should be grateful. You won't have to remember how badly you failed your people." She raised the sword and tapped it against his helmet. "How will history remember you, I wonder? Will your people create some glorious death for you, pretending that you gave your last breath locked in battle with a mighty monster? Or will some sage piece together this scene—a broken man slain with his own sword, begging for mercy amid the wreckage of all that he loved?"

That incredible power flowed through her again, an exhilarating burst of strength and energy. With a casual flick of the sword, she flipped open the knight's visor. The face below was covered with blood and dirt, but the features were unmistakable.

It was Drego Sarhain.

His mouth opened, bloody saliva flecking his lips as he called out. A final curse? A plea for compassion? Thorn couldn't hear anything beyond her own silent scream of fury and the song of triumph that filled her thoughts. The sword was as light as a blade of grass as she raised it over her head, but it was deadly steel as the point struck home between Drego's eyes. She raised her arms and roared at the sky, and the shard at the base of her spine was burning, throbbing as if it were the point of a spear. Pain, anger, and alien joy merged together in a terrifying cacophony, overwhelming all sensation.

Then a hand gripped her shoulder. At the touch, the world around her faded away and fell into utter darkness. The howls in her mind fell silent. There was no sword, no battlefield; she was lying on the ground with a blanket over her face.

"Nyri?" It was Beren ir'Wynarn, the Brelish ambassador. "Are you well, child?"

Thorn reached up and pulled the blanket from her face. Lord Beren was kneeling over her, with Toli right behind him. The light of the moons had given way to dawning sun, and Jharl was preparing breakfast by the campfire. All that remained of the nightmare vision was the piercing pain in her lower back; it felt as if the crystal shard were digging into her spine.

Thorn sat up and laid a hand across Beren's arm. "I'm fine, my lord. Just a bad dream."

"Perhaps the rabbit from last night disagreed with you," Beren said. "I hope not, though. It appears we have the same for breakfast. I supposed I should be grateful that these gnolls are determined to keep me alive, but the quality of that life leaves something to be desired."

Thorn couldn't muster the energy to laugh at the old man's joke, but she managed a smile. "I think I have some Talentan spices in my bag. I do need to take care of my ambassador, after all. Give me a moment to gather my thoughts and I'll see what I can find."

"Bless you, child." Beren beamed. He stood and helped Thorn to her feet. "Olladra smiled when she brought our paths together."

"Yes, I'm sure she did," Thorn replied. Even as she bowed her head to acknowledge the Sovereigns' favor, the words of the dream echoed in her mind. *I am greater than any of your gods. Now we will see what path your people take when this pillar is broken.*

When she opened her eyes, she saw Drego Sarhain staring at her from across the camp.

CHAPTER TWELVE

✠ ✠ ✠

The Jul Kartaal
Droaam
Eyre 18, 998 YK

I t is always a question of blood," the elf said, running a whetstone along the edge of his gleaming scimitar. "Our blood is a thing to be treasured, our bond to the powers of the past. To abandon such a gift to go worship a bonfire . . . I can see why you won't speak. There are no words to defend such an action."

The speaker was Saer Vordalyn, a warrior from the kingdom of Valenar. After the attack at Korlaak Pass, the gnolls had reassigned passengers to the remaining carriages. And so Breland and Thane had been blessed with Vordalyn's company for the last five days, a gift that had made the journey an exceptionally trying time.

The elves of Valenar thrived on conflict in all forms and believed that by fighting, they honored their fallen ancestors. They'd come to Khorvaire as mercenaries during the Last War, only to turn on their Cyran paymasters and lay claim to that kingdom. In the years that followed, they'd sold their services to all sides. While few generals trusted them, the Valenar were, without question, deadly soldiers.

Vordalyn was certainly interested in fighting, whether with steel or words. He'd spent the last five days probing his traveling companions, searching for any sign of weakness or any subject that proved uncomfortable. Minister Luala was his target of choice; she was an elf living among humans, and she had set aside the traditions of her ancestors to follow the Silver Flame. Vordalyn seemed determined to provoke her into breaking her vow of silence, but so far his barbs had shattered against her serenity. The minister simply smiled at his jibes, which in turn pushed the warrior to try harder. This blunt opening was surely just the beginning of a more elaborate and insulting scheme.

Vordalyn watched Luala as he sharpened his blade. The weapon was already honed to a razor edge; it was said that the swords of the Valenar could draw blood from the wind. Thorn suspected that this was just another tactic in Vordalyn's little game. The presence of the naked blade set the bodyguards on edge, while the sound of stone on steel was grating to all. Thorn found it particularly annoying. It might have been her imagination, but the grinding triggered the pain in her skull, the crystal shard grating against bone.

"I don't know, Vordalyn," Thorn said. "I don't think so much of your blood."

The elf turned to face her, a slight smile on his lips. "That's hardly surprising. Clearly your ancestors had little self-regard, to carelessly mingle the blood of two races. Do you even know who it was who brought elven blood into your line, or are you a mongrel with no history to speak of?"

"My mother was an elf," Thorn said. "She came to my father after the Valenar turned on Cyre. She told him that it was impossible to wipe that betrayal away, and that she'd rather destroy her bloodline than pass such treachery on to another generation."

This was a lie. Thorn's mother was an elf of Southern Aerenal, with no ties to the warriors of the north. Thorn had only the faintest memories of her mother, and her father had been loath to speak of her. Whatever had happened between them, it had been a painful parting, and Thorn hated to see her father cry. Nonetheless, she saw Vordalyn's hand tighten around the hilt of his scimitar, and she knew she'd landed a solid blow.

"We did not steal our realm from Cyre. Our ancestors held that ground thousands of years before humans first set foot on Khorvaire. It was ours by right."

"Oh, I see," Thorn said. "Your ancestors—those great heroes whose blood you treasure—conquered the land long ago. And then what happened? They were chased back to Aerenal by goblins, weren't they?"

"Dragons," Vordalyn said, nearly snarling. "Dragons attacked our homeland, and we had to leave Khorvaire to the goblins. My ancestors ran toward battle, not away from it."

"Thousands of years ago. And you've been meaning to come back ever since, but you waited until a civil war was going on and you could stab someone in the back. I understand. Your blood's just not as strong as it was. You wouldn't want a *real* challenge."

Vordalyn hissed and his blade rose an inch. Thorn wasn't worried. Vordalyn couldn't attack her without causing an international incident. He'd spent the last few days trying to provoke someone else into starting a fight. But if Vordalyn struck the first blow, it would be disastrous, and he knew it.

"My ancestors gave their word," he growled. "They would not return to this land until they were asked. The Queen of Cyre called us across the water. She freed us from that oath, and freed us to reclaim our heritage."

"Yes . . . freed you to betray a weakened nation. Is that what those glorious ancestors of yours did? Would they be so proud of what you've done? Do you suppose *your* children will look back and say, 'I treasure the memory of my father, who always turned on his trusting allies?' "

Vordalyn rose in a blur of motion, his blade a gleaming streak as he brought himself on guard. His eyes were locked on Thorn's. She didn't flinch or even move—she just smiled at him. On either side, the gnolls had drawn their weapons. Jharl had an arrow to his bowstring, and Ghyrryn raised his axe.

"Sit down," Ghyrryn said. "We need only protect delegates. You can be fought."

It was the wrong thing to say to a warrior in search of release; Thorn could see Vordalyn tensing in preparation. He *wanted* the gnolls to attack him, to have some excuse to release his anger.

"And what tales will your children tell of this day?" she said, her words low and fast. "Is this the day their father threatened a servant and killed those who sought to protect her? Shall we get someone to paint a portrait?"

Vordalyn's scimitar was poised in the air above her. Jharl had drawn back his bow, and Ghyrryn was ready to strike. Drego Sarhain was watching, but Thorn didn't expect him to reveal his magical powers to the Brelish and gnolls in order to defend her; whatever had passed between them at the Duurwood camp, they were agents of different nations, and he had a mission of his own.

Vordalyn sat down, sheathing his scimitar. Something shifted in the air. A silk cloth attached to Vordalyn's helmet fluttered, and he pulled it across to hide his lower face, leaving only his eyes exposed. He immediately closed his eyes, retreating into private meditation. No apology, certainly. But under the circumstances, Thorn was content with the victory. On the other side of the wagon, Drego Sarhain winked at her, and Minister Luala actually smiled.

✠ ✠ ✠ ✠ ✠

The travelers had been together for six days, and small talk had been exhausted. Had the Brelish been in a wagon of their own, Toli or Beren might have been more talkative, but Toli had no intention of revealing anything in the presence of the Thranes. In the beginning, Drego had told stories to pass the time. But Toli and Vordalyn had no interest in the heroes of the Silver Flame, and it was a poor setting to share war stories. Vordalyn's aggressive comments had driven the conversation for the last few days, and since he had finally backed down, silence reigned in the wagon.

Thorn didn't mind. She had much to think about. The ache in her skull had faded. She rubbed a finger against the stone. *They cannot be removed*, the Jorasco healer had told her. *Cutting them out would cause great damage to the spine. They have become a part of you.*

But what were they, really? Why did the pain come and go? Was it purely physical—the shard rubbing against bone—or was magic involved, or some sort of energy that caused the agony?

The last few nights had been calm. The hunters and their wolves had lived up to their promises; five days had passed with no new attacks. Thorn had done more scouting, studying the other delegates, but with no compelling threat, she'd spent most of her time with her countrymen. The last thing she wanted was to arouse any suspicions. They would arrive at the Great Crag before sundown, and then her mission would truly begin.

She'd slept more soundly since that first night, but the dream still troubled her. She'd tried to discuss it with Steel, but he refused to take interest. *Considering that I do not dream, I'm ill-equipped to offer any insight. Perhaps you should try talking to your bedroll.* She often had dreams in which her actions didn't make sense, but never so vivid. The sensation of watching her body move on its own, of hearing such cruelty in her own voice . . . it still sent a shiver down her spine.

And then there was Drego. Surely his presence proved there was nothing to the dream. The two of them were soldiers on the opposite sides of a conflict. They'd had little private contact since that night. The experience had shown that they could work together, but if it came to it, she would kill him to protect Breland, and she'd expect no better treatment from him. Perhaps that's all the dream was—a dramatization of a possible future. But she still felt a chill when she met Drego's gaze, still felt the sword in her hand as it pierced his skull.

As the hours passed, Thorn sensed that they were drawing closer to the Great Crag. In the confines of the coach, the passengers could see nothing. But Thorn heard the sounds of traffic on the road, of other wagons and columns of troops. There were cries in the air, the calls of wyverns, and a few voices that had to be harpies, though none were raised in song. Minister Luala seemed ill at ease, and Toli kept his hand on his sword. Vordalyn kept his gaze fixed on Thorn. She knew that he was trying to unnerve her, and she had no intention of responding, so she ignored him. Occasionally she brushed a finger against Steel to ask if he could identify a strange sound.

In time, the wagons came to a halt. The rear flap was drawn back, revealing a patrol of armored ogres accompanied by a handsome young man—a human with fine, dark features and wavy black hair. Ghyrryn raised a hand before anyone could speak. The man said nothing; he stepped into the wagon, glanced at Ghyrryn, then looked slowly around the coach, pausing to study each face.

Doppelganger, Steel whispered. Thorn was inclined to agree. While the young man appeared human, it seemed more likely that he was some sort of creature with the power to read thoughts, seeking signs of hostility or treachery. As a Lantern, Thorn had been trained to resist such attempts. Taking a deep breath, she let her thoughts fall into a peaceful pattern, steady waves in the deep ocean. As she'd expected, Thorn felt the faint hint of an alien presence as the youth's gaze passed over her—a touch of curiosity, something she might have dismissed as her own subconscious if she weren't trained to recognize it. The young man turned to Ghyrryn, inclined his head, and stepped out of the wagon.

Soon they were traveling again, rising up a sharp incline—the final approach to the Crag itself, Thorn guessed. She heard dozens of voices outside the wagon—chattering goblins, rumbling ogres, creatures speaking in different languages. Then the voices were drowned out by a loud grinding sound and an impact that shook the ground. It came from the rear of the wagon, and as the coach drew to a halt, Thorn could imagine the source. They were inside the Great Crag, and the doors were closed.

Ghyrryn was the first on his feet. He had a lantern in one hand, filled with cold fire. "Remain together," he said, assertive as ever. "Go where we say. The Crag is full of dangers, and you will not place yourself at risk. Listen to your guards. Obey the Drul. Now follow."

The gnoll threw open the canvas flap, holding up the lantern to light the way. The chamber beyond was pitch black. Most of the creatures who lived in Droaam could see in darkness, and the Crag wasn't designed for those who preferred the light of the sun. Many of the delegates were moving gingerly in the darkness, but Thorn's enchanted ring allowed her to see through the shadows beyond the torchlight.

The Crag was astonishing. The chamber was enormous—the wagons were surrounded by open space, and the curving ceiling was at least fifty feet above her. The walls seemed to be the raw stone of the mountain, but they were too smooth and even to be natural. This was the product of magic or fine craftsmen.

The gnolls led the envoys deeper into the chamber. Goblins scurried about, tending to the draft animals and retrieving luggage. Thorn detected large, hunched figures standing at the very edge of her vision—trolls and ogres. The flickers from the gnolls' torches gave hints about the fearsome weapons they carried. Guards . . . I hope, she thought to herself.

Movement in the air above drew her attention. She looked up, but saw nothing. She was certain something had been there—she'd felt the motion.

An orb hung above them in the chamber, and it began to glow faintly. Its light grew brighter until it shimmered with the pale radiance of a full moon. The light revealed the giant soldiers ringing the chamber, huge creatures dressed in leather and steel.

Below the light, where Thorn had sensed movement, a massive figure stood proudly, feet firmly planted on nothing but air. Pale blue skin gleamed in the magical light, and muscles rippled as he stared down at them. He had the physique of an ogre, the bearing of a barbarian king, and a gleam of intelligence in his eyes. He wore black silk with silver trim, and two horns rose from his forehead. He was handsome and fierce, and Thorn couldn't help but think of the tales of demon princes of Shavarath. But he was no demon. He was an *oni*, an ogre mage —mighty and magical, but still a native of Eberron.

"Honored guests!" His voice was deep and rich, with the timbre of a master storyteller. "You have traveled far and faced great dangers. Your journey is at an end. I am Drul Kantar, and I welcome you in the name of the Daughters of Sora Kell, benevolent queens of the sovereign nation of Droaam.

"I will serve as your guardian and guide in the days that lie ahead. It will be my honor to learn your ways and teach you ours, to help us become one people here and in the world beyond. But let us leave the business of diplomacy to the morrow. You have all made sacrifices to be here, and my queens wish to reward you for your journey.

"Tonight you will be our guests at a grand celebration, presided over by the glorious Sora Katra herself. Lords and ladies, prepare yourselves for an evening that will become legend for centuries to come. We stand on the precipice of history. Now let us *leap!*"

As he spoke the final syllable, the vizier spread his hands wide and fireworks burst forth from his outstretched fingers, brilliant serpents that danced among the delegates below. The ogres and gnolls roared their approval, and a few of the envoys joined in the applause. Thorn was impressed. Whoever this Drul Kantar was, there was no denying his charisma.

"Looks like it's going to be an interesting night," she murmured.

Indeed, said Steel. *Now get to work.*

CHAPTER THIRTEEN

✗ ✗ ✗

The Great Crag
Droaam

Eyre 18, 998 YK

Diplomatic accommodations." Beren snorted, glaring at the tiny chamber. "Boldrei's bloody feet! This isn't a guest suite—it's a prison cell!"

"The Daughters may have more prisoners than noble guests, my lord," Thorn said, setting Beren's bags on the floor. She was accustomed to working in hard conditions, and the journey from Graywall was hardly luxurious, but the Crag had brought this experience to a new low. The bunk in Thorn's room must have been designed for a goblin; she doubted she could sleep without curling into a ball.

Lighting in the complex ranged from dim to completely dark. The oni provided each of them with an enchanted light—a rod suffused with cold fire, providing constant, pale blue illumination. The delegates and their servants were expected to take these everywhere, including their private quarters; only a few chambers or halls had permanent fixtures. It made a certain amount of sense—the tunnels within the Crag had been built by creatures whose eyes could see in the deepest darkness.

Thorn was sure it was a power play. The Daughters of Sora Kell wanted the delegates to be disoriented, to reinforce the power they wielded. The darkness didn't trouble Thorn—if anything, it would be useful when she attempted to explore the subterranean palace. But the ring that allowed her to see in the dark was a tool of her trade, and she needed to be careful not to reveal it; there was no reason for a simple aide to have such an object. She took care to cling to her torch and to stumble occasionally in the dim light.

"Do you need any help?" Thorn wasn't sure where to put Beren's belongings, but she was there to assist him. It seemed the least she could do.

"No need, Nyri. I'm sure you have preparations of your own to attend to." Beren snapped his fingers, and his bag opened of its own accord. Clothes drifted up onto the bunk, where an invisible force carefully folded them. "After one too many jobs where my aide lacked the skills for domestic tasks, I learned a few tricks of my own. You'd be surprised how far you can get with just three spells. For example," he gestured again, and Thorn felt a tingle against her skin as magical energy wiped away the dirt and sweat of the road. The ambassador passed his hand over his own clothes, and stains vanished. "There we are . . . ready for the feast. Not the easiest thing to master, but I wish I'd picked it up long ago. I do believe I spent a year covered in mud and grime when I was fighting on the western front."

"Have you met Sora Katra before?" The thought had lingered in her mind ever since she'd heard that the hag would be attending the feast. Thorn had dealt with her share of princes, and she'd spoken with King Boranel on three separate occasions. But the Daughters of Sora Kell weren't just the rulers of some savage land. Each was a legend in her own right, the stuff of nightmares and children's tales.

Thorn's father had told her a dozen stories of Sora Katra, the clever hag whose gifts always turned on the hero who sought her aid. And her brother Nandon had loved to tell her about Sora Maenya, whispered tales in the dark about the hag who would consume entire villages, the giantess who had—according to Nandon—developed a special taste for tender Khoravar girls. This inevitably resulted in 'Sora Maenya' grabbing her in the middle of the night, though the monster typically chose to tickle her instead of devouring her. As she'd grown older, she'd set these stories aside, along with the legends of the Lady of the Plague, the Lord of Eyes, and the other monsters of youth.

But a decade ago the Daughters of Sora Kell emerged from myth and laid claim to Droaam. And tonight she'd be dining with one of them . . . sitting in the same hall as the Mistress of the Mires, Lord Koltan's Doom, the Spinner of Gold and Lies. And where there was one sister, could the others be far away? Nandon's midnight tales echoed in her mind. *Maenya eats the flesh and drinks the blood, but she saves the soul, binding it forever to the bones of her victim. She sleeps on a bed made from the skulls of children, and their ghostly cries ring through the cavern, now and until the end of time . . .*

"I've never met Sora Katra," Beren said, drawing her from her reverie. "Sora Maenya . . . that's a different story. When I was just a lad, younger than you are now, I was stationed at Lherenstan, one of our keeps along the Northern Graywall. We were fools to try to settle that land, and to try to hold it during wartime. Breland's too big as it is, and we were too far from home. But there were always tales of gold and dragonshards beyond the Graywall, and greed has long outweighed common sense."

"Why were you there?" Thorn said.

Beren laughed. "I know, I know—a tragic waste of such a mighty warrior. My father was to blame. The old man wanted to keep me away from Thrane, to find me a job signing parchments or washing dishes. I knew my duty as a Wynarn. I wanted a sword in my hand, and I found my way to the front lines soon enough. As it turned out, Thrane would have been far safer than Lherenstan."

"What happened?"

"The tide of violence ebbed and flowed. Months passed with no trouble at all, then some settler or prospector would cross a line. The ogres would raid the villages, and we'd take the fight to them. I did my share of bloody deeds those days, on Aureon's word!"

Thorn was accustomed to Beren's stories, to his jovial bluster. But as he continued, she could tell that something was different about this tale. He still smiled, but the fire in his eyes had faded. He pressed on, as if compelled to speak.

"It was Zarantyr of 972 when she came to our gate. She was a refugee. She told us that her husband and children had been killed by trolls. I'll never forget her. Tall and thin, hair as black as a crow's wing and just as ragged, surrounding her like a shroud woven from the night itself. I could see that her skin was flawless beneath the dirt, and her eyes were as dark as her hair.

"But her spirit impressed me the most—the determination that had carried her so far from Sharn and Wroat, the courage that kept her going after her family was destroyed. She said she was hungry, asked if she could stay the night beneath our roof before continuing east. The commander agreed. But I didn't stay for the evening meal. Cainan and I were sent on a scouting mission, to search for our lady's village and track the aggressive trolls."

"And what did you find?" Thorn said.

Beren studied the cold fire dancing along his enchanted torch. "There was no trail to follow. It was Zarantyr, and it had snowed the day before, but there were no tracks save ours . . . and the snow was stained with blood. Yet there were no signs of struggle. No smashed doors, no burned buildings. Just the bones of twelve settlers, picked perfectly clean and stacked neatly by the town well. Every bone . . . except for the skulls. Those were nowhere to be found."

"And the woman?"

"We returned as quickly as we could, but it was past midnight by the time we arrived. I'd called on Dol Arrah, begged the Sovereigns to let that woman be a ghost, a restless spirit who'd simply wanted her remains to be found. But I knew what we were going to find. We'd left thirty people in that fort, veteran soldiers among them. All that awaited us on our return was their bones, picked clean and stacked on the table in the great hall. The skulls were gone. She'd told us the truth. She was hungry."

Thorn had heard such tales before, but never from a man who had actually lived one. She tried to envision the hall filled with bones, but the only thing that came to mind was the battlefield in her dreams, the haughty figure dressed in black and red. The sword descending toward Drego's face.

"Cainan . . . it broke him," Beren said, still gazing into the fire. He wasn't smiling any more. "He tried to kill me. I managed to reach the nearest supply post before collapsing. I don't know if they ever restaffed that fort. A decade passed before I returned to the Graywall, to fight at Kalnor Pass. And I still dream of her . . . those dark eyes, boring into mine. Every night in the Kalnor campaign, I was convinced I'd wake to find her waiting at my bedside. That she'd take my skull next, trapping my spirit until the end of time."

He stopped, and the silence was a weight across the room. The cold fire flickered but made no sound.

"At least we aren't having dinner with Sora Maenya," Thorn said. "Perhaps her sister isn't as fierce."

Beren turned to face her. His eyes were haunted, lost in the past; she'd never seen him look so grim. "I hope so,

Nyrielle. But I'm afraid. I've been trying to forget who we're dealing with . . . *what* we're dealing with. These aren't women. They aren't just monsters. Harpies or medusas I could fight, though I didn't do so well before.

"These are the daughters of one of the first evils of Eberron. They've destroyed heroes, outwitted the greatest minds of Galifar. Tonight I'll be face to face with Sora Katra. Tomorrow I'll be negotiating with her. We couldn't ignore this invitation. We all hoped Droaam would collapse on itself, and it hasn't. But I *am* afraid, Nyrielle. I still see those bones when I close my eyes, and I feel that worse is yet to come."

A sudden rap sounded on the door, and both Thorn and Beren startled. The door opened and Toli stepped inside.

"Our escort has arrived, Lord Beren. The feast is about to begin."

"Very well, Toli," Beren said. He extended an arm to Thorn. "Lady Tam, would you accompany me? I think this is a good night to have the company of friends, and I should like to drink to the memory of Grenn, and those fallen before him."

She took his hand. "Of course, Lord Beren. And I hope that before we leave this place we will be able to lay their spirits to rest."

Arm in arm, torches held in front of them, they walked out of the chamber. Then Thorn remembered that Toli had mentioned an escort.

"Good evening, Lord Beren." Drul Kantar was at least three feet taller than Toli, and his blue skin shimmered in the light of the cold fire. His canines were long and sharp, inlaid with silver sigils. "I hope you are well. I know my lady is looking forward to your meeting. Her sister has told us much about you."

Beren glanced toward Thorn, and she saw the flicker of doubt in his eyes. But if he was afraid, he forced it from his countenance. "Wonderful," he said, grinning at the oni.

"Lead the way—just promise me there'll be something to drink at the other end."

"Have no fear," Kantar said. "At least, not about that."

He laughed to show it was a joke, but somehow, Thorn couldn't bring herself to join him.

CHAPTER FOURTEEN

✳ ✳ ✳

The Great Crag
Droaam

Eyre 18, 998 YK

The halls of the Great Crag were wide and tall, built to accommodate giants. Like the entry hall, the walls were unnaturally smooth . . . yet the angles were irregular, with no signs of block or seam. It appeared more like the burrow of a giant worm than something carved by humanoids.

Drul Kantar was accompanied by ogre guards, and Thorn saw many more of them as they marched through the curving halls. Thorn had encountered ogres before. During the Last War, the dragonmarked House Tharashk had brokered the services of monstrous mercenaries, and a small but significant population of ogre laborers still lived in Sharn and Wroat, where they used their great strength to haul vast weight.

Still, with the exception of a memorable battle in Sharn, she'd rarely been so close to so many ogres, and she'd never really noticed just how bestial they were. She'd always thought of an ogre as a large human, but with the chance to study one up close, she saw many differences. The arms of the ogre were far longer and bulkier than those of a man, while its legs were shorter. The knuckles of the creature brushed the floor, and if its hands were free, she'd almost expect it to move on all fours. Both of their ogre guards, though, carried heavy axes with long, jagged blades. Each ogre's head was a massive, wedge-shaped snout, almost half as large as its torso. Long, pointed ears and a mane of matted brown hair gave the creature a lupine look. Thorn could easily imagine the ogre dropping to all fours and howling at the night sky.

Drul Kantar was something quite different. His arms, too, were longer than his legs, but his bearing was more human. And despite the horns and the two short tusks rising from his lower jaw, Kantar's head was more like that of a man. He was even handsome, in a craggy, barbaric way. Thorn had recognized his nature by his size and blue skin; she'd heard stories from soldiers who had served on the Droaam front. She knew that Kantar was far more dangerous than his bestial cousins, but she knew little of his actual capabilities. She paused for a moment, slipping her arm away from Beren. As soon as the others were a few steps ahead of her, she drew Steel. Hiding the blade behind her back, she whispered, "Oni."

Ah! The origin of the oni remains a mystery, Steel whispered in her mind. He couldn't resist playing the role of sage. *Despite the obvious physical similarities between the two species, onis are quite different from their mundane cousins. In addition to the formidable strength of the ogre, the oni possesses a host of magical abilities. Flight, invisibility, shape shifting, and the capability to heal from any normal wound within seconds are just a few of their powers. In addition, they are far more intelligent than trolls or ogres—or even humans. As a result, many take up the path of the wizard or sorcerer. This one has warded himself against divination, which means he has something worth hiding, and the ability to conceal it. Be careful.*

At that moment, Drul Kantar stopped walking and turned to face her. Surely he'd just noticed that she'd fallen behind; no one could hear Steel's voice except Thorn.

"Is something wrong, young lady?" He sounded truly concerned; his voice was deep and soft.

Thorn slipped the dagger into its sheath and smiled at the blue-skinned giant, moving forward to rejoin the group. "I'm fine, Lord Kantar. I'm just not used to these tunnels. I felt dizzy for a moment. It's passed."

"I understand. You are a child of sun and Siberys, and you miss the air and open sky. My fellows and I are creatures of darkness, and we can forget how hard it is for you."

Thorn nodded as they began walking. "It's kind of you to meet us personally," she said. "If I were more suspicious, I might suspect that you were trying to curry favor with Breland."

"If that were true, I think we'd be in better quarters." Beren smiled to show that he was joking, but Thorn could sense tension in her companion. Kantar's earlier mention of Sora Maenya had set Beren on edge.

The oni chuckled. Thorn found it strange to meet a monstrous creature with such a pleasant voice. If she closed her eyes, she pictured a heavyset priest of Olladra, celebrating the Feast of Fortune with humorous tales and songs. Instead, the voice was owned by a beast who could take off her arm with a single bite.

"I intend to spend time with all the delegates. I've already shown the Thrane and Karrnathi envoys to the hall."

"Thrane and Karrnath?" Thorn said. "And you left them alone? Would you care to lay odds on which side is still standing when we arrive?"

Kantar's smile widened, revealing disturbingly sharp teeth. "Oh, they aren't alone. My ladies have called many of the warlords of Droaam to the Crag for this gathering. You'll see. But I'm afraid you have me at a disadvantage, lady. You are—?"

Beren stepped in to answer. "This is my aide, Nyrielle Tam."

"I see." The giant vizier paused for a moment to look at her, then glanced at Toli before he resumed his pace. "It's fascinating to see whom each nation chose to send. And I am sorry that you lost one of your men in that unfortunate attack."

"And what of that?" Beren said. "I trust you've learned *something* about the attack by now. Are we still in danger?"

"It is not my place to answer such questions," Kantar replied. "Tonight Sora Katra speaks with her own voice, and she will decide what is said. Be assured that the Daughters will not allow any harm to befall their friends."

"And are we friends?" Beren said.

"That's what this gathering will determine."

Beren stopped, and Toli stepped between the ambassador and the giant. "Let me make one thing clear," Beren said. "I am the voice of Breland in this place—your nearest neighbor and the mightiest of the Five Nations of Galifar. I am cousin to King Boranel, and I have fought at his side on the field of battle. Should anything happen to me, there will be dire consequences. Your gnolls knew to keep me alive, and I'm sure that you have the same orders. So don't play games with me, Drul Kantar. I have come here as a favor to your queens, to listen to their plea. We may stand in your castle, but don't think to threaten me. My death would cost you dearly."

The oni stared at Beren, and Thorn felt a faint charge in the air . . . magical power? Then he grinned, and the energy faded. The grin turned into a deep belly laugh. He raised a hand to Toli, whose sword was half-drawn from its scabbard. Thorn realized that she'd already drawn Steel, hiding the blade against her arm.

"Your lord is wise," Kantar said. "Sheathe your weapon, guardian. Yes, we seek the favor of all nations, but Breland is our neighbor and the foe we have fought before, and it is you we most hope to befriend. You are safe here, Beren ir'Wynarn. Enjoy our hospitality, and sleep soundly this night."

Beren gave a curt nod, and they began walking again. Thorn smiled. With the nerve to face down a giant, he'd be just fine without an aide.

✳ ✳ ✳ ✳ ✳

The Daughters had spared no effort on the evening's feast. The hall was a spectacle of colors and sound, an overwhelming sight after the dull stone walls of the rest of the Crag. Sparks of golden light floated in the air, fey flames that drifted just beyond the reach of guests. A team of goblins darted around a central fire pit, preparing and distributing food. After a week of eating rabbits, the rich aroma of spiced meats and vegetables set Thorn's mouth watering. Tribex, gorgon, some sort of crustacean the size of a warhorse—there was enough food for an army, and it smelled delicious.

Long tables were set with Riedran crysteel, plates and goblets with the beauty of carved glass but the strength of iron. Music echoed through the hall, the work of a band of goblins in the far corner. The little creatures were producing a frenzied song on pipes, drums, and lute. A dancer accompanied them. Her skin was jet back, and as Thorn watched, flames seemed to dart across her flesh.

Skindancer, Steel whispered. *Most changelings use their gifts to impersonate other living creatures, but when you can alter your body, there are many other possibilities.*

The skindancer spun in place, and her hair flowed out from her body, taking on a brilliant red hue as it did, as if a cloud of fire had suddenly burst around her. The woman spun faster and faster as the music built to its climax. On the final note, her hair shifted to black and spun in toward her. From a distance, Thorn wasn't certain the woman was wearing clothes; it seemed that she had just painted patterns on her skin.

"We have changelings in Breland—why haven't I seen that before?" she murmured.

Because the changelings of the Five Nations hide their abilities. You know how they're treated, with suspicion and distrust. In a land with harpies and medusas, a shapeshifter isn't so strange. I'd imagine the changelings of Droaam have more opportunities to explore the full extent of their powers.

But as fascinating as it was, the dancer was just one part of the wild celebration. Tiny gargoyles darted around the curved ceiling, tossing spheres of glowing glass in a display of juggling and acrobatics. Around her, delegates spoke with the lords of Droaam. A Mror dwarf dressed in black and gold roared with laughter at the words of an armored minotaur, and Lord Beren was speaking with a woman dressed in flowing robes of white silk with bronzed leather. No . . . as Thorn took in the scene, she realized that the leather was the woman's skin. The living mane that roiled around her shoulders confirmed it. This was a medusa, perhaps the very one Thorn sought. She faced Beren. Clearly, something was blocking her deadly gaze, or there'd be a statue in Beren's place. Again, Thorn was impressed with Beren. Regardless of the setting, it took courage to stare into the face of a medusa.

This sight was enough to shake Thorn out of her reverie. The celebration was a remarkable and overwhelming event, but she had work to do. She had two missions, and she didn't expect to find Harryn Stormblade at this party.

Drul Kantar had said that the Daughters of Sora Kell had called the most powerful warlords of the land to the Crag. Based on the encounter at Korlaak Pass, either some of the warlords had their own plans for Droaam and its relations with the east, or the Daughters were playing a game even their soldiers weren't aware of. Tonight would be her first chance to study the lords of Droaam.

A goblin passed by with a tray of marinated meat on skewers. Thorn grabbed one of the treats as the servant went past. Perhaps it was just her hunger, but the meat was one of the most delicious things she'd tasted; juicy, perfectly spiced, with an exotic flavor she couldn't identify. It wasn't until she reached the end of the skewer that she noticed the small skull wedged down at the base—charred and blackened, but still distinctly humanoid. Pixie kabobs? she wondered. Her gorge rose, and she was half-inclined to let it. Surely they wouldn't serve intelligent creatures as food. She noticed a gnoll licking his jaws, two of the skewers in his hand. She resolved to stick to the tribex.

"Good evening, Lady Tam." The face was familiar, but the voice was a surprise. It was Minister Luala, the Thrane envoy. She spoke softly, but somehow Thorn could hear every word. Drego Sarhain stood just behind her, with the shadow of a smirk on his face. "Now that I am able, I wish to thank you for your conduct and company on our journey."

"I just played the hand I was dealt, minister."

"Nonetheless, your kindness was appreciated . . . especially in comparison to your comrade in arms." Her eyes flickered to where Lord Beren and his bodyguard were speaking to another oni.

"If you mean Toli, I'd be happy to let that subject drop, minister. I'm a diplomat. I choose my words with more care than my companions. But Toli lost friends and family to Thrane soldiers. Personally, I think it's a testament to his restraint that words were all that were exchanged."

The minister looked crestfallen. "I had hoped that we could heal the wounds between our nations—just as I sought to restore Toli to health."

"If you want to magically mend the damage, try raising the dead of Vathirond and Shadukar."

Drego stepped forward. "And what of the Thranes slain by Brelish soldiers? Our nations rose together when the Last War began. Are you somehow placing the blame on Thrane's shoulders alone?"

"Not at all," Thorn said. She sighed. She appreciated what Luala was trying to do, but she understood Toli's anger. "I wasn't asking for forgiveness. I don't expect your people to forget the deaths of those they loved in the space of a few years. I know mine won't. I appreciate your thoughts, Minister Luala. Perhaps a time will come when our wounds can be healed. But right now, we're here for Droaam. I suggest that you don't try to take on too many challenges."

"Wise advice." A woman's voice, low and husky.

The newcomer stood directly behind the Thrane soldier accompanying Drego and Luala. The bodyguard started in surprise and reached for his weapon, but the stranger caught his wrist in one hand and his neck in the other, pinning him in place.

"Don't," she said, addressing Drego and Thorn as much as her prisoner. "I've been told not to kill you, but no one raises a weapon against me and lives."

She released the soldier with a sudden shove that sent him stumbling to his knees. Drego Sarhain had moved between the stranger and Minister Luala, and Thorn stepped to the side, where she could get a good view of the newcomer.

At first, Thorn thought it was the elf she'd seen back at the Duurwood Camp—the hunter with his wolves. The stranger wore the same uniform—loose black hunter's clothes spattered with grey patterns to help blend into the shadows. Pale skin, hair the color of moonlight, the wide eyes and pointed ears of a full-blooded elf. But this was a woman. Older than the young hunter. And only one long elf ear emerged from beneath her hair; her left ear was missing, the wound hidden from view. *My mother sends her greetings*, the young elf had told the gnolls. Thorn guessed she'd just moved up the family tree.

If the son had seemed dangerous, the mother put him to shame. She wore no boots, and she stood on the balls of her feet, arms at her sides, hands open and ready. Elves weren't known for strength, and she wasn't a bulky woman, but she was slender and compact—a perfectly forged rapier set next to the clumsy club of an ogre. But what impressed Thorn the most was the conviction in the woman's large elven eyes. She had the gaze of a true predator. Thorn was certain that the woman had already sized her up and was ready to respond to any action she might take. A chill grew at the base of her spine . . . the same sensation she'd felt when the wolves appeared in the Duurwood.

"I am the warlord Zaeurl," she said. "I believe you've met my children."

CHAPTER FIFTEEN

✗ ✗ ✗

The Great Crag
Droaam

Eyre 18, 998 YK

I beg your pardon," Luala said, carefully studying the newcomer. "You must have us confused with some of the other delegates. I don't know you, let alone your relatives."

"I said my children, not my relatives." Zaeurl was smiling, but it wasn't a pleasant sight. An air of menace hung about this huntress; she was used to being feared, and it had become a part of her. Thorn remembered the way the gnolls had reacted to the wolf pack in the woods; a strange tension had been present then, a sense of an unspoken and deadly secret. She felt that now, mingling with the pain in her spine. "And I misspoke. You may not have seen my children, but they certainly saw you. It was my pack who watched your way for the last five days, shielding you from further attacks. And they told me about you—the silent woman with the silver flame at her throat, and her handsome toy." She glanced at Drego. "That would be you, boy."

"I'd gathered that," he said.

"Warlord," Thorn said. "What does that mean, exactly? Do you command the armies of Droaam?"

"Less formal than that," Zaeurl said, turning her gaze

on Thorn. "I suppose you might say 'baron' in your lands. My fellow warlords all command military forces. Should we return to war, our Queens will guide our actions. It helps to have a commander who can see the future."

"And your soldiers?" Drego said. Thorn could see that he was still on alert, ready to act . . . and it seemed like a wise decision. Zaeurl's eyes narrowed when he spoke, and her muscles stiffened; clearly, she disliked the Thranes.

"Hunters and scouts, mostly. We know the ways of the woods better than anyone else in Droaam, man or beast."

"And what brought you to this place?" Thorn said. "I see ogres, goblins, orcs—I haven't seen many elves in the service of the Daughters."

"Why, the Silver Flame led me to Droaam," Zaeurl said.

Luala frowned. "I beg your pardon?"

"That's twice you've asked," Zaeurl said, and there was steel in her voice. "You could ask a thousand times, and you'd never receive it. Where were you two centuries ago, minister?"

"I beg—" Luala caught herself, and began again. "I served in the library of Flamekeep, tending the scrolls and teaching the young acolytes."

"And were you involved in the war in the west?"

Thorn frowned. Until the Last War, Galifar had been a remarkably peaceful kingdom. There were a handful of uprisings and ambitious lords, but little to earn the title of *war*. Two centuries ago . . .

The Purge.

Drego reached the same conclusion. "Are you referring to the Silver Crusade?"

Zaeurl nodded. "Call it what you will, boy. You weren't alive to see it."

Eberron was a world of magic, and magic took many forms. It might be a blessing or a curse. Sometimes it was both, as in the case of lycanthropy—the force responsible for werewolves, wererats, and other shapeshifters of legend. Thorn had never met a lycanthrope. Since the Purge, they were few and far between.

"And what is your quarrel with the crusade?" Luala studied the warlord carefully.

"Many innocents were killed in your war," Zaeurl said. "I lost my first family at the hands of the Pure Flame."

"Innocents were lost," Luala agreed. "Fear, and the thirst for revenge, drove people to madness. But were you there for the beginning, Zaeurl? Again, your pardon, but you do not appear as old as I. The soldiers of the Flame did not travel to the west on a mere whim. They came in response to the cries of those dying at the hands of the werewolves and their kin."

"Propaganda," hissed the warlord. "Your leaders were only interested in spreading the influence of the Church throughout Aundair. You gave the people something to fear, and then you saved them from a force that was never a threat."

"I cannot claim to know the heart of the Keeper of the Flame," Luala said. "I cannot know if his motives were pure. But I know that it was a time of horrors. The wolf's curse has always been feared, and rightly so. It transforms its victims in mind as well as body. One of my childhood friends tore out the throats of his wife and children after succumbing to the touch of the Rat, before we knew what it truly was.

"Back then, in the midst of the eighth century, whatever power it held was magnified a hundredfold. Even in Thrane, we heard the tales. Wolves that walked like men, slaughtering entire villages. A single bite was enough to turn a man into a monster. If the soldiers of the Silver Flame hadn't responded, the curse would have swept across Aundair and Breland, and then it would have been unstoppable.

"There were casualties, yes. It was a war, and the

infected cared nothing for the lives of others. They did everything possible to mislead our soldiers, to trick them into spilling innocent blood. The tide only turned when the power of the curse itself faded—when it became more difficult for the infected to pass on their affliction. But by then, the people of Aundair were hungry for revenge. And that's when they began to turn on each other, torturing and burning their own in the name of destroying every last shapeshifter."

"I've read the records," Drego said. "It's a blot on the soul of the church. But it was the madness of war. You can't judge the Silver Flame on the actions of zealots who embraced the faith in search of vengeance."

"Don't tell me what I can do," Zaeurl said. "My people were driven from our homeland, burned out of the woods that had sheltered us for generations. My father was butchered before my eyes, and it was the Mockery's luck that allowed me to escape."

"So why didn't you return?" Drego said. "The madness ended long before I was born. The zealots of the Pure Flame are still strong in Aundair, but you'd never see such things happen today."

"I have neither forgiven nor forgotten what was done to me and mine." Zaeurl's eyes burned, and Drego took a step back; though she held no weapons, the woman felt dangerous. "My family was slaughtered by your kind. And you say it's over? You've spent the last century killing one another. How many years do you think it will be before you start again?" She drew back her lips, and Thorn was certain she heard a growl. "This is a dangerous place I have chosen as my lair, but it is an honest one. My children are treated with the respect they deserve . . . and if they aren't, blood is shed. If I ever return to your so-called civilized world, it will be to take vengeance of my own. Perhaps I'll see you there, minister."

Zaeurl kept her eyes fixed on Luala's as she took a step

back, and there was death in that gaze. Then she turned and strode into the crowd. Thorn found that she'd been holding her breath, and she slowly released it.

"Well," Drego said, after a moment of silence. "I'm glad to see that we're making such good friends so quickly. Are they actually going to *serve* this food? Personally, I'm famished."

✠ ✠ ✠ ✠ ✠

Drego's comment turned out to be prescient. Moments later, Drul Kantar's voice rang out across the hall, amplified by magic.

"Lords and ladies! Honored delegates of the eastern lands! Our feast will now begin, and the great lady Sora Katra will soon arrive to address you all. You have been assigned to tables—I ask that you find your seats at this time."

Thorn inclined her head to Minister Luala and flashed a smile at Drego. "I must rejoin my lord. Minister, I thank you for your kind wishes, and apologize if my response was unduly harsh. I look forward to speaking with you and Flamebearer Sarhain in the days to come."

Luala nodded, but her eyes were clouded. The encounter with Warlord Zaeurl was weighing heavily upon her. Drego grinned. "I trust our paths will cross sooner rather than later, my lady."

Thorn made her way through the crowd, pushing past ogre and goblin alike. An armored warrior turned toward her as she approached. His head was a bleached skull, and points of gleaming fire burned in the sockets.

"Karrns," she muttered, moving around the undead soldier. All things considered, it was a good choice for a bodyguard. Animated by magic, it didn't need to sleep and couldn't be enchanted by the magic of a harpy's voice. The idea made her shiver—she'd never been comfortable with the walking dead.

She found Beren and Toli still talking with the medusa. The reptilian woman stood half a head taller than Thorn, and her mane made her seem even taller. The serpents that made up her hair were stretched up in the air, peering around to study Beren. The medusa wore a silver collar with a long pectoral ornament; a Khyber dragonshard was embedded in the pendant, and the large purple gem pulsed with a faint inner light. From her jewelry, her posture, and Beren's interest in the conversation, Thorn guessed that this was Sheshka, the medusa who'd petrified Harryn Stormblade and whose kiss she'd need to free him—if she managed to locate the statue.

Sheshka's death is an acceptable loss, provided Breland can't be blamed for it. Those were Steel's words back in Graywall. Thorn fought the urge to draw Steel; she was dying to know what wards were shielding Sheshka. But guards stood everywhere in the banquet hall, and drawing a dagger near one of the leading lights of the nation didn't seem like the right move at a diplomatic gathering. She held her position behind Sheshka, listening to the conversation.

". . . that we can settle this between ourselves during this gathering," the medusa said. "If not, you would be welcome in Cazhaak Draal."

"A generous offer." Beren raised an eyebrow. "But what would your Sovereigns say about it?"

"The Daughters of Sora Kell have done much for the people of Droaam." The medusa had a musical voice with a pronounced sibilance; her syllables flowed together in a hypnotic song. "They have shown savages the value of civilization, and taught petty tyrants that there is more to life than dominating a wretched pack of goblin slaves. But my people have never been savages or slavers. I am a queen in my own right, Lord Beren, and I held the granite throne centuries before the Daughters came to us. Droaam is stronger today than it was at the start of your Last War.

But I am the Queen of Stone, and I will choose the path of my people."

Interesting, Thorn thought. She'd missed the start of the conversation, but nonetheless . . . back at the Duurwood, Zaeurl's children told the gnolls that there were warlords whose interests clashed with those of the Daughters. Sheshka's name had been mentioned. Could the medusa have been connected to the attack on the bridge? Suddenly, the idea of her death being *an acceptable loss* seemed more appealing.

"I'll bear that in mind, Queen Sheshka. Let us speak on it tomorrow—"

Beren noticed Thorn as he was talking. His expression barely shifted; she detected the slightest acknowledgement, the merest shift in his eyes. But Sheshka noticed. Her serpents hissed softly as she turned to face the newcomer. She wore no hood or veil—nothing to cover her deadly gaze— and although Thorn knew that Beren was still healthy, she instinctively glanced away. *Never look at a medusa.* Everyone knew that.

"Noble Sheshka," Beren said, "This is my aide, Nyrielle Tam."

"Charming," Sheshka said. If a serpent could sing, it would hope for such a voice. "Young. Look at me, child. Let me see your eyes."

I don't think Beren is worried that I'll be petrified, Thorn thought. She raised her head to face the medusa queen.

Sheshka's eyes were closed. The serpents were coiled around her face, staring at Thorn. *Can she see through their eyes?*

"Yes," she said, "charming. Now I suppose we should take our places; it's unwise to anger Sora Katra. We'll speak tomorrow, Lord Beren."

"My thanks for your time," Beren said. "I hope that the interests of Breland and Cazhaak Draal lie on the same path."

"Hope is a fine thing," Sheshka said. "We will learn

the truth of it tomorrow." The medusa turned and walked away. A path opened before her; even the monsters of Droaam respected the queen's deadly gaze.

"Fascinating," Beren said, moving to join Thorn. Nearby, Toli was watching the crowd. She didn't envy the bodyguard. It would be challenge enough to watch for weapons in such a crowd, but half the guests had claws, fearsome teeth, or magical powers. Any of them could become a threat at a moment's notice.

"What was that about?"

"Queen Sheshka wishes to speak privately, tomorrow afternoon," Beren said. He held out his arm and she accepted it. "She was maddeningly vague about the subject, but it seemed that she was suggesting an alliance between Breland and her people, even if we fail to come to an agreement with Droaam as a whole. I'm not sure whether to be grateful that the powers of Droaam aren't completely united behind the Daughters, or worried about getting drawn into some sectarian conflict."

An envelope lay next to each place setting, labeled with a name. This was as formal as a royal gala in Wroat. They found their places at a long table.

"Let's see," Beren said. "Here I am . . . Toli, on my left, good. It looks like they have already accounted for Grenn's death." He sighed, and Thorn remembered that he'd hand-picked the guard. "Nyri, this looks like a mistake. They've put a 'Thorn' on my right. I don't see you at the table at all."

Thorn felt a chill as she looked at the envelope. It was her code name as a Dark Lantern. Who'd written this? Was it a warning? She couldn't help but wonder what name was listed on Drego's envelope.

"I'd rather not be separated, Lord Beren. Why don't I sit here—if this 'Thorn' shows up, we'll worry about it then."

Beren nodded. "Yes, a fine thought. 'Thorn' . . . considering where we are, I wouldn't be surprised if he's some sort of spiny ogre, and Arawai knows *that's* the last thing I need at my shoulder."

Thorn forced a smile and took her seat at the table.

"Well met!" the hobgoblin ambassador struck the table with a fist. "I am Munta the Gray, lord of the Gantii Vus, and—in this place—voice of Haruuc of the Crimson Blade! Who are my companions this evening?"

The Brelish weren't alone at their table. In the wagons, they'd been paired with the Thranes; tonight they'd been seated with the delegates from Darguun and the gnomes of Zilargo. Munta the Gray had surely been a fierce warrior in his youth, but now he was an old man. What must have been considerable muscle was running to fat. He was dressed for war, as befit the reputation of his people; curling horns adorned a steel helm chased with brass, and a light breastplate carried the sigil of a fanged maw wreathed in flames.

"I am Councilor Jolira Jan Dorian of Korranberg." Jolira was young, for a gnome—or so she appeared. The people of Zilargo had a talent for illusions, and there was no telling if the envoy was showing her true face. She was even smaller than a goblin, and more delicate. In many ways she seemed like a beautiful doll, a miniature dressed in lovely robes and decked with jewels. She wore no armor and carried no sword, but her hair was held back with long pins, and Thorn was certain these were charged with magical power. "My companions are Councilor Alidan Lorridan Lyrris of Trolanport and Councilor Mordan Sel Sarin of Zalanberg, together representing the Triumvirate of Zilargo. Ember is our guardian."

This was another surprise. Most nations had sent a single ambassador accompanied by guards or perhaps an aide, but the gnomes had three envoys and a single defender—a warforged. Built by House Cannith during the Last War, the warforged were wood and steel constructs given life through magic. Ember was an impressive figure; he reminded Thorn of a scarecrow, lean and deadly, limbs and torso cast of blackened adamantine. A glyph was carved into his metal forehead, and both this sigil and the eyes of the warforged burned with a fierce crimson light.

Beren made the introductions for the Brelish. That left one more stranger at the table—the man sitting next to Thorn. As disturbed as she'd been by the place card indicating her secret name, her dinner companion proved a worthy distraction. No chair waited at his place, merely a massive bearskin spread out across the floor. His tankard was the size of a barrel, and his crystal plate as wide as a wagon's wheel. The oversized setting was novelty enough, but then the guest arrived.

He was a giant.

No mere ogre, but a true giant . . . a creature Thorn had only heard of in the tales explorers brought back from Xen'drik. As Thorn had seen, the ogres—and even the oni—were quite bestial in appearance; no one could mistake them for humans. The newcomer had no such fearsome demeanor—no fangs, no claws, no horns on his forehead. His skin was jet black, his hair the brilliant red of a bonfire, and he was extremely muscular. Setting aside the color of his skin, at a great distance he could easily have been mistaken for a dwarf of the Mror Holds, a proud miner baron. Up close, it was obvious that he was over three times the height of a man, and that he could crush Thorn's head between his thumb and forefinger. Even sitting on the floor, he towered over the table.

"I am the Warlord Gorodan, called the Ashlord," he said. His voice was bass thunder, and the wine in their goblets shook with the sound. "I am to be your host for this miserable evening. Ask what you will of me . . . but be warned." He set a massive hand on the table, shaking everything on it. "I am hungry and I am cold, and I have no patience for the foolish questions of little men. Now let us EAT!"

The last comment was directed to the room at large. Gorodan's speaking voice was loud enough; when he shouted, Thorn could *feel* the force of it. The command sent the goblins scurrying, and within moments food began to arrive.

After her earlier experience with the pixie sticks, Thorn chose to avoid anything she couldn't identify, but that still left many options. She knew that gorgon was safe, and it wasn't an easy dish to find in Breland. The sauce was a savory blend of wine and firepeppers; Thorn wondered if the Daughters had imported chefs who understood human tastes, or if they ate such food themselves. Beren's tale of Sora Maenya rose in the back of her mind, and she had a vision of the hag preparing a wine glaze for the three children she had just killed; she shivered and tried to force the image away. Suddenly she wasn't hungry any more.

Her companions were pleasant enough. Munta was surprisingly good company; hobgoblins were known as warriors, but Lhesh Haruuc of Darguun had chosen his envoy well. Soon everyone but the giant was laughing at Munta's tale of the goblin smith trapped inside the suit of plate mail. Councilor Sarin surprised them with a war story; not a tale of the Last War, but an account of a battle fought deep within the Seawall Mountains between kobolds and gnome jewel miners. Sarin had begun his political career as a foreman in the mines.

Councilor Dorian had a talent for weaving illusions, and as Sil Sarin told his tale, she recreated it with shimmering figures of light; even the sullen giant was drawn in by the show. At the end, as everyone cheered the clever victory, Sarin scattered a handful of rubies across the table, gems from the very mine of the tales. The councilor asked everyone to take a ruby as a memory of the evening. Even Toli seemed pleased as he took a ruby; while he hated the

Thranes, the gnomes of Zilargo had been strong allies of Breland in the last years of the war.

Clever play, Thorn thought. Beren placed his ruby in his belt pouch, and Thorn slipped it out as he reached for the flagon of wine. Such an object was an ideal target for scrying magic. Assuming the gnomes had a diviner in their party, this friendly gift would allow them to monitor the activities of anyone who kept a ruby. She'd dispose of them later.

Beren and Jen Dorian attempted to draw out the giant. Though still sullen, the warlord's mood had improved as he filled his stomach. "My tale begins in Xen'drik," he rumbled, "far across the Thunder Sea."

Thorn was sure it was a fascinating tale . . . but it was also an opportunity. All attention was focused on the giant. Dropping her hand beneath the table, she carefully drew Steel.

Confirm: the envelope at your seat is addressed to Thorn?

She tapped the blade once with her forefinger.

We're in luck, then.

The warlord Gorodan was explaining how he'd violated a taboo of his people, something he considered to be a foolish, primitive superstition. Thorn used the opportunity. "I'm not sure I understand—could you elaborate on that?"

Sora Teraza is an oracle. It's difficult to determine the full extent of her power—like all the Daughters, the truth is tangled with centuries of legend. We've lost agents in Droaam before due to her prescience. It's not surprising that she'd know your identity. The point is that they know who you are, and you're still alive.

Meaning what? There was a chance they'd have me killed? She had no way to ask this question without raising eyebrows, so she waited for an appropriate moment in Gorodan's story and said, "That is very interesting."

The Daughters had to know the nations would send spies.

They're probably counting on it. They want to make sure that whatever happens here is heard across Khorvaire. So they know who you are and what you are. But if they knew about your secondary mission, they'd probably have taken direct action by now. Have you looked inside the envelope?

Looked inside? She tapped the blade twice. It hadn't even occurred to her. But Steel was right. They weren't just place cards—there was little reason to use an envelope if not to put something inside.

Obviously you shouldn't open it now, since it's not addressed to you. But you'd best take it with you. In any case, about your companions—

Steel's speech and Gorodan's story were both cut off as the floating lights flared and then dimmed, drawing together to create a single pool of light between the tables. A single figure was silhouetted by the spotlight.

Sora Katra. Mistress of the Mires. The crone who wove curses on her loom. Subject of a hundred stories . . . all of which ended badly.

"Let us begin," she said.

CHAPTER SIXTEEN

✼ ✼ ✼

The Great Crag
Droaam

Eyre 18, 998 YK

Though Sora Katra stood below the light, it didn't touch her. It was more than a trick of illumination. Thanks to her ring, Thorn could see in darkness as clearly as day, yet the figure remained in shadow. Sora Katra's voice was equally mysterious. It was firm, clear, commanding. Feminine. Authoritative. The voice of a queen, of a matriarch who has dominated a family for generations. And yet, the moment she stopped speaking, Thorn had trouble remembering the precise sound of that voice. Surely she had the voice of an old woman—but when Thorn looked back on the evening, she heard a younger voice—a voice she'd always associated with her mother.

But when Sora Katra spoke, all questions vanished. Hers was a voice that could not be ignored.

"None of you have met me before. Yet all of you know me. I was with you in your bed when you first heard the tale of Lord Koltan and the story of the Stone Tree. I spent my youth in the Shadow Marches, but I also moved among you; whenever you told my stories, you brought me to your door." Her shadow shifted; Thorn could *almost* make out her shape, but not quite. "We live in a world filled with illusions, a world of changelings and hidden fiends. I myself have worn a thousand faces and more, for each story calls for something new. We have long known each other, yet this is the first time that we truly meet, and I wish you to see who I am."

Her shadow shifted again, and the magical lights faded further.

"So remember that first story. Remember what you feared in the night. Remember . . . and be welcome."

As she finished speaking, she stepped back and fully into the light. A gasp passed through the assembled envoys, and Thorn couldn't help herself; she stiffened, her grip tightening on Steel's hilt. The figure standing before her had stepped out of her nightmares.

Sora Katra was just as Thorn had imagined from hearing the tale of the Forgotten Princess. She was an old woman, and her skin was as pale as her hair, milky white with a touch of green that hinted at rot. Her skin was wrinkled and her flesh withered, but her back was straight, and her movements were smooth and graceful. She wore a cloak of long black feathers over a rough gray robe, bound by a belt made of finger bones . . . trophies from those who'd made foolish deals with her. Her own fingers were unnaturally long, each one tipped with a raven's talon. Despite the distance, Thorn could see her eyes—greenish-white and glowing in the dim light. "Eyes that saw your death as soon as they passed over you," her father had told her. "Saw it . . . or set it in stone."

It's not real, Steel whispered. *She said it herself . . . illusion, and a powerful one. Everyone here is seeing something different.*

Steel's words were comforting, but the unease remained. Though she knew it was a trick, Thorn still remembered lying awake in the middle of the night, clenching her fists every time she heard a bird land on the roof. A young girl terrified that those pale eyes would appear at the window, coming to claim a bone.

"Yes, we know each other, you and I." Sora Katra glanced around the silent room, and it took all of Thorn's resolve to meet her pale gaze. "But do you know this place? Do you know where you are, and why?"

Sora Katra raised her right hand and a medusa appeared in the shadows at her side. Venom dripped from the serpents coiled around her head, and her eyes were wide open; though most knew it must be an illusion, there was a commotion as many of the envoys looked away or shielded their eyes. And Katra wasn't done. She raised her left hand and a troll stepped out of the darkness—a muscular beast, slime and boils glistening on its rubbery green skin. It held a human child in one clenched fist, and it raised the girl to its mouth and closed its jaws around her neck. With that, both images froze, leaving Sora Katra flanked by terrors.

"For a thousand years, you claimed this land as part of your kingdom of Galifar," she said. "But it was never yours, and you knew it. You have numbers, discipline, ingenuity; you have crafted fantastic tools and powerful magic over the centuries. But you have always feared those beings that have powers you can never master. The petrifying gaze of the medusa. The troll's gift to spurn the touch of steel. You fought these creatures in the past, slaughtered them when you could, pushed them away when that was all you could do. You carved out your peaceful sanctuary in the heart of the land, but you never drove the horrors from *this* land. Occasionally, your warriors would cross the Graywall, seeking to make a name, a new legend, to return as heroes of a new story. But you know as well as I how many returned."

Katra lowered her hands and the images vanished. But something lingered in the shadows where they had been . . . a ripple in the darkness.

"Just over a century ago, you tore your great kingdom apart. You have spent decades killing one another, and the heart of Galifar is lost forever. And as you squandered the work of a thousand years, we created something new."

She raised her hand and was flanked by massive figures . . . the bestial ogre guards, and trolls that looked even more fearsome than the one seen a moment earlier—trolls wearing armor and carrying vicious axes.

"My sisters and I each have our strengths. I am the voice. Sora Teraza, the vision. And Sora Maenya is our bloody blade. Alone, we are terrifying. Together, we are far more . . . and that is the lesson we brought to this place. Harpy, medusa, minotaur—any one of them a creature dreaded by your kind. But together, they could be a power this world has never seen. Every fear your people have— standing side by side, using their remarkable gifts in ways never conceived by those living in savagery."

She raised her arms and the walls around her faded away. Harpies and gargoyles filled the air above her. Snarling dire wolves and minotaurs now stood among the ogres and trolls, and Katra was flanked by medusa archers.

"This is where you are. This is Droaam. An alliance of those you fear, of the monsters of your tales. Three years ago we came to you and asked that you recognize our sovereignty. You dismissed us. You had greater concerns, and no interest in the savages to the east. Surely we'd turn on one another within a year . . . or one of you would take it upon yourselves to eliminate this blight once and for all. Yet here we stand."

Sora Katra lowered her hands and the perspective suddenly changed . . . a dizzying, disorienting effect. Thorn felt as if she were rising into the air, looking down upon the army of ogres, trolls, and other beasts . . . an army that grew larger and larger as she gained a greater perspective.

"Three years have passed, and we have not fallen. We are stronger than you ever imagined, and our power grows by the day. We are the nightmare of humanity. And so you have come, in answer to our call. To see for yourselves what power we truly possess. To see the mistake you made years ago. Ignore us, insult us, and this is what awaits you."

Wyverns and manticores joined the beasts in the air, and divisions of gnolls and goblins took positions alongside the ogres and their kin. The army stretched for miles . . .

And then it was gone. Sora Katra stood alone in the pool of light.

"Droaam is the terror that has lingered in the shadows since your civilizations began. Yet we did not destroy your great kingdom. You did that to yourselves. We are easy targets for your fear, but it is time to set aside your primal superstitions and see the world as it truly is."

She gestured, and sparks of light pulled free from the pool floating above her, flying through the air to illuminate members of the audience. The giant Gorodan; the medusa Sheshka; another oni, whom Thorn guessed was Tzaryan Rrac.

"The Ashlord's size may intimidate you, but did he slaughter the innocents of Vathirond? Did he order the burning of Shadukar? We are different from you. But we are no more—and no less—evil than you. Now is your chance to embrace that. Set aside your fears and your prejudice. Accept Droaam as a sovereign state under the terms of the Treaty of Thronehold. Accept us as equals and allies. We offer you this second chance, and we are willing to forget the insult done to us three years ago. But spurn us again and we will become your nightmare, in truth."

The room was utterly silent. To Thorn it seemed that her companions weren't even breathing.

"I'm sure you have questions. Some of you have deals to propose, others have demands to make in exchange for your support. Over the next two days you will have the opportunity to speak to my warlords, to my sisters and to myself. We will discuss the nation of Droaam and the state of your wounded kingdoms, and how we can all live together in harmony. So let me tell you the laws of the Crag."

Sora Katra raised a hand, and an image of the Great Crag appeared beside her. Thorn had been inside the wagon during the approach, and she hadn't seen anything of the city at the base of the mountain. It was difficult to make out details on such a small model, but she saw tents and crumbling ruins scattered between newer, more solid structures.

"We will not tolerate violence, either against our subjects or between delegates. Each of you will have guards assigned to accompany you whenever you leave your quarters; they have been taught to speak your common tongue, which I have sought to spread across the land. Do not wander the corridors of the Crag without these escorts. This may seem rude, but I do not believe that any of you would allow one of my ogres to wander through your royal palaces without guardians . . . and the Crag is more dangerous than any eastern palace.

"You are not to leave the interior of the Great Crag for any reason. Six moons will rise over Droaam tomorrow, a time we call the Midnight Dawn. It is a celebration, a festival, but our ways are not yours, and your life will be in jeopardy if you leave this sanctuary. Heed these warnings, and you will live to return to your homelands. Should you break the rules, I wash my hands of your blood. And as for those of you who have come in hopes of stealing from us, or engaging in acts of sabotage . . . well, perhaps the aide to the ambassador of Karrnath can speak to this."

She reached into the shadows and pulled an object from the darkness. It was a human head, skin pale from loss of blood, stump of the neck jagged and ugly as if torn from the body by sheer brute force. The eyes were glazed and sightless, but suddenly they rolled in their sockets and focused on the crowd. Thorn could swear the dead man was looking directly at her.

"I came seeking a treasure of the Crag," he said, and his voice was hollow, filled with despair. "The Orb of Dol Azur, a powerful artifact which might serve as a weapon in days to come. Sora Maenya ground my bones to dust and bound my spirit so that I might have eternity to consider the error of my ways."

A slight smile pulled at Sora Katra's withered lips, and she tossed the head toward the table where the Karrns were seated. The Karrnathi ambassador was on his feet, paler even than the dead man, his mouth working silently. He instinctively reached forward to catch the head . . . and it vanished as it touched his hands.

"Your man is still alive, Lord Tharsul," Sora Katra said. "He merely sleeps in his quarters, though his dreams are most unpleasant. I would apologize for making an example of you, if you had not brought a spy to my kingdom. Let this be a lesson to you all, for next time it will be no illusion. I welcome you as my friends. Now you have seen what fate awaits those who abuse my trust."

The Karrnathi ambassador sat down, his face as rigid as that of his skeletal bodyguard. Murmurs rippled through the crowd. *The Orb of Dol Azur,* Steel said. *I wonder if he's with Karrnathi intelligence or the Three Faces of War.*

The room fell silent as Sora Katra spoke once more. "You know where you are. You know why you are here. You know what will happen in the days to come, and the laws you must obey. So now, I ask that you enjoy yourselves. Indulge in the delicacies of our land. In the hours to come, you will hear the drums of the Keroine minotaurs and the pipes of the Suthar satyrs. I had planned to give you a taste of harpy song, but in light of recent events, we have set that aside. We are grateful to you for coming, travelers, and tonight is our gift to you. Enjoy it while you can."

She raised her arms again, and the sparks of light above her flowed down, surrounding her in a brilliant funnel. They grew brighter and faster, spinning in a radiant tornado. And then they burst, scattering across the chamber and filling the room with light.

Sora Katra had vanished.

CHAPTER SEVENTEEN

✦ ✦ ✦

The Great Crag
Droaam

Eyre 18, 998 YK

Thorn's bunk was a blanket set atop a slab of stone. *And I was complaining about sleeping on the ground,* she thought. *I'm already looking forward to the trip back.*

"I'll bet I missed a beautiful sunset," Thorn said. It was a code phrase; 'sunset' let other Lanterns know she was concerned about magical surveillance.

We are not being observed, Steel whispered.

"You're certain?"

One of my primary functions is to sense the use of scrying or other active divinations, Steel told her, sounding slightly annoyed. *I've served with thirty-two Dark Lanterns in my time with the Citadel, and I've never been mistaken.*

"At least, you've never had a diviner drop by to *tell* you that you were mistaken."

I've never had a mission compromised by magical surveillance when the Lantern has listened to my recommendations.

"So—no eyes or ears?"

That is correct.

Thorn had remained at the feast long enough to identify the remaining warlords, then feigned indigestion and asked a guard to escort her back to her quarters. She sat on her bunk, running her thumb along Steel's hilt and studying the envelope left for her at the dinner table.

What are your conclusions so far, Lantern Thorn?

"Let's see. I've just seen a childhood nightmare threaten to trap the soul of anyone who tries to steal from her. And I've been told that she knows who I am and possibly why I'm here. So I don't exactly have a conclusion. I've just been wondering whether Sora Maenya will keep my skull on the mantel or use it as a paperweight."

Thorn . . .

"Don't worry," she said, flipping the dagger in the air and catching it. "I've been through worse." She smiled as she spoke. As dangerous as the situation was, she enjoyed the challenge. Considering the problems drove the lingering pain from her mind; the world seemed sharper and clearer.

"So," she said, "let's look at what we know. Sora Katra's position is that Droaam is stronger than ever. She says that Droaam isn't a threat to the east unless we turn down their offer, in which case they'll tear the heads off our children and turn us to stone."

More or less.

"However, we've seen signs that Droaam isn't quite as unified as Katra would have us believe. She didn't explain the harpy attack, but from what we overheard, it was the work of a harpy chieftain in league with another warlord."

Indeed.

"Four warlords are here at the Crag. The giant Gorodan Ashlord. Zaeurl, the cheerful one-eared elf. The medusa Sheshka. And an unfriendly oni named Tzaryen Rrac. Of these, Zaeurl appears to be in favor, but the other three were mentioned as possible traitors. If one of these warlords *is* allied with the harpies, he may still plan to murder the delegates. And Sheshka has asked for a private audience with our Lord Beren . . .

which would be a convenient time to add a new statue to her collection."

Steel wasn't worried. *Your escorts brought a harpy prisoner with them. I'd assume the Daughters of Sora Kell now know which of their warlords betrayed them. Besides, protecting the delegates is a job for bodyguards. You have another mission.*

"Yes . . . the one that's likely to end up with my skull on a shelf," Thorn said. "And then there's this." She tapped the envelope with her code name on it.

Presumably it's a threat, Steel said. *They expected the delegates to come in the company of spies. They just want to make sure you don't engage in any activities beyond basic espionage.*

"Good thing I'm not planning anything else," Thorn said. "Let's see what it says."

The envelope was sealed with a single blob of dark red wax. Thorn pried it off with a fingernail and pulled out a stiff piece of parchment.

"Well, this is an interesting way to send a warning," she said. "Whatever it is, I can't read it."

Let me see it, Steel said.

Thorn laid the note on the bed and passed the knife over it. The sheet was covered with interwoven patterns of lines that seemed more like artwork than language.

It's Draconic, Steel said. *One of the oldest languages in existence. I don't know why they'd expect you to be able to read it. And it's not a warning—not an obvious one, at least. It says, "Nothing lost remains lost forever, not even a bone in an ossuary."*

"Ossuary?"

A receptacle for bones. Often an urn, though the context suggests something larger. A pit, perhaps.

"Of course, that explains everything. They're trying to confuse us to death." She stood up, pinned back her hair, and picked up Steel, flipping the dagger to set the blade against her wrist. "I think the tales of Sora Teraza's madness may be more accurate than those of her foresight. Shall we put it to the test?"

Are you planning to change your clothing?

Thorn was still wearing the gown she'd selected for the feast—the most exotic piece of clothing in her shiftweave wardrobe. It was a lovely, deep blue with azure and silver trim, complete with jewelry and a short train—a ridiculous thing to wear sneaking around an enemy fortress.

"You may have a century of experience with scrying, but I'm not letting a dagger make decisions about my wardrobe."

But—

"The feast is still going on, Steel. From what we've seen, it should be continuing for hours. I've got a plan, but until it comes together, I'd rather be poor Nyrielle Tam, lost in the dark while trying to find her way back to the party, than Dark Lantern Thorn."

Surprisingly wise, Steel said. *But what about your guardian ogre, who's waiting just down the hall to take you back to the party?*

"As to that," Thorn said, "I thought I'd get help from a little friend."

✶ ✶ ✶ ✶ ✶

Thorn slipped out of her room. Her clothing wasn't quite as useless as it appeared— while her boots were fashionably high and pointed, they retained their sound-dampening enchantments, and her heels made no sound when they struck the stone. An ogre waited just down the hall; her chaperone, ready to escort her wherever she might need to go. As she'd hoped, he had his back to her. There was only one way out from the Brelish quarters, and he was expecting people to come from the other direction. He made no move as she crept soundlessly across the hall.

The room she entered was even smaller than her cell, and Thorn winced as the bitter stench washed over her.

A warped wooden board sat atop a stone shelf, two holes carved in the plank. A stranger might have guessed that the smaller one was for children, but Thorn knew it was made for goblins.

The privy, Steel said. *Well, I suppose it's wise to empty your bowels before engaging in a dangerous task. Is that what they teach at the Citadel these days?*

Thorn said nothing. Now that they were out in the open, she couldn't afford to speak. It would have been easier to turn invisible and slip past the guardian. But she'd called on the power to eliminate her odor and any trace of her passage. This spell would last for hours, as opposed to a few minutes of invisibility. Given the number of creatures in the Crag capable of tracking by scent, this was far more prudent.

Especially considering what she was about to do.

They had traveled six days to reach the Crag, and Thorn had spent a few of her evening hours reading . . . specifically, reading the parchments she'd found in the sack belonging to the goblin Kalakhesh. Thorn's father had fought on the eastern front and served with Darguul units. He'd taught her the goblin language between the seasons, and while she couldn't speak it well, she could read it. It had taken her a few days to crack the cipher used by the goblin spy, but she'd succeeded.

Kalakhesh had spent months at the Crag in the guise of a servant. During that time, he'd found a way to move about the fortress—via the latrines. He'd already known much about the layout of the Crag when he arrived. The original foundations of the subterranean fortress had been carved by hobgoblin architects thousands of years earlier, and Kalakhesh had access to an ancient plan. The parchments were his notes, including his initial expectations and the discoveries he'd made as he explored the mountain.

A moment's concentration sent Steel into the mystical pocket inside Thorn's glove, freeing her hands. A second thought and her gown transformed into black garments and leather armor. She'd want the gown back when she found her way out, but the dress wasn't an ideal choice for climbing.

Sifting through the pockets and pouches of her working harness, she produced two small objects. The first was an ivory clip that she pressed across her nostrils. The stench of the latrine alone was enough to make her retch, and she could only imagine how much worse it would be below.

The second object was a loop of leather cord, another object she'd found in Kalakhesh's sack. She placed it over her finger and felt a faint tingle as it tightened against the leather of her glove. Studying the makeshift ring, she pictured a spider web, imagining sticky strands reaching out and wrapping around her palms, feet, and fingers. Thought became reality, and she could feel the invisible threads against her hands. She ran her palm across the rough surface of the latrine wall and felt the threads catch on the surface.

She'd put this off as long as she could. All the preparations were made. Taking a deep breath, she sat down on the privy and lowered herself through the larger opening.

The space below was just as foul as she'd expected. She set her hands and feet against opposite walls and crept slowly down the shaft. The walls were coated with filth and fungus. Though she found herself clutching outcroppings covered in ooze, the spell she'd performed earlier kept the sewage from clinging to her clothing or hair, and it restored anything she touched to its pristine—or filthy—condition. But the spell couldn't do anything about vermin, and as she descended farther into the tunnels, the insects became larger and more numerous. Centipedes landed in her hair, beetles the size of an elf's eye crawled all around her. She'd seen worse in the sewers of Sharn, but she was sure she'd be seeing this scene again in nightmares to come.

Every major intersection bore a few scratches on the wall,

letters carved by the goblin miners who gouged the sewers out of the rock. These were the keys to navigating through the fortress. Thorn wanted to locate Sheshka's quarters and evaluate the area. The medusa hadn't been at the Crag at the same time as Kalakhesh, and Thorn had no idea where to find the medusa queen. But the notes mentioned the quarters of another warlord, and the events of the feast had given Thorn an idea. She just hoped that she didn't find an ogre sitting on the exit.

Fortunately for Thorn, no one was in the privy when she arrived. The room was almost identical to the one she'd left behind . . . just a little larger, designed to accommodate ogres and trolls. The walls were rough stone, marred by a few faint inscriptions long faded with time. Thorn couldn't make out any of the messages. Scandalous rumors? Insulting comments about a hated officer, or professions of unrequited love? The creatures of Droaam might be hideous and fearsome, but the fact that they left messages on the privy walls made her smile. Perhaps Sora Katra was right; perhaps they weren't so different.

She removed the leather cord from her finger, breaking the climbing enchantment. After a moment's hesitation, she pulled the clip from her nose; the scent of sewage was so strong that she nearly gagged. She quickly restored her fine clothing and drew Steel from her gauntlet. As she held the dagger against her wrist, the puffy sleeves of the gown helped hide him from view; if necessary, she could send him back into the glove with just a thought. She gestured toward the door and the hallway beyond.

No magical auras, Steel said. *And no one watching through magical means. That's all I can promise.*

So, you've wandered away from the party, Thorn thought to herself. You've accidentally bypassed dozens of guards without being seen. And you've found your way into the latrine. Perfectly logical. Everyone needs to use the privy sometime.

She slipped around the doorway and into the hall beyond.

The corridor was taller and wider than the guest quarters a few levels up, so multiple ogres or bugbears could walk side by side. She froze as she heard footsteps pounding against the stone. A moment later a goblin sprinted past her, running as if his life depended on it. This being Droaam, perhaps it did. If he even saw Thorn, he gave no sign of interest.

A good start.

Most of the creatures of Droaam were comfortable in the darkness of the tunnels, but few could see very far in pitch blackness, and even then, they saw the world in shades of gray. Because she had an innocent excuse—the poor, drunken foreigner who'd wandered away from the party—Thorn chose passive stealth. The goblin had proved it—she didn't look like a threat, and they ignored her.

She kept close to the wall and walked at a slow and steady pace, doing nothing to attract attention. Catching sight of a large figure at the edge of her vision, Thorn froze in place. A moment later, a troll strode into full view. Trolls were usually savage, brutal beasts, but this one was drawn right out of Sora Katra's illusions. His rubbery hide was covered with armor; a halfling's skull was set into his steel breastplate; and a crest of spikes ran down the center of his helmet. A troll could tear a man apart with his bare hands, but this warrior carried a heavy battle-axe whose blades were notched and worn.

Thorn shivered at the thought of fighting such a brute, and she felt the familiar throb of the shard at the base of her skull, the faint pain returning once more. She remained as still as a statue and the troll walked past her, the claws on his wide, flat feet scraping against the stone. She waited until the sound faded before she moved again.

As she approached her destination, she saw something she hadn't considered: light. Cold fire torches were set in sconces along the walls of the tunnel. It was a good sign. If she'd read Kalakhesh's notes correctly, Thorn was entering the territory of the warlord Zaeurl. The goblin's records described the location of the barracks used by the hunters, and Thorn intended to steal one of the black and gray uniforms they wore. Her gown might serve as an alibi that night, but posing as one of Zaeurl's children would be considerably more useful once the party was over . . . especially if they were all treated with the same respect that the gnolls had shown in the Duurwood.

Even as the thought of the Duurwood crossed her mind, she heard a sound that had become familiar—the whining speech of a gnoll, emerging from an open doorway just ahead of her. A single tooth lay in a pool of blood by the doorway—a fang likely torn from the mouth of the creature she heard.

She slid closer to the doorway and heard the thud of flesh against flesh, and a body striking a stone wall. Then came laughter, and the clear voice of a young man. "I told you we'd be watching. You should have listened to my brother when you had the chance."

The voice sounded familiar, but she couldn't place it. But the next voice she knew well. It was Ghyrryn, the gnoll who escorted her from Graywall. His speech was slurred with pain.

"I would rather die than receive your blessing."

The man laughed, and Thorn knew where she'd heard his voice. He was the young elf from the Duurwood . . . the child of Zaeurl.

"Fortunate for us both, because your death is what we have in mind. I'm just not sure which to eat first—your arms or your legs."

Thorn wore a mithral bracelet on each wrist, hidden beneath the cuffs of her gown. She clicked them together and they unfolded along her forearms, becoming armored bracers.

What are you doing? Steel whispered.

Saying nothing, she stepped into the room.

CHAPTER EIGHTEEN

✗ ✗ ✗

The Great Crag
Droaam

Eyre 18, 998 YK

Ghyrryn had been badly beaten. One of his eyes was swollen shut, and his fur was matted and stained with blood. He'd lost more than one tooth since Thorn had seen him. He was being held against the wall by an ogre, whose snarl revealed a maw filled with long, yellowed teeth. The ogre pressed his forearm against Ghyrryn's throat, and he held the gnoll a foot above the floor. Ghyrryn was gasping for breath, his snout and nostrils flecked with bloody saliva.

The room was a barracks, with bunks for a dozen soldiers. Fortunately for Thorn, only two other creatures were in the room, and all eyes were focused on the ogre and his prey. A young man stood between Thorn and the gnoll—a man in black and gray. He was the elf from the Duurwood, as she'd suspected; he held a curved steel blade in one hand, and the scimitar's tip was stained with blood. The other occupant of the room walked on four legs—a lean gray wolf, sniffing at the captive gnoll.

Thorn gasped in horror, raising her hand to cover her mouth and bringing her other arm up to her chest, keeping Steel hidden against her bodice. "What . . . what is going on?"

All eyes were upon her. The ogre snarled, and for an instant Thorn thought his teeth were *growing*, but it was surely a trick of the light. The elf spun to face her, lowering his sword and raising a hand to admonish the ogre. "Don't!" he snapped at his companions. "You have your orders!"

"Who *are* you?" Thorn said, filling her voice with shock and terror.

"This is not your concern," the elf said, taking a step toward her. The wolf padded over to stand next to him. Not threatening, not yet, but an intimidating physical presence, yellow eyes boring into her own. "How did you get here?"

As the elf spoke, a second voice echoed in her thoughts. Steel.

Get out of here. Now!

Thorn stood frozen in place, her eyes wide. A chill began at the base of her spine, the same sensation she'd felt in the Duurwood and when facing Zaeurl. It was painful, but it held a promise of energy and anger waiting to be unleashed. She held her ground, watching the elf, studying the way he moved, the way he held his blade.

She knew little about the hunter, but he was a man used to having his way; she'd seen his pride in the forest clearing. She was trusting that he wouldn't kill her right away. He apparently had his orders, and she might actually be a diplomat broken free from her guards. As long as she remained silent, he couldn't classify her as enemy or innocent, and she could see the frustration building in him.

"Speak, woman!" he snapped, taking another step toward her. "What are you—"

That step was all she needed. Steel flashed in the torchlight as Thorn raised her hand and lunged forward. He was quick, and he tried to dodge as soon as he saw the glint of metal. But he'd come too close, given Thorn too much time to anticipate his motions. The dagger went straight into his left eye, and Thorn struck the pommel with the heel of her free hand, driving it deep into his brain. His right eye widened in shock, and for a moment it seemed to change, the white becoming darker, orange—then his muscles spasmed as the news of his death spread across his body.

In a situation like this, the first death was always easy. She had surprise on her side, time to study her foe, the chance to set the pace of things. That was over. She planted a hard kick in the chest of the dying elf, using all her strength to force her blade free from his skull. The gray wolf was leaping for her throat, a streak of fur and muscle. Thorn flung her arm up and the wolf sank its teeth into her forearm, only to grind against the mithral bracer. Thorn pushed against the wolf, pressing her armored limb into its jaw, and it staggered back and released her, spitting and choking.

What happened next made no sense, even to Thorn. She'd forced the wolf away, but she'd taken her eyes off the ogre. The brute dropped Ghyrryn and lunged for her. All she saw was a massive fist reaching for her face as the creature prepared to crush her head with its bare hands. She had no time to dodge, but she didn't have to.

Thorn felt a surge of power, as if her blood were on fire, then she realized that she'd caught the ogre's fist with her own tiny hand. It should have been impossible—the beast had more muscle in its right arm than she had in her entire body. Yet she'd stopped the blow and hadn't even felt it. She closed her hand around the ogre's fingers and felt flesh and bone give way. Then, throwing all of her newfound strength into the motion, she spun around, pulling the ogre and sending it tumbling into the snarling wolf. A startled yip mixed with a curse in the tongue of giants. Thorn lunged, driving her dagger into the ogre's kidney, and she felt the blade sink into the flesh of the fallen beast. Whatever the burst of strength had been, it passed; she landed a solid blow, but it wasn't enough to finish the job.

"Unwise." The ogre drew an enormous cleaver as he rose to his feet. Next to him, the wolf circled around her, seeking to flank her, to force her into a position where she had to give one of them an opening. Thorn saw no communication between the two; the animal was well-trained in the art of war. "You become our meat tonight. I even follow orders. I need no blessings for you."

At least Steel was silent; whatever his opinions, the dagger knew better than to distract her in the middle of a battle. Thorn said nothing. She just waited, dagger in hand, as her two enemies circled her.

The wolf moved first. It had slipped behind her, and now it sought to tear at her tendons and drop her to the ground. But it underestimated her speed and her awareness of her surroundings. The beast's teeth tore at her dress, and she felt its breath against her leg, but she pulled away just in time. Turning in place, Thorn set her hand on the wolf's back and vaulted over the creature. The ogre's cleaver descended at the same moment, and he nearly struck his ally. As she spun through the air, she made a single thrust, catching the wolf at the base of his neck and pulling free as she landed.

It was a perfect stroke. She felt the blade against the spine; it wasn't a killing blow, but it should have removed the beast from the battle.

It didn't.

The wolf's fur hid the wound, but it spun to face her, and in her surprise she barely avoided its snapping teeth. *Did I imagine—*

She had no time to think. She was outnumbered, and both her enemies were upon her. The wolf charged again, and this time she jumped over the strike. She landed directly on the small of the beast's back and called on all her strength. She tried to leap up and over the ogre, to buy more time, to find a better position.

She failed.

Pain flared through her as the ogre's blade smashed into her chest, knocking her out of the air. A moment later, she slammed into the ground, her head bouncing against the stone floor. She was lucky—her foe had struck her with the flat of the blade. If he'd caught her full on, he might have split her in two. Thorn tried to gather her wits, to force herself to her feet. But the wolf was already leaping for her throat—the wolf that should have been dead. Teeth gleamed as they dived for her neck. She caught a flash of silver as warm blood spread across her chest.

It wasn't hers. Ghyrryn was standing above her, and he'd just driven a metal point through the wolf's throat. It collapsed atop Thorn, hot blood pouring from the wound and the stench of its flesh filling her nostrils.

Ghyrryn had saved her life, but there was a price to be paid. He'd left himself open to the ogre. Sparks flew as the cleaver struck Ghyrryn's shoulder. Blood dripped from the gnoll's mouth as he cried out in pain. His battered steel armor held, but the blow had dented the plates, driving them into the muscles of his arm.

The gnoll went on the defensive. His axe had two blades—the longer crescent blade and the smaller, curved spearhead he'd used to kill the wolf. Blocking the ogre's next blow, he retaliated with the smaller blade, slashing his enemy's arm. But the situation was hopeless. Ghyrryn was too seriously wounded. Blood was streaming down his injured arm and he was limping . . . and his enemy seemed to be an unstoppable wall of muscle.

But Ghyrryn was clever. He wasn't trying to fight; he was getting the ogre to move. As he parried and cut, Ghyrryn was circling, forcing his foe to turn . . . and then the creature's back was to Thorn. She was still on the ground, pinned beneath the fallen wolf, and he had forgotten her.

She pushed the wolf aside. Her ribs ached and the room spun as she rose to her knees, but she forced herself to focus. As she climbed to her feet, Ghyrryn fell; the ogre knocked the gnoll's weapon out of his grasp and forced him to the ground. She had no more time: setting aside her doubt, pushing away the pain, Thorn threw Steel.

The ogre raised his blade. The blow would surely shatter Ghyrryn's skull. But he paused at the height of his arc and the blade slipped through his fingers to clatter to the floor. Steel was lodged in the base of his neck, and this time the blow was good. The ogre's fingers flexed convulsively, and his limbs went limp. The floor rumbled when he fell.

"And I wanted . . . a challenge," Thorn said. She sat down on the floor, struggling to catch her breath.

✷ ✷ ✷ ✷ ✷

Gnolls were a tough lot, and Ghyrryn rose to his feet. He picked up his axe and prodded the body; the beast was dead. He looked at Steel, and Thorn raised her hand. *Return*, she thought, and the dagger pulled free from the corpse and flew to her fist. "Smaller than a crossbow," she said. She gingerly rose to her feet, waiting to see what the gnoll would do.

Ghyrryn knelt over the ogre for a moment, his fingers working at its jaw. He grunted in satisfaction and threw a small object toward her. A bloody tooth landed on the floor and skidded into her foot. "Take it," he said. "He waits for you in the world to come."

It was the tradition he'd told her about on the first day of the journey . . . keeping trophies as a way of placating the spirits of the fallen. She reached down and picked up the tooth.

"You fought for me." Blood dripped from his mouth as the gnoll removed his damaged armor.

"You defended me at the Korlaak Pass," Thorn said. "You saved my life."

"True," the gnoll said. "Explain your purpose."

Thorn studied the wounded gnoll carefully. She could

feel Steel's presence buzzing in the back of her mind, and she sheathed the dagger before it could speak.

"I'm searching for a statue," she said. "And I want to know where Queen Sheshka resides."

"Describe the statue."

She'd kept the golden tome hidden in her left gauntlet throughout the journey. Now she drew it forth, flipping through until she found a picture of Harryn Stormblade.

Ghyrryn studied the image. Then he looked at her. For a moment both were silent, the bruised and bloody gnoll studying the Dark Lantern. Then he spoke. "The statue was on display. It was moved, at the request of a warlord. Where, I do not know. We will pass Sheshka's quarters on the way to your own."

Thorn gestured at the bodies around them. "This . . . what will you do?"

"I will speak to my brothers. The Children of Zaeurl do not sleep when the moons are high. This will not be known."

"But why were they going to kill you?"

The gnoll made a gesture with his hand, palm flat and horizontal. "You have saved my life, and I yours. I care nothing for a statue. But I hold the honor of my brothers, and this I cannot speak of. There is a . . ." He paused, searching for a word. "Disease, the darkness that spreads. I do not like what I see. But it is not my place to challenge the rules of war."

Thorn inclined her head. "I thank you for my life, noble Ghyrryn."

"We have shared blood." He glanced at her. "You need new clothing. Take what you will from this place."

Thorn was surprised, but she wasn't going to argue with this good fortune. The gnoll knew what he was doing. He wouldn't reveal secrets, but he seemed willing to trust her. She searched the footlockers until she found a hunter's uniform that would fit her, with a sack to hold it.

"A final gift," he said. "We have shared blood, but you placed yourself in danger when you had taken no vow. We are brothers." He held out his long axe.

"That's all right," she said. "I don't really need it."

"You will," he said. He glanced at the dead wolf, but said no more. Thorn remembered the feel of Steel piercing flesh—a blow that had done no harm.

She took the axe and drew it into her right glove.

CHAPTER NINETEEN

✠ ✠ ✠

The Great Crag
Droaam

Eyre 19, 998 YK

Goblins stared at Thorn as she and Ghyrryn made their way through the hallways of the Crag, but a snarl from the black-furred gnoll was enough to send the servants scurrying. Ghyrryn needed only a few minutes to find a squad of gnoll soldiers. Thorn couldn't understand their whines and chittering howls, but four of the warriors loped away following Ghyrryn's instruction; she imagined that they were going to deal with the mess they'd left behind.

The other two helped Ghyrryn and Thorn reach a dormitory held by the Znir Pact. At least twenty gnolls filled the long room; some were tending armor and weapons, some sparring, others playing a game that involved pitching teeth into an outline chalked on the floor. The arrival of the wounded Ghyrryn created a stir, and the pack crowded around him, hooting and crying in their strange tongue. The elderly healer pushed the others aside and forced Ghyrryn to sit on a bunk.

"You stay," Ghyrryn told Thorn. For the moment, she welcomed the chance to sit down. The pain in the crystal shards had faded to the usual faint ache, but her side was a mass of bruises and her head throbbed where she'd struck the ground.

The healer came to examine her. His fur was patchy and graying, but his green eyes were sharp and alert. Still, Thorn remembered him applying broodworms to open wounds in the Duurwood camp, and she wasn't eager to trust her health to a gnoll medicine man. She held up her hand, keeping the healer at bay.

Ghyrryn snarled at the old gnoll and a debate ensued . . . or so it seemed to Thorn. Perhaps they were discussing the weather, but if so, the gnoll language was quite dramatic. Then Ghyrryn turned to Thorn. "Please." It was the first time she could recall him saying something that wasn't an order. "This is Fharg. Let him help."

Well, I've come this far, she thought. She stretched out on the bunk, her bruised muscles resisting the movement. "Very well. But you tell him—no worms."

Thorn had been treated by halfling healers, which was strange in its own way. Seen in blurred or peripheral vision, a halfling was much like a human child, and it was strange to wake up surrounded by children who appeared to be playing the healer.

Working with Fharg was something else entirely. She'd spent the better part of a week in the company of gnolls, but something was disturbing about having a creature with such bestial features sniffing at her wounds. She trusted Ghyrryn, but a primal part of her was afraid that Fharg would suddenly take a bite out of her.

His treatment was surprisingly effective. Fharg rubbed a numbing oil into her bruised skin, then applied a salve to her wounds. She felt her skin tingling beneath the greasy lotion, a sensation she recognized from the healing potions of House Jorasco; she realized that Fharg used a magic tonic. Then she understood the argument between Ghyrryn and Fharg; the gnolls undoubtedly had a limited supply of such goods, and the healer would be reluctant to use his stores on a human.

Fharg had little interest in conversation. He was quick

and efficient, surprisingly so for his age. He paused when he discovered the two crystals embedded in her flesh. "Hurt?" he said, running a finger across a shard and the scarred flesh around it.

Nothing your salves can help, she thought. The memory of that mission flashed through her mind. Hundreds of dragonshards had orbited the eldritch core of Far Passage, serving both to empower the mystical weapon and to prevent Thorn and her companions from reaching it. The pain she felt still was nothing compared to the agony when those shards had torn into her flesh—crystal shrapnel ripping through leather and cloth. When she finally woke from her coma, the healer had removed most of the shards from her flesh . . . all but these two, which had fused to bone and nerve. At least they were stable; the halfling assured her that she wasn't in any danger.

Mayne hadn't been so lucky. He was the only one who'd remained conscious after the explosion, and Mayne had dragged Thorn to safety. He wasn't hit as hard, but the damage was worse in the end. The shard that lodged in his flesh didn't stay in one place—it burrowed deeper and deeper until it reached his heart. The healers couldn't reach it, and he was dead long before Thorn had risen from her coma. She'd never had the chance to thank him. He would have told her it wasn't necessary. He was just doing his job, and she'd have done the same thing. But Mayne had risked his life to save hers. And she was alive, and he wasn't.

The stone throbbed as the gnoll's hand passed across wounded flesh, and Thorn silently asked Olladra why *she'd* been the one to survive. She'd asked the question a thousand times before, and she received no new answers this time.

"It's fine," she said.

Ghyrryn seemed more concerned about Thorn's health than his own. He'd ordered Fharg to use his healing salves on her, and she felt almost as good as new. He was still battered and bloody when Thorn rose to her feet, but he didn't want her to waste any time.

"You will go now. We return you to your place."

"You need rest," she said.

"Another will lead you." He whistled and whined, and a familiar figure emerged from the pack around her, carrying a rough cloak of brown wool.

"Jharl!" Thorn said. It was the tracker who'd ridden in her wagon—the hunter who'd cooked rabbit for six days straight.

The gnoll whined in return, then spoke in the common tongue. "Ghyrryn has explained. Put this on and follow me."

Thorn looked back at Ghyrryn.

"Go," he said. "We are done."

It seemed that sentimental farewells weren't a gnoll tradition, so she took the cloak from Jharl and followed him into the hallway. It had been made for a gnoll, and on her smaller frame, the hem dragged along the ground. But none of the passing creatures paid any attention to the hooded figure or her gnoll escort.

Jharl spoke first. "You have befriended the wind," he said.

"Hmm?"

"It does not carry your scent."

Well, at least that's still working, she thought. It seemed unlikely that Zaeurl could learn of her involvement in the fight, unless she forced it out of the gnolls. The protective spell had even kept the wolf's blood from staining her clothes. "It's good to have friends," she said.

Jharl was silent for another hundred paces, then he spoke again. "Ghyrryn told me that you were searching for the statue of the warrior."

"A statue of a warrior, yes. I imagine there are others."

"I do not know where it has been moved. But the medusa queen spent much time with that one. It has meaning for her."

"Meaning?"

Jharl cocked his head for a moment; from what Thorn had learned over the last week, this was much like a human shrugging his shoulders. "Perhaps it is her trophy, as we keep the memories of the fallen. She has spent time with it, watching."

"I see. I appreciate you telling me."

"It is no secret."

"What about Ghyrryn? Why did Zaeurl's children attack him? And the ogre—"

Jharl came to an immediate halt. He turned toward her and made the same horizontal hand gesture she'd seen from Ghyrryn. "It is not our place to speak of this. Our Pact was here long before the coming of the Three and the call to the Crag. This is a time of change. We will remain. You do not fight the storm. You wait for it to pass."

"What are you saying?" Thorn said. "The Daughters are placing Droaam in danger?"

"The Daughters *are* Droaam," Jharl said. "Droaam is change. There is opportunity, and there is danger."

"But what do *you* want?"

Jharl indicated a passage to his left. "This tunnel leads to the abode of the medusa Sheshka. She sets guardians at the gate when she rests. We cannot go closer."

Thorn stared at the archer for a few moments, but he said nothing more.

"Fine." Thorn studied the tunnel. "By the way, do you mind if we stop at the nearest latrine? It's embarrassing, but these things happen."

Jharl saw her safely back to the guest wing, then returned to his duties. Thorn glanced through the crack in Beren's door, but the envoy's bed was empty. Quite the party, Thorn thought.

She returned to her chamber and sat on the bunk. Curious, she drew the axe Ghyrryn had given her out of her glove and examined it, testing the balance and considering how to effectively use both blades. The long crescent was forged steel, but the spearhead was a different metal; it was lighter in color and weight, and the edge wasn't quite as sharp. Some sort of silver alloy?

She lay the axe on the bed. Enough stalling. She drew Steel from his sheath and sighed. Let's get this over with.

Explain your actions. The dagger's voice was even colder than usual.

"Why?" Thorn said.

You endangered this mission, and I would like to know your reasons.

"I *endangered* the mission? Without me, there is no mission." She set the dagger down on the bunk next to her. "Perhaps you'd like to accomplish it on your own."

She waited a minute, then picked up the dagger again. She heard his voice the moment she touched the hilt.

I have worked with thirty-two Lan—

She dropped the dagger and the voice faded. "Thirty-two Lanterns. I know. And I'm just one of them. Zane told me that you would advise me, and you've been a great help so far. But I don't answer to you, Steel. Sometimes I'm going to follow my own instincts. And I believe I did the right thing."

She waited a few minutes, then picked him up again. This time, a few seconds passed before he spoke. His voice was softer.

Please explain your decision, Lantern Thorn.

"You've worked with many Lanterns, Steel. But I've worked with people. I spent six days with Ghyrryn. I watched him fight. I saw him dealing with the hunters. I believe that he's a man . . . gnoll . . . of his word."

Reports suggest that the Znir Pact has long been a neutral force within Droaam, Steel acknowledged.

"We need allies. I was confident that Ghyrryn would stand by someone who saved his life, and I still am. He wasn't willing to reveal all the secrets of Droaam, but I don't think that he'll tell any of the warlords about me."

That's all?

"I think it's enough. I've learned where Sheshka's quarters are. I know she has guards that frighten the gnolls. And I know that Harryn's statue was recently moved at the request of one of the warlords . . . and that Sheshka is fascinated by the statue."

You think Sheshka had the statue moved to her quarters?

"It seems like a logical assumption," Thorn said. "Sheshka shows up for this gathering, gets her room set up, asks to borrow her favorite toy to add a little color to the place." She glanced around her barren cell. "Olladra knows this place could use it."

Yes. Another moment passed, then Steel spoke again. *I apologize. I have known you for less than a month, and I was told . . . I was told that you might be unstable as a result of your last mission. I should not have questioned your judgment.*

"You can question it all you want," Thorn said, flipping the blade in the air and catching it in her left hand. "I never said I was stable. But I told you before: I don't take orders from a dagger. If you want to be partners, that's different."

Perhaps you won't die on me, she thought, trying to ignore the pain of that image.

Very well. Steel's mental voice was calm and quiet. *What do you intend to do now?*

"I know you hate it when I do these rash, crazy things, but I was considering sleep." She stretched out on the cot, feeling the hard stone beneath the blanket. "On the other hand, with a bed like this, *considering* it might be as close as I'll get." She remembered the axe. "What can you tell me about this?"

She passed Steel over the axe Ghyrryn had given her.

It is difficult to say with absolute certainty, but it appears to be an axe, Steel said. *Albeit an unorthodox design.*

Thorn rapped Steel's hilt against the bed. "I know that. Tell me about the enchantments."

It's not enchanted.

"I don't understand," Thorn said. "I struck the wolf with you—a solid blow—and it kept coming. Ghyrryn stabbed it with the spearhead and it fell. And he insisted I take the weapon. There has to be something unusual."

Nothing that I can perceive.

"Could you be mistaken? And I've already heard about the thirty-two Lanterns, so spare me."

Of course I could be mistaken, Steel said. *Magical auras can be concealed. If that's the case, however, I can't help you. I suggest you stab something and see what happens.*

"What about the metal? The two blades are made from different alloys."

That could be relevant, Steel said. *There are creatures or spirits who can heal from wounds inflicted by mundane metals, yet can be hurt by unusual alloys. Droaam is the primary source of an ore known as byeshk, which is effective against certain monsters found in the underworld of Khyber. And there are the tales of the lycanthrope and its vulnerability to silver . . .*

Steel's voice trailed off. "What is it?" Thorn asked.

The wolf. Its body. Did anything happen when it died?

"Other than the bleeding? No. It fell on top of me, but it acted like you'd expect a dead wolf to act. Why?"

A pause—Steel was thinking. Thorn hated that the dagger had no expression, no face she could study for clues.

Most shapeshifting creatures revert to their natural forms when they're killed, he said at last. *It's supposed to be true of werewolves.*

"I thought all lycanthropes were exterminated by the Church of the Silver Flame. As I recall, that was the subject of our entertaining party chat."

And given that our dead wolf was just a dead wolf—if strangely difficult to kill—that still seems to be the case. I'm afraid I don't have an answer. I suggest you get some sleep.

"I don't take orders from daggers," Thorn said. Then she smiled. "But I suppose I can take your advice."

CHAPTER TWENTY

✷ ✷ ✷

The Great Crag
Droaam

Eyre 19, 998 YK

Ridiculous," Beren growled. "This entire affair is a waste of time. Two weeks in a thrice-damned wagon just to listen to an idiot giant parroting speeches he clearly doesn't understand about the 'flaws' in the Code of Galifar."

Thorn would have said that the ambassador had woken up on the wrong side of the bed, if the beds were large enough to have two sides. Instead, he'd obviously woken up on a stone slab in Droaam, which amounted to the same thing. He'd enjoyed his breakfast more than Thorn; many of the inhabitants of the Crag were carnivorous by nature, and they'd been offered a selection of dried meats and fish. Both Beren and Toli had wolfed down a surprising quantity of this jerky, while Thorn had to struggle to find something she considered edible.

Perhaps it hadn't agreed with Beren after all. Whatever the reason, he'd been in a foul mood ever since, restless and aggressive. Toli hadn't shaved, and he was unusually sullen; Thorn wondered if there'd been another argument with the Thranes after she'd left the feast. When she made a joking inquiry about the late night, the two simply grunted and shrugged it off.

So far, the day had been a tedious one. As Sora Katra had promised, the envoys were given the opportunity to talk to the warlords about matters at hand. The oni Tzaryen Rrac discussed issues of trade and tariffs on Droaamish goods. Gorodan Ashlord was debating the merits of the Code of Galifar—confirming that citizens of Droaam would be protected in nations that operated under the code, and debating the relative merits of adopting the system in Droaam itself.

To make matters worse, the crystal shard at the base of her spine was troubling her. Thorn's neck burned with anger, but the lower stone was an icy dagger grinding against the bone. Finally she excused herself and left the conference hall, walking until she was out of earshot of any guards.

"Living in these caves, you'd probably never see a sunset," she muttered.

Steel picked up on the code. *We are not being observed.*

"That you know of." Thorn lowered her voice until she was barely whispering.

Correct. When do you plan to take action?

"Even if the statue is in Sheshka's quarters, I can't just haul it out through the latrine. I'll need her there to break the enchantment. So—tonight."

Reasonable, Steel said. *Why are we out here?*

"Because if I had to spend another minute listening to Lord Tharsul trumpeting the virtues of the Code of Kaius, we might have had an assassination on our hands. And where are the Darguuls? I haven't seen Munta all day."

Not a good sign, considering Sora Katra's demonstration last night. Is that your only concern?

"No." Thorn had spent much of the morning retracing the events of the previous night, and something was troubling her. "During the fight last night, when the ogre tried to grab me . . . I felt a surge of strength, of tremendous physical power. Were you responsible for that?"

No. I can do nothing to enhance your prowess in combat, aside from serving as a sharp object.

"And you don't know what happened?"

It's difficult to study magical auras when you're being thrust into the eye socket of an elf. Could you have imagined it?

"Possibly . . . except for the part where I threw the ogre across the room." What truly bothered her was that the sensation had been familiar. Her muscles felt as if they were on fire, as if she were filled with a power her flesh could barely contain.

The feeling she'd had in the dream, when she killed Drego Sarhain.

She had nothing more to say. As she neared the diplomats' hall, a handsome man in black attire stepped out of the chamber.

"Lady Tam," Drego said. "I hoped we could have a moment alone. You left the feast quite early in the evening."

"I shouldn't have taken a chance on the shellfish, I suppose. I spent most of the evening in the privy."

He reached out, placing a hand on her arm. Thorn didn't pull away; she could feel the tension in the air and in his touch.

"Nyrielle," he said, his eyes locked on hers. "We began something in the Duurwood. I'd hoped we could continue it. I know you were defending your countryman the other day, but if we want the war to be over, we need to work together."

"And what did you have in mind?"

"During the Duurwood incident, the elf implied that one of the other warlords had turned on the Daughters—and might threaten the delegates. I had some trouble with indigestion myself last night, but I chose to walk it off."

"If I could turn invisible whenever I wanted, I might have done that as well," Thorn said.

"I wanted to know more about Tzaryen Rrac. I felt some hostility during the feast. Certainly, he wasn't telling us everything. So I followed him after he left the hall."

"Considering that all the envoys seem to be alive, should I assume that you defeated him in heroic battle?"

"Of course," Drego replied, raising his chin in mock arrogance. "Then I resurrected him so no one would guess. No, I saw nothing suspicious at all. No unusual behavior or secret conversations . . . he doesn't even have an army here. I don't think he's the target."

"That leaves the medusa and the giant, if the elf is to be believed."

Drego raised a finger to her chin, gently turning her face up toward him. Bold, Thorn thought. One set of instincts suggested that she drive her heel into his instep and follow with an elbow to the throat. Another part of her had different ideas. He was confident, handsome—and, it seemed, good at what he did.

"What about you?" he said. "Did you learn anything last night?"

"You *really* don't want to know what I saw last night." She gently pushed his hand from her chin. "It's nothing relevant to our shared goals."

"So you do have your own agenda!" he said. "Just like that unfortunate Karrn. Let it go. You saw what Sora Katra threatened to do to him."

"And will you just abandon your mission? What—you think I didn't know about it?"

She didn't, of course. Until now. Drego was good at what he did—very good. But he shouldn't have touched her. Nothing showed on his face, but he couldn't keep the twitch from his hand. And he knew it. He let go of her arm, looking faintly crestfallen.

"Well played," he said. "So if I tell you, then what?"

"Then you're placing your mission at risk based on the fact that you like me. Perhaps you haven't been at this for very long, but that's not usually the way to get ahead in this game."

"Perhaps I don't consider it a game."

Thorn knew that Steel would be shouting at her right now, but she didn't touch him to find out. Drego was an enemy spy. He was practically volunteering to share information. And she was pushing him away.

"Do as you see fit," she said. "But I'm not promising anything in return."

He glanced from side to side, then closed his eyes for a moment—probably using his powers to search for scrying. He took a step toward her; barely any space was left between them. He whispered, "I'm here to kill the Daughters of Sora Kell."

His proximity was distracting, his words calm and committed; it took a moment for them to register.

That was ridiculous. Sora Maenya alone was said to have broken a battalion, and Sora Katra had different powers in every tale. If Drego were that powerful, surely she'd have heard about him . . . then she realized what he was doing.

"I'm supposed to release Khyber, myself," she said. "At least we're not at odds."

He chuckled. Thorn had been right the first time. Drego was good at what he did, and he wouldn't give the game away after a single night in the woods. But she'd still come out ahead. She knew he had a secret . . . and she'd seen him lie. In time, she'd learn to read him. Until then, she could feel the energy between them. He might put his nation first, for now. But the desire was there.

The door of the conference hall opened, and delegates began to emerge. Drego leaned close to whisper. "The giant or the medusa. Which do you want?"

She could feel his words against her neck, and it took several moments for the question to register. I'm just leading him on, she thought.

"Medusa," she said.

"Flamebearer Sarhain?" Minister Luala had spoken. Drego pulled away from Thorn.

"My apologies, minister," he said, his dashing smile in place. "I left the hall to look for a latrine, and then I found myself in the midst of a story." He glanced at Thorn. "I do hope there'll be an opportunity for me to finish telling it."

"As do I. Minister, Flamebearer, if you'll excuse me, I must find Lord Beren. Olladra be with you."

"Let the light of the Flame be your guide," the minister said.

Thorn took hold of Steel's hilt as she made her way through the crowd.

So now he knows what you'll be doing tonight, Steel said.

"But won't be in my way," she muttered.

So you hope. I'm just glad that you're not being seduced by his gallant ways and handsome features.

"Of course not," Thorn said. And in truth, it wasn't the feel of his breath against her skin that stayed in her mind.

It was the vision of a sword flashing toward his face.

Beren ir'Wynarn was speaking with Drul Kantar. The oni wore a robe of dark blue silk bedecked with golden stars. Around his neck, a golden chain bore six crystal spheres of various sizes and shades . . . the six full moons, Thorn realized. She wondered if he had other crystals representing the other moons. Seeing a monstrous creature dressed in such finery was very odd. Kantar had a gentle manner, but he every bit as muscular as the ogre Thorn had fought on the previous night.

Beren scowled. "There you are," he snapped. "I don't expect to be kept waiting by my *aide*." If Drul Kantar noticed the unusual emphasis Beren placed on the final word, he didn't show it.

"My apologies, Lord Beren," Thorn said. "Are we joining the others?" The rest of the envoys were already being ushered away by the ogre guards.

"In time," Drul Kantar said. "At the moment, someone wishes to speak to you."

Thorn moved toward the oni. "Drul Kantar, have you seen Lord Munta of Darguun today?"

Kantar chuckled. "Have no fear, my lady. Lord Munta's head is still on his shoulders. I'm afraid that the chuul served at the feast disagreed with him. I believe his warriors are standing watch over his sickbed."

They made their way down the dark, winding halls of the Crag. Thorn felt like she was walking through the body of some enormous beast; the tunnels were as indistinguishable as blood vessels. And I've already been through the bowels, Thorn thought.

They came to an arched entrance. Drul Kantar raised a hand.

"Give me a moment," he said, stepping through the archway. Before long, they heard his voice. "Was this necessary?"

"Yes." It was a woman's voice, beautiful yet assertive. Familiar, but from her distance, Thorn couldn't identify it.

"I've brought the Brelish ambassador. Can I leave you alone?"

"Are you questioning my loyalty, Drul?"

"Only your restraint."

There was a low hiss. "Don't worry," the voice came at last. "I won't do anything that can't be undone."

It's likely a show, Thorn thought. Drul and this woman want us to hear the conversation. They're trying to intimidate us.

A moment later, Drul emerged. "She's waiting for you," he said. "For your own safety, I suggest you keep your eyes fixed on the floor. An escort will be waiting for you when your business is concluded."

Despite Thorn's suspicions, the giant's concern seemed sincere. She took the lead, keeping her eyes low as she turned the corner.

A statue stood in the way—a large, bulky figure carved from stone. Slowly raising her eyes, Thorn saw that it was one of the armored ogres that served as diplomatic escorts. His left arm was maimed; the jagged scar suggested that the damage was recent.

"Come in." Another sound bloomed behind the woman's voice. Distant rain, or the voices of a dozen hissing serpents. This was accompanied by a more disturbing sound . . . powerful jaws working at flesh.

Thorn recognized the speaker: Sheshka, the Queen of Stone.

CHAPTER TWENTY-ONE

✷ ✷ ✷

The Great Crag
Droaam

Eyre 19, 998 YK

Even though she was shielded behind the petrified body of the ogre, Thorn let her gaze fall to the floor.

"Our thanks for your hospitality, noble Sheshka," she said as she stepped out from behind the statue. She stressed the last word, making sure Beren and Toli heard her. Both hastily lowered their eyes.

As soon as she recognized Sheshka's voice, Thorn had entertained the wild hope that the statue of Harryn Stormblade might be in the chamber. But these weren't Sheshka's living quarters, and the unfortunate ogre was the only effigy in the room. This was simply a smaller conference room, apparently chosen for its distance from the main halls.

The chamber was as barren within as the hall without. A single cold fire torch spilled dim light across the small room, and a few sturdy wooden stools were spread before a round table sculpted from granite. Thorn could hear the medusa's snakes hissing softly, and she easily pinpointed the creature's location on the opposite side of the table. The other sound—the chewing—came from beneath the table.

"Sit," Sheshka said.

Toli's job was to secure the area, and he took charge. He pushed Thorn aside with a little more force than she'd expected, and she stumbled on a piece of debris lying on the floor. As Toli examined the surface of the table and pulled out a stool, Thorn glanced down at the object that had almost caused her to fall. It was oblong, crescent-shaped, and a little longer than the palm of her hand. Curious patterning covered it; bending down, Thorn realized that these were the lines and wrinkles found on skin.

A stone finger. Likely torn from the hand of an ogre.

Thorn was still processing this discovery when Toli leaped backward, swearing and drawing his sword. The ghostly shield expanded from his ring, shimmering into existence around his right fist. Thorn glanced over to see what had caused his reaction—and found herself staring into the eyes of a basilisk.

It was small for its kind, not much larger than a wolfhound, and it was curled under the table, contentedly chewing on a chunk of ogre. Its scaled hide was emerald green, and it was flexing the claws on all six of its legs. Its eyes were milky white, with no pupils. And, according to the legends, its gaze was as deadly as that of the medusa. Thorn snapped her eyes shut, knowing it was too late; she'd met the creature's gaze dead on. But nothing happened. She felt no loss of sensation, no chill of her limbs turning to stone.

"*Sheathe your weapon!*" Sheshka's voice was fierce. Her serpents hissed violently, but Thorn still heard another blade being drawn—a sword in Sheshka's hand. "Lord Beren, if this guard of yours hurts my Szaj, I will have his head!"

"Toli, stand down!" Beren commanded, and fury blazed in his voice. "What is going on?"

"Dorn's teeth, sir!" Toli swore. "There's a thrice-damned *basilisk* down there!"

"Szaj will not harm you!" Sheshka snapped. "If he

frightens you, look away. Raise your eyes and let us speak face to face."

Anger infused her voice, but she'd dealt honestly with them at the feast. "Let me," Thorn said. She looked up and opened her eyes.

As Thorn expected, Sheshka had closed her eyes. The medusa queen projected quite a different image at this meeting. She still wore the silver collar with the smoldering Khyber shard. But in place of her gown of white silk, Sheshka wore a light shirt of fine chain mail, along with vambraces protecting her forearms and long shin guards. She held a curved sword in one hand, and her mane of serpents writhed around her head, hissing her fury.

"Now lay your weapon down," she said.

"Toli—" Beren said.

"No, sir!" Toli snapped. "I'm not letting you put your life in her hands. I want this lizard out of here, and a blindfold on this bit—"

"*Enough!*" Sheshka roared.

Thorn saw the medusa's eyelids opening, and turned away in time. Caught up in his rage, Toli wasn't so lucky. Thorn saw his eyes widen and his muscles go rigid. Black threads spread across his skin, growing and intertwining, spreading from skin to cloth to sword . . . and then he was gone, replaced by a statue of polished black marble. And he was falling. Toli had been taking a step forward when he meet Sheshka's gaze, and the statue was tipping. Thorn leaped and caught him, straining against the weight of the stone. She couldn't stop the fall completely, but she managed to slow his descent and push him against a stool. He struck hard, but nothing broke.

Beren swore, and to Thorn's surprise he reached for his sword. Despite his past, Beren had achieved more as a diplomat than he ever had as a warrior, and she'd never seen him lose control during a negotiation. Last night, he'd faced the medusa queen with no qualms whatsoever. She seized his arm before he could draw his blade. Behind her, she heard Sheshka sheathe her sword.

"My eyes are closed," the medusa said.

"I should tear them out!" Beren cried. For an old man, he was surprisingly strong.

"Be calm, Lord Beren," Sheshka said. She had regained her composure. "Your man should have known better. Would you allow someone to speak to your king in such a way? I will restore him when our business is concluded."

"He was just acting to protect Lord Beren from your basilisk," Thorn said. "How did you expect him to react?" Thorn knew it was unwise to push the issue, but she was as angry as Beren.

To her surprise, the medusa shook her head. "I forget how little your people know of the world and its wonders."

Her voice had actually softened. A few of the snakes hissed in a strange pattern, and suddenly the basilisk retreated from under the table, moving over to settle next to the medusa queen. She leaned down and dropped something on the floor . . . another petrified finger.

"Szaj is young. His gaze is unlikely to transform a creature of your size. Beyond that, the gaze of the basilisk is dangerous only when its eyes are fully exposed. If you met Szaj's gaze, you'd have seen the pale membranes across his eyes." Sheshka ran a hand across the lizard's head; the finger it was chewing on had somehow become flesh and blood. "He is being trained to be around others without harming them."

Beren was staring at the statue of Toli, and the muscles in his jaw were twitching. Thorn spoke before he had the chance.

"You couldn't have expected Toli to know that," she said. "He believed you were trying to kill us. So did I, for that matter. Surely you could have foreseen this."

Six serpents hissed at once, watching her closely. "So

you've never heard of Cazhaak Draal? You didn't think we would speak at this summit?"

Beren was still bristling, but he had regained enough composure to speak. "Make your point."

"You aren't in your Five Nations any more," Sheshka said. She had sheathed her sword, but her voice was deadly. "You have come to *my* home. Your soldier threatened me with a blindfold. A *blindfold*, on *my* soil. Would I come into your castle and strip away your sword, or demand that you wear chains? If I found a hunting hound in your chamber, would I try to kill it, or would I assume it was under your control?"

"We can't kill with a glance," Beren said.

"And that excuses your threat to pluck out my eyes? Should I cut off your hands so you cannot strangle me?" The medusa's eyelids fluttered, but remained closed. "Hand, tooth, steel—we are all deadly, Beren ir'Wynarn. If you had studied the creatures of our land, you would have known that Szaj posed no threat. Or you simply could have trusted that I wouldn't allow a diplomatic envoy to come to harm. Instead, you drew a weapon and demanded that I cripple myself for your benefit. I am queen of my own kingdom. You cannot make demands of me, and you should consider yourself lucky that I am willing to restore him. If one of my kin acted in such a way in the presence of your king, I doubt you'd be so merciful."

A storm brewed in Beren's scowl. "Your kingdom would amount to little more than a city in Breland," he snarled. Once again, Thorn was surprised by his aggressive tone. "Your leaders called us here. You want to join *our* alliance. We aren't bargaining. We're listening to the pleas of beggars."

Sheshka's serpents hissed, lying close to her skull. Thorn was ready to push Beren to the floor the instant the medusa opened her eyes, but Sheshka kept her composure.

"This is futile," she said. "Beggars. Monsters. You cannot trust us unless we are crippled and chained. We reach out to you and you spit on us. I had hoped to discuss the common ground between us, but now I see there is no such thing. I will waste no more time on you. *Guard!*"

"Wait," Thorn said. She heard an ogre moving behind her. "Toli—"

"Take his hands." Sheshka walked around the table. As she moved closer, Thorn could see that the queen was wearing a headband beneath her serpent mane; copper and silver disks glittered in the torchlight as she approached. "If he strikes at me again, I will snap off his arm and feed it to Szaj."

Beren said nothing; he merely glowered at the medusa. Thorn took hold of Toli's wrists. Then Sheshka bent alongside the petrified man. Her lips brushed the surface of his neck for a moment, then she stepped back. Her serpents hissed and the basilisk trotted to stand at her side.

Nothing happened, and Thorn wondered if this was all a game; she felt a fool clutching the arms of a statue. Then the stone grew warm beneath her touch, softened, and color flowed across the dark stone like the sunrise against a deep night. The instant his consciousness returned, Toli threw his strength against Thorn, struggling to break free of her grip. His lips drew back in a snarl, and it was all she could do to contain him.

"Toli!" she cried. His eyes were wild, and he gave no sign that he had heard her. She couldn't risk releasing his sword hand, but she let go of his other hand and slapped him across the cheek. "Toli!"

"Stop." Beren's voice was firm and steady, and it brought Toli back to himself. His breath came in deep, ragged gasps, and his eyes darted wildly about the room. "We are leaving. Sheathe your weapon."

Toli shook with rage when he caught sight of Sheshka, and his head darted to the side. Her eyes were closed, but the bodyguard wasn't taking any chance. He managed to slow his breathing, and Thorn released his sword. He turned to

174 • KEITH BAKER

Beren, who nodded, and Toli slowly sheathed his sword.

"Take us away from here," Beren told the ogre. "Our business is done."

Thorn took one glance back at Sheshka, preparing to turn away at even the hint of an open eye. The medusa watched them, eyes closed, idly stroking the head of her basilisk. She was a cold one, and Thorn couldn't tell if Sheshka was disappointed in this outcome, or if it was what she had anticipated all along.

Well, at least one thing came of this, she thought as they returned to the hall. I know she can restore her victims. Now I just need to find the right one . . .

✯ ✯ ✯ ✯ ✯

Beren's mood grew darker as the day wore on. In the final meeting of the day, Drul Kantar opened the floor to demands, hearing what the envoys of the east expected in exchange for alliance. Many of the delegates had conditions or concerns. Minister Luala wanted assurances of full religious freedoms for the people of Droaam, including a pledge to erect a shrine to the Silver Flame in the Great Crag itself. Lord Tharsul of Karrnath wanted to know which ruler the Daughters believed held the greatest right to the throne of Galifar. Kantar laughed off both of these, telling Luala that religious freedom was why there *wasn't* a Temple of the Flame in Droaam, and that the Daughters weren't asking for an alliance with Galifar; they sought a place among the Thronehold nations.

Beren ir'Wynarn said nothing. Thorn was certain that he'd been sent with a list of demands; Breland was Droaam's closest neighbor, and Beren's story of Sora Maenya was just a taste of the Brelish blood that had been spilled over the years. Yet he maintained a grim silence.

After the session, he opened up slightly. "I apologize for my behavior, Nyri. I . . . I'm not feeling well. I barely slept last night, and I don't think the food here suits me."

"Should we find a healer?" The thought of Fharg examining Beren brought a faint smile to her lips in spite of her concern. Surely the Daughters would be prepared to care for the needs of their guests—all the more so given the dangers of the region.

"I can examine him," Toli said. He might not be an adept of House Jorasco, but Thorn had seen Toli's talents when he bound his own wound in the Duurwood.

"Then I think we'd best retire," Beren said. "I'm trusting you to represent Breland at dinner, Thorn. This is a time for charm, and I don't have that in me."

The evening meal was interminable. The medusa Sheshka was notably absent, and Thorn yearned to set her mission in motion, to match wits with the medusa queen. But Beren's orders were equally important. She might be a Lantern, but she was also an agent of Breland—and at the moment, her country needed her charisma as well as her blade. And so she laughed with the gnomes over the soup, discussed the aerial races of Sharn with the ambassador from the Mror Holds while enjoying a course of braised boar, and heard about the troubles with the Q'barran lizardfolk while considering the dessert.

Sora Katra chose not to make an appearance that evening, and Drul Kantar was the master of ceremonies. He moved from table to table, talking with envoys about the issues raised at the final debate. The oni paused at Thorn's table, where she was talking with the Q'barrans. "Is Lord Beren in need of assistance?" he asked.

"He slept poorly last night," Thorn said. "All he needs is rest."

"Good advice." Drul smiled, revealing his tusks and pointed teeth. He was still wearing his robe of stars and necklace of moons, and the crystal spheres seemed to pull in the light. "I fear the people of the east have no stomach for the ale of Droaam. Perhaps we went too far with last night's festivities."

It was as good an explanation as any, for Beren wasn't alone in his absence; a number of delegates and their guards were missing from the hall. Drul chuckled, and there was something about his tone that bothered Thorn.

"What's funny?"

"Tonight is a special night for the people of Droaam, Lady Tam. The Midnight Dawn."

Right—the convergence of the moons. Hence, the necklace. "And?"

"The celebration on the streets of the Crag this evening will outshine last night's gathering as a full moon does the new moon. I was simply imagining how you easterners might take to the celebration of the Midnight Dawn, if you couldn't even stomach our welcome." He placed a hand on her shoulder and smiled again. "Please, Lady Tam, I meant no disrespect. I hope that we will someday share a meal in the palace at Wroat. Then you can show me how the Brelish enjoy themselves."

"Let us hope so, Drul Kantar. And with that in mind, I think it's time for me to take my leave," Thorn said, rising from the table. She smiled at the Q'barran delegation and curtsied to the oni. "Good night to you all."

Drul Kantar assigned a guardian ogre to escort her back to the Brelish dormitories. Walking alone through the corridors with the massive brute brought back unpleasant memories of the previous night, but this creature was peaceful enough; he was simply slow and ponderous, perhaps frustrated that he should be shepherding a little half-elf when he could be dancing beneath the moons. Thorn had to restrain the urge to run ahead of him, but eventually she was back in her chamber and alone.

"Sunset?" she said, drawing Steel.

You are not being observed through magical means.

A smile spread across Thorn's face. "Then let's prepare for our audience with the queen."

CHAPTER TWENTY-TWO

✳ ✳ ✳

The Great Crag
Droaam

Eyre 19, 998 YK

Thorn spread her tools out on the bed. If everything went as planned, she'd be leaving the Great Crag tonight in the company of Harryn Stormblade. She had to take everything she'd need with her, but she wanted to leave enough behind for her disappearance to seem truly mysterious. As they'd been warned many times, the Great Crag was a dangerous place. Thorn wanted her hosts to believe that she'd wandered off the path and fallen prey to one of the lurking threats. So she was leaving behind a locket with images of someone's family, and a diary chronicling recent events in the life of a young diplomat named Nyrielle Tam.

Thorn considered the equipment laid out before her. She was wearing the black and gray uniform of the hunter that she'd stolen the night before. She studied her hands. Her bracers were fully extended, the interlocking plates of blackened mithral unfolded to cover her forearms. Ghyrryn's axe was hidden within her right glove, and the mystical book was in her left. Thorn still wasn't sure what she'd need it for, but until she found Harryn, she couldn't leave it behind.

She wound a coil of lightweight silk rope around her

waist. She expected to leave through the latrines, and in all the stories she'd heard of Harryn Stormblade, none had involved descending down sewers; she guessed that he'd need all the help she could provide. Next she fastened her dark cloak over her doublet, brushing her hand across the hidden pockets to make sure everything was in place. Thunderstone, poisons, darts, the bottled spiders and other oddities she needed to work her spells . . . the basic necessities of life.

Sitting on the bed, Thorn picked up Kalakhesh's notes and studied them again, making sure she memorized the proper path. She'd made Jharl take her to a latrine when they'd passed Sheshka's quarters, not because she needed to use the privy, but so she could identify it—placing it within the context of the goblin's sewer map.

With a little deduction, she'd found a line that led directly into the medusa's private chambers. This luxury was a relatively recent addition to the network, and according to Kalakhesh's notes, it was too small even for a goblin to crawl through.

Luckily for Thorn, he'd provided another solution. She'd found a few glass vials wrapped in the rags in his sack. Between Steel's analysis and the goblin's notes, Thorn concluded that drinking the liquid would transform her into a ghostly, mistlike form—allowing her to pass through the pipes as if she were pure gas. The effect wouldn't last for long, but it would be enough to reach the medusa's lair. This was powerful magic, and it was a lucky find for Thorn. Kalakhesh had been saving these supplies for a desperate situation. But Thorn couldn't imagine a greater need . . . and she wouldn't have to justify using the potion to some goblin quartermaster.

Thorn picked up Steel. "So, faithful advisor. You told me before that you could offer protection against the gaze of a medusa. What's the secret?"

You'll need your masking bag, Steel said.

"This doesn't sound like the magical solution I was hoping for," Thorn said. She reached into a pocket of her cloak and produced a black silk bag. The hood was used to restrain prisoners; it was placed over the head and then secured with drawstrings, preventing the captive from observing his surroundings.

Steel's next words confirmed her fears. *When you have subdued Sheshka, you can use the masking bag to eliminate the threat of her gaze.*

"Yes . . . but I was hoping for something that would protect me from medusas and basilisks *while* I was subduing her."

Steel's voice was a calm metal whisper. *For the first stage of the mission, you will wear the masking bag yourself.*

"Because . . ."

If you cannot meet the medusa's gaze, her power cannot affect you.

Thorn laughed. She couldn't help it. All the tension that had been building over the last day burst out of her. The sight of the basilisk chewing on a fleshy finger, the tension with Drego, the disturbing encounter with Sora Katra . . . for a moment, she let it all float away.

Eventually, the stream of mirth slowed to a trickle and stopped completely. "So," she said. "What's the plan?"

For the first stage of the mission you will wear the masking bag yourself.

Thorn had taken Steel's calm statement to be part of the joke; it was the voice of the straight man telling the perfect punch line. But it wasn't as funny the second time, especially when Steel still didn't see any humor in it.

"But won't that make me blind?" she said. Perhaps she was missing something.

Of course. That is the purpose of the bag.

"Set aside fighting here—how am I supposed to find Sheshka if I'm blind?"

She felt a faint buzz in the back of her mind . . . Steel's

sigh. *How have you found your way through the tunnels of the Crag when there have been no lights?*

"My ring allows me to see through darkness." Thorn couldn't see the connection.

And how did you locate Drego Sarhain when he was following you in the Duurwood?

"I . . . don't know."

Try.

"I heard him moving," Thorn said. "I *felt* his presence. I felt the motion in the air."

Place the masking bag over your head.

Thorn sighed. Trust the advisor, I suppose. She pulled the black cloth over her face and the world fell into darkness.

Now throw me into the corner of the room, Steel said. *Then get up and find me.*

"How—"

Do it.

Fine. Thorn was happy to throw the dagger away. She heard it clatter against the stone and hoped that the sound wouldn't wake Beren. Part of her was tempted to leave the dagger on the floor, to forget this mad mission and go to sleep. But the shards still burned in her back, and she remembered the voice of her father. *Why do you go to war?* she'd asked him. *What makes it worth the risk?* His words had been the light that had brought her down this path; she wouldn't let him down.

She stood up, spreading her fingers and holding her hands out low at her sides. The layout of the room was strong in her mind; it was barely large enough to hold the bed, with little floor space to speak of. She knew how she'd thrown Steel, the trajectory and the force she'd used. It wasn't hard to calculate where he should be . . . and when she bent down, she found the dagger exactly where she'd guessed.

"Memory won't help me in a room I don't know."

It's not your memory, Steel replied. *Your memory wouldn't have found the invisible sorcerer in the Duurwood. The ring doesn't just sharpen your eyesight. It provides a tighter focus for all of your senses.*

It seemed impossible, but she had been able to sense Drego's presence in the woods. And earlier that day, she'd known exactly where Sheshka was from the sound of her serpents. "Vague impressions aren't a substitute for my eyes."

It can be more. You've only touched a fraction of this ability. You need to let your instincts guide you. Scent, sound, the pressure of air on your skin—let these paint a picture of your surroundings. Stop trying to see, and allow yourself to feel.

"And how do I do that, exactly?" Thorn turned in place. Stop trying to see. She opened her eyes. She'd been holding them closed behind the hood, and that alone was a distraction. With her eyes open, there was still nothing around her but darkness. She turned around. The room's too small, she thought. How can I not know what's inside it?

Thorn spun around, faster and faster, until she felt the touch of vertigo. She stopped moving, trying not to stumble; she didn't want to touch any surface. She'd play Steel's game until she could show that it was madness.

But it wasn't.

As the dizziness faded, she *knew* where the door was. She could feel the faint flow of air around the frame, and the scent of the latrine across the hall painted a clear outline. As she moved forward, she could *feel* the wall ahead of her. It was hard to take hold of any one sense, to seize on the sensations and analyze them. But if she just acted, her instincts told her what was nearby. It wasn't a new sensation; in the Duurwood, she'd scoffed at Drego's flawed invisibility, thinking how his noisy footsteps gave his presence away. Now she realized that Drego wasn't an amateur; she hadn't known the power he possessed.

Anger flared inside her. "Why didn't you tell me this

before?" She'd been given the ring just before she was sent to Far Passage. If she'd known about it then . . .

The ability to see in darkness is a simple thing. There's nothing simple about this. Your mind needed time to adjust to it, for it to become instinct before you tried to force it.

"I would have liked to know about it before my staring contest with the basilisk."

Steel didn't apologize. *Beren and Sheshka will remember your fear. Should Sheshka survive, that will be important. Furthermore, as useful as this gift can be, it has many limitations.*

Thorn could see the truth in this. She could feel the presence of the door and the bed. She'd known the location of the invisible man, and that might help her fight a medusa. But the details were limited. She might be able to feel the presence of a shelf of books, but she'd never be able to tell one book from the next. And Drego had been nearby when she'd noticed him. This might be enough for close work, but it was no substitute for sight. Still, close work was what lay ahead.

"Very well," Thorn said. Sheathing Steel, she removed the hood and tucked it into her belt. She'd need to see the markings on the walls to find her way to the medusa's chambers. She sorted through her belongings one last time, gathering her remaining tools and tucking the goblin's notes in a pocket. Finally, she produced the vial of dark liquid, unsealed the top, and swallowed it.

Everything seemed to fall away from her. For a moment, Thorn was afraid that she'd lost her clothing and gear. But looking at her hand, she could see the leather glove, mithral bracer over her wrist—and she could see through them. When she moved her arm, there was no muscle tension, no sensation of skin against cloth. With her expanded senses she could feel the slightest shift in the air, but little more.

Rather than trying to walk, she imagined her body flowing toward the door, thinking of herself as a simple gust of wind. She focused on the narrow crack beneath the door, and then she was drifting down, the mist that was her body compressing to pass through the narrow opening. The ogre guard was looking away from her room, and Thorn glided across the hall and into the privy chamber.

Her journey through the sewers was far simpler this time. They were designed to channel gases and odors, and she flowed down through the maze. The only challenge was that she couldn't refer to Kalakhesh's notes; they were made of vapor, and her hand passed through them. She had only her memory to guide her through the foul labyrinth, and she couldn't even brush aside the scum covering the wall markings, or the insects crawling across every surface.

Patience and caution prevailed. It was easy to spot the newer stonework splitting off from the old; the walls were smooth, lacking the layers of scum built up over the centuries. The inscription on the wall was clear; the narrow path ahead would take Thorn to her final destination. She rose up through the narrow passage, through the opening of the latrine itself, and into the chambers of the medusa queen.

She emerged slowly, keeping her eyes tightly closed until she was certain there was no one around her. Opening her eyes, she examined the room. The brass mirror on the wall came as a surprise. It was a common myth that a medusa could be petrified by its own reflected gaze . . . then again, it would be difficult for a species to survive if they turned one another to statues. It made far more sense for the medusa to be immune to its deadly power. The only other feature of the chamber was a pit filled with fine, dark sand.

Does she bathe in it? Thorn wondered. But she discovered a greater concern—the faintest ripple in the air above the floor around the latrine, a whine just on the edge of hearing. Sheshka had considered the danger posed by the sewers; a mystical ward lay on the surrounding floor. Odds were good that the field rose from floor to ceiling, and even in her gaseous state, Thorn was likely to set it off.

I can't work like this, she thought. Thorn imagined a great weight spreading over her, lead flowing across her body. It was a trigger, a way to break the enchantment of the potion. As she contemplated the idea, vapor returned to flesh and blood. Her feet were set on either side of the latrine, and she struggled to maintain her balance in the wake of the disorienting sensations. Within a moment, the vertigo passed.

Kneeling carefully on the edge of the privy, Thorn studied the floor, watching for the shiver in the air that indicated the presence of magic. Steel could analyze the ward, but she didn't need the dagger for this; she'd learned to deal with mystical countermeasures long before she'd been told to work with Steel, and she enjoyed solving the puzzle. She reached into a pocket and produced a pinch of silvery powder. She tossed it into the air, mouthing three syllables as it fell. The silver immediately vaporized, and she studied the eddies of the vanishing mist.

An alarm, she thought. The mystic field wouldn't harm the person who touched it; they wouldn't even notice it. But it sent a magical warning to the person it was attuned to—likely Sheshka herself. If she were sleeping, it would certainly rouse her.

Let's do something about that, she thought. Thorn ran her fingers along the hem of her cloak, pulling on a stud and producing a length of mithral wire. Next she found a tiny vial—nightwater, fluid charged with the energies of Mabar, which had a dampening effect on many forms of magic. She considered the whirling mists she'd seen a moment ago; there were tiny gaps in the ward, and she needed to pass the probe through one of those openings. In the corner of the room above her, a tiny gray spider spun a web as Thorn extended her wire through the invisible wall of magic. Many breaths later, it touched the floor. Thorn's eyes were locked on the probe, but there was no spark or shimmer in the air around it; she'd been successful. Breaking the seal of the vial with her teeth, she let the nightwater flow down the wire, pooling on the floor. She saw a ripple . . . and then the air was still.

Thorn released her captive breath, returning the probe to her cloak. Only one more thing to do.

I hope you're right about this, Steel.

She took the masking bag out of its pouch and pulled the hood down over her face. Pulling on the strings, she tightened it around her throat; it wouldn't do to have it pulled free.

She felt as though she knew what was around her . . . but until a moment ago, she'd been able to see it, and it was still clear in her memory. She stepped down from the privy and removed Steel from his sheath.

I know you cannot see details, he whispered in her mind. *If you need information, rub your thumb along my hilt in a circular pattern.*

She tapped the hilt once and crept toward the doorway. The door was slightly ajar, and as Thorn leaned against the wall next to the opening, she found that she could feel what lay beyond. She could sense the width of the hallway, the height of the ceiling, and the presence of a familiar smell . . . Sheshka, a musky odor she now recognized from their earlier meeting.

She slid through the gap without touching the doorway. The short passage held two archways, both open. One led to a larger chamber; Thorn couldn't clearly sense what lay beyond the doorway, but the feeling of space suggested that it was the main room of the suite. The room to her right was smaller, more likely a bedroom. But she shivered as she sensed a shape in the doorway, blocking the passage. This was no wolfhound. It was easily as large as a pony, and it could barely fit through the arch. Another distinctive smell struck her nostrils, and Thorn knew what she was facing even as Steel confirmed it.

Basilisk, he said.

CHAPTER TWENTY-THREE

✹ ✹ ✹

The Great Crag
Droaam

Eyre 19, 998 YK

Thorn was pressed against the wall, and the beast gave no sign of detecting her. She quietly slipped Steel back into his sheath. The dagger wouldn't solve this problem, and she needed both hands for what she had in mind. Her hood protected her from the gaze of the basilisk, but it was a massive beast with armored hide and powerful jaws; it could sever her arm with a snap. And if Sheshka were asleep, the sound would surely wake her.

But noise was an enemy Thorn could defeat.

Thorn's cloak was an arsenal lined with weapons and tools. She had half a dozen blades to choose from, and she settled on a thin stiletto, balanced for throwing. It wouldn't end the fight, but it was a good opening. She slipped her hand into a hidden pocket and her fingers closed around a small globe of glass.

The basilisk raised its head and grunted. Thorn froze, and the strangeness of the experience washed over her. She couldn't actually see the creature. She didn't know if its deadly eyes were exposed. But she could feel its motion, the shifting of displaced air as it moved its blunt, wedge-shaped head. When she tried to think about the scene, it collapsed. It was as Steel had said—her subconscious mind understood her senses. She just had to accept it.

The beast shifted against the floor but didn't rise to its feet. Thorn slowly removed the sphere from her cloak, and as she did so the basilisk lowered its head. She felt a slight pang as she raised the stiletto. She'd killed people before in the service of Breland—more than she cared to remember. This was a dumb brute, just a strange sort of animal. Yet it reminded her of Boros, the hound she'd had as a child. When her father was off to war, Nyrielle and her brother Nandon had spent most of their nights curled up with Boros. The basilisk wasn't an enemy soldier or spy; it was a loyal beast protecting its mistress as she slept, as Boros had watched over her.

But this wouldn't be the first innocent that she'd killed, man or beast—and it wouldn't be the last. Thorn hurled the knife, hoping to hit one of the creature's deadly eyes. Before the blade struck its target, she dashed the glass globe to the floor. The stiletto pierced the thick hide of the beast and it rose to its feet, thrashing its tail and bellowing with rage. It roared, but no sound echoed through the room.

The shattered sphere was a product of the master alchemists of Zilargo. The fluid was atomized, spreading its effect into the air when it was released. In this case, the mystical gas absorbed all sound in the area, lasting a few minutes before dispersing. It would have been useful when dealing with the harpies, but even if she'd had the sphere at hand, Thorn would have been hard-pressed to explain how Nyrielle Tam came to possess such a thing.

The basilisk was loping toward Thorn. She could feel the vibrations as its eight legs padded against the floor, and though she couldn't see its expression, she could imagine saliva dripping from its jaws. As soon as she felt the hot breath of the beast, Thorn leaped into the air. She brushed against the rough scales of the basilisk, and even though she heard no sound, she felt its teeth click together, just missing the hem of her cloak. By then she'd reached the apex of her jump and began to fall.

Thorn held out her hands, and Ghyrryn's long axe shimmered into existence, the silver spear extending from the head. Locking her hands around the haft, she drove the spear through the spine of the basilisk, bringing her full weight and the velocity of the fall to the blow. The beast jerked and spun, but six of its legs weren't moving; the battle was almost done. The convulsions threw Thorn to the side, but she kept her hands locked around the spear haft and pulled it with her. One blow with the crescent axe was all it took to end the struggles of the crippled basilisk. It shuddered for a moment, and then lay still.

Thorn could smell the creature's blood as it spread across the floor. It would have chewed off her limbs if she'd given it the chance, but the image of Boros still lingered in her mind.

The mystical gas absorbed all sound as she crept forward, but this was a handicap. Thorn couldn't hear anything stirring in the room ahead of her. She slid along the edge of the wall until she reached the open arch. Thorn still found it difficult to trust her newfound senses; it seemed like madness, as if she were simply guessing what lay ahead of her. But her instincts told her that a small room lay beyond the archway . . . and that Sheshka was stretched across a warm, round bed. She caught no scent of feathers or silk in the air, just stone, sand, and coals. And Sheshka wasn't alone. The smaller basilisk Thorn had seen at the meeting was curled up at her feet.

A thought sent the axe back into Thorn's glove. She drew Steel, letting her thumb trace a circle on the hilt.

The effect of the silence barely extends into the room, Steel said. *No wards or watching eyes. A significant aura is hidden below her hand . . . a weapon buried in the sand, capable of causing fearsome wounds. The pendant around her neck is a powerful source of magical energy, but I cannot identify its purpose.*

Thorn returned Steel to her sheath, then untied the masking bag and pulled it from her head. The only light in the room came from the dying embers laid around Sheshka's sand pit. After her time in the bag, the light was dizzying. She took a moment to orient herself.

The medusa queen was stretched out on the black sand, naked except for the silver pectoral pendant that hung between her breasts. Most of her body was covered with gleaming coppery scales, but her breasts and belly were paler, slightly iridescent, like the underbelly of a true serpent. The snakes of her mane were spread out around Sheshka's head, coiled on or around small stones scattered across the pit; their tiny black eyes gleamed in the remnants of the firelight. The basilisk, Szaj, lay next to his queen, curled up like a dog, one of its eight legs kicking slightly against the sand.

Thorn pulled up her mask to hide her lower face, and raised the hood of her cloak. Though she intended to blind Sheshka, she saw no sense in taking unnecessary risks. She hadn't studied medusa anatomy, but most humanoid creatures had the same basic vulnerabilities. With Sheshka spread-eagled as she was, a number of nerve clusters were available to choose from. One blow should take her down for at least a minute, she reasoned. Bag her, deal with faithful Szaj, then bind her and locate Harryn.

It was a good plan. Even beyond the magical field, Thorn's footsteps were as silent as moonlight. Szaj didn't stir as she approached with the hood in her hands. Sheshka was resting peacefully.

But her hair wasn't.

Thorn was halfway to the bed when she realized that one of the serpents had shifted position. The viper stared right at her. All of the snakes had their eyes open. She hesitated, and that moment of doubt saved her life. When Sheshka's eyes snapped open, Thorn saw only the faintest glimmer of golden light before she closed her own eyes. She leaped back and Steel was in her hand, ready to throw.

"Who dares?" Sheshka said, her voice low and deadly. She was standing, and Thorn could hear the blade in her hand as it cut through the air, and the hissing of her angry vipers. The basilisk snarled. Thorn's intuition painted a picture in her mind. The medusa queen was standing in the middle of her sand pit, Szaj at her side, a storm of serpents writhing around her face. She held a short, curved sword—the same weapon she'd threatened Toli with.

"Be calm, great queen." Thorn lowered her voice. It wouldn't do to have the medusa recognize her as the Brelish attaché. "I am here to negotiate."

Sheshka hissed, and Thorn didn't know if it was anger or a medusa's laughter. "Lay down your weapon, envoy, and open your eyes. Then I'll hear your plea, if you have voice left to speak."

As angry as she was, Sheshka had not attacked, and the basilisk remained at her side. Curiosity or concern, this was promising.

"I will not surrender without a fight, Queen Sheshka. And believe me, you do not want that battle."

"And why is that, assassin? You think you can best me with your eyes shut? Once I have crippled you, I will cut away your eyelids." Sheshka's serpents hissed in strange patterns, one after the other; it was a strange and distracting sound.

"I'm sure that I can't defeat you, mighty Sheshka. But I assure you of one thing." As she spoke, she threw Steel toward the ceiling, then plucked the spinning dagger from the air. Now Sheshka knew Thorn could fight without her eyes. She was surrendering a tactical advantage, but she didn't want to fight. "Should we cross blades, I *will* kill Szaj."

"What do you want?" Sheshka hissed, her voice colder than any serpent.

"I seek the return of someone stolen from our lands. Free him, and we can end this peacefully."

"And my compensation for this indignity? Do you offer me gold? The goodwill of your nation?"

"Would that work?" Thorn's mind was racing as she spoke. She knew nothing about Sheshka's skill with the sword, but her title of warlord was hardly encouraging in that regard. And although Szaj was a young basilisk, she'd still be outnumbered.

"No." Sheshka was considering the situation; Thorn could hear it in her voice. Thorn knew little about Sheshka's abilities, but the medusa knew nothing about her talents, either. The fact that she'd gotten so close to her had to concern the queen.

"Just as well," Thorn said. "I'm acting on my own, and I neglected to bring my vast personal fortune. You couldn't just consider this a favor?"

"I might consider a trade," Sheshka said. "I free your friend and keep you instead. It would amuse me to keep my would-be assassin close at hand."

"Fine. Free him, and I'll stay with you."

"Him? A lover, perhaps? No." Sheshka was growing more confident. "Speak the name of this love of yours, and then open your eyes. I may grant your request, but you will never see him."

"Why should I believe you?"

"You are in no position to bargain, girl. You are at best a failed thief, at worst a would-be assassin. I am Queen of Cazhaak Draal. I will keep my word, should I give it. Who is it you wish freed?"

The medusa was barely six feet away. It would be hard to strike a nerve cluster without opening her eyes, but Thorn would have to take that chance. She traced the scene in her mind: Lunging forward, striking Sheshka with an elbow, then sweeping her blade down into Szaj's neck. The pain should incapacitate Sheshka for at least a few moments, long enough to take her down and knock her blade away. But she needed the medusa to lower her guard.

I'll have to tell her eventually, Thorn reasoned. "Harryn Stormblade."

Silence settled across the room. Sheshka's vipers became still.

Thorn leaped forward. But as she drew back her arm to strike, she realized something was wrong.

Someone else was in the room.

Her eyes still closed, Thorn had only instinct to guide her. Silk and flesh, a streak of steel—and it wasn't aimed at her. Instead of using her elbow, Thorn slammed into Sheshka with her entire body. A razor wind nicked the back of her hood, passing through the space once occupied by the medusa's skull.

Thorn winced as she felt three pairs of tiny fangs sink into her shoulder. No time to worry about that. Szaj was snarling and leaping at the intruder, who had drawn his long blade to deal with the threat. Thorn staggered backward, pulling free of the vipers and getting a wall against her back. Her shoulder throbbed, but she could tell that Sheshka had turned her attention to the newcomer. The clash of blade against blade echoed off the walls.

It must have been the silencer, she realized. I didn't hear him come in. She could tell—smell?—that the stranger wasn't a medusa, and he'd just tried to spill Sheshka's blood.

"I'm going to pluck out your eyes and feed them to you." The voice was deep, rough, masculine. Filled with hatred and cruel joy. It was enough to make Thorn's eyes snap open. Medusa or not, she had to see the truth of this.

It was Toli.

CHAPTER TWENTY-FOUR

✦ ✦ ✦

The Great Crag
Droaam

Eyre 19, 998 YK

Thorn saw three of them. The first stranger was a Valenar elf dressed in silk and mithral, spinning a double-bladed scimitar. Thorn opened her eyes just in time to see the blades dance across the neck of the rearing basilisk; blood spurted from the lizard's throat, and Szaj fell backward. The elf's face was hidden behind silk and a mask of black gauze, undoubtedly protection against the medusa's gaze. Thorn wondered if it was Saer Vordalyn or one of his companions. Whoever hid behind the mask was a fearsome warrior.

His companion was a muscular hobgoblin, and his steel breastplate bore the fanged maw of the Gantii Vus. He was one of the soldiers who accompanied Munta the Gray. Fresh blood spattered his breastplate and his battle-axe; he'd already seen a fight that night. As the elf struck at Szaj, the hobgoblin charged forward. He roared as he leaped into the air, flinging himself at Sheshka. He'd barely sounded the battle cry when he fell silent, orange flesh becoming gray stone; he'd met the eyes of the medusa queen and paid the price. Sheshka took a step to the side to avoid the statue that crashed to the floor, its limbs shattering on impact.

As the battle unfolded around her, Thorn's eyes were

locked on the third member of the trio: Toli. He advanced into the room with his sword drawn and ghostly shield forming a broad circle. A vicious light gleamed in his eyes, and his lips were drawn back in a cruel sneer.

This was madness. Toli couldn't be working under orders of the Citadel; Sheshka's death would make Thorn's mission impossible. Besides, he wore the uniform of a Brelish guard. He wasn't a trained assassin. He couldn't know if the room was free of scrying eyes. And he didn't have any protection against her power; he'd already been petrified once and should know the threat he faced. If he were killed, the Daughters would surely assume that Breland had tried to assassinate one of their leaders. Sheshka's death was an acceptable loss . . . *as long as Breland couldn't be blamed.* Those were her orders.

Take him alive, Steel whispered. *Magic is at work. Don't let Sheshka kill him.*

And who keeps Sheshka from killing me? Thorn thought. Her shoulder burned from the viper bites, though so far she seemed to be fighting off the effects of any venom. For the moment, Sheshka was occupied with the Valenar swordsman; as long as he could avoid her gaze, Thorn had a chance.

Toli circled around Sheshka, searching for an opening. He'd raised his shield so he couldn't see her face and was keeping his eyes on the floor. Toli's attention was focused on the medusa, and he didn't see Thorn as she slipped behind him and wrapped her arm around his throat. But Toli was no common soldier. He was a Shield of the King's Citadel, and as Thorn had been trained to spy and kill, Toli had been taught to defend. Surprised as he was, Toli still reacted before Thorn could tighten her grip. He dropped his chin to block the hold and slammed the edge of his shield into her stomach. Despite being formed of magical energy, the shield was as hard as iron, and Thorn staggered backward, gasping for air. Toli turned to face her, fury in his eyes.

At least I don't have to worry about him killing Sheshka, Thorn thought.

The Valenar and the medusa whirled in the darkness, blades singing, and Sheshka's serpents hissed and spat as they struck at her foe. Thorn turned all of her attention to Toli. He was relentless, striking with both sword and shield. She was handicapped by her shorter reach and her desire not to kill him.

"A shame," Toli snarled. His thrust missed her throat but grazed the side of her neck. "I wish I had more time to savor this, Nyrielle."

Nyrielle? Thorn was hooded and masked, and she was dressed in the clothes of a Crag hunter. How could he——

The distraction cost her dearly. The world went white as Toli's shield smashed into her face. She tried to leap back, out of range, but the world was spinning and her legs would barely hold her. Pain washed over her, and she felt the sickening sensation of steel grinding against her flesh and bone. His sword had pierced her right lung, and warm blood spread across her skin as he pulled the blade free. She fought against the pain as she dropped to one knee, trying to keep from fainting. She saw Toli's white teeth gleaming in the darkness, his sword raised for another blow.

A rage built inside Thorn as she fought for control. She wasn't going to die. Not like this. Not at the hands of a Brelish soldier. She had barely enough strength to lift her arm, but she grabbed at Toli's chest, hooking her fingers into his chain mail shirt.

Toli screamed. For a moment, Thorn thought she was on fire; a burst of heat engulfed her hand and flowed up her arm. But it was more than heat; it was strength, a surge of energy. It swept over her body and the pain of her injured lung evaporated before it. All the while, Toli howled in agony.

He pulled free of her grasp after several seconds, but it

felt like eternity. He fell to his knees, and his skin was pale and sweaty. He lay still for a moment, staring at Thorn, the steel flashing behind her as medusa and Valenar continued their dance.

Then he changed.

His eyes were the first thing she saw. They weren't human eyes anymore; they turned orange and black, the eyes of an animal. His jaws lengthened, pushing forward from his skull, sharp fangs gleaming in the light. Then he seemed to *burst*, his human skin and clothing falling to the floor to reveal a creature standing in his place.

A wolf.

He recovered his strength during the transformation and leaped at Thorn in a blur of fur and fang. But Thorn's muscles were still singing from the surge of energy. For her, the wolf seemed to move in slow motion; it was a simple matter to roll out of its way and rise to her feet. The beast skidded against the stone floor, snarling and spitting. Whatever this was, it wasn't Toli, and Thorn didn't hesitate; she drove Steel into the creature's neck.

The blow didn't stop the wolf; instead, he twisted his head and snapped at her wrist. He was surprisingly strong and knew how to use his weight to his advantage; in an instant, he'd pulled Steel from her grip. The dagger buried in his neck didn't seem to bother him, and Thorn saw only a tiny trickle of blood.

Wolf. Steel doesn't hurt him. Shapechanger . . .

It all became clear. As the wolf leaped at her, Thorn held her ground and raised her hands. Ghyrryn's axe flashed into her grasp, and Thorn lodged the haft between the jaws of the beast. She used her training, spinning and slamming the beast to the ground. As the wolf gasped for air, she raised the gnoll's weapon and drove the spearhead into the beast's exposed belly, aiming for the heart. The wolf howled, and blood flowed out in a dark fountain. The spear had a cutting edge, and Thorn placed her foot on the wolf and drew the blade toward her, slashing deeper into its chest. The howl faded, and the room went silent.

Caught up in the frenzy of battle, a few moments passed before Thorn realized what that silence meant. As she pulled her weapon free from the bloody wolf, she caught a glimpse of something out of the corner of her eye. A blade made of black marble. The blade that had belonged to the Valenar elf. The only sound in the chamber was the furious hissing of Sheshka's vipers . . . directly behind her. She felt the point of a sword pressing against her back, and the touch caused more pain than mere steel could account for.

"About that deal . . ." Thorn said.

"You hold a myrnaxe," Sheshka said. Her voice was cold but steady. "Where did you get it?"

"It was a gift," Thorn said.

"From whom?" For a woman who'd just been surprised by assassins twice in one night, Sheshka was disturbingly calm. She might have been discussing the price of tribex.

"A friend."

Thorn winced as the point of the blade dug into her back. Though it was just a single motion, it felt as if Sheshka were carving into her flesh and pouring salt into the wound. Steel had warned her about this sword; apparently, it was as dangerous as he'd claimed.

"Enough games. Tell me why you are here. Who sent you? And what do you know of these others?"

"Yes. About that—"

Thorn never got to finish her sentence. The silencing mist was still effective, and she'd heard nothing from the hall. But she saw a flash of motion. A woman in the archway, wearing a dark cloak fastened with a blue pin. Hands outstretched before her, fingers twitching . . . magic. War magic.

Fire filled the room, sweeping everything away in a wave of light and heat.

✼ ✼ ✼ ✼ ✼

The air was scalding, and the smell of scorched flesh was overpowering. Thorn pushed past the nausea and fought to overcome the pain . . . only to realize that there was no pain to overcome. Her flesh, her clothes—the fire hadn't touched her. She'd felt the blazing heat, but she wasn't burned; her hair wasn't even singed.

Illusion?

No. The damage to the room around her was real. Her intuition told her that Sheshka was crumpled on the ground behind her, and the wolf . . .

. . . wasn't a wolf any more.

The body on the floor in front of her was badly burned. A wound gaped in its chest, and Steel protruded from the corpse's neck. But it was unmistakably the body of a human man. Even beneath the facial burns, Thorn could see it was Toli.

She'd make sense of all this in the hours ahead. But she needed to deal with the assassin who'd tried to broil her right away.

Thorn took an instant to send the axe back into her glove, then snatched Steel from the scorched corpse. The sorcerer had ducked behind the doorway, and Thorn approached the arch carefully, ready for her enemy to leap out again.

"What do you see, Steel?" She kept her voice low.

Searching now, Steel replied. *I don't feel anything out there, but the aura of the silencer may be hiding weaker signatures.*

Thorn spun around the corner of the door, thrusting at the level of the woman's kidneys. Nothing. The hall was empty. But Thorn could *smell* her—flesh and wildflower perfume, a lingering hint of sulfur and guano. She'd fled toward the main room. Thorn followed, switching Steel to a throwing grip.

The great chamber held chairs, tables, another pit of sand, and a large hearth. A statue of a harpy with outstretched wings filled one corner, while a more abstract sculpture of crystal and marble lay next to the fireplace. She found no sign of the woman. The main door to the chamber stood open, and Thorn could see the body of an armored medusa lying in a pool of blood in the hall beyond. Thorn sniffed the air, trying to trust to her new-found senses. Was the sorcerer using invisibility to hide from her?

Despite her newfound gifts, Thorn was no bloodhound. But it seemed that her trail led back to the door—that the woman had fled. She started to follow, but Steel's voice stopped her.

Let her go. You must tend to Sheshka. She cannot be allowed to die until you have completed your mission.

Sheshka! Thorn ran back to the silent hall. She closed her eyes before entering the bedchamber, but there was no need. The medusa was sprawled motionless on the floor, and the smell of blood and burnt flesh filled the air.

CHAPTER TWENTY-FIVE

✱ ✱ ✱

The Great Crag
Droaam

Eyre 19, 998 YK

Sheshka?" No response came, and the serpents were silent. Thorn held Steel over the body of the medusa queen. "Steel, is she looking at me?"

No, Steel replied. *I fear this may be a lost cause.*

Thorn opened her eyes to a dire sight. The basilisk Szaj had suffered the worst, and charred bones protruded from his corpse. Sheshka had been partially shielded by the statue of the Valenar elf, but that had simply spared her from instant death. Many of her scales had been burned away, leaving blackened flesh below. Her breathing was slow and faint. She had a deep cut on her left bicep and a piercing wound in her right thigh. The Valenar might have lost his battle, but he'd stained his blades before he fell. Sheshka had defeated her opponent, only to be taken by treachery.

There's nothing to be done, Steel told her. *In all likelihood, the wounds are already infected. Even with the aid of a healer, she would need days to recover.*

"No," Thorn said. "There has to be a way. The gnolls—they had healing salves. Perhaps—"

You know nothing of the relationship between the gnolls and Sheshka. She seemed suspicious that you were carrying a gnoll's weapon. For all you know, they want her dead. And in either case, she is a warlord of Droaam. Once she's in the hands of the guards, you won't get close to her again.

Thorn was still recovering from the chaos of the battle, and many things were only beginning to sink in. "Why am I still alive?"

"What do you mean?"

Thorn ran a hand along her side, pulling at the fabric for a better look. The blood on her doublet was still wet, but the flesh below was smooth and unmarked. "Toli punctured my lung. I should be dead, but I'm not even hurt." She touched her shoulder. "Even the snakebites are gone."

And yet the wound from Sheshka's blade remains, Steel observed. It was true. Despite the pain she'd felt at the touch of the sword, the wound wasn't deep, but the blood was still fresh. *When you were fighting Toli, you touched him and he cried out in pain. What did you do?*

"I . . . don't know. I was angry, in pain. Then I felt a rush of energy flooding through me, and the pain stopped."

It appears that you stripped away his life force and used it to heal yourself.

"But how is that possible?" Thorn said. "Could it happen again?" She looked at her hands. Was she in danger of killing anyone she touched?

We don't have enough information, Steel said. *Perhaps it was a curse placed on Toli, and not on you.*

"And about Toli . . . "

We don't have time to discuss this now, Steel said. *If we can't heal Sheshka, you'd best kill her and leave before someone arrives.*

"Kill her?"

Suddenly, the pieces fell into place. Sheshka saw Toli, a Brelish soldier. If the medusa lived, she could blame the attack on Breland. If Thorn took his body, the blame would fall on Valenar and Darguun. Trouble surely—but they couldn't allow this to be set against Boranel.

Thorn shook her head. "No, there has to be another way"

We have no time to debate. Kill her. You can dispose of Toli's body in the sewer,s and we'll reevaluate the situation.

Thorn considered her hands again. Moments ago, she'd stolen Toli's strength to heal herself. If only she could reverse that, to give Sheshka some of her own life force. But she had no idea what she'd done. As Steel had said, perhaps the power wasn't in her at all.

Then she saw the answer.

What are you doing?

Thorn knelt beside the burned medusa. "Carrying out my mission. Which means saving her life."

How—

Thorn sheathed the dagger. She found a patch of unburned scales on Sheshka's back, pulled off one of her gloves, and set her palm against the medusa's skin. Then she concentrated, trying to remember the instructions of the provender at the Citadel.

"You can move it if you need to," he'd said. "You just have to want it."

She felt as if her flesh was actually crawling. The tingling, creeping sensation moved up her leg, shifted across her stomach, and flowed down her arm. Finally, the energy appeared on her hand. Were it holding still, it would appear as a tattoo, an abstract pattern of colored lines. Instead, the energy danced around on the skin of her palm. It was a healing tattoo—the mirror of the one that had saved her at the foot of the Korlaak gorge. When she'd been given the assignment, the provender had placed two designs on her skin, and she'd seen the symbols crawl from his flesh to hers. Now she needed to force the tattoo onto Sheshka.

The symbol didn't want to leave her; it responded to conscious thought, and Sheshka wasn't welcoming it. But Thorn made a wall with her mind, imagining the space on her hand shrinking. The lines of the tattoo compressed as it tried to fit into the ever-smaller space. Then it burst away, spilling onto the scales of the medusa.

Well, that's the easy part, Thorn thought. She knew little about the force that empowered living symbols, and she'd had trouble activating the tattoo when it was on her own skin. But this time her mind wasn't fogged with pain . . . and the success of her mission rested on healing Sheshka. With her palm pressed upon the symbol, she considered the scorched body of the medusa queen.

You have to want it.

Thorn thought about the imperious woman she'd seen earlier that day, the proud voice she'd bargained with mere minutes ago. She had fire in her, will to live. Thorn had to draw it out. She shoved Sheshka, pushing down on the sigil.

"Do you want to die?" she said. "Are you going to let go so easily?"

She pushed Sheshka again, trying to channel her own growing anger into the symbol.

"I survived this. A puny softskin. You're going to fall to a fire that didn't even touch me? You're going to let these murderers get away with this? Damn you, they killed Szaj!" She pushed down on the tattoo.

Was it growing warmer?

"Get up!" she shouted. "Live, you coward!"

Sheshka's back arched beneath Thorn's hand, and the medusa queen gasped for air. The tattoo dissolved into a shimmering light, spreading across Sheshka's scorched flesh and healing her wounds. As the glow passed over her head, her snakes began to move again, a few hissing weakly.

Thorn stood up and stepped back into the sand pit, closing her eyes as she did so. She'd taken the sword that was lying next to Sheshka, and she set it point first in the sand.

"Welcome back to the living, your highness," she said.

"You'll forgive me if I don't help you stand. The last time I saved your life, your hair bit me."

Sheshka rose up on one arm, her breathing still ragged, and from the sound, Thorn could tell that the medusa was looking at her. Sheshka's voice was rough, still unsteady. "Why . . . did you . . . save me?"

"I told you before. I came to negotiate."

"You wear the colors of Zaeurl's children." She was gaining strength, slowly. "Why?"

Zaeurl's children? The wolves. "These aren't my clothes, Queen Sheshka."

The medusa rose to her feet. "Open your eyes," she said.

"And you'll release Harryn Stormblade?" Thorn said.

"Open your eyes."

As dangerous as it seemed, Thorn had seen Sheshka in a number of different circumstances. They'd bargained. She'd heard the medusa's righteous anger when she fought with Beren. Now her voice was soft, almost gentle. Praying that this wasn't some cruel trick, Thorn opened her eyes.

The medusa queen stood before her, looking at the floor. The healing tattoo had done a remarkable job. Sheshka seemed slightly unsteady on her feet, but her burned scales were completely restored. Five serpents studied Thorn as they bobbed and weaved around Sheshka's head. Thorn could see a faint golden glimmer at the edge of Sheshka's eyes, but her gaze was fixed on the floor.

"What is your name?"

"You can call me Thorn."

"And what do you want with Harryn Stormblade, Thorn?" This time, she wasn't demanding. Her voice was steady and quiet.

"I told you. I wish to return him to the eastern lands, to his home."

"Then I release you from our bargain." Sheshka raised her head, but she closed her eyes as she did so. "You have saved my life, Thorn. If you can keep me alive, I will give you Harryn Stormblade."

"Keep you alive . . . you say that as if you expect it to be a challenge."

"I do." Sheshka knelt by a large stone chest. Reaching inside, she produced the armor she had worn earlier and began dressing herself, drawing the chain mail shirt over her torso and binding the vambraces and shin guards to her forearms and legs. "I caught only a glimpse of the woman who produced the flames. What became of her?"

"She escaped," Thorn said. She'd had a close look at the sorceress, and what she'd seen was fixed in her mind . . . the blue dragonhawk of Aundair pinned to her cloak. She was one of the Aundairian envoys.

"The Crag is large, and they likely think me dead." Sheshka paused, using her teeth to tie the cords on her bracers. "But guards will surely be here soon to make the shocking discovery. If I'm still alive, I suspect that they'll be prepared to finish the job. And my death would be a tragedy for both of us, it seems."

"Why would the guards of the Crag want to kill you?" Thorn said.

Sheshka buckled a sword belt around her waist. She held out her hand without looking behind her, though two of her vipers fixed their eyes on Thorn. "What do you think just happened here?"

"Four people tried to kill you—and would have succeeded if not for me." Thorn tossed the curved sword toward Sheshka. The medusa snatched it out of the air and sheathed it.

"And I'd like to know exactly how you survived," Sheshka said. She placed a diadem around her head, the band hidden beneath her serpents. An array of metal disks dangled from the silver band. "But now is not the time for that discussion. Who were these assassins?"

"A Brelish soldier, a Valenar elf, a Darguul hobgoblin."

"And how would you interpret such a group?" Sheshka said, straightening the diadem.

She'd already thought this through. "The Gantii Vuus fought alongside Brelish troops in the Last War, and the Valenar will fight for anyone. I'd conclude that someone in Breland wanted you dead."

"Yes. Neither the hobgoblin nor the Brelish was protected from my gaze. Both wore the clothes of their nations—hardly an intelligent action for an assassin, as you seem to have concluded."

"So they *expected* to be petrified, then the wizard fills the room with fire, killing you, leaving the corpses intact and the blame on Breland." Thorn's mind raced. So was *Aundair* behind this? The sorceress wore the Aundairian crest, but Breland and Aundair were allies. "But why would Toli agree to this?"

Sheshka wound an arm ring around one bicep. "Because his true loyalties lie elsewhere, of course. You saw what he became."

"A werewolf." Thorn knew almost nothing about these creatures. Legends said they were all but extinct.

"Yes," Sheshka said. She placed a ring on her finger and hissed sharply as she released it, as if it caused her pain. She turned to face Thorn, closing her eyes as she did. "And Zaeurl and her children have always been loyal to the Daughters of Sora Kell."

"So you think the Daughters want to kill you and make it look like Breland is responsible?"

"I believe they already have," Sheshka said. Sheshka paused for a moment near Szaj's corpse, then strode out of the room. Thorn followed her into the main chamber. "The evidence is here, and all they need to do is ensure my death. My people will certainly demand vengeance. Why they would want war with the east I cannot say, but it seems inevitable. I don't know what stakes you hold in such a conflict, but there's nothing we can do alone."

"Ber—" Thorn caught herself before she said the name. Surely Sheshka knew she was one of the envoys, but didn't know which nation she was from. "What about my companions? I can't leave them here."

"There is nothing to be done for them," Sheshka said. "If the Daughters are behind this, we will be lucky to escape with our lives. If your comrades are diplomats, it's more likely that they will be kept as hostages than killed. If you help me escape, I can get word to my people. We cannot stand against the full might of Droaam alone, but I can help you. At the least, I may be able to find Harryn Stormblade, though I fear it won't be easy."

Only then did Thorn realize that she'd been throughout the medusa's chambers and had seen no petrified warriors. "So Harryn isn't here."

"No. Until recently, he stood in the Great Hall. Two days ago he was moved beyond the walls of the Great Crag, at the orders of the warlord Drul Kantar. If you are willing to remain until my soldiers arrive, we might be able to find him. But until then, he could be anywhere in the city. Searching for him would be . . . what is your phrase? Like searching for a tree in a forest."

"Or a bone in an ossuary," Thorn said glumly.

Sheshka's reaction surprised her. The medusa's head snapped toward her, and her snakes coiled back as if preparing to strike. "What did you say?"

Thorn took a step back, closing her eyes. Something dangerous lurked in the medusa's voice. "It would be like finding a bone in an ossuary. It's a container for holding—"

"I know what an ossuary is," Sheshka said. "Why did you say it now?"

"A note was left for me at the welcoming feast. That's what it said."

"Let us go." A rack of weaponry hung in the main room, and Sheshka selected an ornate short bow and quiver. She turned to face Thorn. Her eyes were closed, and she had regained her composure. Bow in hand, armor gleaming, she was every inch the warrior queen. "We may not survive the journey. The gates lie above us, and they will be guarded. I can no longer say who in this place can be trusted, but we will not die alone."

"Could we use the sewers?" Thorn said.

Four of Sheshka's serpents turned to look at her, their posture suggesting surprise. "I suppose . . ." she said. "There must be a path leading out. But I do not know the way, and it would be a gruesome journey."

"Honestly? I've seen worse," Thorn said. "Besides, I know a ritual to help with that, and to keep trackers from following. If you'll allow me, your majesty."

Thorn had held back from casting the shielding spell, because she'd hoped to include Harryn Stormblade in its effects, but it seemed she'd need its defense now. She whispered the syllables of magic, tracing the pattern to include the medusa, and she could sense Sheshka's odor fading from the room. "It's done."

"Then ready yourself for battle," Sheshka said, nocking an arrow to her bowstring. She nudged the door open with her foot, revealing the corpses of two guards. One lay in a pool of blood; his head had nearly been severed from his body, likely by the blades of the Valenar elf. The other had been felled by magic. A focused burst of flame had melted her steel breastplate and charred the muscle beneath, leaving metal bound to seared flesh.

"You'll need the myrnaxe," Sheshka said. If the sight unnerved her, she gave no sign. "This is a night for silver."

CHAPTER TWENTY-SIX

✷ ✷ ✷

The Great Crag
Droaam

Eyre 19, 998 YK

Thorn had already intended to use the sewers as her escape route, and—thanks to Jharl—she knew exactly where to go. She led the way at a hard run. With only a few hundred feet to go, speed seemed more important than stealth. And it was. Thorn was less than ten feet from the privy chamber when she heard the sound of thunder rolling down the hall—iron-shod boots pounding against the stone. She darted into the latrine and pressed herself tight against the wall. Sheshka followed close behind her, taking the other side. Moments later, a troop of armored ogres stormed past them, loping toward Sheshka's quarters.

"Skullcrushers," Sheshka murmured, once the sound had faded. "The elite guards of the Crag."

So she was right, Thorn thought. Either the Aundairian had been caught and then confessed, and the guards had been sent to save Sheshka—or they'd come to finish what she started. Either way, trouble lay ahead. "Olladra, Aureon, smile on your servant Beren," she breathed.

Thorn thought that Sheshka might need the rope and climbing tools she'd brought with her, but the medusa knew what to do. She'd slung her bow and was sliding down through the ogre's latrine.

The last time Thorn had passed through the sewers, she'd been a gaseous cloud. That had many advantages—floating through the air was far easier than clinging to scum-encrusted walls while trying not to slip and tumble into the sewage below. And in her ghostly form, she'd lost her sense of smell. This time, Thorn was solid, and her senses were sharper than ever. In her haste to follow Sheshka, she'd neglected to use her nose clip, and the odor was horrific. She struggled to keep from retching, which was no help as she fought to keep her grip on the wall.

If the stench bothered Sheshka, she gave no sign of it. The medusa was cool and efficient, descending at a steady, methodical rate. Her serpents had settled against her back and shoulders, coiled quietly against her skin.

Thorn had plotted the path the night before, and she knew exactly where to go. But it was one thing to plan this journey in bed, and another to actually crawl through the foul pipes, surrounded by flowing water and scuttling insects. Yet even bad things come to an end, and eventually they dropped into the main sewer line—an underground river of filthy water, flowing deep below the Crag. A path ran along the edge of this subterranean canal, but the pipe Thorn and Sheshka were in opened up immediately above the water, and they had to swim through the ghastly tributary to reach the walkway.

"Thank Aureon for magic," Thorn muttered. Thanks to her masking spell, the waste hadn't clung to her, but she didn't know if she'd ever be able to drive the odor from her mind. She reached into her cloak and found her nose clip. Better late then never.

"And praise to his Shadow," Sheshka said. The common myth of the Sovereign Host was that the god Aureon had been the first among the Sovereigns to master the art of wizardry, but in his quest for knowledge, Aureon had given malevolent life to his own shadow, and that force was responsible for all manner of dark magic, along with the creation of many monsters. Thorn had heard that many of the people of Droaam worshiped the Shadow, but she'd never pictured them being so nonchalant about it.

"This way," Thorn said. She produced the axe again. Sheshka said she'd need it for what lay ahead . . . presumably, that meant more wolves. The myrnaxe was a heavy weapon, designed to be wielded by an eight-foot gnoll. With effort, Thorn could carry it in one hand. She'd gone too long without consulting with Steel, and she wanted her partner's opinion about their situation. She pressed her hand against the dagger's hilt.

You should have brought Toli's body, he said. *There would have been nothing left to link the incident to Breland.*

Damn it. At the same time, if Sheshka was right, the bodies were essentially a formality. "He would have slowed us down," she whispered. "And it would have been exciting meeting those ogres with a corpse over my shoulder."

"What?" Sheshka was close behind Thorn, her bow in her hands. Thorn had been muttering, and it was unlikely that the medusa heard her exact words, but she'd clearly heard enough to be curious.

"Sorry. I talk to myself when I'm nervous," Thorn said.

Why should you be nervous? Steel said. *We're only looking at war between Breland and Droaam.*

"But why?" Thorn frowned.

"Why what?" Sheshka said. "If you're nervous, explain your fears."

"This makes no sense," Thorn said. "You said that To—the assassins were werewolves."

"Not necessarily," Sheshka said. "The Dark Pack is largely made up of the Children of Zaeurl—wolves. But there are wererats in the Crag, and I've seen boars, bears, even fierce lizards. The curse can be bound to any predatory spirit."

"Fine," Thorn said. "Shapeshifters. The assassins were

shapeshifters. But from what I've heard, these creatures were exterminated hundreds of years ago. The assassins were all members of the other diplomatic delegations. How long have they been planning this?"

A torrent of filth rained down into the canal as they passed a set of drains.

"I don't know," Sheshka said. "A few among them have the power to pass their affliction to others. But it takes time for the magic to seize hold—a week or more."

"Why do you call it an affliction?"

"They call it a blessing," Sheshka said. "But I've dealt with members of the Dark Pack, and I remember the past. The power changes the people it takes root in. It's not always bad—I know an ogre near Cazhaak Draal who is wiser and more serene than is typical for his kind. He has little desire for the company of others, and he has never harmed one of my kin.

"But in others—the change it brings is terrifying. The Children of Zaeurl may wear the skin of wolves, but the wolf doesn't hunt other creatures for sport. It takes no pleasure in tormenting its prey. Not so the wolves of the Dark Pack."

She said she remembered the past, Steel said. *Find out what she meant.* Thorn dutifully repeated the question.

"My people live far longer than yours," Sheshka replied. "I remember a time when skinchangers came down from the great woods of the north. My people have never been touched by the shifting, but I saw many others who were— ogres, goblins, even trolls. Those corrupted by this power turned on their own kind. Fortunately, they were few in number and we kept them at bay.

"Decades later, Zaeurl came south with her kin, along with worgs and dire wolves. But unlike those who had come before her, she sought only to be left alone, to roam with her pack and hunt the beasts of the wild, or occasionally the humans on the western frontier. She didn't seek to spread her affliction. And so the warlords left her alone."

She's talking about the Silver Crusade, Steel said. *The same event Minister Luala described at the feast. It sounds like the Droaamish fought their own battle against lycanthropy. Fascinating.*

"I don't know if Zaeurl had dealings with Sora Katra in the intervening years; many of us dealt with the Mistress of the Mires. But when the Three Sisters called the warlords to the Crag, Zaeurl arrived with her full pack and was the first to swear fealty to Droaam. The Dark Pack and the Znir Pact have always been the staunchest allies of the Daughters—hence my suspicion when I saw you holding the myrnaxe."

Many things were bothering Thorn, but in the meantime, a new problem appeared. A metal grid blocked the tunnel—at the border separating the sewers of the Crag from the city surrounding it. No signs of corrosion were visible on the bars.

Adamantine. The goblins and hobgoblins who'd carved their kingdom into the Great Crag used little in the way of magic, but they were master architects and metallurgists. Adamantine was the most durable alloy ever discovered. Thorn wouldn't be able to force her way through these bars. A hinged gate was set into the metal grid—heavy bars held in place by a hefty lock. Thorn had trained on Dhakaani locks, and she'd rather have had to break a warding spell.

"This will take some time," she said, drawing an assortment of wire probes and other tools from her cloak. She started testing the tumblers. "I still don't understand something. You said Zaeurl is loyal to the hags."

"Since the first days of their reign, yes. Sora Maenya's skullcrusher ogres and giants are the iron fist of the Daughters, but the skullcrushers are a blunt tool. The Dark Pack are hunters, subtle and skilled."

"And the Dark Pack and the ogres tried to kill you. To

start a war with Breland." A pick snapped against the adamantine workings of the lock.

"It seems likely," Sheshka said. "My people are one of the most powerful factions in Droaam, and while I respect what the hags have done, I am still weighing whether we wish to walk their path. If they want war with Breland, my death would enrage my people and bring them to the front lines, turning a possible enemy into a valuable ally."

"But if they want a war with Breland, why not start a war with Breland? It's taken them months to set up this summit. Why go to the trouble?"

Sheshka had no immediate answer to that.

"And these assassins. Even if they somehow infiltrated Darguun, Valenar, Breland— how could they know their spies would be chosen for this mission?"

"If there was more time, I'd think they had been turned while at the Crag," Sheshka mused. "Those who suffer the affliction become loyal to their new pack. But I told you— the change takes days at its fastest, more likely weeks. A chance of succumbing whenever there's a full moon in the sky, but only a chance."

"You're sure Zaeurl couldn't be acting on her own?"

"Anything is possible," Sheshka said. "But she's always seemed so fiercely devoted. It's difficult to imagine."

The lock finally turned. Thorn opened the gate and they stepped through.

Another thought lodged in Thorn's mind. "Blessing," she said. "One of the gnolls I dealt with said something about that. 'A blessing more common by the day'—or something similar. It made the wolves angry enough to kill him."

Sheshka's vipers hissed in the shadows, the sound rising over the gurgling of the sewer. Thorn still had much to learn about the ways of the medusa, but she could recognize surprise.

"What is it?"

Hsssss. Finally Sheshka answered. "Nothing I should speak of."

"I would have thought we were past that, since they tried to kill you too."

"I don't know your nation, but you are not of Droaam. We may soon be at war. Would you tell your secrets to your enemy?"

"Do you want war?" Thorn said.

Hsssss.

"I told you before. Zaeurl has lived in the west for over a hundred years, and she never sought to spread her affliction beyond the members of her pack. I spend my days in my own domain, and I know the Daughters do not regard me with perfect trust. I am not told everything that they do. But I have heard rumors that they have called on Zaeurl to share her 'blessing' with members of the skullcrushers. And they are building up a squad of giants and ogres with the added power of the predator."

Memories flashed through Thorn's mind. *Don't,* the elf had told the ogre. And *I don't need my blessing to deal with you. Don't . . .* Did he mean, "Don't change shape?" He'd tried to take Thorn into custody . . . did he not want the ogre to reveal his power in front of a delegate? Sheshka said the gnolls were allies of the Daughters, and Ghyrryn served in a company assigned to the Crag. If the hags didn't share all of their secrets with the Queen of Cazhaak Draal, it was possible the gnoll did know more than Sheshka.

"How many of these blessed ogres do you think we're talking about?" Thorn said. They'd reached a ladder, and Thorn began to climb. The Great Crag was surrounded by the ruins of an old goblin city, which the Daughters were reclaiming. Kalakhesh's notes were sketchy, but if they spoke the truth, this opening would let them exit at the inner edge.

"From what I've heard, it's just an experiment,"

Sheshka said. "I'd be surprised if there were more than a score of them."

A stone lid appeared at the top of the ladder. Thorn pushed hard against it, and it finally shifted. Light spilled down onto them, and for a moment Thorn thought it was day. Then she realized that it was the light of the full moons. Looking through the hatch, she could see two gleaming orbs in the sky above. She reached up and pulled herself onto the surface. She saw four more moons in the sky, far brighter than the Ring of Siberys. And she heard voices, chanting and shouting. And more than that. The roar of beasts. Bears, perhaps? And the howling of wolves, echoing off ruined walls.

Hundreds of wolves. All around them.

"Sheshka?" Thorn reached down to help the medusa up the ladder. "About those numbers? I think you're going to be surprised."

CHAPTER TWENTY-SEVEN

✠ ✠ ✠

The Crag's Shadow
Droaam

Eyre 20, 998 YK

Thorn called forth her myrnaxe and prepared for battle. But the voices of the wolves had been carried by the winds. Thorn and Sheshka stood amidst ruins and rubble. The shattered stone face of a hobgoblin priestess regarded them with her one good eye, her mold-encrusted headdress carved into the stone of a nearby pillar. No one else appeared to be watching.

"You're right," Sheshka said at last, four of her serpents turning to face Thorn. "Far more than twenty. Zaeurl has brought the full force of the Dark Pack to the Great Crag. But not even the pack has so many dire wolves, and I hear the bellowing of steelbone bears. The rumors are true. They've been recruiting."

The tumult continued—the rumbling of ogres chanting in their native tongue, the piercing howls, the cries of other creatures, and the occasional heart-wrenching sound of a harpy's song—but whether celebration or ceremony, the noise was a safe distance away.

"Are we in danger?" Thorn had set her back against a weathered wall, and she held the myrnaxe in a flexible grip, ready to strike with either spear or crescent blade. It occurred to her that she was looking directly at a medusa;

if Sheshka opened her eyes, Thorn would be a statue. Time to work on peripheral vision, she thought.

"I do not know." Sheshka strung her bow and set an arrow against the string. Her eyes remained closed, but her serpents twisted about, searching for signs of movement. "Because the assassins were wolves, we can only assume that Zaeurl is my enemy, and thus any beast may threaten us. If Zaeurl acts in the service of the Three, anyone who lives in the Crag's Shadow could turn against us."

"Lovely," said Thorn. "At least it's not a very *big* city."

"If your magic has done its work, they will be unable to track us . . . and I'd be surprised if word has reached the Pack yet. The skullcrushers are likely still puzzled by my absent corpse."

"So. Now I know our enemies. Do we have allies? You said we needed to get word to your people. I hope at least some of your people are here in the Crag."

"All too few, I am afraid. I was instructed to bring a small guard, so as not to frighten the visitors. An inconvenient request, but I have grown used to the fear of your kind."

Just as we were told to bring only four envoys, Thorn thought. Convenient, if you're planning to seize the delegates. "Give us time."

"How much time?" Sheshka said. She was looking away, and somehow Thorn knew that the medusa had opened her eyes. "I have dealt with your people for centuries, long before the coming of the Daughters. I have faced your crusaders and champions, crossing the Graywall to battle the monsters. Yet never did I send my soldiers against your cities."

"Until the Last War," Thorn said. She knew that medusas had taken part in the battles along the western frontier.

"Yes," Sheshka said, drawing out the word. "I did join my forces to the banner of Droaam. After centuries of silence, I felt it was time to speak. Now . . . I am still uncertain."

A new chorus of howls rose into the moonlit sky, and this time they sounded closer.

"As much as I enjoy discussing politics . . . you said you had few allies here. I'm hoping 'few' isn't 'none'."

"Have no fear, Thorn. My people are masters of stonework; it may be the ogre's strength that shifts the blocks, but it is the medusa's eye that places them. Together we will find the foreman. His companions will be architects and artists, but even the Dark Pack will be careful about falling under their gaze. Follow me. Silence is the wisest course for the journey."

Thorn nodded. She hated to let the medusa take the lead. This was exactly the sort of operation Thorn was trained to handle. But Sheshka knew where they were going. Thorn would have to be satisfied with staying out of sight and keeping the queen alive. To that end, she returned the axe to the space within her glove and drew Steel. If they fought a wolf, she'd pull the silver. But for now, she wanted something she could throw.

"Lead the way," she said.

Thorn was little more than a ghost in the moonlight. Her cloak was enchanted to gather the shadows, and her gray and black clothing blended into the broken stone. Though the surface was rough and uneven, Thorn left no trace of her passage, made no sound as she moved. She was a Dark Lantern of the King's Citadel; stealth was her armor. But Sheshka was a surprise. The medusa queen might be no match for Thorn, but she was no clumsy aristocrat. She was as comfortable in the ruins as she'd been descending the slick tunnels of the sewers. Sheshka might not be a spy, but she was certainly an accomplished huntress.

Sheshka seemed to find every shadow, clinging to cover wherever it could be found. All too soon, they stumbled upon the revelers. Thorn had seen the people of Droaam at play in Graywall when ogre fought minotaur in the pit of the Bloody Tooth. Compared to the Midnight Dawn, the scene at the Bloody Tooth had been as calm as a noble's picnic.

Gargoyles darted through the sky, striking at each other with feathered rods. A trio of changeling skindancers was spinning around, flesh shifting with every step, accompanied by frenzied orc drummers. Goblins leaped through rings of fire. Trolls wrestled, using full force of tooth and claw. These beasts healed at an astonishing rate, and most of their wounds were sealed as soon as they were opened. They possessed terrifying strength; a roar went up as Sheshka slipped past a fighting ring, and Thorn saw the victor brandishing the arm of his opponent over his head.

Farther on, several giants were flinging chunks of rubble at one another. The rock-throwing seemed a sport, and the brutes had a knack for snatching stones out of the air just before they struck. The scent of blood was strong, and Thorn soon saw a giant clutching his shattered arm; apparently the game was just as dangerous as it appeared.

Trolls, ogres, giants, goblins, orcs, harpies, gargoyles . . . and wolves. Wolves were everywhere, in all shapes and sizes. Some were the gray wolves Thorn expected to see preying on the sheep of Eldeen farmers. But there were black wolves. Dire wolves the size of horses, with thick hides and fearsome claws. Wolves seemed to be *speaking* to others around them. Other beasts were in the streets, but a wolf lurked in every shadow, snarling or howling at the moons.

Thorn felt sweat bead on her skin as they slipped through the city. Time and again a wolf raised its head to taste the air as she moved past. Yet time and again, luck, skill, and magic saw her through.

But luck never lasts, skill can be matched, and magic fades away. They were finally moving away from the celebration when they passed under a strange shadow.

This doesn't make sense, Thorn thought. With all the moons in the sky, no darkness was terribly deep; buildings were casting shadows in all directions. But they'd crossed into a patch of darkness that was simply too wide and too deep for the structures around it; this was a pool of gloom.

Sheshka noticed it as well, and paused to study the ground. Then they heard the snarl behind them.

"Good fortune for me," the voice said, the growl of a beast twisted into words. The wolf was the size of a pony. The night was warm, but its breath steamed as it spoke, and its pure white fur was rimed with frost. "I sense you are no member of the Pack, little half-elf. I will freeze your blood before—"

It turned to white marble. Except for its eyes, it was hard to tell the difference.

"You could have let it finish its threat," Thorn said, trying to cover her surprise with a smile. She would need some time to get used to that.

"I suspect it was going to crack your bones and suck out the marrow," Sheshka said, stepping into an alley. "I've heard it before."

✳ ✳ ✳ ✳ ✳

They were almost at the edge of the city, and the sounds of revelry had fallen behind them. A few goblins were clustered around campfires, eating rats and beetles roasted on sticks, but wolf and ogre seemed to have been set apart.

"Your people seem to like their solitude," Thorn murmured.

"There is a reason they chose this place," Sheshka said. "But you are correct. It is not in our nature to share our lives with other creatures. As with the Children of Zaeurl, so it is with us—our power is also our curse. It is difficult to live among creatures so fragile that one angry glare can bring death."

"But you can restore those you turn to stone," Thorn said. A tower surrounded by scaffolding stood up ahead; Thorn guessed it was their destination.

"It's not as simple as it seems." Sheshka's hand brushed against the silver collar that hung around her neck. "I am Sheshka, the Queen of Stone. To you, that may seem an arrogant title, an affectation of a woman who governs a city smaller than your Wroat or Passage. But it is not just a title of nobility. It is a statement of fact. I am the Queen of Stone. I hear the whisper of marble and granite. I have the power to release those who meet my gaze, if I so choose. For others of my kind, this takes skill with the arts of magic. Few possess such talents. Most of the time, the prison of stone is final."

Fascinating, Steel whispered. The dagger had kept silent, not wanting to distract Thorn, but for now the danger seemed to have passed. *Zane will want to know about that.*

"We have arrived," Sheshka said. "Be welcome in our keep."

The tower was a slender structure of white stone. It reminded Thorn of the trunk of a tall tree. A spiral ramp led up around the tower, and the pattern of a serpent's path was engraved into the stone.

"Perhaps I should go first," Thorn said. "Just to make sure there's no danger."

"And will you meet the angry gaze of my countrymen? No, this is my home, Thorn. I shall lead the way."

Sheshka strode up the ramp, holding her bow in one hand as if it were a scepter instead of a weapon. Thorn followed, keeping Steel close against her wrist. She closed her eyes; she wanted to stay as close to Sheshka as possible, and she didn't want to end up like the white wolf. Something troubled her . . . a smell in the air. But she couldn't place it; she still had much to learn about her keen senses.

A door waited at the top of the ramp, and it stood ajar. Sheshka walked beneath the marble arch. Her serpents hissed in a strange pattern, and Thorn wondered if it was some sort of language. With her eyes closed, she couldn't see through the entrance, but she had the sense that a number of small stone objects were scattered about the floor, perhaps the remnants of a sculptor's unfinished project.

"Greetings, my cousins!" Sheshka said. "This is a dire time indeed, and I call on you for aid and sanctuary. We must—"

Something lay on the floor in front of Sheshka. It was a granite statue of a rat . . . a rat the size of a small dog. The beast's snout was at least four inches long, its mouth frozen in a snarl that revealed razor teeth. One leg was raised, claws clutching the air. It was an ugly thing, pure feral rage frozen forever in stone.

But it wasn't the statue that had silenced the medusa queen. It was the shapes in the darkness beyond, the claws and teeth tearing at flesh and bone. All too late, Thorn realized what the strange scent was.

"Rats," she said.

CHAPTER TWENTY-EIGHT

✶ ✶ ✶

The Crag's Shadow
Droaam

Eyre 20, 998 YK

As Sheshka's words died in her throat, the room came to life. Thorn's intuition told her of movement in the darkness, of the creatures crawling on the shelves and tables, the huge rats gnawing on the four corpses spread across the floor. She could hear the scrape of claws against wood and stone, the click of tiny teeth, and the chittering voices of the vermin all around them. The stones scattered on the floor proved that the inhabitants of the tower had put up a fight; they'd taken many of the creatures with them. But in the end, the eyes of the medusas were no match for the numbers they had faced.

"Back!" Sheshka hissed. She held her bow in one hand and her sword in the other. "*Don't let them bite you!*"

It was too late for that. The rats were already upon them. Thorn killed the first one that leaped toward her with a single stroke of Steel, but ten more followed in its wake. The creatures were all over her, clawing and biting. Each scratch was trivial, but the pain was a distraction. As she scattered the little beasts, something heavy landed on her back, claws digging through the mystical field formed by her bracers. It was one of the larger rats, and its teeth were long and sharp. Thorn hissed in pain as the creature sank its fangs into her shoulder, but she didn't stop moving. She thrust Steel over her shoulder, simultaneously slamming her back against the nearest wall. The impact pried the rat loose, and she felt her dagger sink into its flesh. Twisting around, she flung the speared beast to the ground.

The rat should have been crippled, if not instantly dead. Instead, it landed on its feet and scampered back toward her. Cursing, Thorn called the myrnaxe forth from her glove. She had only one hand free, and she couldn't make a true thrust; instead, she let gravity take over. As the rat darted forward, she simply dropped the axe, guiding it as best she could. The spear point slammed through the beast's back. It screeched and lay still.

Wererats, she thought. Lovely . . .

"Sheshka!" she shouted. "We need to *leave!*"

The ordinary rats were all around her; the only mercy was that the sheer numbers of the smaller creatures were keeping the large wererats at bay. Sheathing Steel, Thorn set both hands against the axe and pulled it free from the corpse; the oversized rat was already shifting, transforming into a pale goblin. Next to her, she heard the crash of a stone rat striking the floor, the sound of Sheshka's sword spilling blood. But this wasn't a fight they could win.

"*Now!*" Thorn cried. She swung the axe with all her might, sending rats sprawling across the room. Then she turned and charged out the door, leaping off the ramp and into the air, falling toward the ground below. Thorn spun in midair, twisting to get her feet beneath her; it was a hard landing, but she was standing within a second, searching through the pockets of her cloak.

Sheshka was just behind her, and she leaped from the ramp with the grace of a trained acrobat. A half-dozen rats clung to the medusa's armor and scales, but her serpents were snapping at the vermin even while Sheshka was falling. Thorn saw a viper sink its fangs into a rat and tear the creature loose. The medusa rolled out from the impact, rising next to Thorn.

"Follow me," she said, breaking into a run.

It was one thing to outpace a normal rat, but the shape-shifters had speed to match their size. When Thorn glanced back, she could see the massive rats pouring out of the tower, loping across the ground with the speed of hounds. The fugitives had a head start, but it wouldn't last.

Thorn held a wooden vial in her left hand. She pulled at it with her teeth, prying off the lid to reveal a delicate glass tube inside. With one sharp motion, she dashed it to the ground, never breaking her stride. The instant the glass shattered, the magical effect began spreading out behind her. This one temporarily transformed earth and bare stone into thick, sloppy mud, and Thorn heard a surprised screech as the first rat stumbled into the muck.

It bought them time, nothing more. The rats would soon make their way through the bog. But every second was valuable, and Sheshka seemed to have a destination in mind. They had left the heart of the city behind, but a building stood up ahead, a ruin painted in the multi-colored light of the moons. It was a stockade made from stone—a few defensive walls set together to form a barricade, presumably an outer watch post for the old city. The walls were crumbling and shattered in places, but Thorn could see the silhouettes of guardians standing on the walls, the shapes of halberds and arbalests set against the night. No one was challenging Sheshka's approach; it seemed that she had friends after all.

Thorn could hear the rats screeching behind them, claws tearing at the earth. The mud had slowed them down, but they were closing in once more. The women would reach the barricade before the rats, but then it would come down to battle. Thorn hoped Sheshka's allies were good at their work. They gave no indication of being interested in the situation; the archers weren't firing, and the halberdiers were standing steady.

A great gap yawned in one of the walls, and Sheshka leaped over the broken stone and into the compound. "Follow!" she hissed. Thorn saw that the structure wasn't a fortress at all; rather, the walls were raised around a wide staircase that descended into the earth. Soldiers stood around them—hobgoblins and bugbears in full armor—but none of them moved or spoke as Sheshka darted through the troops and down the stairs.

The passage stretched down for at least thirty feet, and Thorn struggled to keep from tripping on the steep, curving steps. They reached a wide tunnel. Once, a gate had sealed the passage, but it had been knocked from its hinges long ago; all that was left were fragments of rusted metal and splinters of ancient wood. Soldiers stood around, but as before, they showed no interest in the intruders.

Sheshka spun around, gazing up the stairs. Thorn caught a brief glimpse of her glowing golden eyes as she turned, but it wasn't enough to cause harm. Sheshka had sheathed her sword, and her bow was drawn back, one arrow to the string, two more clutched in her fingers. Thorn didn't know what was going on, but she took a position at Sheshka's side, ready to thrust with the tip of the silver spear.

"Wererats?" Thorn said. "*Wererats?*"

"I told you there were rats in the Crag," Sheshka said. "I doubt they'll have the courage to follow, but we should wait a few moments to make sure."

"The courage?" Thorn said. "What is this place?"

"This is the Ossuary," Sheshka replied, her eyes fixed on the stairs above. "And we're here to look for a bone."

The Ossuary was a goblin garrison, carved into the earth by the same masons that had hollowed out the tunnels of the Great Crag. It was built for creatures that could see in the shadows, and there was no source of light in the depths. Once again, Thorn was forced to rely on the vision granted by her ring, which cast the world in shades of gray. So it took her a moment to realize why the hobgoblins and bugbears around her still hadn't reacted to her presence.

They were all made of stone.

"What happened to them?" Thorn said. Presumably, they'd been petrified, but something about the situation felt wrong. The Valenar soldier in Sheshka's quarters, the rats in the white tower—they'd been caught in the midst of battle. By contrast, no signs of fear showed on the faces of the soldiers around Thorn—no sense that they'd seen this threat approaching. One of the hobgoblins had been petrified in the middle of speaking to his comrade; he held his pike at rest, not at the ready.

"They fell in the war that destroyed the goblin empire, thousands of years ago." Sheshka still watched the stairs, waiting for any signs of motion. "They faced one of the lords of madness, the daelkyr Orlassk, who some say was the creator of the cockatrice and the gorgon. It was Orlassk who destroyed Cazhaak Draal so long ago; then he came south to the Crag. He rose from Khyber, from tunnels that lie deep below this very fortress, and as he drew near, his sheer presence turned the guardians to stone. He petrified thousands across the city, and his troops killed ten times as many. And then, somehow, he was defeated and driven back into the depths."

"Petrified thousands across the city? I didn't see many statues . . ."

Sheshka turned away from the stairs, apparently satisfied that the rats had abandoned the chase. She began walking down the wide hallway, ignoring the frozen sentinels. "You would have, had you been here twenty years ago. It is why the Great Crag stood empty for so many millennia. The city and the lower levels of the Crag were filled with the effigies of the fallen. People said it was cursed—that the spirits of the fallen remained trapped in the stone, crying out for vengeance." She paused and brushed a finger across the cheek of a hobgoblin sergeant. "Surprisingly perceptive."

"You're saying it's true?"

"Of course it's true. You want me to restore your virtuous knight, don't you? Where do you suppose his soul has been all of these years? When you die, your soul flees your body and goes to Dolurrh, where it can rest and find peace. But our power traps the soul in stone. A few centuries may leave no mark, but these soldiers have been bound for thousands of years . . . and they fell in battle against one of the daelkyr, the destroyers of reason. There is no rest for their spirits. The only thing worse would be if the statues were broken."

Thorn's foot struck an object and it skidded across the floor . . . the frozen face of a bugbear, fallen from its statue. Sheshka smiled.

"The storytellers spoke truly when they said the spirits were trapped and tormented. Where they erred was their assumption that these unfortunates had any power. According to the tales, their ghosts would reach out from the stone to kill those who moved among them . . . or they would turn the offenders to stone, drawing them into their eternal nightmare."

"But that part's *not* true," Thorn said. The image of the faceless bugbear was lingering in her mind.

"People surely died, disappeared, turned up as statues in the ruins of the Crag. But this is Droaam. Savage trolls and wild cockatrices are a far more likely explanation. Still, the tale kept people from the Crag . . . until the Daughters of Sora Kell chose to make it the capital of their new nation."

"So what happened to all of the statues?"

"See for yourself."

They'd been making their way along curving tunnels, moving deeper and deeper below the surface. As Sheshka spoke, they stepped into a cavernous chamber—a hall that stretched far beyond the scope of Thorn's mystic sight. Pillars were spread throughout the hall like trunks of enormous trees. And there, in the darkness, were the petrified guardians of the Great Crag. Hobgoblins in armor, turned to stone in the midst of battle. Goblin peasants, their faces transfixed in fear. Mighty bugbears. Savage trolls. Beasts of war and burden—dire wolves, tribex, even a small wyvern with its wings broken off. Walking forward, Thorn could see no end to the chamber or to the legions of stone. Some of the statues had been positioned with great care, arranged in military formations. Others had been stacked in heaps that rose up to touch the ceiling. Many were missing limbs, or had been disfigured in other ways by the passage of time or malicious intent.

"Here are the thousands that fell at the hand of Orlassk," Sheshka said. "Along with some petrified in later days. The Daughters have called on the powers of my kin in the past, and in the early days of their rule, more than a few were turned to stone to serve as warning and example, and ultimately condemned to eternity in the Ossuary. And now the Stormblade has joined them."

"What makes you so sure? You said he could be anywhere."

"You came to this place in search of the Stormblade, yes? And you were given a message at the welcoming feast. What did it say?"

Thorn thought back. "Nothing lost remains lost forever, not even a bone in an ossuary."

"There is your answer. You have come in search of something long lost to you. He has been taken from the Crag. And he is here. You should not doubt the words of Sora Teraza."

"That's ridiculous," Thorn said. "If Teraza knew why I was here, why would she *help* me find Harryn?"

"Because she is Teraza," Sheshka replied. "Sora Maenya

is hunger, the strength of the Three Sisters. Sora Katra is cunning, and she is their voice. But Sora Teraza . . . she is fate. She watches the wheels of time. She convinced me to come to the Crag, when Droaam was born. Katra's words serve the Daughters and Droaam, but Teraza serves a higher power, and she always speaks the truth."

"This is the same woman who tried to have you killed, yes?"

A ripple passed across Sheshka's mane of vipers—was this a medusa's shrug? "The Daughters of Sora Kell may be seeking my death, yes. And if Sora Teraza has seen it, it will come to pass. Her words to you will still be true. Harryn Stormblade is here . . . one more bone in the Ossuary."

"I assume the wererats were afraid of the stone ghosts," Thorn said. "Is that going to last?"

"I do not know," Sheshka said. "But I am troubled. From what I know of the rats, they are mostly goblins. Many served on the Graywall in the recent troubles. I know that they serve the Three Sisters. But they have never been bound to the Dark Pack. They struck my cousins in the same way that I was attacked, ensuring I would have no sanctuary. They may lack the courage to follow us, but I fear they are working for another. Whether it is Zaeurl or the Daughters themselves, this place will not be a sanctuary forever."

The task seemed hopeless. Thousands of statues filled the rooms, and the women didn't even know which hall held Harryn. Thorn was about to draw Steel, to see if the dagger had any ideas, when the answer occurred to her. She knew where Harryn was. She'd already seen him.

"You've been down here before, right?" Thorn said.

"Many times," Sheshka replied, studying the frozen faces around them. "But in those days, the Stormblade stood in the Great Hall of the Crag."

"I'm not looking for the Stormblade," Thorn said. "I'm looking for something else. What's the largest statue down here?"

Sheshka's snakes coiled and flexed as she considered this. "There are two giants—one to the north, and one to the south. Then there's a broken wyvern. Three griffins. But the largest would be the hydra. It must have been raised down here—I don't think it could fit through the tunnels."

Thorn nodded. "And is one of the griffins close to this hydra?"

A few of the vipers hissed. "Yes. How did you know?"

"Take me there."

As they walked, Sheshka's tales of spirits trapped in stone stuck in Thorn's mind, and she wasn't sure which disturbed her more—the soldiers who stood ready to strike, or the severed heads and broken faces scattered around the hall. Worse still was the utter lack of vermin. The hall was too clean, too quiet. What could keep even the insects away?

"There it is," Sheshka said.

The hydra was frozen in black marble. It was an awe-inspiring sight, with eight reptilian heads coiled back and ready to strike. Thorn couldn't help but think of Sheshka and the nest of vipers twisting around her head. But the hydra was a huge creature; each of its heads was nearly as large as Sheshka was tall. A griffin had been set across from it, rearing up on stone legs. Thorn had seen this tableau before . . . the picture on the last page of the golden book.

And there, standing in front of the griffin, was the figure of a man in armor, his arms at his sides. Thorn couldn't see his features, but she already knew it was the Knight of Storms.

Sheshka recognized him as well. "There!" she cried. She started to run forward, but Thorn tackled her after only a few steps, taking her down to the ground. A serpent snapped at Thorn's face, but this time she was ready. She batted the snake aside with her open hand.

Sheshka whirled to face her, and Thorn snapped her

eyes shut; she could feel the queen's anger. "What are you doing?" she hissed.

"Possibly saving your life. Again," Thorn replied. She'd seen it just in time. A faint ripple in the air—the telltale sign of a magical ward, and a powerful one at that. "Whoever carried the statue down here didn't leave him unprotected."

Thorn slowly stood up, drawing Steel from his sheath. "What can you tell me?"

"I know nothing of such things," Sheshka replied. "I have never encountered a ward down here before."

Thorn ignored her; it was Steel's analysis that she wanted.

This is no simple alarm, he said. *This is strong offensive magic. Poetic. It's set to petrify anyone who crosses the boundary. Seek a statue, become one yourself.*

Thorn sighed. She hated being right. A pinch of silver dust gave a momentary glimpse of the shape of the ward . . . a mass of wavering glyphs floating in the air like snowflakes, whirling around the Stormblade statue. It was one of the largest she'd seen; whomever had woven this trap had tremendous mystic skill. Sora Katra? Sora Teraza? Did they send Thorn expecting that she'd join the stone army?

Thorn considered her tools—the picks, powders, and oils that she used to disrupt magical energies. She let a few drops of nightwater fly across the boundary. They evaporated instantly.

It was too powerful, too well woven. She considered the pattern again; it was flawless. It had no gaps to exploit. She couldn't break it.

But she had another option.

Tucking her tools into her cloak, Thorn stood up. "Sheshka?"

The medusa seemed to know what she was thinking. "This is not an ending."

Thorn stepped forward, across the line of the ward. For an instant she saw the glyphs shimmering around her. Then she felt the touch of magic, chill tendrils spreading through her bones.

And then she felt nothing at all.

CHAPTER TWENTY-NINE

✠ ✠ ✠

The Ossuary
Droaam

Eyre 20, 998 YK

She found no darkness, because she had no eyes to see. Neither pain nor the lack of pain; she had no nerves or muscles. She couldn't even give form to these ideas, for she had no mind to channel her thoughts. All she could truly feel was a sense of loss, that everything had been stripped away from her . . . even though she could no longer explain what "everything" had been.

She felt no sense of time. Years might have passed, or seconds. She couldn't trap memories in the stone pathways of her mind; she knew only that once it had been different.

Then something changed. A thousand sensations passed over her in an instant, along with the awareness that there *were* such things. Pain. Cold. Fear. And then Thorn was back in her body, struggling to stand on legs that were suddenly able to bend.

A stone knight stood before her, his open hands spread at his sides. He was a large man, tall and muscular. He wore no helmet, and his features were rough, but handsome. His was a face that had seen many battles, hardened by fire and steel. He was dressed in plate mail, and it was the armor of a soldier on the battlefield, not the ornate gear of a jousting knight. The only adornments on the armor were the dents and scars from the hundreds of blows it had turned aside. That the man could fight in such heavy armor was a testament to his strength. The only decoration he wore was the symbol on his tabard, barely visible on the statue. The cloth was torn, but Thorn could see the outline of a shield on his chest, bearing a simple silhouette of a crown. The Shield of the Crown.

Harryn Stormblade.

Memory followed sensation, flowing back into Thorn's mind. With this came the realization that Sheshka stood directly behind her; a serpent was brushing against the back of her head. "Help him! Quickly!"

In studying the trap, Thorn realized that she couldn't disable it. But she could sense the power within the ward, and that it would take time to rebuild its energy after being discharged. Only a living creature could trigger the effect; she couldn't have thrown a rock through the field. Knowing that Sheshka had the ability to restore her flesh had given her the answer. Her sacrifice had drained the ward. They had only seconds to act before the magical field was restored.

Sheshka leaned close to the petrified knight. It was the image Thorn had seen on the last page of the golden book—the knight standing before the griffin, the hydra with its heads coiled above the medusa. Sheshka pressed her lips against Harryn's neck, and stone became metal and flesh.

Thorn waited. The instant she saw the change, she grabbed the man's arm, pulling him out of the petrifying trap. He followed, confused, staggering in his heavy armor.

"Sheshka!" Thorn shouted.

The petrification glyphs have been restored, Steel said.

Thorn spun around, barely remembering to close her eyes. Sheshka tumbled into her, and the two fell to the ground. Although she'd lost her balance, she was still flesh and blood. The medusa's snakes hissed and snapped at the air. Steel scolded her for trusting their fate to Sheshka's hands. Caught between them, eyes squeezed shut, Thorn found herself laughing . . . something she'd had little opportunity to do in Droaam. She continued to chuckle as Sheshka pulled free, struggling to regain her footing and her dignity. To her surprise, the medusa queen extended a hand and helped pull Thorn to her feet.

"Thank you," she told the medusa. "You could have just left me—you promised only to restore Harryn."

"You have spilled the blood of my enemies. You called to me when I stood on Dolurrh's doorway. You were not born in my egg-clutch, and I offer nothing to your nation. But you are my sister, Thorn." Her voice was weary, and the motions of her vipers were sluggish. It seemed that the act of restoration was an effort for her.

Thorn pulled back her hood and drew down the mask covering her lower face. "It's Nyrielle," she said. "Nyrielle of Breland."

If Sheshka was surprised, she gave no sign of it. "I am honored by your trust, Nyrielle Tam. But it is as Thorn that you saved my life. And it is Thorn who must face the road ahead. You have your prize. Now you must decide what to do with him."

It seemed strange that the knight had remained silent throughout her conversation with Sheshka. On the other hand, he didn't know her, and he was undoubtedly confused. She turned to speak to him, but her voice died before it left her tongue.

Harryn Stormblade stood before her. At least, his body did. His face was as blank and expressionless as it had been when it was cast in stone. His eyes were unfocused, staring vaguely ahead.

Thorn took a step toward him, gently waving a hand before his face. No reaction. "Harryn?" she said. "Lord Stormblade, can you hear me?"

Nothing. He stood up straight, and he'd followed when Thorn had pulled his arm. But there was nothing to suggest that a single conscious thought floated in his head.

"You said a few centuries wouldn't hurt him," Thorn said as she drew Steel, holding him out toward the placid warrior.

"I said that mere centuries of imprisonment would leave no mark on the soul," Sheshka said, and there was true sorrow in her lovely voice. "It has not. You see him as I saw him last, so many years ago."

"What are you talking about?"

"The Stormblade and I . . . we knew each other for a time. Centuries ago. I was young, and I sought adventure and excitement as all youths do. There was darkness in the land, and while it could not threaten Cazhaak Draal, I had followed it south. I met Harryn. In another time, we might have been enemies, but he had a different quest." Sheshka's eyes were closed and her serpents were very still; they were draped down around her shoulders, so still that they could have been mistaken for hair. "I let fear gain the upper hand and I parted our ways before he faced his final foe. The next time I saw him, he was in this condition."

"And it didn't occur to you to mention this earlier?"

A few of Sheshka's vipers rose up around her shoulders. "You asked me for the Stormblade, and I have given him to you. I have lifted my gaze from him. What afflicts him is none of my doing. I have fulfilled my promise."

Steel had taken a long time to study the serene knight, and he whispered in Thorn's thoughts. *This may have been the work of magic, but there is no ongoing mystical resonance. This isn't a curse that can be broken. A spell isn't clouding his thoughts—his mind has been taken away.*

Taken away. Thorn thought about the stories her father had told her, the tales of the Shield of the Crown. The Stormblade. "What happened to his sword?"

"You see him as I found him," Sheshka said. "Unarmed and helpless. I could not take him to Cazhaak Draal. There would have been no place for him there. But he was a brave warrior, and I did not wish him to be taken by the beasts of the land. So I changed him and I left him, another guardian among the stone ghosts of the Great Crag."

"It's the thrice-damned *sword,*" Thorn said. Three keys, and I found only one.

"What makes you so certain?"

"I read it in a book," Thorn said. " 'Without his sword, he was bereft of his past, and so he met the Queen of Stone.' It said that I'd need to find 'his sword and his past.' If you don't know where his sword is, it seems like a lost cause."

Sheshka's serpents had risen around her head—not hissing, simply watching, tongues flicking out to taste the air. "Tell me of this book. I do not see how anyone could know of such a thing."

"No need to tell when I can show." The tome was still stored in her left glove; a thought brought it into her hand.

Sheshka's reaction was as dramatic as it was unexpected. She took a step backward, and as she did so, all of her vipers spread out to their full length, baring their fangs and hissing. Venom dripped to the floor. Her eyelids flickered, and Thorn sensed that it took effort for her to keep them closed. "Where did you get that?"

"An acquaintance," Thorn said. "No longer with us, I'm afraid. He didn't give me any details."

"His death is no surprise to me. You have carried this thing through Droaam and lived to speak of it! While standing before Sora Katra herself!" Her snakes were writhing wildly as if in pain.

"What *is* it?"

"I know the people of the east tell tales of Sora Katra

and Sora Maenya. I'm sure you've heard how Maenya binds the souls of her victims to their skulls, and sleeps on a bed of the damned. But it seems you know little of Sora Teraza."

"As I recall, she's the one who's not so bad—the one who gave me the helpful note."

"She follows a different path from her sisters. That makes her no less dangerous. She is the oldest of the three, and her ways are mysterious even to them. It's said that she has a library in the Crag, filled with the lives of heroes and prophets."

Thorn frowned, more puzzled than angry. "There's a room in the library of Wroat filled with the lives of prophets. What's so strange about that?"

"Not accounts of their lives . . . the lives themselves. Until now, I have heard this only as rumor, and I could be mistaken. But the face on the book is just as I have heard. Teraza must have claimed him, taken his story from him—and left this shell behind."

Thorn looked at the leather-bound book, the stern face staring up at her from the cover. Strength lay in that face, a sense of purpose that was missing in the vacant expression of the man standing behind her.

"Stealing from Sora Teraza . . ." Sheshka's snakes were twisting about nervously.

"You said it yourself. I had the thing in my hand when Sora Katra was only half a room away, and nothing happened. But I don't need a story. I need his past. I need his sword." She considered the gilded tome again. The proud face. The silver sword gleaming on the spine. "You say she took his *story* away."

"Yes."

"But he's missing his sword. And he's Harryn *Stormblade*. His sword *is* his story. And his story is his past."

Thorn turned to face the knight. He still stared at her, his expression vacant as ever.

"Take it," she said. She thrust the book at him, holding it so he could see the spine. "Take it back."

Harryn's eyes focused on the gilded sword. His hand twitched, and then he slowly raised his arm and reached for the book. The moment his fingers touched the leather, it slipped free of Thorn's grip. It should have fallen to the ground—Harryn didn't have a firm grip on it. Instead, it hung in midair. Mist flowed out from the pages, a gray mist lit from within by a pale blue light.

A blinding flash lit the room, and a crash of thunder sent Thorn staggering back. When her vision returned, the hall was illuminated by the shimmering blue light. But the light emanated from the furrow running down the blade of a gleaming silver greatsword. Harryn's sword was as beautiful as his armor was plain. The blade was perfect, polished to a mirror finish, not a nick on its edge. The knight held the weapon in both hands, and his face had changed. He wore the stern expression Thorn had seen pressed into the black leather. His eyes were hard, and when they fixed on Sheshka, they flashed with anger.

"You!" he cried. Blue-white energy crackled along the blade as he drew it back. He dropped his gaze to the ground, and Thorn knew what would come next.

He lunged forward, but Thorn was ready for him. The knight had turned his back on her, and as he started his charge, she slipped behind him and tripped him, sending him tumbling to the ground.

"Sheshka, go!" she shouted. "Let me deal with this!"

The medusa was already darting away, disappearing into the silent ranks of the stone army. Harryn tried to rise and follow her, but a swift kick put him back on the ground.

This is one of the greatest warriors of old Galifar? she thought. *Well, he's been asleep for a few hundred years . . .*

Her overconfidence was nearly her undoing. The knight had been distracted by Sheshka, but his attention shifted to Thorn. As he rose, he was ready for her kick. He caught her foot with one hand and pulled Thorn toward him; it was all she could do to keep from falling.

"What are you?" he growled. In the light of his sword, she could see his eyes, a deep and vivid blue. "Are you one of Drukan's creatures?"

Thorn broke free from his grip and backed away. She kept her hands out before her to show that she wasn't holding a weapon. "I don't know what you're talking about. You've been cursed. I just released you from its effects."

"More lies," he said. She could sense his pain and confusion. He was trying to focus on her, but his eyes were glancing about the room.

"Do you know where you are?" Thorn said. She continued to back away, and he followed her. Thorn wanted to move him away from Sheshka and the petrifying ward. "Do you know how you came here?"

A flicker of doubt crossed his face, but his blade was steady, and he leveled it at her chest. If he charged at Thorn, no one could protect her. "Who are you?" he said.

"I am Thorn of Breland, Dark Lantern of the King's Citadel."

"The King's Citadel." His eyes narrowed. In Harryn's time, the Citadel had served the king of Galifar, not the ruler of Breland, but he knew the name. "And how can I know you haven't been corrupted by Drukan?"

"Because I don't even know who that is," Thorn said. She tried to project all the sympathy and sincerity she could muster. "If you are Harryn Stormblade—you've been petrified for over two hundred years."

Harryn's eyes were fixed on hers. His mouth opened to protest, but he could see the hundreds of statues all around him, mute testimony to Thorn's tale. He stared at her, searching for the slightest hint of deception. She stared back, willing him to believe her.

A sudden sound broke the tension. The howling of wolves, and the deeper call of the dire wolf.

The Children of Zaeurl had found them.

CHAPTER THIRTY

✕ ✕ ✕

The Ossuary
Droaam

Eyre 20, 998 YK

Harryn's eyes never left Thorn's as the howls echoed throughout the hall. From the sound, the beasts were at the entrance to the Ossuary, still some distance away. The fact that they were announcing their presence suggested they saw this as a game, a hunt to be savored.

"Wolves," he said. "Your enemies?"

"Yes," she said. "But they're worse than wolves. They're—"

"You need not explain." He lowered his sword. "I am Harryn of Thronehold, called the Stormblade. You have an honest face, Thorn of Breland. And it seems we have a common foe."

"Yes. That we do. And about that foe, they aren't wolves. They're—"

"Shapechangers."

"Yes. Why would you guess that?"

Harryn was studying the chamber, and she could see the wheels turning in his mind. He was judging the field of battle, looking for ways to turn it to his advantage. "If two centuries have truly passed, it appears there's been little progress. And I fear that your dagger is a poor weapon for the work that lies ahead."

"Well, " Thorn raised her hand and summoned the myrnaxe out of the air. "We've made *some* progress."

Harryn's eyes widened slightly. But he had no time to discuss magic; the enemy was closing fast. They heard a woman's voice, faint and far off, at the distant entrance to the great hall of statues.

"Spread out. Forgahn, right. Ghass, left. Farhn, guard this post. The rest of you, with me."

The light from Harryn's blade faded. It wasn't entirely dead, but it wouldn't reveal their presence. Harryn whispered, "Tell me about this place."

"I know of only one exit to the surface," Thorn said, pointing toward the passage. "And it sounds like it's being watched."

Harryn tapped a statue. "These are everywhere?"

Thorn nodded.

"Then we'll use them." He made his way through a column of hobgoblin soldiers. Ahead of them, vast numbers of broken statues had been piled together in heaps; the result was a series of makeshift walls formed from the shattered corpses, a hedge maze built from lost souls.

"What about Sheshka?" Thorn whispered. She didn't plan to leave the medusa to the mercy of the wolves.

Harryn's face was turned away, but she could see the muscles in his neck tighten. "What was she doing here?"

"She released you. I don't know what happened between you, but it's been two centuries, Harryn. She risked her life to save you."

"As long as you're Thorn, call me Stormblade," he said. "And you're correct. You don't know what happened."

Thorn opened her mouth to retort, then closed it and pointed. A light flickered up ahead—the glow of a torch. The wall of statues blocked their line of sight, but the torchlight shone through the gaps in the heap of granite goblins, flickering across frozen faces and clutching hands. Thorn studied the motion of the light, the shadows that she saw . . . two figures. One humanoid, holding the torch, and a wolf, sniffing for a scent they hadn't left. She signaled Harryn, pointing at the enemy, indicating the path she planned to take. He nodded, and she stepped away.

She was finally on her own.

Sheshka was a huntress, but she was no match for Thorn. And legend or not, Stormblade was a soldier, slowed by his heavy armor; Thorn could hear him as she slipped away. If Thorn could hear it, the nearby wolf likely could as well—she had to act quickly. Her enemies were exposed by their torchlight, but Thorn was the hunter in the dark, slipping among the statues. Stormblade was leading their enemies away, backing deeper into the hall, while Thorn was closing in behind them.

Thorn slipped around a wall of stone, avoiding an outstretched hand frozen in granite. She saw them—an ogre carrying the torch, and a gray wolf padding along at his side. They moved cautiously, the wolf leading the way. It hadn't howled yet, but that could come at any moment. Thorn leaped up onto the mass of goblins, moving soundlessly along the wall of stone corpses. The wolf and its companion crept along the wall. Thorn drew ever closer.

And then Harryn Stormblade stepped into view, blue sparks crackling around his silver blade.

The pair had been sent to hunt Sheshka. At the least, they were surprised to see the knight with the gleaming sword, and Thorn seized the distraction. She dropped down from above, the silver tip of her spear flashing in the torchlight.

The wolf never had a chance to howl. Pulling the spear free from the creature's spine, Thorn swung the axe blade in a low arc, hoping to slash the muscles in the ogre's leg. The axe was plain steel, but this was just an ogre . . .

Except that it wasn't.

Thorn had only seen the beast from behind. He walked on two legs, and he wore the armor of a guardsman of the

Crag. But up close, she saw the bristly black hair along his arms. His posture was hunched, more than most ogres. And his head had a strange shape, long and blunt, with great tusks rising from his mouth. It looked as if a sculptor had taken a clay figure of a fierce boar and forced it into the form of an ogre, retaining as much of the beast as possible.

Her axe cut into the creature's flesh, but it didn't have the impact she'd hoped for. Her enemy was still on his feet. He turned to face her, and she felt flecks of spittle on her face as he snorted and raised his cleaver. But the blow never fell. A flash of light blazed as Harryn's sword cut through the blade of the weapon and into the arm of the beast. The ogre flailed wildly at his foes, but it was no use. Thorn danced away from the clumsy blow, while Harryn swatted it aside with his blade.

The ogre was still a fearsome foe. Thorn remembered how much trouble it had been to bring down his cousin in the Crag, and this creature had the added muscle of the boar. Thorn took a deep breath, ready for a long, hard fight.

Harryn stepped to the side, slashing at the beast, handling the greatsword with the speed and dexterity of a rapier. No single cut caused much damage, but he forced the beast to turn, building its rage. The ogre was snorting and spitting, and Thorn was completely forgotten, until she sank her silvered spear into its back, piercing lung and heart. Blood flowed down the haft, and the creature roared in pain and anger.

Thorn felt the pulse of the heart, and she knew the wound was mortal. But the ogre-boar wasn't willing to fall. He spun around with such force that it tore the spear from her hands, and he charged at her, bloody foam flecking his lowered tusks. Harryn's blade was gleaming in the darkness, but there was no time for the Stormblade to reach her. Thorn rolled to the side, drawing Steel and flinging the dagger with all her might. It caught the ogre in the right eye, and the creature staggered sideways. He caught himself with one massive hand splayed against the floor, then collapsed, his tusk snapping as it struck the stone.

The beast was transforming as Thorn retrieved Steel. She pulled the myrnaxe from the ogre's side, the bone twisting as the features of the boar faded away.

"How can you still be fighting these creatures and not know of Drukan Moonlord?" Harryn whispered. "Just tell me . . . tell me that Galifar has survived, that these things have not destroyed our glorious land."

"Well, *these* things haven't destroyed Galifar," Thorn said. She pushed forward before Harryn could respond to her hesitant tone. "I told you, I've never heard of this Moonlord, and I've never seen a werewolf until today. According to the stories, they were wiped out over a century ago."

"How?"

Thorn wanted to move. The other hunters had surely heard the ogre's death cry. But Harryn had locked his hand around her wrist, and his grip was a vise.

"I know this is strange for you, Stormblade, but I wasn't even alive then. From what I've heard, it was a bloody mess that spread across the west. Soldiers from the Church of the Silver Flame organized the defense, standing against these shapeshifters until the tide turned."

"At what cost?"

Thorn slipped her free hand down to Steel's hilt; history wasn't one of her strengths, but the dagger whispered details into her mind.

"Tens of thousands. Aundair suffered the worst of it. Farmers, mostly. The shapechangers spread out from the woods and across the east. Thousands more were lost to the persecution of innocents after the fact. Can we save the history lesson for when we don't have wolves at our heels?"

"No," Harryn said, his voice low but steady. "I must know now. I need to know what lies beyond that gate. You say that you haven't seen these wolves before, that you thought they were wiped from history. And yet it seems that there are many of them. You are certain that you haven't heard of the Moonlord?"

"No." Thorn tried to keep watch for approaching torches. "Who was he?"

"A mage in the dark lands of the west. Some said he was a wizard, a student of Mordain the Fleshweaver. But as I pursued him, I learned a different truth. He was not a man at all, but a shapeshifter, a tiger in human flesh. He served an ancient power, a darkness from the very dawn of time, a force that embodies all our fears of the wild.

"I have known shifters. And I have even met werewolves who were not creatures of evil, who were simply drawn to the woods. But all who carry that mark can be brought under the sway of Drukan's ancient master. Six moons—that was what he sought. Under the light of six moons, he could shake the bonds of the slumbering fiend, empower the skinchangers, and bring them under his sway. They would spread the curse across the land, and as their power grew, so would that of the chained demon, until he could finally burst his shackles and usher in an age of savagery."

Harryn paused, his eyes clouded.

"I fought monsters and minions. I seized the Orb of Olarune. I made my way to the ancient mountain fortress, but I could not find his tower of shadows. And that is the last thing I remember . . . standing in a field of statues, knowing the moons would soon rise."

He shook his head.

"At least the horror was contained. Even at the cost of thousands of lives. At least Galifar survives."

Thorn had been drawn in by the story, and she found herself at a loss for words. She could sense Harryn's pain.

But this was not the time to try to explain the Last War. And there was something else . . .

"Wait," she said. "Did you say *six* moons?"

Harryn's answer was cut short by snarls.

Thorn and Harryn were in a wide alleyway, bordered on either side by piles of shattered statues. Now dark shapes emerged on either side of them, light flooding the area as the Aundairian sorceress threw a glowing sphere into the air. A massive gray wolf stood alongside the woman, and four wererats stared at Thorn with hungry eyes. On the other side, three wolves were spread around a truly terrifying figure. Once, it had been a giant troll—fearsome enough, possessing tremendous strength. But its features were blended with the worst aspects of the bear. Ursine eyes glared out of sunken sockets. Its snout bristled with yellowed fangs, and its long and twisted fingers were tipped with vicious claws. He roared, and his breath was thick with the scent of blood and flesh.

"I don't know who you are," the woman said. The dragonhawk crest gleamed on her breast, and energy crackled around her fingers. "But your answer to my next question will determine just how long it takes for you to die. Where is the Queen of Stone?"

CHAPTER THIRTY-ONE

✷ ✷ ✷

The Ossuary
Droaam

Eyre 20, 998 YK

Y ou will have no answer from me," Harryn said. "I
know you for what you are, and I pity you."

So much for talking our way out of it, Thorn thought.

The woman laughed. "Bold," she said. "I like you. If
there were more time, I should like to keep you. I think
you'd sing a different tune after I'd had a taste of you. But
the moons grow closer with each moment, and there is
much to do. Kurlun, take them. The rest of you, keep them
bound in this place."

The wolves and rats spread apart, forming living
walls to seal off the alleyway. Any doubts as to Kurlun's
identity were dispelled as the trollbear lunged toward
them. It moved with terrifying speed, and sparks flew
from the stone as Thorn leaped over its blow. She brought
the myrnaxe spear down on the troll's hand, hoping to
pin the beast to the ground. But to her surprise and
dismay, the flesh beneath the trollbear's ragged fur was
as hard as iron, and her strike slipped aside. Surprised,
she was unprepared when the beast lashed out with
the back of its hand. Its strength was astonishing, and
even this glancing blow sent Thorn staggering into the
heaped statues.

Stormblade fared better. "For Galifar!" he cried, and lightning flared around his blade. Thorn didn't see the stroke, but she heard the impact and the troll's hiss of pain. She knew the legends of that sword, the blade that struck with the force of a thunderbolt and shattered all lesser weapons. Hope soared as the tales flashed through her mind, and she pushed herself back to her feet, searching to land the perfect blow. Then the troll turned, slashing at Harryn, and Thorn saw that the wound he had inflicted was almost completely healed.

For a moment she considered fleeing. Using her magic, she could easily vault over the piled statues and disappear into the darkness. The thought struggled to take hold, and then it was gone. Thorn had been sent to claim the Stormblade. She was too close to victory to surrender, and if something had happened to Beren, she intended to salvage her mission. She leaped at the troll, landing a solid blow where its kidneys should be, but once again she was unable to pierce its hide. The best she could do was scratch it, and scratches healed instantly.

Stormblade was holding his own, but it couldn't last. The sorceress laughed as the troll's claws tore Harryn's tabard from his chest and left deep gouges in his armor. The blows that missed sent scattered fragments of stone goblin flying across the hall and seemed to shake the floor. The trollbear dug its claws into Harryn's armor, grabbing the knight and pulling him close. Stormblade had no room to bring his sword to bear, and the troll set its jaws against either side of Harryn's skull.

Thorn didn't try to fight the troll any more—she couldn't hurt it. Instead, she studied the sorceress and listened to the vibrations in the rock and the sounds in the hall. The Aundairian smiled at her.

"You've seen reason," she said. "You have a choice. Tell me where to find Queen Sheshka, or watch Kurlun crack your friend's head between his teeth."

"It's not Sheshka you need to worry about," Thorn said. She smiled, and it was all she could do to keep from laughing.

"Then what should I be concerned about?" The sorceress flexed her fingers again, tracing patterns of fire in the air. "You can't beat Kurlun."

"That's what the hydra is for." Sheshka's voice rang out from behind the sorceress. She stood on the back of the great beast, which was stone no longer. Eight heads snapped forward, and gouts of steaming acid burst from the hydra's many mouths, engulfing the trollbear. The creature howled in agony, releasing Harryn from its jaws, and the knight slammed both feet into the troll's chest, rolling free from its grip.

The sorceress was stunned. The hydra was huge, and it had left a trail of shattered stone in its wake, but distracted by the battle with the troll, no one had seen or heard the black-scaled hydra approaching in the shadows. As she watched the troll collapsing, whimpering in agony as its flesh melted away, the Aundairian was even more surprised when Thorn's spear passed through her throat. Thorn hadn't been idle—she had turned her attention to the wizard, recognizing the tell-tale signs of shielding magic and anticipating the sorceress's next move. The Aundairian never had a chance to release a spell; she crumpled to the ground as Thorn pulled the spear free.

The rest was chaos. The healing powers of the troll were no match for the acidic bile of the hydra, and soon bones were all that remained of Kurlun. Rat and wolf howled and snarled, and Thorn carved a path through the storm of claw and tooth. A clap of thunder echoed as Harryn's blade struck the dire wolf. Then the hydra was upon the unfortunate creature, two separate heads tearing it apart and swallowing the pieces.

It was over within moments. The corpses were still shifting as the hungry hydra devoured them. Sheshka slid down from the creature's back, keeping her eyes closed. She ran a hand along the hydra's nearest neck, murmuring in a language Thorn didn't speak.

"Now I'm embarrassed," Thorn said. "I leave you alone for a few minutes and you come back with a hydra. The best we could do was a wretched troll."

"There was nothing wretched about that troll," Sheshka said. Her serpents seemed limp, her movements sluggish. "That was a war troll of the Great Crag, one of the personal host of Sora Maenya. I'm certain you noticed the skin of steel, and the speed at which it healed."

"I've never been an expert on trolls."

Sheshka staggered, falling against the side of the hydra, and Thorn took a step forward.

"What's wrong?"

"I'll be fine," Sheshka stammered, though her voice quavered as she spoke. "Used more . . . energy . . . than I anticipated."

"You saved us." Thorn glanced over her shoulder, where Harryn was staring down at the bones of the troll. "Stormblade. Are you injured?"

"I've suffered worse," he said. He ran his fingers across the new gouges in his armor.

"Then I'd consider it a personal favor if you thanked our savior."

Sheshka's vipers all turned at once, shifting to look away from the knight. Stormblade hesitated, but he approached the two women and dropped to one knee, laying his sword before him.

"Lady Sheshka—"

"Queen Sheshka," she said softly.

Thorn was skilled at reading people—tells were as vital as spells, and she always watched others' emotions. Harryn Stormblade was a stern and serious man, and he hid his feelings well. But he was taken off guard. Something ran deeply between these two.

"Queen Sheshka," he said at last. "I thank you for the risks you have taken on my behalf. There is no token of my gratitude I can give that I haven't offered before. I am unaware of much, and I trust you will forgive my ignorance."

"Will you forgive me?" she said. Her serpents peered backward over her shoulders, as shy as vipers could be.

Stormblade hesitated, but his voice was firm. "No."

"You'd be dead if not for her," Thorn said. "Twice."

Harryn looked at Thorn, and she could feel the storm twisting within him. "I know nothing of this. Centuries have passed. Perhaps things—and people—have changed. But I am still living in your yesterday, and I cannot change how I feel so quickly." He looked at Sheshka. "I am sorry, my lady—your majesty—but I cannot forgive you yet."

A few of the snakes hissed quietly, but Sheshka looked at him kindly. "I understand."

Thorn didn't, but she had other concerns. "Sheshka, I need to get Harryn back to Breland. I know that you have troubles of your own—"

"Let us travel north together," Sheshka said. "I can call a winged messenger and send word ahead to Cazhaak Draal. We can have you astride a wyvern and on your way back to Breland within three days."

"Can you bring your scaly friend?" The hydra was sniffing around the alley, looking for more corpses.

"He's too large to fit through the tunnel to the surface. I fear I shall have to petrify him again. I don't want him to starve."

"What about the moons?" Harryn Stormblade had risen to his feet, and his voice was grim.

"What do you mean?" Thorn said.

"How many moons are in the sky?"

Thorn hesitated. "Six."

"Don't you see? It's happening again. This is why I have been restored." His fingers tightened around the hilt of his sword. "The Wild Heart reaches out to the world above. Tonight, as the six moons pass over his tower, the Moonlord will taint them with his magic, and that evil will spread to all the skinchangers. That cannot be allowed to happen. This is destiny."

"And yet you failed before," Sheshka said. Thorn could tell that the ghosts of the past were haunting the conversation. "You were stripped of your identity and left for dead. But the world survived. The soldiers of the Silver Flame did what you could not. This is not a task for one man . . . or two women."

Stormblade's voice rose with his retort, but Thorn wanted to hear another voice. She took a step back, giving Sheshka and Harryn room to argue, and ran her fingers along Steel's hilt.

I was beginning to wonder if you'd forgotten about me.

"I've been busy," she muttered. "What do you think?"

Intriguing. Much about lycanthropy remains a mystery. As Sheshka said, some lycanthropes are driven to murder and depravity, while a few live solitary, peaceful lives. We know that during the Silver Crusade, the curse became far more contagious, and its victims more violent. Harryn is attributing this to the work of the Moonlord . . . and saying that it could happen again. If so, the surge was contained before. But according to the records, most of the lycanthropes exterminated during the purge were humans and shifters—infected people of Aundair and Breland. These trolls and ogres are another matter.

"And that time, we had a united kingdom," Thorn murmured. The Church of the Silver Flame might have provided the soldiers, but under old Galifar, the church was expected to pursue supernatural threats across the breadth of the realm. Now, the bulk of the military force of the church was aligned with Thrane. Even if the Keeper of the Flame made the offer, the Brelish wouldn't welcome the presence of Thrane troops. And if Breland stood alone, how long would it be before other nations took advantage of its weakness? The Cyran refugees could see an opportunity to seize land for their people. The Darguul goblins were always a concern. Even Thrane might use the presence of the plague as an excuse to cross the border in force.

"Stormblade!" she called.

Harryn paused in mid retort and glanced at her. "Yes?"

"Say that I agree with you. What must be done?"

"Queen Sheshka says we are already past the midnight hour. If the threat is real, the ritual must be underway. The Moonlord will be in the tower of shadows."

Thorn nodded. "And where is that, exactly?"

"I don't know."

Sheshka's snakes hissed derisively.

"That could explain why you didn't find it before," Thorn said.

"The text I found was unclear," Harryn said. "The tower is a relic of the first age of the world. It is difficult to translate the writing of fiends. It seemed to say that the tower was destroyed long ago, but its shadow remains—and the tower itself remains in the shadow."

Thorn was about to make a clever remark about wasting time searching for destroyed towers when Steel whispered in her mind. *Such a thing is possible,* he said. *The fiends of the first age possessed immense powers. It would operate on the same principles as your gloves—pulling a pocket of space out of the world. The question would be finding the portal.*

"So you're saying that the castle is *in* a shadow?"

"Exactly," Harryn said.

Possibly, Steel qualified.

"So with six moons in the sky, we're going to look for . . . a shadow."

"According to the text, it's the shadow of the tower," Stormblade said. "The ghost of a shadow."

"Well, that makes it—" the words died in her throat.

The ghost of a shadow. When she and Sheshka had traveled across the city, they'd passed through a patch of unnatural gloom. The shadow of a building—with no building to cast it. "I know where it is."

Stormblade smiled—the first time she'd seen a gentle expression on his face. He struck his hip with an armored fist. "Destiny! Let us fight, then, Thorn of Breland. Together, let us fight for Galifar."

You'll have to tell him sometime, Steel said.

"Yes," Thorn said. "For Galifar. Sheshka, this isn't your battle. If you want to stay here, I understand."

The medusa's serpents were coiled proudly about her head. "I will join you, sister Thorn. I am not the child I was. And while I do not understand why the Daughters would welcome this darkness, I do not believe that it belongs in our lands. You may fight for *Galifar* . . . but I seek to defend Droaam and Cazhaak Draal."

Thorn called the myrnaxe from the glove and raised it in the air. "Very well, my friends. Let us see what fate has in store for us."

As they prepared for the struggle ahead, one thought lingered at the back of Thorn's mind. If Sheshka were correct, Sora Teraza had stolen Stormblade's identity so long ago. And Sora Teraza had told her where to find the petrified knight.

Were they following the path of destiny . . . or dancing to the tune of Teraza?

Chapter Thirty-Two

The Ossuary
Droaam

Eyre 20, 998 YK

"Chew these," Harryn said, handing her a few leaves.

Though he was eager for battle, Harryn was no fool. He sought to treat their wounds before challenging whatever enemy lay ahead. The knight had some skill with the healing arts and a few salves in his bag; his work did not draw from magic, but he was likely a match for the gnoll Fharg.

The leaves were sharp and bitter, and Thorn grimaced. Harryn was bandaging the rat bite on her shoulder, which was the worst of her injuries.

"What is this?" she said.

"Wolfsbane."

She spat it out. Time to go back to Fharg, she thought. "That's poisonous!"

Harryn looked at the leaves. "Don't worry. It's a small risk, but it's better than the alternative."

"He speaks the truth," Sheshka said.

Harryn returned to his work, examining the scratches on Thorn's leg. "The rats, the wolves. You've been bitten, and that means the curse was likely passed to you. The wolfsbane should drive it out of your blood."

"So I could turn into a *rat?*"

Sheshka said "No," just as Stormblade said "Yes."

Thorn looked at Sheshka. "You first."

"Only a few of the Children of Zaeurl have the power to pass on their 'blessing,' and even then, it needs time to take root. Even if you were infected, you would not change until tomorrow, if then."

Thorn glanced at Harryn. "Now you, poisoner."

"What she says would be true, any other time. But not beneath these six moons. If the Wild Heart truly stirs—and if the moons are in the sky—the curse is stronger than it has been in over a century. Any of the cursed can pass on their affliction with a bite, and only those with tremendous will can resist its power. Those who fall to the curse will become subjects of the Feral Master, driven to spill the blood of those they once loved. Under the light of these moons, the change could occur within moments." He had finished his work, and he slung his pack across his back and picked up his sword. "I have done all that I can. Battle calls."

Thorn was troubled. As they made their way to the surface, she moved closer to Sheshka. "Do you believe what Stormblade says?"

A few serpents turned to regard her. "I do. I told you of the skinchangers who came to this land before Zaeurl and her children. They were a dangerous breed, and those they touched turned on their own kind. The greater horrors came after the Stormblade left us. Perhaps, if I'd remained at his side . . . things would have been different."

"But it doesn't make sense," Thorn murmured. "You said that Zaeurl wasn't like those others . . . and that she was loyal to the Daughters of Sora Kell. Why would *they* want their people to become subjects of the Wild Heart?"

"I do not know. But Zaeurl cannot be acting alone. The skullcrushers and the war ogres are the troops of the Great Crag."

Thorn shook her head. "Perhaps. But it still doesn't feel right."

The moonlight was dazzling as they emerged from the mouth of the Ossuary. All around them, stone hobgoblins stood ready for battle, waiting for a war that ended thousands of years before. Ahead of them, they could still hear the shouts, drums, and howls of the revelers. Drul Kantar had told the truth; the welcoming feast was nothing next to the excitement of the Midnight Dawn.

"Stormblade, tell me more about the Moonlord," Thorn said as they climbed over the ruined walls of the fortress. "Do you suppose someone's taken his place this time? You said he was a tiger—could this be a woman with the soul of a wolf?"

"I know little about the Moonlord," Stormblade replied. "He claimed to be chosen by the Feral Master himself. He had power over those who were touched by the wild. He could drive them to madness or force them to do his bidding. But I don't know if these were gifts of his own, or tied to the orbs."

"Orbs?"

"The lunar orbs. Crystal spheres, relics of the first age. I know even less about them than I do about Drukan. I know only that there was one for each moon, and that Drukan sought them all."

"Silence upon you," Sheshka whispered. "We approach the city."

"This time I know where we're going," Thorn said. "I'll take the lead."

After the battle in the Ossuary and the rats in the tower, Thorn was expecting resistance. But it seemed that the Aundairian and her troops were all that the mysterious Moonlord deemed necessary to deal with the medusa queen. Goblin children chased one another through the outer ruins, and once Thorn was disturbed to meet the gaze of a rat in the shadows. The rodent appeared ordinary, but a stroke of Steel made it a moot point.

They reached the strange pool of darkness, and she

stepped into it. It was as she'd remembered—a massive patch of gloom that defied the light of the moons above. Looking at it with Harryn's tale in mind, she could see it for what it was—the shadow of a vast, strange building, a structure that could not be seen. She studied it more closely, tracing the walls down to where its foundation should be. But there was a large plot of open ground, dark and wet, a patch of mire in the midst of the city—poor ground to build on, certainly. Ironweed and chunks of sharp stone rose up from the muddy surface. The swampy soil was reason enough for it to be left barren, but Thorn guessed there was another reason.

She made her way to Sheshka and Stormblade. The two had paused near a crumbling wall covered in goblin graffiti—scrawled words that might have been written in dried blood.

"I've found our shadow," she said.

Neither of them responded. They were breathing, but aside from that, neither one had moved since she returned. Even Sheshka's snakes were frozen in place. As this registered in her mind, Thorn caught a familiar scent in the air. She turned, placing her back against the ancient wall.

"What are you doing?" she said.

"I think your answer to that question must be more interesting than mine, Lady Tam. I'm pursuing the interests of my people. You appear to be working with a medusa warlord. And a changeling with a disturbing fixation on Harryn Stormblade."

The voice was as familiar as the scent—Drego Sarhain.

"You don't know what's going on here, Drego."

"So tell me. You know how much I enjoy our moonlit talks."

"They're not nearly as pleasant when I'm talking to the air."

"True," he said, and then he was beside her.

If he'd truly been there all along, his skills with concealment had improved considerably. Scent and sound told Thorn he was nearby, but she hadn't been able to pinpoint his location. Yet everything else about him seemed the same. He was dressed in black and silver, his hair shone in the moonlight, and there was laughter in his eyes. But something about him was different. Like his scent, it had always been there, but she hadn't been aware of it until then.

Familiarity.

It was something in his eyes, the way he spoke, his laughter . . . she'd seen him before Droaam. Spoken with him. But she couldn't remember where; the more she thought about it, the more it seemed like a dream. But she felt as if she knew him . . . and he seemed to feel the same way about her.

He smiled at her. "So what is this, Nyrielle?"

"The warlord Zaeurl is about to unleash chaos on the Five Nations. Zaeurl was the traitor all along."

Drego laughed. "That's ridiculous."

"I know it seems that way, but it's the truth. She's a werewolf, Drego—"

He placed his hand over hers, gently brushing his fingers across her skin. "I know."

Then she saw it all. Toli. The Aundairian. Steel flashed into her hand, and she let the point dig in just below his chin. "You're one of them."

He smiled and slowly raised his chin, just enough so he could open his mouth. "You're wrong. And you should know."

"And how's that?"

"You have a stone at the base of your spine, a crystal shard."

Thorn let the dagger touch his throat again. "How do you know that?"

He ignored the threat and the question. "When we were

in the woods that night and the wolves approached—did you feel something in the stone? A chill, perhaps?"

She said nothing.

"And when you saw Zaeurl at the Great Crag?"

"I felt that same chill all day yesterday," she said.

"Yes . . . when you were with your comrade Toli, I suspect. But do you feel it now?"

He was right. Thinking about it, she'd only felt that chill in the presence of Toli, and later at the Ossuary. Now, the stone was calm. "If the pain means something—if it reveals werewolves—I think I'd have noticed during the week I spent in the wagon with Toli."

"Or, perhaps, he *wasn't* a werewolf then."

Thorn lowered the dagger and Drego smiled. It was a lovely smile . . . though it froze when she set the point against his heart. "I'm still listening. For someone who's not a werewolf, you know a great deal about them."

"Silver Flame," he said. "It comes with the church. As for Toli, I think it would be obvious. He was taken after the welcoming feast, along with some of the other delegates. It's a good thing you had an early night—otherwise you might be howling at the moon yourself."

"But you said Zaeurl wasn't behind this."

"She's not. She's a werewolf—she doesn't have a choice in the matter. She needs to obey when her master calls."

Master. Then it came to her. *He had power over those who were touched by the wild; he could drive them to madness or force them to do his bidding.* "The Moonlord."

"Yes."

"You knew about him?"

"Yes, I did." Drego's voice was calm.

"And you're here to stop him?"

"No. I'm afraid that's where we have a little problem."

"What are you talking about? He's trying to spread a plague across the Five Nations! The same plague your people fought so hard to stop!"

"Exactly." Drego seemed, if anything, pleased—as if she'd just solved the puzzle.

"What do you mean, 'exactly'?"

"The same plague we fought so hard to stop. And *did* stop. Don't you see, Nyrielle? This is exactly what the world needs. I didn't come here to stop it from happening. I came to make sure it *did* happen."

Thorn pressed the blade against his skin. "Give me one good reason to let you live."

"The end of war." He smiled at her surprise. "Don't you see? This is exactly what we need. A common enemy, a threat that compels us to join forces. The first crusade against lycanthropy brought hundreds of thousands to the Church of the Silver Flame. The second will reunite Galifar, as people remember what saved them before."

"Convenient that it's Breland and Aundair that stand on the front line of this new threat, and Thrane that holds the seat of the Silver Flame."

Drego shrugged. "I did say I was pursuing the interests of my people. They just happen to coincide with yours. Be reasonable, Nyri. Tens of thousands died in the Silver Crusade. Perhaps more will be lost this time. But how many died in the Mourning? This is a chance to force reunification without war. The people will demand it."

He could be right. Steel was in her hand and his voice was in her head. *The most zealous followers of the Silver Flame are Aundairians, as a direct result of the crusade. The battle against the shapechangers is one of the fundamental things people know about the church. If there's a new plague of lycanthropy, people may turn to the Flame.*

"You don't know that," Thorn said. "People might band together to face the common threat. Or they might turn on each other. And the Church may not be strong enough to face this challenge again. You're gambling with the fate of the world."

"I like the odds. And we shatter Droaam in the

process. The Moonlord is no friend to the Daughters of Sora Kell. He'll tear their forces away and turn these beasts against each other. Come on, Nyrielle. Don't you want to change the world?" He smiled, and a part of her *wanted* to work with him, wanted to turn her back on everything she'd done before. But that was a tiny spark that flickered and died.

She thought about Beren's tales of fighting on the Droaamish front. She remembered Sheshka's tales about the dark times of her youth—the infection that turned its victims against their loved ones. And she imagined the trollbear smashing through a Brelish village, how many common soldiers—men like her father—would fall fighting such a beast.

"Not like this," she said.

One moment, her knife was against his chest. The next, he was six paces away from her. Magic was at work, and his spell was still active. He was standing right in front of her, but he was flickering, wavering. With her enhanced senses, she could feel him slipping in and out of existence.

He's shifting between planes, Steel whispered. *Any attack or spell may pass through him, and if he needs to, he can slip away through solid matter . . . walking through a wall while he's on another plane.*

"I don't want to kill you, Nyrielle," Drego said, and his voice was warped by the spell, rising and falling. "When the sun rises, this will be inevitable, and we'll be able to fight on the same side. But I can't let you stop it."

"It's not up to you." Thorn charged forward, spinning on her heel and aiming a kick for Drego's temple. By the time the sun came up, it would be over, one way or the other. Though they came from different nations, relied on different skills . . . she felt a bond to Drego. Somehow, whatever it was, she didn't want to kill him.

He blinked out of existence just before she struck him, and her foot passed through empty air. He reappeared a few feet away, holding his hand toward her. The air rippled as a field of energy took shape in the form of a giant hand. By the time she knew what it was, it was already wrapped around her, pinning her limbs with iron strength.

"It's over," Drego said. "I'll have to bind you, I'm afraid. As for your companions, the medusa is supposed to be dead already. And as for Stormblade—if he is truly who he appears to be, I'm sure that Thrane could use another champion."

"My sword belongs to Galifar." Perhaps Thorn had distracted Drego; perhaps it was an indomitable will finally breaking its bonds. Harryn Stormblade was striding toward Drego Sarhain, and lightning crackled around his greatsword.

Drego grinned. "If that's true, shouldn't it be broken?" His next word struck Thorn's ears with physical force. She felt a moment's pain, but the impact on Stormblade was far more severe. His armor rattled, but his sword was the target of Drego's spell. The metal shivered and shook, and for a moment it seemed like it would shatter. And then the moment passed.

"That's quite a sword," Drego said. The blade flashed in Harryn's hands, but once again, Sarhain vanished just before the blow landed. He returned a few feet away. "Let's try again. I've got time."

All the while, Thorn was struggling against her bonds, but to no avail. The ghostly hand might as well have been made of stone. Her muscles simply couldn't match the magic. All she could do was watch the battle between Drego and Harryn, the sorcerer and the knight.

Then, as she watched, she saw another battle. Another knight. An armored warrior with Drego's face. *How will history remember you, I wonder?*

With that thought, power flooded through her, fire blazing through every tendon. She flexed, and the silver hand holding her shattered into a thousand pieces and was gone. Steel was already in her hand as she charged forward. Drego flickered back and forth, slipping away from Stormblade's blows. But Thorn could sense the motion of the air. She could *feel* the currents shifting away from where Drego had been and the place he was going to be. She tried not to think; she let her instincts guide her, and the spy appeared just before the point of her blade. He was looking away from her when the blade passed along a rib and into his heart. But she heard his voice, faint and bloody.

"Well done . . . Sarm . . ."

He never finished the last word. Thorn had barely pulled Steel free when she felt his flesh harden beneath her touch. His doublet of black silk became black marble. Thorn knew what had happened even before she heard the hiss of Sheshka's serpents.

It had to be done. Thorn knew it was necessary. Her mission was to retrieve Harryn Stormblade and to protect Breland. But as she turned toward the long shadow, she saw a pair of laughing, familiar eyes in her mind, and for one moment, she hated her job.

CHAPTER THIRTY-THREE

✶ ✶ ✶

The Crag's Shadow
Droaam

Eyre 20, 998 YK

Sheshka and Stormblade had heard everything. Drego's spell had paralyzed their muscles, but it had done nothing to their ears. Harryn said nothing. Thorn guessed that he was dedicated to the mission, and that for the moment everything else was secondary . . . even the state of Galifar. She could hardly blame him. He'd just lost more than two centuries of time; how could this seem like anything but a dream? The last thing he remembered was the fight against the Moonlord, and he was fighting that battle once more.

But the medusa queen had other plans.

"You heard him," she hissed. "This Moonlord is no friend to the Daughters of Sora Kell. And Zaeurl is his slave. The Daughters were never my enemy. Someone is seeking to shatter Droaam beneath their eyes."

"And we're approaching that someone's palace in the shadows right now."

"When I thought that all in this place stood against me, I was prepared to die at your side. But the Daughters must be told." Sheshka was too angry to close her eyes, though she was looking away. Her serpents were seething, a roiling mass of rage.

"It's too dangerous. We're almost at the shadow now. And we don't know how many of the Crag Guards have been turned."

"I told you before," Sheshka said, "that I would fight for Droaam and Cazhaak Draal. We choose our battles. You have yours. This will be mine."

"Your power could make all the difference," Thorn said.

"I trust that it will," Sheshka returned.

Thorn looked at Harryn. "Do you have anything useful to add?"

The knight inclined his head, solemn as ever. "You have always chosen your own path, Queen Sheshka. I hope that you are making the correct choice this time."

"As do I." Sheshka's serpents had quieted, and she closed her eyes. "Shadow hide you, Harryn Stormblade. And you, sister Thorn."

"Aureon light your way," Harryn said.

Thorn said nothing. She held out her hand, and for a moment, Sheshka pressed a palm to hers. Then she turned and made her way toward the moonlit city and disappeared within the ruins.

✠ ✠ ✠ ✠ ✠

Stormblade gazed at the mire. "There it was, just waiting for the moons to rise. To think that I was so close . . . so long ago."

"We're not inside yet," Thorn said. "This could be a clever illusion designed to trick people into wandering into the Crag's only swamp."

"No. I can feel the truth of it. I held the Orb of Olarune in my hand . . . it seems like only hours ago. The lunar orbs are close. This is where we are supposed to be."

Lunar orbs . . . the final piece she'd been missing. Suddenly it all fell into place. She knew who the Moonlord was. "Drul Kantar," she whispered.

"Look to the sky," the knight said. "Look to the moons that have passed above the tower. They are already stained with blood."

Thorn followed his gaze. A ruddy mist was drifting across the sky; the moons that lay above it were distorted by the crimson cloud. Thorn knew nothing about the weather of Droaam—possibly, this was a natural phenomenon, but it was certainly an ill omen. "You say you can feel the lunar orbs. Can you find the gate to this tower?"

"We shall soon see." Sword in hand, Stormblade strode through the shadow cast by the tower. Curious, Thorn grabbed a chunk of stone from the ground, and as they drew closer, she hurled it toward the muck. She was disappointed to see it drop into the mire, scattering mud around the point of impact. At the same time, it made sense; if the tower was merely invisible, surely thousands of people would have noticed it.

They stood on the very edge of the barren land. Harryn studied it, eyes half-closed as if listening for distant music.

"Take my hand." He set his sword against one shoulder and held out his right hand.

Thorn didn't bother asking why.

"Close your eyes and follow me."

He pulled her forward, and as he did, everything changed. Thanks to her ring, Thorn was perfectly comfortable with her eyes closed. Scent, sound, and vibration all combined to paint a picture. And with one single step, the picture changed. Smooth stone replaced cold mud, high walls took the place of open air. Something was awful about it, like the fading memory of a nightmare—then understanding bloomed just beyond her conscious mind. The walls are built from terror, she thought, but she didn't know how or why. But the tower was the least of her concerns.

They were no longer alone.

A great cat was waiting when she opened her eyes, as if it wanted the intruders to see it before it attacked. It was a nightclaw tiger, larger than the stone griffin in the Ossuary. Thorn had seen a nightclaw only once before, when a beast had emerged from the King's Forest of Breland. By the time King Boranel and his huntsmen had brought it down, fifty-three people lay dead.

Thorn had no idea what hidden powers this beast might possess, but the chill at the base of her spine told her it was no normal animal. Beyond the nightclaw, a pack of wolves blocked the lone hallway leading deeper into the tower. Thorn couldn't even see how she and Harryn had entered; no gate stood behind them.

She had no time to ponder that question—the cat was already in motion. The nightclaw was a blur of muscle and fur as it darted toward them, claws scraping against the strange, rough stone of the floor. Fierce as it was, a more fearsome creature stood in the chamber. Harryn Stormblade's life had been stolen from him, and returned centuries later. He had awoken in the dark, among thousands of lost souls, and had been forced to fight war trolls and sorcerers. It had taken time for the hero of old to rise to his senses.

That hero had returned. A crack of thunder and a blaze of light erupted as Stormblade slashed at the beast. He moved with remarkable speed despite his heavy armor, and when the werewolves joined the fray, he slipped among them, spinning and slashing. A living whirlwind, he filled the creatures with fear and despair. Thorn joined the fight, lashing out with her silver spear, but she might as well have watched the battle. Nothing could stand in the Stormblade's way. His guard was all but impenetrable, his stamina without limit. Bear, wolf, rat, troll—all fell before his shining blade.

Until they reached the heart of the tower.

The chamber was huge. Thorn could barely see the far

side of the hall. The walls were formed of rough red crystal that pulsed with a bloody light, a disturbingly unsteady beat. The roof was a vast chimney, a hollow tube that opened to the sky. The golden face of the moon Nymm lay directly above them, and the crimson mist was beginning to overtake it.

A bizarre contraption lay below the moon-tunnel, a blending of crystal, iron, and what appeared to be molten brass, flowing and twisting through the air with no apparent support. Thirteen stone slabs were spread around the strange crystal flower—prison beds built for giants. But today, delegates and diplomats lay stretched out on the platforms, held in place by unseen manacles, or magic that froze the mind. There was Beren of Breland, Tharsul of Karrnath, Munta the Gray of the Gantii Vuus. And there was Jolira Jan Dorian of Zilargo, her throat cut and her blood flowing down her slab, seemingly absorbed by the pulsing crystal. Three of the delegates were already dead—one for each of the moons that had already passed over the shadowed hall.

A lone figure stood at the strange machine, adjusting the crystals and the flow of blood. He wore a long blue robe studded with golden stars, and around his neck the lunar orbs glowed with the power of the moons above. Drul Kantar, the Moonlord, glanced at the intruders and spoke. His voice was deep and gentle, the kindly teacher admonishing a tardy student.

"Leave me, children, and I will elevate you in the world to come. Soon hunter and prey will be divided. Leave me to my work and I will welcome you into my pride. Proceed with this impudence and you will brand yourselves my prey."

"I know you by the orbs you wear, Drukan." Harryn raised his sword above his head, and the blade flashed and rumbled. "I swore to stand against you and your master, and tonight I will see that oath completed."

Drul laughed, a calm and gentle chuckle. "But I have no interest in fighting you, Harryn. Though I suppose I can spare these dogs." He raised his hand and six of the envoys rose from their biers. They groaned as their bones twisted and muscles warped. To Thorn's horror, she saw Beren pulled into the shape of a lean gray wolf as he approached her, while old Munta the hobgoblin became a mighty boar. The newly transformed lycanthropes growled and grunted, until a gesture from the oni sent them loping across the floor.

"Don't kill them!" Thorn cried out to Harryn. It was no simple task. As a man, Beren was old, kind, and generous. As a wolf, he was driven by hatred and hunger, a mad desire to kill. Thorn smashed the beast in the side of the head with the flat of the axe. As long as they weren't striking with silver, the supernatural stamina of the creatures helped them shrug off the blows.

Stormblade resorted to crippling blows against the four who attacked him, breaking legs so the enemy could be left alive but helpless. Thorn focused on Munta and Beren. She refused to get blood on her spear; instead, she struck with the flat of her blade, using the long reach of the myrnaxe to hold the wolves at bay, and striking at crippling nerves whenever an opportunity arose. It was slow and dangerous, and time and again she caught tooth or tusk on the haft of her axe or against the mithral of her bracers. But she believed in her victory. She knew she could not lose. And while her unnatural strength didn't return, in time both boar and wolf collapsed and remained still.

"Drukan Moonlord!" Harryn called again. "Your doom approaches. Two centuries I have waited. No more!" The blue-white light flared as the knight raised his sword above his head and charged at his enemy.

The oni chuckled. "Harryn Stormblade. The storm is a thing of the wild—learn that lesson now." He casually waved his hand and a mighty gust of wind swept across the hall. The gale knocked Thorn off her feet, smashing her against the far wall. Stormblade held his footing, but he couldn't move against the terrible force of the wind.

Drul raised his left hand, and thunder rumbled in the chamber. Blue-white light flashed again, but this time the lightning was the weapon of Drul Kantar. Bolts of energy rained down from the distant sky, ricocheting off the walls of the high tower before striking the battered knight. There was no escape. *Crack!* and Harryn staggered. *Crack!* and he dropped to his knees. *Crack!* one final bolt and he fell heavily to the floor.

Drul clenched his fist again, and *Crack!* Another bolt of lightning flared around Harryn. The knight was still. The pale blue giant seemed almost disappointed. "Who knew destiny could be so easily thwarted?" he murmured.

"Not I," Thorn said, thrusting her spear into his spine.

The wind had died when Drul had begun his fierce assault on Harryn. Thorn had neither the strength nor stamina of the knight, but stealth was her gift, and the oni never saw her approach. He howled with rage and pain, and Thorn pulled the spear free as he turned to face her. His howls changed from rage to mirth.

"A silver spear?" He roared with laughter. "A *silver spear?* You might as well move the ocean with a spoon, child. You know not what you face. But I shall grace you with a vision of glory before you die."

Another burst of wind threw Thorn backward. For a moment, she thought the ogre had exploded; he was surrounded by a cloud of blood and smoke. Then she realized that his wings had knocked her back, wings that seemed like flames—vast, leathery wings stained in red and black. He has the soul of a tiger, Harryn had told her, and so he did; he also had the head of a tiger, with bloody crimson stripes separated by bands of bottomless darkness. The only things that resembled the ogre lord were his size and mighty physique, and the collar of glowing orbs bound around his neck.

"Gaze upon true wonder," he roared. "Drulkalatar Atesh, the Feral Hand, speaker of the Wild Heart. Immortal and perfect, soldier of the first age and the age to come." Lightning danced around his outstretched arms, wreathing the hooked talons that tipped each finger.

Thorn was stunned by the spectacle before her, torn by conflicting emotions. The most powerful of all was fear. She had seen many horrors in her life—she had faced a demon and survived. But she had never encountered anything with the sheer *presence* of Drulkalatar. He wielded the primal power of the predator—the feeling of the newly-shorn sheep staring into the eyes of the dire wolf. Yet there was something else.

Familiarity.

Thorn had never seen this creature before. She knew that, just as she knew she wouldn't be alive if she had. And yet, its shape, its voice, the light in its eyes, even the sense of fear . . . she'd seen it before. And there were voices, words in the back of her mind, whispers she couldn't quite hear.

She had no time to search her memory. As she'd stood frozen in fear and confusion, Drulkalatar had finished posturing.

"Had I the appetite, I would feast on your flesh, little half-elf." The chamber shook with the sound of his voice. "Instead, I will give you to the storm."

As he raised his hands, time slowed to a crawl. Thorn could *see* the lightning flashing down toward her, brighter and stronger than anything he'd flung at Harryn. She *knew* the bolt would incinerate her, leaving burnt flesh and charred bones. She wanted to flee, but she was moving even more slowly than the lightning. She had no escape, just the delayed horror of watching . . .

Waiting . . .

When the bolt finally struck, it was almost a relief. *Almost.* The pain was beyond anything she'd ever felt. It tore through her, and she could feel her muscles snapping, her joints coming apart.

Then her mind exploded.

It lasted less than a second, but to Thorn it seemed a lifetime. When the smoke cleared, nothing remained of the Brelish spy.

In her place stood a dragon.

"Storm?" she said, and her breath was sulfur and heat. "I prefer fire."

Chapter Thirty-Four

✯ ✯ ✯

The Crag's Shadow
Droaam

Eyre 20, 999 YK

When the lightning struck her, Thorn gave in to madness. For a moment, everything fell away from her, and when it returned, every sensation was wrong. Her blood was on fire, searing heat spread throughout her veins, but there was no pain. The blaze within her was a comfort, warming her soul. She rose up and spread her wings, and only then did she realized that she had them. Her wings . . . her neck . . . her *tail* . . . what had become of her?

Two constants stood amidst the chaos. A needle of pain—the sharp agony of the stone set into the base of her skull. And the warm glow from the crystal at the base of her spine. Together they served as spiritual poles, as anchors for her thoughts. Clinging to these points made it easier to let go of the rest. It was akin to her sharpened senses; part of her already understood it, and Thorn only needed to surrender conscious thought to these instincts. This didn't feel new. It was as if she'd always had wings . . . and she'd somehow forgotten.

Storm? I prefer fire.

She only realized that she was speaking as the thought passed through her head; she wasn't sure where it came from.

But it snapped her back into the moment. Drulkalatar. The fiend still stood before her, but now he was looking up at her; mighty he might be, but she towered over him. She could feel his emotions, fear and surprise pouring from him. And he was speaking again.

"*Sarmondelaryx!*" he shouted. "Begone from this place!"

Anger flowed through her. Confused as she was, her memories were quickly returning. This beast was threatening her nation and possibly the entire world. He had taken pleasure in striking down her friend, and he dared to threaten her. She opened her mouth, intending to hurl an angry word at him—

—and the room filled with fire. It was more than ordinary flame; it was Thorn's fury given elemental force. She heard Drulkalatar scream. When the fire faded, she saw why. The fiend had folded his wings across his body, creating a shield to protect himself . . . and Thorn's flames had seared through skin and flesh, leaving charred gaps in his wings.

"Not so perfect anymore," she said.

Drulkalatar howled, and the winds took up his cry. The gale struck Thorn with the force of a hurricane, knocking her from her feet and slamming her to the floor. She felt a stone bier shatter beneath her, shards grinding against her armored skin. Thorn the woman would have tried to rise to her feet, struggling against the winds. But she was Thorn the dragon, and instinct drove her down a different path. She lashed out with her tail, and the blow flung Drulkalatar across the room. She heard the crack of snapping bone as he struck the crystal wall.

Silence reigned as both combatants rose to their feet. The fiend spat a broken tooth from his mouth, and his blood steamed as it struck the floor. "Why are you doing this?" he said. "You know what I want. Leave me be, and together we will revel in the savage time that lies ahead."

Thorn realized that he wasn't speaking the common tongue of the Five Nations any more. She didn't even know what his language was. But she knew what he was saying, and if she spoke without thinking, the words came to her.

"What are you talking about?" she said, and the words were like thunder echoing through the room. "Who do you think I am?"

It was only a moment of confusion, but it was enough for the fiend. He howled again, and a blinding flash of lightning seared the air. Thorn had no time to brace for the blast—but the blow never fell. Thorn's blood burned in her veins, and she could *feel* the power of the fiend shatter against her. He raised a hand, and thick, thorny vines burst up from the floor, seeking to surround her and crush her. But they shriveled before they could touch her. It wasn't merely fire that flowed through her blood; it was unbridled magic. And the spells of this demon were no match for this pure power.

"You cannot hurt me," Thorn roared. She hoped he would accept her word; the lightning hadn't touched her, but she ached from the impact with the floor. "Surrender, Drul Kantar. Or I will end this, and you with it."

The beast hissed at her, and crackling blades of lightning rose from his fists. He leaped forward, blades flashing toward Thorn's eyes. She couldn't avoid the blow—he was too fast, and her body was huge and unfamiliar. She tried to raise her hand, but her wing rose up. The shock was excruciating, but she rode the pain, lashing back with her wing and flinging Drulkalatar to the floor.

"Fool!" Drulkalatar snarled. "At least I know what I am." He rose to his feet, spitting hot blood. "I am the Voice of the Wild Heart. I am rising terror and lingering fear."

He howled again, and a horde of beasts took shape around him, creatures seemingly called by his rage alone. Lupine trolls. Giants with the features of nightclaws, and nightclaws with the simian traits of the giants.

"I have prepared for this for two hundred years, and I will not wait again!" Drulkalatar cried. He raised his hands, lightning crackling around his claws as his troops rushed forward.

But Thorn was ready. She didn't pause to think; words and actions came to her as one. "I know what I am," she said, "I am the Angel of Flame. And your plans end here." Fire flowed from her mouth, engulfing the oncoming horde. When the flames settled, Drulkalatar's minions were ash, and the fiend himself was scorched, the flesh nearly flayed from his bones. Before he could cast another spell, Thorn pounced, her massive forepaws pinning him to the floor as a cat might trap a mouse.

"Why?" he said, staring up at her. "Why would you do this?"

"I don't know yet," she said. It was the truth. "But I will."

"I cannot die," he said. "You, of all creatures, should know that. I will return, Sarmondelaryx. And you will pay for this."

"I don't think so," she said. "And my name's Thorn."

Reaching down, she caught the crippled fiend between her jaws. She raised him up in the air, slowly crushing him. And then, as she felt his resistance fading, she unleashed her anger. Fire flowed through her teeth, and Drulkalatar was at the heart of it. His bones melted away, his body vaporized in the intense heat. But she could still feel the last trace of his presence . . . the essence of his evil. His spirit. And before he could slip away, she swallowed him. She felt a flash of pure hatred, surprise, and fear. And then he was gone.

The walls of the castle began to shake and fade. Thorn's world dissolved into chaos once more. Nothing seemed solid. The walls and floors around her, her very flesh—everything was in motion. One moment she was flying, then she was falling to the earth, and her only anchors were the burning pain in her skull and the soothing warmth at the base of her spine.

✯ ✯ ✯ ✯ ✯

Mud. Cold earth. The stink of fetid water. And the sounds of battle, now fading. Thorn was lying face-down in a puddle of muck. She was weak, barely able to push herself out of the mud. She was in the patch of swamp, and though the moons were still in the sky, the long shadow had disappeared. The moons themselves were free of the ruddy hue Stormblade had attributed to the Moonlord's curse.

Harryn! Looking about, Thorn saw the knight on the ground nearby, his sword stuck in the mud. The swamp was littered with bodies, some still breathing, others merely the remains of bloody deeds done in the shadow. The delegates were strewn about, both the living and the dead. Thorn staggered to her feet and began dragging the bodies to solid ground. At last, she reached Harryn. His breastplate covered his chest, and she couldn't see if he was still breathing. When she tried to move him, his body was cold.

"Harryn." Her throat was raw, and though she tried to yell, what came out was little more than a whisper. "Harryn!" She slammed a hand against his chest, but his face remained as still as when it was stone.

"Listen to the water, child."

Thorn hadn't noticed the old woman standing behind her. Bent with the burden of years, she was dressed in stained gray rags. A weathered hood was pulled down to hide her eyes. Her skin was so wrinkled that it seemed it might crumble if she were to smile. Thorn couldn't make any sense of what she'd just said, but she spoke with utter conviction.

"My friend needs help," she said. "Many here need help. Is there a healer in the city—"

"Life and death are part of the same stream," the woman said. "What is it like to swim the river twice?"

"I don't know what you mean," Thorn said. "I need—"

The crone raised an admonishing finger. "Help comes, soon enough for those who will live. Until then, I have gifts for you and yours."

"Gifts?"

The woman took Thorn's hand, and there was surprising strength in her withered arms. She pressed a small object into Thorn's hand. "Never a gift at all, you see. This was not the gift you were given, and what you were given was not a gift."

"Yes . . . of course," Thorn said. She was surprised a madwoman could survive in the Shadow of the Crag; the locals didn't seem likely to be overflowing with charity.

The crone kept one hand on Thorn's, holding her fist closed around the mysterious gift. But she knelt next to Harryn. "Not yet time for rest," she said. "There are pages still unwritten. What I once took, I give once again."

She placed her hand over Harryn's heart. The faint gleam of mystical energy appeared, and Harryn stiffened, gasping for air, his fingers clutching at the mud.

"Harder this time, yes," the woman murmured. "And harder still to come."

Harryn's eyes snapped open, and he was gazing into Thorn's face.

"Thorn . . ." he choked, and tried again. "Thorn . . ."

"Nyrielle," she whispered. He nodded, and a faint smile touched his face.

"Harryn," he said.

"Sister!" A new voice rang across the swamp, bold and powerful. "Didn't mother teach you not to play with your food?"

Soldiers were approaching, a troop of ogres. Thorn tried to pull free, but the ragged crone had a grip of iron. "Listen to the water," she said. "This story is almost done."

"She speaks the truth," said the newcomer. "You are in no danger. The Warlord Sheshka sent us to find you, to bring the survivors back to the Crag."

The stranger came closer, and when Thorn caught sight of her, she knew exactly who she was. *Tall and thin, hair as black as a crow's wing and just as ragged, yet surrounding her like a shroud woven from the night itself. I could see that her skin was flawless beneath the dirt, and her eyes were as dark as her hair.* The dark-haired woman went straight to Beren and picked him up as if he were a child. She opened her mouth, and as Thorn had guessed, rows of razor sharp teeth hid behind her flawless smile.

"Don't worry," she said. "Lord Beren and I will not finish our business this year. Now bring your wounded knight and come with us. We are grateful . . . at least for today."

The old woman released Thorn's hand and accompanied the younger woman as the ogres gathered up the delegates. Thorn helped Harryn to his feet.

"Can you walk?" she said. "It seems that Sheshka was successful. Unless they're just bringing us back for a public execution."

Harryn was weak and had to lean on her. "Were . . . we successful? Drulkan—is he dead?"

"Look at the moons," Thorn said. "It seems that all is well. At least, as well as it will ever be in Droaam."

Harryn nodded and focused on walking, leaving Thorn alone with her thoughts. Harryn didn't see the defeat of Drulkalatar. And Thorn . . . could she trust her own memories? Could it have been a dream? If not, what did it mean? *What is it like to swim the river twice?*

She still clenched her fist around her unknown gift. She glanced down and opened her hand.

It was her ring—the magic ring she'd been given just before her mission to Far Passage. The ring that allowed her to see in the dark and sharpened her other senses. But she wasn't wearing it, and she could still smell Harryn's scent, feel the motion of air and the vibrations of every footfall.

Never a gift at all, you see. This was not the gift you were given, and what you were given was not a gift.

What did it mean?

CHAPTER THIRTY-FIVE

✳ ✳ ✳

The Great Crag
Droaam

Eyre 21, 999 YK

Sora Katra studied the man before her. "I give you this final chance to change the fate of nations, Lord Beren. What is your will?"

They stood in the Great Hall of the Crag, the audience chamber of the Daughters of Sora Kell. All three of the sisters were present. They stood on a raised dais, but it held no thrones; rather, a dead tree spread its limbs above and around the sisters. The significance was lost on Thorn, unless it was supposed to be as gnarled and tough as Sora Teraza.

Lord Beren ir'Wynarn had been chosen to speak for the surviving delegates. "Sora Katra, I am astonished that you even ask. While under your roof, my compatriots have been kidnapped, cursed, and some of them killed. If not for the graces of the noble Minister Luala, many of us would still be afflicted with lycanthropy. There are yet a few who could not be cured, and who have suffered permanent psychological damage. And you still dare to raise the question of your petition?"

Sora Maenya stood behind Katra, and her laughter was deep and troubling. She'd chosen to remain in the form of the hungry woman from Beren's tale, but she'd let her hands slip. Her skin was as pale and smooth as that of a noble woman, but her fingers were unnaturally long, and her cruel claws were crusted with dried blood.

"I do, Lord Beren," Katra said, showing no signs of guilt or remorse. "We live in uncertain times. Things happen that cannot be controlled. This is one moment that you can control, and I suggest that you choose wisely. You have seen the power that we possess. Do you truly want us as an enemy?"

And there it was. The previous day, Sora Katra had claimed that the actions that had cost the lives of delegates were the work of Drul Kantar, the warlord governor of the Crag. According to Katra, none knew of Drul Kantar's influence over lycanthropes or the army he was building in secret. Drul's power enabled him to subvert the Warlord Zaeurl and many members of the Skullcrusher Guard.

Now that Drul Kantar was gone, Zaeurl was a trusted ally again. And since the conjunction of moons had passed with Kantar's ritual a failure, the power of lycanthropy had returned to prior conditions. Only a few among 'the blessed' could spread the affliction, and the hags claimed to have no plans to craft more shapeshifters, lest it empower Drul Kantar's mysterious overlord.

But even if the Daughters created no new lycanthropes, they had no intention of disposing of the ones already in their armies. With the defeat of Drul Kantar, the Skullcrusher Guard was once again fanatically loyal to the Daughters of Sora Kell. If war erupted between Breland and Droaam, trollbears might be tearing across the Graywall.

Lord Beren bowed slightly. "No, Sora Katra, I do not. I hope that Droaam will enjoy a long and peaceful relationship with Breland. But it takes more than military power and intimidation to earn the respect of the Thronehold nations."

Except for Valenar . . . and Darguun . . . and some days, Karrnath, Steel observed.

Thorn was the only one who could hear Steel's remarks, and she struggled to keep the smile off her face as Beren continued.

"During this journey, you and your people have forced me to reconsider my views of humanity. It is all too easy for us to fear the unknown or that which is dangerous. Many of your people deserve our trust and respect instead of our fear, but that means nothing if you, as the rulers of the nation, cannot distinguish between the two. The fact that you could allow this event to occur is sufficient cause for us to decline your petition at the present time."

"The present time is the only time, Lord Beren. There will not be another."

"Be that as it may, Sora Katra, we have made our decision. And we will expect reparations for the losses we have suffered on this journey."

"You and your comrades will be given safe passage to Graywall, Lord Beren. Beyond that, I offered you the chance to change the fate of nations, and you have. This will have consequences, Lord Beren. I wish you well . . . until we meet again."

Sora Maenya's laughter echoed through the hall as the gnolls escorted the delegates out.

✕ ✕ ✕ ✕ ✕

Ghyrryn and Sheshka had both come to bid the travelers farewell.

"Few of you survive, so fewer wagons are needed," Ghyrryn explained. "I now serve a greater need in the Crag."

"Well, at least our loss is your gain." Thorn produced the myrnaxe. "Do you wish to take this back?"

"You will not return a gift," Ghyrryn said, surprised. "We are brothers. And you may need it again."

Whatever had happened, it might as well have been a dream. She'd tried to become the dragon again. She'd even picked a fight with an ogre, to see if it was something triggered by combat. She had no success. Perhaps it was just madness, the crystal shard digging into her brain. But she was haunted by the memory of fire flowing through her vein, and the recognition in Drulkalatar's eyes when he looked at her.

What is it like to swim the river twice?

She felt a thought pressing its way into her mind, and she let it in. She felt the mental signature of her handler, Zane.

Thorn—Situation in the Eldeen. Griffin and provender will be waiting at Twilight Palace. Expect immediate briefing and transport.

Too many mysteries filled the world. Too many unanswered questions. But she had a job to do. A country that needed her. And perhaps, she'd find her answers along the way.

"King and country," she said, passing her hand along Steel's hilt.

In the shadow of the Last War, the heroes aren't all shining knights.

PARKER DeWOLF

The Lanternlight Files

Ulther Whitsun is a fixer. When you've got a problem, if you can't find someone to take care of it, he's your man—as long as you can pay the price. If you can't, or you won't . . . gods have mercy on your soul.

Book 1
The Left Hand of Death

Ulther finds himself in possession of a strange relic. His enemies want it, he wants its owner, and the City Watch wants him locked away for good. When a job turns this dangerous, winning or losing are no longer an option. It may be all one man can do just to stay alive.

Book 2
When Night Falls

Ulther teams up with a young and ambitious chronicler to stop a revolution. But treachery may kill him, and salvation comes from unexpected places.

July 2008

Book 3
Death Comes Easy

Gangs in lower Sharn are at each other's throats. And they don't care who gets killed in the battle. But now Ulther had been hired to put an end to the violence. And he doesn't care who he steps on to do his job.

December 2008

But all of these—drinking with Sheshka, sparring and joking with Harryn—were just ways to ignore the things that were truly bothering her. So much about that final day made no sense. Clearly, Sora Teraza had known about Drul Kantar's plot. Presumably, she'd known that this would result in the failure of the summit. Had she truly withheld this information from her sisters? Or had Sora Katra known how things would turn out from the very beginning?

And the ring. *Never a gift at all.* After dwelling on this, Thorn had no doubt: her enhanced senses had nothing to do with the ring. Even with the ring in the palm of her hand, her eyes could still pierce the deepest shadows, and she could feel the slightest shift of the wind against her skin. Both Zane and Steel had told her the ring was the source of this power. She'd received the ring before she'd crossed paths with Steel, so perhaps he knew as little as she. Or perhaps both of them were lying to her. Why? What was happening to her?

And what of the dragon?

After waking up in the mud, she'd pushed the battle from her mind, forced herself to complete her mission. Part of her wanted to believe that it had simply been a moment of madness, some strange effect of the tower of Drulkalatar. No one had seen her change; perhaps it was just a strange living nightmare. But as much as she wanted to believe that, she knew it was a lie. For a moment, she'd been a dragon . . . and it had felt so natural, so true. The feel of fire flowing from her throat, of her wings spreading around her—it was more real than any dream, and every time she thought back to the battle, she felt small and empty.

Sarmondelaryx, the demon had said. The name from her dream, and one she knew from stories. The Angel of Flame, a terror from the dawn of Galifar. But what did it have to do with her?

"I suppose I may." It saddened her to think that they might meet again on opposite sides of a battlefield. "Good hunting, brother."

Sheshka waited nearby, her eyes closed. She touched her palm to Thorn's. "Trust a gnoll to see a brother when one clearly has a sister," she said.

There was little more to say that had not already been said, and Beren, Stormblade, and Thorn climbed aboard their wagon. Sheshka, Thorn, and Stormblade had spent much of the previous night talking and sampling the strange liquors of Cazhaak Draal.

In light of her service, the Daughters had offered Sheshka the title of Warlord General, a position second only to the Three. While she had always had doubts, and a desire to rule a greater territory alone, Sheshka found that she had come to believe in Droaam. She might find a sister in Thorn, or a friend in Stormblade, and they would always be welcome in Cazhaak Draal. But her people would always be feared in the world beyond. In Droaam they had the chance to create something magnificent. Thorn could feel the tension that remained between Sheshka and Harryn, but whatever lingered there, it was something neither intended to discuss openly.

As for Harryn Stormblade, the news of the Last War and the fall of Galifar was a great blow. But he believed that the kingdom would rise again, and given his experiences in Droaam, he was likely to see Breland's claim in a positive light, which was exactly what the Citadel wanted. If and when the war began anew, having the Shield of the Crown as Boranel's champion would be a powerful propaganda tool. The challenge, of course, would be to keep Harryn from realizing just how he was being used. For the moment, he was a handsome and upstanding man, he owed Thorn a considerable debt, and they had a week's wagon ride to Graywall ahead. She looked forward to seeing what developed.

An action-packed tale of adventure and
intrigue from one of the EBERRON®
line's finest authors.

DON BASSINGTHWAITE

Legacy of Dhakaan

From the ashes of the long-collapsed Dhakaani Empire, a new
king of the goblins will do whatever he can to see the kingdom
of Darguun recognized. The Five Nations may not have much
love for the descendents of Dhakaan, but they must respect the
bloodthirsty warriors.

Book 1
The Doom of Kings
August 2008

The Dragon Below

In the dark places of the wild, there are terrors older than
the nations of men. When a chance rescue brings bitter rivals
together, two warriors team up on a mission of vengeance.
But the enemy waiting for them in the depths of the Shadow
Marches is far more sinister than any they've faced before.

Book 1
The Binding Stone

Book 2
The Grieving Tree

Book 3
The Killing Song

RICHARD A. KNAAK

THE OGRE TITANS

The Grand Lord Golgren has been savagely crushing
all opposition to his control of the harsh ogre lands of
Kern and Blöde, first sweeping away rival chieftains, then
rebuilding the capital in his image. For this he has had to
deal with the ogre titans, dark, sorcerous giants who have
contempt for his leadership.

VOLUME ONE
THE BLACK TALON

Among the ogres, where every ritual demands blood and every ally can
become a deadly foe, Golgren seeks whatever advantage he can obtain,
even if it means a possible alliance with the Knights of Solamnia, a
questionable pact with a mysterious wizard, and trusting an elven slave
who might wish him dead.

VOLUME TWO
THE FIRE ROSE

Attacked by enemies on all sides, Golgren must abandon his throne
to undertake the quest for the Fire Rose before Safrag, master
of the Ogre Titans can locate it and claim supremacy
over all ogres—and perhaps all of Krynn.

December 2008

VOLUME THREE
THE GARGOYLE KING

Forced from the throne he has so long coveted, Golgren makes a final
stand for control of the ogre lands against the Titans . . . against an
enemy as ancient and powerful as a god.

December 2009

Never been to the FORGOTTEN REALMS® world?

SEMBIA: GATEWAY TO THE REALMS

Opens the door to our most popular world with stories full of intrigue, adventure, and fascinating characters. Sembia is a land of wealth and power, where rival families buy and sell everything imaginable—even life itself. In that unforgiving realm, the Uskevren family may hold the rarest commodity of all: honor.

But even the most honorable family is not without its secrets, and everyone from the maid to the matriarch has something to hide.

THOMAS M. REID

The author of *Insurrection* and The Scions of Arrabar Trilogy
rescues Aliisza and Kaanyr Vhok from the tattered remnants
of their assault on Menzoberranzan, and sends them off on
a quest across the multiverse that will leave
FORGOTTEN REALMS® fans reeling!

THE EMPYREAN ODYSSEY

BOOK I
THE GOSSAMER PLAIN

Kaanyr Vhok, fresh from his defeat against the drow, turns to hated Sundabar for the
victory his demonic forces demand, but there's more to his ambitions than just one
human city. In his quest for arcane power, he sends the alu-fiend Aliisza on a mission
that will challenge her in ways she never dreamed of.

BOOK II
THE FRACTURED SKY

A demon surrounded by angels in a universe of righteousness, Aliisza makes what
decisions she must to survive. So how did an angel make
such simple choices so complicated?

(November 2008)

BOOK III
THE CRYSTAL MOUNTAIN

What Aliisza has witnessed has changed her forever, but that's nothing compared
to what has happened to the multiverse itself. The startling climax will change the
nature of the cosmos forever.

Mid-2009

*"Reid is proving himself to be one of the best up and coming authors
in the FORGOTTEN REALMS universe."*
—fantasy-fan.org